ROBERT ALAN JAMIESON was born in Lerwick on Up Helly Aa, 1958 and grew up in the crofting community of Sandness. He attended the University of Edinburgh as a mature student and subsequently held the William Soutar Fellowship in Perth. He was a co-editor of *Edinburgh Review*, 1993–98, and writer in residence at the universities of Glasgow and Strathclyde, 1998–2001. Since then he has tutored creative writing at the University of Edinburgh. He is the author of three novels, three collections of poetry and two plays, and has edited a number of anthologies. Through his occasional work with the organisation Literature Across Frontiers, his poetry in Shetlandic Scots has been translated into more than a dozen languages, and he has translated over twenty contemporary European poets into Shetlandic Scots.

Robert Alan Jamieson is one of this country's finest, most distinctive writers, and Da Happie Laand *is his best work yet. Vast in scope but understated in tone, big in ambition and beautifully rendered from beginning to end, if there's any justice this potent tale of a very unreal world and another very real one should find a wide audience of readers who will come away feeling inspired and uplifted.* RODGE GLASS

Epic and ironic, tragic and humorous, encyclopedic and confessional, realistic and fantastic, Da Happie Laand *relates a stunning journey across an invisible archipelago, combining Ulysses' zest for geographical exploration with Penelope's superior ability to weave a story-cloth – a beautiful Shetlandic lace of memories and voices that will haunt long after you turn the last page.* CARLA SASSI

Finally, Shetland has the novel she deserves – big in scope, rich in ideas, uncompromising in execution. Jamieson explores metafiction, ethnology, history, linguistics, existentialism and sheer irrepressible humanity with imaginative zest, encyclopaedic knowledge and a wry, subtle humour. This intimate, multifaceted epic puts you in mind of such literary greats as Allende, Nabokov and Marquez and will swiftly be recognised as a great addition to the wise and quietly dignified bookshelf of Northern European Literature. KEVIN MACNEIL

Coupled to a quiet and unobtrusive experimentalism, [Jamieson] has produced a work of power and originality. SCOTTISH REVIEW OF BOOKS

DA HAPPIE LAAND

Robert Alan Jamieson

Luath Press Limited

EDINBURGH

www.luath.co.uk

First published 2010
This edition 2011

ISBN: 978-1906817-86-2

The publisher acknowledges the support of

 Scottish
Arts Council

towards the publication of this volume.

The paper used in this book promotes sustainable forest management
and is PEFC credited material.

PEFC

Printed and bound by
Martins the Printers, Berwick Upon Tweed

Typeset in 9 point Sabon

This book is dedicated to three late mentors,
great encouragers all –

John J and Laurence Graham of Shetland
and Hugh Nolan of Australia

Thanks to

my father: JRP Jamieson, for telling me what no research could uncover

those who provided shelter of one kind or another during the writing:
my family; the William Soutar Fellowship, Perth;
Lister Housing Cooperative, Edinburgh; the Scottish Arts Council;
the universities of Glasgow, Strathclyde and my alma mater, Edinburgh

those who have listened to much talk about this book:
Mary Blance, Richard Browne, Alex Cluness, George Gunn,
Wilma Jamieson, Murdo Macdonald, Lorna J Waite

those who saw early drafts, and said what was needed:
Jenny Brown, David Goldie, Duncan McLean,
Jennie Renton, Robin Robertson

those who read the first full draft, and said it was nearly done:
Rajorshi Chakraborti, Rodge Glass, Wilma Jamieson,
Kevin MacNeil, Randall Stevenson

those who read the final draft, and said it was ready:
Belica-Antonia Kubareli, Jordan Ogg, Carla Sassi

those who have made publishing easy:
Tom Bee, Leila Cruickshank,
Gavin MacDougall, Jennie Renton

What follows, arranged in these pages, are the various contents of an outsize brown manila envelope delivered to me by one of the elders of the Church of Scotland in Craigie, Perth, Scotland, in 2003, soon after the death of the former incumbent minister of that parish, who was for a number of years my next-door neighbour there. This man, the late Reverend Archibald Nicol, was a cultured and sophisticated individual despite his essential and unshakeable belief in the ineffable and inexplicable, with whom I had a number of interesting conversations during my time as William Soutar Fellow in 'The Fair City'.

My interest in the contents of the envelope was spurred by the realisation, when I had read Reverend Nicol's accompanying letter, that I too had met the barefooted bearded stranger who, as I quickly came to understand, had briefly entered the old minister's life with such a dramatic effect. This stranger had, in fact, knocked on my door first and asked me for directions to the manse, which I duly gave him, so I was in direct causal relationship to what this envelope contained.

I have arranged these papers to mimic the order in which I found them, to present the fabula contained within more or less as I encountered it. I cannot tell whether this order was the true and full intention of Reverend Nicol, or to what extent it is the product of chance. However, I have included much that to Reverend Nicol's mind was merely a footnote, or background to the story, including his own correspondence; and, in editing his typescript of James Gabrielsen's history, I have allowed certain passages to stand which the Reverend Nicol had himself excised as digressive, by rulering lines through them. This I do in the belief that he too has become a player in this drama – to which, in view of the content, I have given the title *Da Happie Laand*.

I have included an amount of ephemera where that material is mentioned in the letters – essays on the colony of New Zetland, its history and language, interviews and other notes which were sent to the Reverend Nicol. For the general reader, these may be quickly passed over, yet I believe they have their role in the story as a whole, and so have included them where they occurred in the related correspondence, as Nicol had attached them. As to the sources for the Reverend's version of Gabrielsen's history, this script appears to be a palimpsest of different writings. It is possible to detect an original nineteenth-century style which I presume to be Gabrielsen's in much of the reportage, even in those passages where Nicol does not acknowledge him, while other sections seem to suggest a more twentieth-century mindset, in style and vocabulary – we presume Nicol's own interventions. It is clear one or both of the authors made free use of the records of both the Truck Commission and the Crofters Commission, in addition to the journals of Sir Walter Scott and the young Robert Louis Stevenson. I also found reference in the marginalia to *The Zetland Book* by AT Kuliness, published in 1954, and therefore a source of Nicol's and not Gabrielsen's.

RA Jamieson

Note: The observant reader will detect considerable variation in some of the names, apparent elisions in the text, as well as inconsistencies in some of the dates and details. These are issues that cannot be resolved. The recorded past is essentially unstable. All versions suffer from partiality, presumption and occasional error. There is no 'gospel truth' here, no authority to refer to, for true and final judgement. I present the mysteries as I have found them.

Perth
10th January 2002

Dear Mr Jamieson

You will, I trust, remember we were neighbours in Wilson Street, Perth, while you were community writer-in-residence there a few years ago, and that you and I spoke at some length about literary matters. I have now a request to make of you, if you are willing and able, which I hope will not be too onerous a task.

I am entrusting to your care the enclosed scripts which have preoccupied me in the last few months. I wonder whether there is, in your opinion, anything of merit that might be salvaged? I feel that among the fragments I have collected there is a story of genuine interest, a mystery relating to the death of Rod Cunninghame, or Scot, and the disappearance of his son David; yet the writing of that has confounded me, just as the truth has. You will, I trust, understand as you read.

Perhaps you, as an editor, may be better placed to do the work of collation and I am happy to pay the labourer his worth. I enclose copies of the correspondence between myself, Philippa Gabrielsen of New Zetland and Peter A Scot of Miami, as this may help in explaining the background.

Please excuse brevity – I was recently seriously ill and writing is almost too great a task now. I am no longer in Wilson Street either myself these days, but in a retirement home across the river.

Best wishes to you and your family

Yours faithfully
Archibald Nicol (Rev.)

21 June 2000 – Train

If I close my eyes, a red light flashes – it's the light that tells me a message has been received. What it doesn't tell is whether the message is complete or coherent, if the caller has left their name, their number, whether the automaton will chant *the other person has cleared, the other person has cleared* – or if a voice will speak.

That light is flashing on the inside of my eyelids now. Press *Rewind*, *Stop* and *Play*. Four rings, a pause and then a very English voice.

'My name is Hart. Doctor Peter Hart. I'm calling about your father. My number is …'

The tape fuzzes before it runs out. I replay it over and over again. The mumbled number becomes clearer. As do the lost words, when I call him back:

I'm afraid your father has
    disappeared

Carbon Copy retained of a letter from the
Rev. Archibald Nicol of Perth, Scotland, sent presumably to
Philippa Gabrielsen of Tokumua (New Zetland)
and Peter A Scot of Miami
February 20th 2001

Dear

I am writing to you as I found your name and address in an envelope containing papers pertaining to the late Mr Rod Cunninghame, along with an unfinished manuscript of 'A History of the Parish of Norbie and Thulay in Zetland', written by one James Gabrielsen, a schoolmaster in that parish, presumably in the late nineteenth century, and various documents relating to the Gabrielsen and Scot families of that parish.

These papers came into my possession by chance some months ago and they have presented me with a moral dilemma which I am now attempting to resolve. I apologise in advance for what is liable to be a very longwinded explanation, but I trust you will bear with me as this is a matter of the utmost importance to me.

I was visited recently by a young man I believe is David Cunninghame, the remaining son of said Rod and his wife Ella, though he did not volunteer his identity and I was thus unaware of who he was until after he left. But I first must also tell you who I am, and what my relationship is to the Cunninghame family.

I am a Church of Scotland minister, recently retired through ill health, and the family was once amongst my congregation. Indeed, Ella was organist in our church for many years, but she, her son Martin and now her husband are with the Lord now – David is the sole remaining child. It was this David who came to see me, I realise in retrospect. He stood there on the threshold of the manse, barefooted, a pair of brown brogues in his hands. I thought he was some wandering tramp who had come to the manse looking for Christian kindness, and so I took him in. He was clearly distressed, and so I tried to counsel him. He told me, in fragments, of a recent bereavement, though he didn't specify who had died. He was so distracted I couldn't extract from him the details. When I asked for his name, he merely said he was a pilgrim, 'the son and heir of being lost', and when I asked where he was going, he laughed and cried out, 'Jerusalem!'

David stayed three nights with us in the manse. He slept for most of that time, as if fevered, muttering all the while. On the fourth morning, I opened my eyes to see him in our bedroom, peering down at me, where I lay, half-awake, with a most disturbing expression on his face. He made neither excuse nor apology, but simply smiled, then left the room silently as if he had every right to be there.

What mischief – if any – he had in mind, I cannot say, but the experience confirmed a growing unease I had felt at his presence, since his bare and blistered feet first crossed the threshold, and he sat down to share our plain dinner of boiled fish and potatoes that Friday evening. He had looked at me that first night as if he knew something which I didn't – as if he knew me. It was most disconcerting. But now, realising who this bearded wanderer was, I can see that the tension between us arose from my failure to recognise him – an infant I had baptised, yes, but a child I had known well enough too, as a choirboy. Now he is a grown man, a stranger to me – and I feel I have failed in some final test of my duty of care.

When I finally arose and went downstairs that day, ready to confront whatever troubled mind awaited me, I found he had gone, as if risen from the dead, leaving behind the unmade bed, and on it a old brown leather briefcase, containing the various papers I have described.

So you see, I hope, why I write to you now, as you are one of only three contacts I have with the mystery which David left – from among all these papers which he carried with him when he came, and left behind him when he went. I would like to trace this man and help him if I can, and if God wills it.

I would appreciate, at your earliest convenience, any information you may be able to give me on the Cunninghame family, particularly the whereabouts of the said David.

I am
Yours sincerely
Rev. Archibald Nicol (retired)

PS – If you are indeed the person who supplied the copies of Gabrielsen's history, you should already have these, but I will enclose a set in case you have it no longer. I do not know if this is a full copy. It seems to end very abruptly, and chapter nine is merely a few notes?

21 June 2000 – Train

I lay my head back on the railway seat and try to shut it out. I try to close my eyes and drift away, but there's Gran with her white perm and gold-rimmed glasses, at home in Blair. I'd phoned her, trying to be tactful, to ask if she'd seen him. But she sensed there was something wrong, and I had to tell her. She kept on at me to go. And so I agreed. I agreed to go to the island where he'd last been living. I had a few days holiday due. She said I was to be sure to let her ken.

I open my eyes slowly, on the North Sea. The intercity express is skirting cliffs above a rocky coastline near Johnshaven, where my father's Ford Cortina blew a cylinder head gasket on a family trip to Aberdeen. Martin and me watched the inshore fishermen while the village mechanic howked under the bonnet and my mother disappeared to visit the village church. That was her hobby, visiting churches.

The window flecks with drizzle. In the seats behind me, four men are drinking cans of super-lager, joking and sharing stories from the rigs. This is oil country now. The fishing boats have gone. The grey horizon hides platforms, pipelines, supply vessels, helicopters, hard hats, mud, drilling bits, accommodation blocks, four square meals a day. All hidden from the traveller till the next Piper Alpha lights up the sky.

I close my eyes. Press *Rewind*, *Stop*
and *Play*

Letter from Philippa Gabrielsen
to Rev. Archibald Nicol,
August 12th 2000

Bon Hoga
Sellafir
Tokumua
NZ

Dear Archibald

Of course I don't mind you writing to me, in fact I'm rather glad you did! I have been expecting a message from Rod Cunninghame for a few months and was wondering if something had befallen him. But it wasn't me who sent Gabrielsen's history, I'm afraid, although the writer is an ancestor of my husband's. It really is most interesting to both of us. Rod had mentioned that he had located the original and was to send a copy to me.

I'll explain myself a bit for your benefit. I first got in touch with Rod through a common contact in Zetland, a man by the name of Peter Frazer who is a local wise man and expert on genealogy. It turned out that both Rod and I were researching the same two families but from opposite ends. So we have had a lot of correspondence over the last year or so and Rod was planning to visit Tokumua, or New Zetland as the locals here still insist on calling it.

I myself am not a local here but came as a schoolteacher about twelve years ago, from Wellington. I had never been here before and 'Piri NZ', as they sometimes call New Zetland in Tokumua, was just a few dots in the midst of a great ocean on the map to me, notable only because it had a similar name to New Zealand, but I knew little more than that. I had no idea about the Zetlandic colony or the weird cultural mix that there is and to begin with found it very strange and hard to adjust to, in so many ways quite different from Wellington. But I am now quite active in trying to preserve that very history as vice-president of the Heritage Society. We have a new project to create 'A House of Memories' in the oldest house here, once the home of Captain Jack Kulliness, the original Zetlandic settler.

I personally have become particularly interested in the history of our little school here, and its founder, my husband's great-grandfather, a Zetlandic minister called Thorvald Gabrielsen, who came out here as the leader of the first big shipload of settlers in 1877. He was a son of your historian, James the schoolmaster at Norbie in 'old' Zetland, where the majority of those settlers came from. He was really both minister and schoolteacher to them, you see, and led the expedition with all the zeal of a pilgrim father. In fact, they called him 'The Minister', and that is how he is known today. The statue to him in Serrafir bears that name.

His father, your James Gabrielsen, besides devoting his life to the education of his fellow men, was a great scholar and correspondent, and acted as the agent for emigration to New Zealand for a number of years. He was also an acquaintance of the very first Zetlander to arrive in Tokumua, this Jack Kuliness I mentioned, a sea captain who had visited the archipelago a few times as a young sailor aboard whaling ships, and then was commander of a whaling station there during the 1830s. Though the station folded when the sealing and whaling moved on, 'Kapiyaki', as he was called, stayed on, trading as he had always done and making the occasional voyage to New Zealand and Australia. Over time he built himself a fine wooden house which he named Sellafirt after his native village in Zetland, but no sooner was the house finished than off he went in his ship.

For a year the house lay as it was, guarded by a few men he had recruited from among the local Murikavi people, and so long went by they thought he might have been killed by pirates, but then one day he sailed back into the harbour in Sellafirt with not only a new ship but a new wife – a Maori woman from the Bay. This couple were the key to the Zetland colony. Around their fine wooden house a shanty-town began to grow, which took the name Serrafir, and in time, when the colonists came out in 1877, it began to grow to be a proper town. Where I now live!

Anyhow, I didn't mean to go on like that. You see how 'teacherly' I am, without even trying! But I will send you more material, if you like. One thing I know you will be interested in is something I am going to do this summer.

There is a woman who is now in her hundredth year, by the name of Mimie Jeromsen. Mimie is the oldest person in the Zetlandic community and what will be really interesting to you is that she once worked as a maid for the Scot-Cunninghame family. I have arranged to go to see her in three weeks' time.

Best wishes

Philippa

ps – hope you like the enclosed postcard – new design!

---

21 June 2000 – Ferry/Town

And so I'd phoned him back.

'Your father hasn't been seen for four days. I thought he might have decided to travel south, perhaps, to visit you?'

'I haven't seen my father for years. But who are you exactly, Dr Hart?'

'I own the chalet …'

'Chalet?'

' … where he lives.'

'His landlord?'

'More of a friend.'

I stop the memory tape. My father has disappeared. And what kind of friend is this landlord? I run my fingertips over railway seat fibres. They bristle harmlessly.

I let the tape run back to the time when I knew him best. The time when he was there, and he lifted me up to his huge shoulders and set me there to see the world from a place higher than he himself could reach.

Then he was Daddy. But the shoulders are narrow now, and my fingers won't stay still. I press *Fast Forward*, let the spindles turn, to the time when he stood bent and balding at my brother's graveside, the moment when the orbit of my family exploded, when its central star imploded and turned us all to a scattering. Yes, things reassure – a note at Christmas, a card.

The message is received. But when somebody I haven't seen for years disappears, have they not disappeared already? Or was I always conscious of something tangible, even in absence, being there?

No, I deny the existence of a being such as 'Daddy', whose child I am. A father, maybe, possessed by me – my father.

I think about that letter and pull it from my bag. Why had I never replied? It was so obviously a plea for forgiveness. But I couldn't find it in me.

The ferry takes all night. The sea is quite calm, they tell me, but I can't sleep. The cabin is far too hot and I feel I can't breathe. I left in such a hurry, brought nothing to read, and the only book to hand is a Gideon's.

At last, I hear people moving in the corridor, the sounds of morning, and I rise. A steward brings me a bowl of lumpy porridge in the ferry café, with milk that sways around as the waves collide with the ship. It's liquid within liquid. I am made of liquid, my body merely water, swilling around. I try to eat, hungry and nauseous at the same time, lift a spoon, then stop.

A lighthouse appears, then land like paradise promised but so long in coming that it's hardly believed when glimpsed in the distance. I shove the porridge bowl away. That's all I can stomach.

The sound of a foghorn draws me out through a doorway to the deck. There's the white lighthouse clinging to a sharp cliff and a bare conical hill behind, the smell of hot engine oil blown by the gusting breeze. The engines slow. The ferry glides into harbour through a morning mist, past a town-bound midsummer morning.

Seagulls flash by, squabbling over scraps dumped in the harbour water. The ferry comes alongside. The little town offers the ship a rope, thrown up from the quay by a stocky island docker. A door in the side of the ship opens and I rejoice at reaching the promised island, take my rucksack and descend. Immediately the sickness eases a little.

Streetlamps yellow the morning mist. I walk towards one, hoping for illumination on this strange place, this quest.

Out of the fog a taxi appears and the driver takes me into the town, where the folk are waking. I wander along the crooked main street, no wider than a bus, imagining my father here, walking through this place he chose to go to, as far north as he could get in Britain.

What was he looking for
     here

A History of Zetland with particular attention to the
Parish of Norbie, Valay and Thulay, as transcribed
from the unfinished 1899 original of James Gabrielsen
(schoolteacher), and supplemented by
Rev. Archibald Nicol, MA, DD, of Perth

CHAPTER ONE

'THE BEAUTIFUL ESTATE OF NORBIE'

My intent is to lay before the reader a brief history of the parish, as my
research has revealed it. I make no pretence of expertise in this field. My
study tends me towards a better grasp of Abraham's Moriah, of Sinai, the
summits of Gerizim and Ebal, or glorious Carmel, than it does the boreal
peaks of my native land. Indeed it is only since my retirement from the
ministry that I have ventured into the northern territories of this realm. I
am neither expert as historian, nor in the area of our scrutiny. The distant
isles of Zetland I was unacquainted with until my 73rd year, and venturing
imaginatively there I came upon a land such as I had never glimpsed even
in moments of reverie. Nonetheless I will attempt, with the aid of various
authorities and quotations, to establish this particular parish in the mind
of the reader.

To begin I might turn to the advertisement description from *The
Scotsman* of July 31st, 1894, the year in which this history will end, when
the estate was sold by the ancient family who had fallen on hard times:

ZETLAND

For Sale by Private Bargain

THE BEAUTIFUL ESTATE OF NORBIE, in the parishes of Vass
and Saness, on the West Coast of the Mainland of ZETLAND,
comprising lands on the well known Harbour of Valaysund
to which high-class Passenger Stamers (sic) run weekly, in
24 hours from Aberdeen, and 14 hours from the railway at
Thurso. The Estate is within 22 miles of Larvik by good road,
and it is intersected by good county roads.

NORBIE HALL, which contains Dining-Room, Drawing Room, Six Good Bed-rooms, Large Kitchen, and Servant's Accommodation, Patent w.c. and bath, Store-room, Stabling, and Out-houses, and Good Walled Gardens attached, is situated under the shelter of Westness Hill, on a beautiful bay, with splendid views of the large islands of Papay and Thulay, and the islands of Magnus Bay. It occupies one of the finest positions in Zetland, the Rock Scenery being superb.

The Estate is estimated to contain about 15,000 acres. The Home Farm is in the Proprietor's hands, and the remainder of the Estate is let to crofters and farmers, who pay their rents with regularity.

The sport upon the Estate is good – 250 couple of Snipe, 45 brace of Wild Duck, and numerous Wild Fowl, Rabbits, and Seals have been shot in a short season. The Sea Trout as well as the Loch and Burn Trout Fishing in numerous Burns and Lochs is the best in Zetland.

This most picturesque of sketches we may assume tends slightly to the rose-coloured, as it was no doubt intended to sway the purchaser by its charm. We find a different kind of portrait in the press of 1869, in a letter (to which we shall later return) by our primary source for the history that follows – James Gabrielsen, the local schoolmaster, begging funds with which to build a new schoolhouse:

Norbie, situated on the north-west of the mainland of Zetland, is about three miles long by about one and a half miles of average breadth, is bounded on the south by a ridge of hills, the chief of which is Westness Hill, rising 1,000 feet above the level of the sea; and its shores are washed on the west, north, and east by the waves of the Atlantic, of the Sound of Papay, and of Magnus Bay; and is separated from the neighbouring parish by a large tract of wild waste moorland. It is the prettiest parish in the Zetland Islands; and contains a population of upwards of 600. The inhabitants are fishermen, crofters, and common sailors and there are very few well-to-do families among them. The gales of October 1867 utterly destroyed their crops, and this year's fishing turned out a complete failure, so that they are at present seriously embarrassed.

These glimpses of the past are as yet distant futures to our narrative, however, for the building of the parish school and the sale of Norbie estate are far progressed from the beginning of our tale. The land-owning family who fell from power at the end of the nineteenth century and the peasantry around them had a much older relationship and their common history is an example of an identifiable period in Zetlandic society.

We might properly begin our story in 1469, the point at which Zetland is pawned by the Danish government to the Scotch, for it is the coming of the Scots to Zetland which is the key theme of this story, and our family is by coincidence named 'Scot'. But to do so would be to ignore the earlier history and, before any of this, I would gladly paint for you a picture of the early Christian missionaries, voyaging northwards bearing the glorification of Our Lord and his servant St Ninian of Whithorn like torches before them in the dark, barbarian islands. I wish you might see them now as I do, as they pilot their tiny coracle craft around the steep and haven-less west side of Zetland – a speck of bobbing flotsam passing between the fabulous cliff-isle of Thulay rising a thousand feet sheer out of the Atlantic ocean on the horizon, its three-step northern face stark against a setting sun, and the dramatic Red Sandstone cliffs of Deepdale scarred with waterfalls at Westness to landward.

I would have you apprehend, as they did, when rounding the ultimate western headland and passing through the fierce tidal passage between the Zetland mainland and the island of Papay, the welcoming green, flat meadows of Norbie, lying in the mouth of a sheltered vale, with two large freshwater lochs and numerous streams running into them from the mountain above. You, like them, would wish to draw your boat ashore on the perfect curve of the sandy beach, and consider this a good place in which to found a church. So 'St Ninians' was established there, in a time before record, perhaps as long ago as the Fall of Rome – and though nothing now remains of this building, the field where it stood is still recalled locally. According to one of the elders of the parish, no grass would ever grow where the pulpit once stood – the sacred spot resisted secular use. In recent times a local crofter, under duress from the authorities who had heard of his prize, presented the Zetland Museum with the original font, a hollowed-out granite block which he had been using as a water trough for his home flock of sheep.

What these courageous Christian pioneers found in Zetland, we can but guess. Earlier peoples had inhabited the isles, had built their round 'brochs' or 'burgs' for defence from weather and foe, but whether they remained when the missionaries arrived or whether they had left, chased south by worsening climate or killed by some famine, I cannot tell. Whatever the case, Zetland was firmly Christianised, we know, by the time the heathen Norsemen began to arrive from western Scandinavia around 800, before the Scots and Picts became one people under Kenneth McAlpin in 843, with his coronation in the heart of the country at Dunkeld.

Little the inhabitants of this remotest parish would have known of that, or any of the other significant events shaping Scotch history for the next four hundred years, for it and the rest of Zetland was then amongst the Norwegian empire centered on the city of Bergen – first as part of a vast Norse 'Jarldom' (earldom) of the Orcades, stretching over the whole western seaboard from Ireland to the north of Europe; then, after the Norwegian king confiscated it from the Orcades' jarls, under direct rule from Bergen.

I will not dwell on this Norse era. The Orcadian writer Mr GM Brown has written at length on this period and has presented an excellent, if creative, life of the great Orcadian Christian figure of St Magnus Erlendsson, the jarl who was killed in 1117 by his cousin.

Suffice to say that, from 1195 when the Orcades and Zetland were separated, the former became increasingly Scotch, passing into the hands of the Earl of Angus in 1231, while the latter remained staunchly Norse, so that when King Haakon massed his fleet of two hundred warships in preparation for the long voyage southwards to engage the Scots in battle in 1263, he gathered his fleet in an eastern harbour of Zetland not as a beach-head in a foreign land, but as the outer reach of his own secure country.

By then, another strange people had begun to frequent the Zetlandic shores during the long summer days – the 'Dutchies', traders of the Hanseatic League – drawn by the riches of fish around the distant archipelago.

With such links to Scandinavia and the continental coast, it is safe to assume that the great victory of our national hero William Wallace would have been of less immediate interest to the natives of our parish of 1296 than, for instance, the news from Bergen of progress in the building of the Apostles' Church, funded largely from Zetlandic and Faeroese rents. At this time, Zetland was closer in culture and politics to its mountainous northern neighbour than the gentle green slopes of the Orcades, or the land of the Scots.

Yet Scotland impacted on Zetland ever-increasingly from this point onwards, with Viking-like raids on the islands by marauders from the south in 1312 demonstrating the danger. Having arrived at the subtle acquisition of the Orcades jarldom, and having won independence from England under Bruce at Bannockburn in 1314, no doubt the distant shores of Hjaltaland (as it was in Norse times) held an appeal for the political Scot of the period, particularly if the northern seaboard could then be fortified against further incursions by belligerent Norwegians.

As it was, the balance of human power in all these places was to be challenged by a tiny organism rushing northwards from the Mediterranean, the so-called Black Death.

In Scotland, John of Fordun records that in the year 1350 there was in the kingdom of Scotland, 'so great a pestilence and plague among men … as, from the beginning of the world even unto modern times, had never been heard of by man, nor is found in books, for the enlightenment of those who come after. For, to such a pitch did that plague wreak its cruel spite, that nearly a third of mankind were thereby made to pay the debt of nature.'

In Norway too, the effect was devastating. The disease was brought on a ship from London. The crew discovered the infection, and quickly succumbed – two days was the usual extent of the dying process. Finally the vessel ran aground somewhere off Bergen. The local people went out to the ship's aid, only to discover the awful cargo. A number of the well-to-do families tried to escape by going to the mountains, with the aim of founding a new settlement, but the killer followed them and all died but one. A girl was found, many years later, running wild like a dog and shunning human company, as if still terrified by the spectre of plague.

Beyond this tragic, miserable time, in the vacuum we may assume prevailed, a powerful figure rises in the northern islands, a man whose life verges upon myth – Henry Sinclair of Rosslyn. As with St Magnus, much has been written of Sinclair, and heated arguments about his deeds persist. There are some who say he was the conqueror of Zetland and Faroe, a voyager to Iceland, who built up a great navy and travelled the old Norse route to America in the company of two Genovan navigators and cartographers. To them, he was one of the outstanding men of his century.

Others are less convinced. But that Henry Sinclair was invested by King Haakon of Norway as the Jarl of the Orcades and Lord of Zetland on the 2nd of August 1379 is a matter of record. In so doing, Haakon reunited the two archipelagos, though in practice Sinclair had to win his lands. He finally took Zetland following the suspicious killing of his rival Malisse Spera at Tingwall in 1391, after a protracted struggle for supremacy. The following year King Robert III of Scotland acknowledged Sinclair's power and his control of access to the waters of the North Atlantic. The Norwegian empire was in serious decline at this time, so an opportunity existed for Sinclair. When, in 1397, Norway and Denmark were united under Christian II of Denmark, the power that was once Bergen formally diminished – it had waned for decades prior to that. The Black Death left so few alive that positions in the church could not be filled – and this lack of vigour led to the appointment of the first Scot as Bishop of the Orcades, William Tulloch, in 1418.

The rise of a powerful king in Edinburgh far to the south, James I, with an intense determination to weld his country together by whatever means required, and the desire to encourage trade with Holland and Scandinavia, must have made the seabound Sinclairs, with their powerful estates and northern connections, seem attractive allies.

To allow the reader to gauge the potency of the potentate, William Sinclair, known as 'Prodigus', who began the building of Rosslyn Chapel in 1446, was 'Prince of Orknay, (Duke of Holdembourg), Earle of Catness (and Stratherne), Lord Zetland, Lord Saintclair, Lord Nithsdale, Sherieff of Dumfriese, Lord Admiral of the Scots Seas, Lord Chief Justice of Scotland, Lord Warden and Justiciar of the three Marches betwixt Berrick and Whithorne, Baron of Rosline, Baron of Pentland and Pentland Moore in free forestrie, Baron of Couslande, Baron of Cardain Saintclair, Baron of Herbertshire, Baron of Hectford, Baron of Grahamshaw, Baron of Kirktone, Baron of Cavers, Baron of Newborugh in Buchan, Baron of Roxburgh, Dysart, Polmese, Kenrusi, etc., Knight of the Cockle after the ordre of France, and Knight of the Garter after the order of England, Knight of the Golden Fleece, Great Chancellour, Chamberlain and Livetenant of Scotland, etc.'

'Titles to weary a Spaniard', as one commentator phrased it. Sinclair was also one of the claimants to the vacant Norwegian throne in 1449, and although unsuccessful in that endeavour he was made Lord Chancellor of Scotland in 1454 and was rewarded with the new Scotch Earldom of Caithness by James II in 1455.

Our quiet remote parish has habituated many generations during the previous pages. Little of all that I have described, perhaps not even the plague, will have made its way out here on the very edge of Europe.

However, momentous events at the highest level of society are about to bring Norbie into recorded history, with the Danish king's promise of the isles of Zetland and the Orcades as surety on a sum of dowry due to the Scotch king, James III, on the occasion of his marriage to the Danish princess. Zetland's price was 8,000 florins. When the sum was unforthcoming, the Scots quite gleefully annexed the islands, along with the Orcades, to the throne.

William Sinclair, son of 'Prodigus', had to surrender his title, and within eleven years, was declared 'incomposmentis et fatuus' and 'a waster of his lands and goods for sixteen years previously'. Thus, by 1482, the Scotch crown had taken the dangerous and debated lands of the north to itself, and the power of the Sinclairs was waning. Though Lord Henry Sinclair was granted a thirteen-year lease of the Orcades and Zetland, the custody of Kirkwall Castle and the offices of Foud and Bailie, in 1489, the land and the right to grant it now belonged to the Scotch crown.

The era of the Scots was beginning in Zetland – and in our parish, as a precursor to what will follow, we find Jopinn Sigarsen and Hans

Sigurdsson at the Bergen lawcourt in 1489, defending their lands at 'Norbie, Hjaltaland' against a counterclaim by a Scot – named Sinclair. Though the Norsemen were successful in this case, in time the law would cease to be Norse, the courts would no longer be administered from Norway, and 'Hjaltaland' will become, slowly, 'Zetland' – and Scotch.

---

21 June 2000 – Norbie

I get the bus to Dr Hart's estate at Norbie. The road heads north past the ferry terminal, then turns up a treeless hill. The coach creeps slowly out of the little town, then freewheels down the other side of a long peat hill to a bridge, then climbs up and over another treeless peat hill into the next valley, and down to a huddle of houses. When the driver stops at a junction and tells me it's my stop, ahead there's a derelict Victorian villa and down by its fence, a man with his sheepdog, watching a flock of sheep with their lambs.

He says, 'Aye, aye,' as I approach, then, 'Fine day.' He's grizzled, brown teeth sticking out beneath his curled lip, a pipe between them, eyes hooded and doleful.

I ask the way to Dr Hart's.

He looks at me curiously. 'Oh, just you follow the road. Keep right on till the end of the road and you'll see the sign. Carry on to the top of the hill, then you'll see a junction by an old phone box. Go right at that, an carry on doon towards the beach. You'll see the laird's hoose fae the top o the hill. Norbie Haa. It's the big wan by the shore. What we call the big hoose here. It's a mile or two yet, though.'

So I set out along the road, ignoring the NORBIE PRIVATE ESTATE signs. I haven't gone far when a vehicle approaches from behind, slows down, and when I turn to look it's the same old man, driving a green van, with his dog, tongue out, panting on the passenger seat. He stops and slowly screws down the window.

'I was wonderin, maybe you'll be wantin a lift?' he says. 'I can drop you. A'm the shepherd.'

I tell him I'll just walk, thanks. As if he's disappointed, he lifts his head and girns, then drives off. I walk on. Keep right on to the end of the road, he said, so I do just that, whistling that very tune. One of Gran's.

The sun is breaking through now, the mists are clearing and in the distance I recognise the landowner's house, positioned so that it overlooks his estate, this Norbie Hall.

Five storeys tall, dwarfing the scattering of low-roofed tenant crofthouses, facing the sea, walled gardens around them, even a few gnarled trees. It's a beautiful situation, this Norbie, but it's a house of feudal masters, and the residence of the man who called and caused the red light to flash – and he is expecting me. I wander up the gravel driveway to the house, to the front porch, ring the bell and hear barking. An old balding man appears inside, surrounded by four dogs, two Alsatians and two Corgis. They whirl about his feet, barking, as he opens the door, cursing their howl.

'Hello,' he says. 'David. Would have recognised you. You're like your father.'

It's the voice from the recorded message, but now it isn't threatening, it's warm, and he takes my hand.

'You're Dr Hart?'

'Hart, yes. Your father's friend,' he says, smiling. He shakes my hand. He's very jolly this and jolly that, despite everything, as he leads me into the hallway of the Hall, followed by the dog pack. The house has a feel of old Empire, the very smell of colonialism I know from big houses in Perth, the same assortment of carvings and trophies, models and maps of exotic provinces. Here, the focus is on Selangor and Malaya.

'I have to tell you, I don't think that there's a great deal you can do. But of course you're welcome to stay in the Haa as long as you're here.'

We go upstairs, into a lounge on the first floor. The room is far smaller than I'd imagined. The deep window cavities tell why – walls of solid stone, feet thick, surround us.

He offers me a seat, then sits himself, as the dogs file in around their master's armchair, to lie down as if rehearsed. Through the dirty panes of glass, I see the views to the beautiful arc of silvery beach and the knobbly finger of dark land, pointing out to sea. And on the horizon, a strange island with a three-step outline materialises from the clearing mists.

'Can I offer you something to eat?' he asks. 'There's steak pie the cook made, would only take a few minutes to heat. My own beef.'

'No, no thanks, I've eaten. I've been eating all day. Anyway, I'm a vegetarian.'

'Ah! I'll tell her that. Would have come to pick you up from the bus if you'd called, you know.'

Then, suddenly gruff, Dr Hart apologises for not having acted sooner. He is worried about my father. They often talked. They played chess together.

'He was rather good. Tell you the truth, one can get a little lonely here, which is why I so value your father's company. Having an intelligent well-read man around, one appreciates that.'

Then Dr Hart offers me a dram. I hesitate, but he's already on his feet, moving towards the ornate sideboard, where the decanter stands. He brings it and two glasses, fills them and leaves the decanter standing there on the table between us.

And I picture my father, sitting here in the drawing room of this obviously lonely laird, drinking his whisky, warmed by the fellowship of the bottle. Soon another whisky is poured in my glass, even though I don't want it, and I've told Dr Hart so. I take a sip or two as he rambles on about Malaya, rubber, his life, and how he came to be here. I just nod now and then, my eyes nearly shutting. I can't keep awake any longer. I'm too tired to listen. So I leave the whisky and make an early exit.

He leads me up through the lower floors till we come to a narrow spiral stair. I think of David Balfour at the House of Shaws, one of the stories my father read me, and how that image stuck in mind, the steps twisting higher through the stairwell till it reaches the one where the night sky waits – that step out into flight.

But there's a landing, a tiny door and a room, the smell of damp, a bed covered with a yellow candlewick. A table, a bedside lamp, and a window onto the light, the midsummer sky still a crystal blue above, now studded with stars.

'I had Mrs Mitchell put you in here,' he says. 'Servant's quarters, really, but the big rooms take so long to warm. If I'd had more warning you were coming ...'

'Really, this is fine,' I say. 'Thanks.'

After his slow steps have gone quiet, I lie on the little bed and drift into a dream that my father is an ANZAC, and that I am the Red Cross.

There's a knock on the door.

'Are you there?'

It's him, the old laird. Across a chasm of rest, he calls me out of sleep again.

'Yes?'

I hear him shuffling on the stairhead. 'Dinner will be ready in half an hour,' he says.

Water needles my neck. I adjust the temperature and stand there, soaking it in, soaking in that goodness, that fresh steaming hotness, emptying my mind. After yesterday's madness, I'm trying my best to mend myself again, to draw the splintered pieces together into one whole. And the water helps. It seems to wash away what's inside as well as out. The heat eases the pain and when I step back out, into the chilly dampness of the bathroom and shut the taps off, I feel better. More like myself again. I go back to my room and put on a clean shift, as Gran calls it. A shift into something new, untarnished. I dry my hair with a towel, absorbed in the present again.

The table's set for three, proper cutlery and wine-glasses and all that. There's the laird and a guest. The guest's got his back to me at first, but when he turns round I see a churchman. And he stands up smiling, black curly hair on top of his head, dark eyes sparkling.

'I'd like you to meet Reverend Shand Pirie,' the laird says as the minister holds out his hand to me.

'Oh, please, Peter. Let's forget the formality. Call me Shand.'

And I shake Shand's hand. The skin feels soft but the grip is firm. Has this been set up, for my benefit, this meal, this visit?

'I'm very sorry about your father.'

'But we mustn't jump to conclusions.'

No.

A woman comes in with a big tureen. Dr Hart thanks her, introduces her as Mrs Mitchell, sits down, beckoning us to do likewise. She sets it in the middle of the table and lifts the lid off, then starts spooning into my plate. The strong aroma of onion rises on the steam in the damp air of the old house.

'French onion soup. My own onions,' the laird says. 'Absolutely no meat extract, isn't that so, Mrs Mitchell?' he adds, to the minister. 'Rod spawned a vegetarian,' he adds. 'Although you eat fish, don't you?'

And then the minister starts.

'Our Heavenly Father, we thank thee for this, our daily bread, and pray that those who are cold and hungry tonight will find a place to sleep and food to eat, by Thy Grace. Amen.'

This is the first time I've heard anybody say grace over a meal in many years and it releases the memory tape. Spinning out come a hundred family meals, my grandmother presiding. The clink of spoons on china, the blue willow patterns round the lip of the plates, the formal place settings, the smell of the soup, all loaded with remembering. Wash your hands before dinner, now sit up straight, don't play with your cutlery. Don't fiddle with your fork. The bairn inside is cowed down, polite, waiting for the sign.

You may begin.

But Reverend Pirie takes a first spoonful of soup and places the spoon on the middle of the empty plate, then stares at me.

'Are you a churchgoer?'

'No, not for years.'

'So you share your father's scepticism?'

'Scepticism?'

'Oh, he and I have had many an argument. Always friendly, mind you.'

I ask, was my father interested in religion?

Dr Hart and the Reverend exchange glances. 'Your father is, I think, a kind of instinctive Christian. That is to say, he lives according to the Christian doctrine, although he was never quite able to accept the idea that Christ was God Incarnate. Now, he isn't alone in that, by no means. Some of the foremost scholars of our age have had difficulty with just that idea. You may have heard of Don Cupitt? No? A television series a few years ago? No? Well, as I see it, it is the teachings of Christ that are the fundamental things. Don't you agree, Peter?'

Dr Hart nods. The minister carries on. I'm watching his shining eyes, so cool, so at ease in themselves and the way they see the world. Through certainty. Through a definite belief.

'Whether or not one chooses to believe that Jesus really was the Son of God, whatever that may mean, whether or not we can accept the Biblical version of events, there's no dubiety over the teachings themselves. Your father agreed on that.'

'On what exactly?'

'The Christian call for compassion. The ideals of faith, hope and charity. Kindness to one's fellow man. The aspiration towards goodness. Turning the other cheek. Seeking out the mote in one's own eye, rather than judging others.'

He lists these like they were self-evidently true. I finish my soup and put my spoon down. He's leaning forward towards me as if he expects me to say something.

'You're familiar with these ideas?'

'Oh, I remember the teachings. But there's one thing that always bothers me. The whole Imperialist approach. Subjugation and the suppression of so-called heresy. That's why I can't take God or the church seriously.'

The minister is still smiling, as if he's heard all this a thousand times and he's got an answer at the ready. But all he says is: 'I sense at this moment in time, you're in need of faith, you're seeking something.' He laughs, as if he expected a comment, anticipated it and had the response ready. 'Not just your father, but Our Father. And the way to Him is through his Son. All it takes is for you to open up your heart to Jesus, to ask Him to come into your life and immediately the pain you feel will ease. I know, believe me.'

As he speaks he takes my hand in his, the touch of a concerned friend, or a lover, sensing the pulse of emotion inside. And for a moment, he has me, caught in a reflex, a pattern of physical call and response that I know so well, from my mother, her friends, the church in Perth. His eyes have the look of genuine compassion.

Mrs Mitchell comes back carrying a silver platter with a salmon on board, and starts to portion it out. The Reverend Pirie leans away, his serious hanging face with him for a moment, before he looks up, transformed to happiness again.

I take my plate in turn, and the three of us begin to eat.

'I was reading earlier today,' the minister goes on, talking with his mouth full, 'a man called Joseph Campbell. Do you know his *Hero with a Thousand Faces*?'

I shake my head, although I do.

'No? Oh, he's a wonderful scholar. Really, you should read him. He spent his whole life studying the world's myths. There was a television series based on his work a while ago.' He's chewing and eating as he talks, excited by the sound of his own voice, while Dr Hart looks on admiringly, supping his wine with more enthusiasm than he has for eating the big fish.

'It's just that when you mentioned the settlers in America earlier, Peter, it reminded me of where he quotes this New England preacher of the late eighteenth century. I can't recall the exact words, but the image is one of the bow of God's wrath, with the arrow ready on the string, and he says that justice is bending the arrow is towards you. And that it's only at his pleasure that the arrow isn't fired. Now it's a poetic metaphor, obviously, but one senses that impending doom that hangs over us all. Whether it's our own lives, or our children's, or our parents', at any time, without the slightest warning, that arrow can shoot out and destroy all your certainties. That is what happens. People drift along quite happily as long as the arrow doesn't shoot out, then suddenly they find themselves in need of help. That's my vocation, to help in that hour of need, to help them find the path to God. To let them see that despite everything, God's promise is kept, that we can trust in Him, in His will, that every sorrow can and shall be overcome in time.'

He chews away at the forkfuls of salmon and salad, watching me. So I just eat. I eat, I nod politely, sit up straight and clean my plate. Dr Hart keeps filling his glass. And by the time the salmon's eaten, the minister's flagging, his words are drying up, the storm is passing. He's giving into the silence, quietude has swallowed him, though still he's talking,

and I

drift

'Split the stick and there's Jesus,' he says and turns to me, his dark eyes dancing, as if I must surely share his amazement. But I've no idea what he's on about.

'It's a Gnostic aphorism. God at the heart of everything, even the dumb, inanimate wood. It's like the teachings of the Koran, wherever you turn there is the presence of Allah.'

'Ah …' says Dr Hart, and fills his glass.

The Reverend Pirie hesitates, remembering. 'Peter, you recall we were discussing this Bible Code book the other day. Another question which arises concerns whether or not the code is written in stone, so to speak. You've heard of this, David, I expect? It has been spot-on in predicting future events which took place after its first writing but which, to us, happened in the past. The thing is, what of our perceived future? Eh?'

He quickly takes a few bites of his meal, chewing furiously, desperate to return to his subject, as if food is just an obstacle. 'Now, Roger Penrose suggests in his book that it is only our consciousness which requires us to perceive a flow of time and that to a physicist space and time are interchangeable. Time is no more required to flow than is space. And if time truly doesn't flow, then it is reasonable to assume that a being of sufficient intelligence, possessing the technology capable of producing something as complex as the Bible Code, would be able to view the whole fabric of time in one complete picture.'

With the timing of a master orator, Pirie bides his moment, then continues: 'My dear friends, the reality of what we creatures down here on earth experience may only represent a tiny part of the whole and be no more significant than any other part of the picture. No more, in fact, than a single thread within an intricate complexity making up this weave of time.'

The Reverend takes a breath. The echoes of his sonorous tone die out. I am listening.

'Is the code predicting just one possible and unchangeable future, or is it presenting us with probabilities based upon what is happening in our perceived now?' Dr Hart asks.

What's he making of this, the laird? Or Mrs Mitchell, in the kitchen? Is she eavesdropping, or oblivious?

Pirie takes another bite, considers. then continues: 'We don't know. The Bible Code contains the interlinked phrases "It was made by computer" and "The writing of God engraved on tablets." This suggests that computer technology was required to unlock the code, which was in fact the case, though it seems bizarre.'

Again, he eats a few furious mouthfuls. 'Sir Isaac Newton was obsessed with the notion that there was a code in the Bible and spent much time trying to prove it. No doubt if he'd had access to a modern computer, he could have found it.'

The minister stops and gazes round. The laird suddenly lifts his head from the careful deboning of his salmon. 'So, tell me, if the code is a way of warning us of possible future catastrophic events on our planet, how do we go about putting it to good use? How can we know what to look for, Shand?'

The Reverend Pirie, Shand, considers. He looks at me with those excited dark eyes, challenged by the thought, delighted to be so questioned. 'What we might do is to examine carefully the current events we believe may be shaping our future in a significant way and then look for these in the code, and search for surrounding clues as to what might happen. It may be in our best interests to do just this. For just as the code told of comet Shoemaker-Levy smashing into Jupiter, naming the comet, the planet and the date exactly, it also encodes "comet" with the Hebrew year 5766, our 2006, and "Year predicted for End".'

I just eat, silently, listening. The minister is barely halfway through his meal. The laird is listening silently, drinking, a frown on his face, as he picks the bones from his big fish.

'Yes, I've heard of this,' I say, finally.

'Remarkable, isn't it?' the laird asks.

'I have a few notes here,' the minister says, and pulls from his pocket a folded paper, which he flattens and reads, indicating quotations with his fingers.

'Comet is also encoded with 5772 or 2012 – "Earth annihilated" and "It will be crumbled" and "I will tear to pieces". All in here.' He taps the page. 'Great earthquakes are forecast for Japan in either 2000 or 2006, as well as for Los Angeles in 2010. "World war" is encoded with 2000 or 2006, as is "atomic holocaust". There's more, but even that should be enough to make us sit up and take notice.'

The laird puts down his knife and fork. 'If it is real, it could be the very mechanism which saves us from some future catastrophic event,' he says, but do I detect a wink in the look he throws me?

Pirie doesn't see it, however. He continues reading from his notes. 'It even suggests this itself where, along with "world war", "atomic holocaust" and "end of days" the phrase "code will save" is found. "Code will save", eh? Now what do you think of that?'

No one answers.

But in my head the phrase resonates. I like it, the idea that
CODE WILL SAVE

Mrs Mitchell comes in to clear the table. I jump up and lift the plates in a clumsy pile and ask her where I should put them. Dr Hart's glare suggests I've broken the rules, but the kitchen is warm and sweet after the pointless table-talk, the pointless formality, and I want to linger there. Mrs Mitchell begins scraping plates into a tall wastebin. She turns to me and smiles again, grey hair and pencil-dark eyebrows contrasting.

'I get the feeling you've heard enough for a while,' she says. 'He does go on. I'm Mary, by the way.'

Her hospitality is a welcome surprise, and I nod. She leans back against the wall and wipes her forehead with the back of her hand.

'I suppose you see it all from a different perspective,' I say.

'What?'

'Dinner parties. Guests.'

She shakes her head. 'Oh I don't mind that side of it all. No, I like that side of it. Though I don't think I'd like to spend a whole night listening to the minister drone on.'

I laugh. 'Have you worked here long?'

'A couple of years. Since I came back from the mainland. I was away from here for twenty years.'

'What brought you back?' I ask.

She smiles, sighs. 'Ah well, that's a long story. But my mother's getting on and I was too far away to help. And things changed, where I was.'

'Where was that?'

'Glasgow. I worked for a firm of solicitors. I'd been there for years.'

She lifts a packet of cigarettes and a lighter.

'Do you mind?'

I shake my head and stand watching as she places the cigarette in her mouth, flicks a gold lighter, then takes a long draw.

'So what about you? How are you feeling?' she asks.

I shrug. 'All right, considering. I'm a bit disorientated. Dislocated.'

And she makes a face, a face of pity. I feel like I could talk to this woman. Confess even.

'Right. Coffee,' she says and stubs out a half-smoked cigarette.

Both of the diners look at us as I follow her in, bearing the silver tray like one of the staff, rather than a guest. I'm breaking the boundaries, crossing the divide between master and servant.

The Reverend Pirie can't contain his tongue for more than a few seconds. He's immediately on to me again. 'I was just saying to Peter, your father is an irascible old chap.'

'Irascible?' I say.

'Rather quick-tempered.'

'Oh yes?'

'We've had a few arguments, haven't we?'

And he looks for confirmation towards Dr Hart, who raises his eyebrows and refills his glass. He's on the second bottle. His eyes are looking glazed, like he's elsewhere, just going through the social motions. But Pirie isn't bothered, he's happy to answer his own questions, he's a man of many words, a talker for a living, a one-man dialogue.

'I remember one evening we started on the subject of pacifism. Your father was telling me about some poet he knew who'd argued against the Second World War, and he and I ended up in, well, a very heated discussion, let's say.'

And he looks at me as if maybe I'm disappointing him, not performing as he had expected the child of the father to do. Just sitting quietly, eating crème brûlée, letting it all wash past, maintaining silence while the minister wants me to open up, to reveal myself, my beliefs, so he can challenge me, overcome me, prove me wrong by his superior knowledge and intellectual reasoning. But tonight I'm an intellectual pacifist, not interested in conflict. And he's not my spiritual leader, he's an apparatchik, a trained talker, his head full of received ideas. I'd rather be washing up with Mrs Mitchell. Just let him rattle on, talking about this, that.

Bible codes? Apocalypse?

I make apologies before the brandy, saying I'll have a stroll before turning in, just to take the air. As I'm going out, he stands up to shake my hand.

'There's a service tomorrow at eleven. I'd be very pleased if you'd come. And if there's anything I can do, if you feel that you want to talk, or pray, then please, let me know. It's what I'm here for. The manse is right by the church.'

This beautiful northern summer light is still strong though it's late. Half ten. The tide is high tonight. The waves roll further up the beach.

And I think of him, here, my father, talking over dinner with this verbose minister and the laird of old Empire. Where he stood between them. But then I've always wondered that. When he was bound to the burghers in Perth, he followed the party line, writing his editorials to suit the mood of the town, following, not leading. And I always wondered how he really felt about some of the issues he was covering, how they squared with his early politics, the radicalism he was fond of bragging about. I always thought he had rejected those beliefs in favour of something more utilitarian. Sad that it was only when he gave up all his responsibilities and ties to family and community, he could be that free.

But as long as there are other folk who don't believe as we do, who won't turn the other cheek, who would stab you in the back or spit in your eye, what use are those loving, Christian pacifist principles? Just to be hung on a cross, stoned to death, thrown to the lions, cast out into the wilderness like my father when at last he finally did stand up for something he believed in, after all those years of writing what folk wanted to hear.

Apocalypse? I lived with that terror, that Hiroshima hollowness. From the time when my mother's skirts and my father's shoulders could no longer shield or support me, I lived with that.

And I remember my mother describing her vision of heaven before she died, the way she pictured it, a distant shore somewhere over the water, a beautiful misty shoreline that you could only get to by relinquishing the life you knew. An emigrant's dream, of a kind, an Australian dream, a colonist's vision.

But now that isn't sustainable. Barring the immediate arrival out of that clear sky of a shining cigar-shaped craft, I'm lost for explanations. Just a speck under stars, daring to look up and wonder, daring to take into myself true knowledge of the scale of things, the sheer vastness of it all, to be frozen by the sense of inadequacy and helplessness that this knowledge entails.

And yet, there are things, worlds smaller, all that subatomic stuff, tinier than I can get an image of, spinning right through us, somehow constituting us as it does. A miracle, really a miracle, that I can even think about it, that I can sit here on this quiet beach and even begin to think about it.

That I could look up at that crescent moon and think specks like me have travelled there.

Here on this northern island, there's nothing between me and the stars, no trees for shelter, no tenements. Just this beach with the tide moving slowly

in

And then, back across the beach towards the laird's house I see him, the man of the cloth, a black crow, following me. The minister is at the end of the road staring in my direction, about a hundred yards away,

calling out and

waving

Letter from Peter A Scot
to Rev. Archibald Nicol,
September 7th 2000

Dear Reverend Nicol,

In response to your letter, I must apologise for the delay in responding.
I was indeed the person who supplied James Gabrielsen's history to
Rod Cunninghame. I am shocked to hear of his death. Rod and I had
corresponded infrequently ever since I first wrote to him in the fall of
1993. I had not heard from him for some while.

To explain, in my retirement I became very interested in genealogy.
Many colonials were transplanted with myths of family wealth which
they in turn left like heirlooms to their children's children, and our
family had a tradition that, at some point in time, we had owned a large
in estate in northern Scotland, called Norbie.

My great-aunt Margaret Jean had a watercolour of the old family
house which hung in her hallway throughout my childhood, and after
her death I inherited this painting. I realised that I had almost always
known about this house and what it represented, but that the true story
was never openly discussed. It was Aunt Margaret Jean's death which
spurred me to inquire.

Piecing together the evidence from various sources, I came across a
branch of our family which had gone to New Zealand, and which had
taken the name Cunninghame for some reason. I was surprised and
delighted to discover Rod's existence, and even more so when he replied
to my letter. It turned out that he knew nothing of the changing of the
name. I think it came as something of a bombshell to him to find out
that he was not a Cunninghame at all but an original 'Scot with one t',
like myself. The mystery of the splitting of the branches of the family
puzzled us both. What had happened, to cause this parting so severe that
it sent us to separate continents, living under different names?

And what had this to do with the estate of Norbie, and the family's fall from wealth, if that part of the myth were to prove true? Rod knew nothing of this either, of course, until we made contact, and I remember he wrote that it came as a shock to him to discover that his Scotch roots were not firm in the heartland of Scotland in Perthshire, but gripping to its very edge. It was as a result of our correspondence that he chose to move to Zetland, indeed, to Norbie itself. How ironic that he should now have died there, in the place of our common ancestors. I, having in a way sent him there, almost feel responsible – but it was in reality Rod's own curiosity that sent him northwards. He wanted to know the full story, being a journalist by habit and by training.

When I came across Gabrielsen's history, that helped to fill many of the gaps. I obtained it, after a long search, from one of his descendants who had, ironically, also settled in New Zealand, but in the South Island. It turned out to be quite a famous lost document among the historians of Zetland, as it had been referred to in Gabrielsen's obituary in 1899 but never came to light – because it was in Christchurch in a box of old family photos, ignored for years.

If you have read Gabrielsen's history, you may well have figured out for yourself what the family connections are, but just in case you are still puzzled, I'll map these out for you and put them into this letter.

Rod's forebears are Albert and Robina. I have spoken with one person who remembered them – another great-aunt. She was in her eighties by the time we met, but could recall visiting them once when she was about six or seven. She remembered Robina wrapping her in a lacework shawl – a 'hap', as the Zetlanders call them – and made a point of how beautiful Robina herself was, how graceful, even as an old lady.

I suppose one thing you won't get from Gabrielsen is what happened to the Scots after they left Norbie. I don't have all the facts, but I can tell you Albert's interest in motor cars continued, not as a manufacturer but an entrepreneur of a kind. He was the first man to bring an automobile to New Zetland, then later he opened a garage. Rather a change for the young laird, the boy who had driven his princely gig around the few miles of road in Norbie.

Perhaps the family feud was the reason why he wanted to cut the ties with his old life, who knows? Nonetheless, the family story goes that Albert and Robina Scot-Cunninghame were happy in New Zetland. The evidence shows they certainly stayed together till his death in September 1937.

Regarding the matter of the mysterious David, Rod did once write to me about his family. I believe the two had fallen out at some stage, around the time of the death of his wife. I can quote you the few lines he wrote, which I guess must be about David: 'My other son, unlike Martin with his musical gifts, seems to have no particular quality to distinguish him. He dropped out of university and has a child with a girl he doesn't live with. He doesn't get in touch often.' He adds the following, 'It is sad and strange how families explode, when the centre cannot hold, as Yeats phrased it.'

I'm afraid I can't personally help you in contacting David, though I can and do understand your concern. The Cunninghame side of the Scot family, as I encountered it, consisted only of Rod and his mother, and I wouldn't know where to begin to look now that Rod's gone. But if the son's name is indeed David Cunninghame, you may be able to trace him these days using the worldwide web. I will see what my son-in-law can do, with his computer knowledge.

I would like to have a look at the contents of these notebooks you kindly offered to copy for me. Is this a kind of journal David wrote?

If I can be of any further assistance, do please let me know. I do understand your desire to find your lost sheep. The Lord's ways are manifold and mysterious.

Yours in faith
Peter A Scot

Letter from Philippa Gabrielsen
to Rev. Archibald Nicol
September 20th 2000

Bon Hoga
Serrafir
Tokumua

Dear Archibald

I thought you may be interested in this little piece on New Zetland
penned by one of our members in the Heritage Society for this new
website, which recently was launched by a friend of a friend in the US.
It's a revolutionary idea which may never catch on, an encyclopaedia
anyone can add information to!

There will be much more to follow in due course. We are very keen
to present our community using the new technology as a means of
attracting visitors and boosting tourism. Tokomua is isolated, but such a
beautiful place to visit.

Btw (computer speak for 'by the way') you really should get a
computer. Then you would get my messages instantly!

I hope you're in better health than when you last wrote.

Best wishes

Philippa

Tokumua ('old rock') formerly **New Zetland**, is an island nation located in the South Pacific Ocean, 47 S 179 W, to the east of <u>Dunedin</u> in <u>New Zealand</u> and south of the <u>Chatham Islands</u>. Although self-governing, Tokumua is in free association with New Zealand, meaning that the Sovereign in Right of New Zealand is also Tokumua's head of state.

In schools, the <u>Tokumuan</u> language is taught alongside English and both are used in business and communications. The primary vehicle for business is a creole, known as '<u>Alroki</u>'. The people are predominantly Polynesian, though 19th century settlement by people from <u>Zetland</u> in Scotland has created an interesting ethnic mix in the southern islands of Yer and Unsi. These settlers have maintained the language and the customs of their European forebears and visitors may still hear the old <u>Zetlandic</u> language spoken in the quaint little capital Serrafir, where some stone dwellings that were erected in the Zetlandic style still stand today.

TOKUMUA

SERRAFIR

NEW ZETLAND

Coordinates – 47 S 179 W
Capital – Serrafir/Sellafirt
Official Languages –
Alroki
Zetlandic
English
Demonym – Tokomulan
Government – Constitutional monarchy
Head of State – Queen Elizabeth II
Premier – Toke Faka Gabrielsen
Associated State – Constitutional Act 1974
Total area – 1,469 sq. miles
Water – 7%
Population – 2000 est. 22,679
Currency – New Zealand Dollar
Internet TLD – .tk
Calling Code – + 683

HISTORY

Tokumua was first settled by Polynesian sailors around 900AD and by further settlers (or invaders) in the sixteenth century. It is regarded as the ancestral home of the Murikavi people, the second wave of Polynesian migrants *c.* 1500, a people remarkable for their pacifism. Their specific origin is uncertain, and debate continues as to whether they were part of an early Maori migration.

The Murikavi population of Tokumua was estimated in 1800 at around 2,000, scattered through a number of inhabited islands, each with their distinct identity. At that time there was no national leader of government. Chiefs and heads of families exercised authority over small regions. Around 1800, perhaps due to the increasing presence of foreigners, the viki, the practice of kingship began, with the patu-iki ruling over the whole archipelago and presiding over an annual council of island representatives at the sacred round-tower of Mu-Ra.

The first European to sight the island group was Captain James Cook in 1774, but he was refused permission to land by the natives and continued his voyage. He reported a richness of seals and whales around its shores and in time this drew a great quantity of whalers from Australia and America, as well as Britain. They centred their activities on the island of Yer, where a substantial shantytown had grown up by 1800. However, the thirst for profit was so great that within thirty years the trade was exhausted and the interest moved to Macdonald Island and MacQuarrie Island. It was not until around 1850 that the sealers returned, this time in greater number.

A tense stand-off existed between Viki and Murikavi. The natives were afraid they might lose everything if they did not make friends with the strangers, and so made contact through an interpreter. This man, a young Scotch sea captain, John or Jack Kuliness of Zetland, established himself at the former shantytown, which he called Sellafirt, in the wake of the whaling era. It had been the site of a substantial station, and Kuliness cleverly used the timber left behind to build himself not only a pleasant bungalow but a small chapel and a trading post.

Captain Kuliness had learned to speak Murikavi and proved himself useful to the natives in negotiation with the viki, subsequently providing both tools and knowledge the Murikavi considered of genuine benefit. In time Kuliness brought his wife and child to live at Sellafirt. Their house was extended in ever more grand ways, and they lived a contented life there, accepted and respected by the Murikavi and profiting by their trade.

Kuliness brought a number of his countrymen there to work and a small community of Zetlanders grew up, each farming their own land and fishing, just as they had done at home. Despite the fact that these islands were on the other side of the world, the climate and the latitude were not too different. The Zetlander might thrive here.

Captain Kuliness's life came to an abrupt and shocking end when he was eaten by cannibals in Vanuata while engaged in 'blackbirding' – taking native islanders to work in the sugar plantations of Queensland, an activity barely distinguishable in the worst cases from the slave trade. He had financed his colonial pretension in Tokumua by the dirtiest of methods. Captain Kuliness's widow Isabella returned with her child to live in Zetland, where she sold the property her husband had purchased from the local Murikavi chief to a laird keen to move some of his tenants. She it was who christened the island as 'New Zetland' in her advertisements.

So it came about that, a decade later, on sponsored passages, eighteen families from the northern Scotch islands of Zetland arrived in Sellafirt, New Zetland, led by their minister, the Reverend Thorwald Gabrielsen, to settle virgin land. They found that all the huts and sheds they had intended using as immediate shelter had been taken apart and carried off, used to build rudimentary wooden boats or shacks, so they had no choice but to live under canvas till new structures were built.

The early days of the new settlement were thus difficult and a number of families left for the Southland of New Zealand, but those who persisted in time profited from the rich fishing around the islands.

In 1887, fearing annexation by a less benevolent colonial power, King Farak-iki, who reigned from 1887 to 1897, ceded sovereignty to the British Empire. By the year 1900 the new settlement had begun to thrive. Kuliness's embryonic Sellafirt grew rapidly by the subsequent settlers' efforts and attracted more immigrants from Britain, including another wave from Zetland prior to the First World War, when assisted passages resumed in 1904.

As this influx progressed, the majority of Murikavi retreated to the west and the north of the archipelago. As a people they were greatly afflicted by the diseases the Europeans had brought. A group of elders went as far as the outermost island of Fu Ra, no more than a sea-cliff rock, in the hope of escaping these pestilences, but even there the evil was among them. The last Murikavi of full blood died in 1923.

Nonetheless Kuliness, or 'Kapiyaki' as he was known, was a well-respected figure among the native Murikavi and the tale of the coming of Kapiyaki is still told in Tokumua today.

ORAL RECORDING – DATED 12.3.1954

TRANSCRIPTION AND TRANSLATION FROM TOKUMUAN BY JOHN INKSTIR

For twelve generations the Murikavi were in Tokumua and no one came. They loved the land and lived in peace there, for after the Rorikratira battle it was decreed there should be no more bloodshed among us, that disputes should be settled by individual combat which would end when blood was drawn.

Then the great wooden ships of the Viki began to come among us. They killed many sealfolk and took the calving whales. They butchered them on the shore and boiled them into foul-smelling potions, carried them away in their wooden ships, in barrels.

At first the Murikavi kept their distance from the strangers. They withdrew from the place where the Viki made their longhouses and watched from a distance. But they brought powerful tools with them, a spear that threw a tiny burning stone and killed us from afar, and they sent illness to strike us down in our sleep.

So the elders gathered and agreed we must talk with these powerful strangers, find out what they want and give it to them so they will be at peace with us.

Only one among them knew how to speak – Kapiyaki, who later came to live among us. He told us their demands were slaves and land, women to lie with them, the food from our gardens, that they were not to be trusted.

When the seal and the whale left our shores, the Viki left too, to hunt them wherever they went, even to death. But Kapiyaki stayed with us and taught many useful things, like how the Viki weave their nets and make their kreels, and how to fuse wood with nails. He told us he was not like them, but a Yetlaani man, who were a people of peace like the Murikavi. He told the Elders he could bring more Yetlaani to Tokumua so they could teach the Murikavi how to use wooden ships. He would show them how the Yetlaani weave sails, and how their animals grow threads to weave the magic patterns of his gansi. Kapiyaki said he would bring a man to teach them how to write their words and how to find eternal life.

So the Yetlaani came in a big wooden ship as Yaki had foretold and built their Toon at Serrafir. They brought their flocks of Yows, whose hair was thread. He proved to the Murikavi he was a man of trust. The Yetlaani were a people of peace as he had said. Some of them were accepted by Murikavi families as sons and children were born with two tongues, who spoke both Murikavi and Yetlaani.

Kapiyaki was the chief of the Yetlaani all of his life. No young warrior dared challenge him. He was the wealthiest man in the world. He built the school and the kirik at Serrafir so all people of Tokumua could live forever in heaven with Jesus Christ our Lord.

All was well in Tokumua. The Viki had gone and the Yetlaani had come. They taught the Murikavi many things and the Murikavi taught them many things. Together they became strong as one.

But when Kapiyaki was eaten by the people of Malitia, Serrafir became dark and stormy. Miss Kapiyaki went back to the homeland of the Yetlaani, and many Yetlaani went to other lands. Some grew sick and died. They left Tokumua to the Murikavi again, except the children who stayed with their Murikavi mothers, the children of two tongues.

But when the wooden ship with the Minatir arrived the peace was broken. He brought many of his sheep, the Kiriki people, and they ravaged the plants. Soon the land of Yer was bare, and nothing grew but ferns. The Kiriki were full of anger and mistrust and measle poison. The Murikavi elders knew they did not know how to give eternal life, like Kapiyaki. The measle poison spread to the Murikavi and so many grew sick and died.

The elders of the Murikavi who were left gathered and held coonsil. They decided to launch the canoes which first brought them to Tokumua and retreat to the island of Fu-ra, which lay towards the morning sun, and could be seen sometimes on the edge of the ocean, like a great rock, strong and safe. On the rock of Fu-ra, the sickness and the firespears of the Viki would not reach the people. They mourned the passing of Kapiyaki, the only one of the strangers who knew how to speak.

22 June 2000 – Norbie

I open the skylight window on deafening birdsong. Gulls arching up and round the big house from down at the beach. There's a skylark singing high up. I breathe in deeply, cold northern air giving urgent signals to my lungs, to work harder. I breathe in. My heavy eyes are opening fully. Breathe in again, deep cold air. After breakfast we go to the place where my father last lived. The place he has disappeared from.

Where could he have gone, leaving a frozen chicken to defrost, till the stink was unbearable and the old laird began to suspect?

Last night Dr Hart said they got on well together, my father having grown up in Australia, Dr Hart in Malaya. Two children of the Empire, now in retreat. The laird liked him, they played chess. They talked about all sorts of things, family was just one.

But Dr Hart said he detected, yes, from a very early point, his moodiness, the deep depression that at first he tried to cover up. It was connected to his family, yes, he was sure he felt old, rejected, useless – no longer able to do anything for anybody. Service was important to him, the idea of serving a community. It was an instinctive form of socialism, a pure form. 'Not that we agreed politically,' the laird had stammered, when boozed.

Dr Hart drives an old Land Rover that smells strongly of dogs and alcohol, veering to one side of the narrow road, then the other. I wonder how early the sun is over the yardarm with him, if indeed it ever moves at all, or if it sits permanently at glorious sundown on his empire, as we drive up the hill away from the big house, to the phone box, then right, round a corner and along a narrow track cut into a steep hillside. No trees.

The doctor is quiet, maybe a little uncomfortable after last night's exuberance. To make conversation, I ask about a ruined building near the beach.

'Is it an old Celtic church? It says St Mary's on the map.'

It's a habit of my mother's, asking about churches.

He grunts non-committally, says, 'Nearly there,' and points towards a wooden house in the distance, set above the sandy beach. As we approach, I can see that it's not just one but there's a row of three, and that the middle one is a burned-out shell, with only the concrete foundations and the charred lower spars still standing.

'What happened here?' I ask.

'A fire. Couple of months ago, around Easter. Luckily no one was in at the time. But it completely destroyed the place. Takes so long for the fire brigade to arrive here from the town. Really thought the other two would catch light. I fetched the garden hose from the house and we kept that playing on the roofs till the firemen came. By a piece of good fortune, it was the first day in a month when there wasn't a wind. Flames went straight up. Gave everyone an awful fright, though.'

'No wonder.'

'Your father was something of a hero, actually. Went in and rescued a few things. Tenants are a young couple expecting their first child. They'd bought various bits and pieces. Your father helped them pull some of the more valuable things out. Must clear this up.'

My father, the hero. We stop and get out, go up to the shell and look in at the mess of burned wood and melted household items, a metal bed frame, a sink. The air is cold, and the wind whistles now. Dr Hart fumbles in the pocket of his tweed jacket for a key. Except for the fact that the middle one is now a shell, these chalets would have been identical, three timber shoeboxes, with glass fronts pointed towards the view to the beach. They're old and have doubtless been battered by many a northern gale. They're tinder.

Somebody peers out the window of the other remaining chalet, from behind the curtain, only a clothes line away, a man staring intently at me through the glass. For a second, we look directly at one another.

I turn to face the three concrete blocks that form the steps up to the door of my father's residence. Dr Hart unlocks it and steps back, gesturing to me to go first. I hesitate on the threshold. The smell still lingers from the rotting chicken. The chalet has a sitting area with two cheap wooden-framed chairs, a coffee table covered in cup-rings and a basic settee. Behind is a tiny kitchen with a breakfast bar and a couple of high stools for happy holidaymakers to sit up on. The floor is covered with worn linoleum. Dingy floral orange curtains skirt the windows, a faded Renoir print hangs above a stove.

Nothing to say that this place is my father's, no sense of him at all, until I see the papers underneath the scratched coffee table. I recall him with papers spread everywhere. For years I thought that's how everybody's house was. Piled up with magazines, newspapers, books. It wasn't till I started going to friends' houses after school that I saw ours was different. They might have a bookcase or a magazine rack, all neat and well under control, but our house was the victim of a disease, a printed-word disease that was eating into the rooms like some kind of virus running loose through a body. Everywhere, my father's papers. This is so unlike him, this neat little pile under the coffee table.

And then in one corner of the chalet, I spot a fishing rod in its case with a lovat-green hat hooked over the top, and a pair of green wellington boots. I'm still on the step peering. Dr Hart, standing two steps behind me, grunts. 'Well? Shall we go in?'

But well is what it is not. In no sense. No crystal water waiting to be drawn up in a bucket. No mineral spring. No sense of health, good fortune, of comfort. But there is a welling, a springing up of feelings, a fountain-head of emotion inside, of me regressing, as the old laird ushers me in. Press

Rewind

I'm a child again, at the door of my father's study in Perth, waiting for him to open it as I knock. Daddy, can I come in? I can hear the scrape of his chair legs on the floor as he pushes it back from the desk. The step of his shoes on the floorboards. As ever, I shift a language gear, get ready to speak properly.

He hates me using slang.

'YOU-SING!' ... 'ing'. Like 'sing'!'

But this isn't his study in Perth. This place stinks so badly I think I'm just going to wait till Dr Hart's gone, then torch it, burn the whole lot, like the place next door. Like tinder it'll burn, whoosh: it has went up in flames, daddy. And I hear

has GONE up! Not 'has went'!

His Australian-Scotch accent flaring.

But I can't not go, can't but go in, creeping like he was still there, like it was still Perth, and he's grinning and offering me a seat, saying sit down, I want to talk to you. Serious, like he has some deep truth to impart, some ancient wisdom to be transmitted across his desk to me. In Perth there was always that between us, that barrier strewn with papers. And yet I loved that desk. When he sold the house, I wanted that desk. I wanted it for my own. Even though I hardly use it now.

My head spins. I've been travelling since the previous morning, the train, the ferry. I smell the rotten chicken and my stomach churns up the thought of the sea, swelling, swaying, swilling about.

But I do go in. Dr Hart is at my back, with his bunch of keys. He sniffs, grunts, then strides confidently across the floor, like it's his place and not my father's. Which it is, of course.

He gives me a look of deep distaste.

'That smell! It's a little better now. But when I opened the door the other day, it was ... I really thought that ...'

He doesn't have to say. I can smell the obvious thought: there's something dead in here. But I know there's no body. Instead I'm struck by the bareness, the absence of things, as if his life is clear, purer. I sit down in a rickety old wooden chair. The elastic straps under the cushion have broken.

Dr Hart goes to the sink and pushes the window above it fully open.

'Can't leave these open because of the wind. I think I'll have to get some sort of heavy-duty disinfectant.'

I peer at him, muttering away to himself, inconvenienced by my father's disappearance, and I wonder just how deep this friendship he boasts about really goes. When the fire's over, when the disappeared are found, dead or alive, he's still the landlord with a property to maintain, new tenants to find, bad smells to evacuate. He turns and sees me watching him, gives a twisted grin.

'So …'

'So indeed.'

We stare at each other a moment. He jangles keys.

'The police should be here today. Promised they would arrive yesterday but no one came. I called the station and complained. The officer said they were undermanned. Undermanned! Can you believe it? Summer holidays, he said. Summer holidays indeed. All too typical of the state of this country these days. Personally I don't think they're taking this seriously. In the meantime, we shouldn't touch anything. But if you want to have a look round, I suppose that'll be all right.'

'I'd just like to sit here a while and think.'

Dr Hart is hovering at the door, his form a black shadow against the sunlight coming through the glass. 'All right. I've got business to attend to. I'll leave you here a while. Shall I come over when I've finished and give you a lift back?'

'No, I'll walk back. I won't stay long. And anyway I like to walk.'

He's taking a key from his bunch and looking uncomfortable, like it's painful to part with even this bit of his empire.

'Well then, I'll see you back at the house?'

'Fine then. I'll just take a look around.'

He goes out, glancing back like he isn't sure he's doing the right thing, as if he doesn't really trust me.

I watch the laird leave, turning his Land Rover in a three-point turn, squeezing round and away up the gravel road, weaving about, dodging the potholes. Alone, his black shadow gone, I chill. I look around at my father's stuff, aware for the first time of his disappearance as a fact. Not his not being near me. That I've had for years, his absence from my life. This is his absence from his own. Then this lump swells in my throat and keeps growing bigger. My hands go forward as if detached from my brain, begin raking through issues of the local paper piled up under the coffee table. *Readers Digest. National Geographic.* A couple of yellowed broadsheets from weeks before, *The Scotsman, The Times.* Magazines, advertising leaflets for double-glazing. A religious tract titled 'YOUR SOUL'. 'What is God's Plan for us?' it says. 'Having ignored my Sustainer, presumed on His resources, broken His laws, dishonoured His property, may I remind you that there is a day coming when God will judge the secrets of men.'

I sit there a while in the chalet, still feeling the effects of the trip on the ferryboat, swaying up and down like I'm still on board. In the damp kitchen cupboards there's a mountain of tin cans, of fruit, rice pudding, baked beans. Spaghetti hoops and cooked ham. But what dominates is a mass of cans of soups of all varieties. Lentil, tomato, chicken, minestrone. Tins piled upon tins. I laugh at that – my father, the man who went out into the wilderness hunting, shooting, fishing, who loved red meat, who never understood why I became a vegetarian, and why I wouldn't help him light the barbecue, now eating out of tins.

Then I catch sight of a small brass key on the window ledge, and pick it up. Just a key, but it must open something, a cupboard, maybe. But after a while of looking I've found no lock for it to open, so I stick it in my pocket. I sit a while. A long while. Emptying my mind till at last there's peace and I wonder what it was that happened to him after he had left the south and started wandering. The truth is that he'd changed so much from the man we knew, the one we rebelled against, the one we hated when he seemed to want to direct our lives, when we were leaving home.

Don't do this, do that.

Watch me, see how I do it.

Right, now have a go.

No, no, no. Not like that. You aren't paying attention.

I go outside, leave the glass doors open and sit on the topmost step. The air's moving seawards, away from the land. It's cold here – it smacks of disappearance, a vacuum, as if the contents of the atmosphere were drifting out to sea along the finger of land. Low cloud moving quickly, patches of shadowy darkness lifting and shifting, moving over the hills rapidly. There are so many spaces for wandering thoughts to fall into, gaps like holes in the solid earth. Before I can grab them, they slip into
        the void

I go inside and fill the kettle and put the cooker on, take a mug from the cupboard and wash it, break up the crystallised mass of instant coffee in the jar with a spoon, and lift out enough for a cup. I drink it black and, sitting down, start to go through my father's papers systematically. This here, that there, like with like, as my mother taught me: a pile of things to look at, and one of distractions. Possible clues and worthless pap.

Here's a notebook, filled with shorthand. I run through the pages, but I can't read it. It was always his way of keeping things secret. Notes to himself I always thought were about me, or Martin. And then from the pages of this notebook, a postcard falls out. It's addressed to him, stamped in Australia, the picture showing a barren landscape of red rock and desert on the back. The writing is small and hard to make out.

> *Dear Rod,*
> *Glad to hear all's well with*
> *you in your northern territory*
> *posting. But if you are still*
> *planning on coming over*
> *I'd be really happy to put you*
> *up. Can't promise luxury, but*
> *as you well know, there's plenty*
> *of sun and sand*
> *Love, P*

So had he been planning to go back to Australia? To complete the circular journey of his life, from Australia to Scotland, back to Australia? And who's this 'P'?

He'd have told Dr Hart, surely he wouldn't have gone without bragging about it, he wouldn't have left the chicken to rot. His razor sits in a glass by the sink. He didn't take that either. I pick it up. The blade hasn't been washed. The foam and the spikes of beard have dried in a white-flecked line under the blade.

None of it makes any sense. I stare at the finger of land pointing away southwards, out to sea. Was it a view to have inspired him to leave, to go back south with the aim of remaking what he could of his life? I don't know. For years I haven't seen the world from his point of view, I've blocked out any light that tried to filter through from the blackout I'd imposed on his existence. But I force myself to focus on this barren place. I can't resist it any longer, my father's life is part of mine. And I want no police poking around in here with uniformed efficiency, examining everything.

That's my job. It's why I've been called here.

So I pocket the shorthand notebook and the postcard. Then I see five unused notebooks, his own favourite 'Lion' brand. I take them too.

The chalet door rattles. A huge figure, his back to the light so I can't see his face clearly, opens it and comes in.

'Jesus!' I say.

He steps forward slowly, seems to fill the whole of the little room. 'You should not take the Son of God's name in vain,' he intones, in a deep slow voice. He turns sideways and I see his profile, long hair ranging from a balding head and a full beard like a fringe to his face, extending down over his chest. He sits down as if he owns the place and glowers at me, eyes bulging in a not quite aligned stare. Like a junkie.

'"And he opened his mouth in blasphemy against God, to blaspheme His name." Revelation 13.6,' he says. The slowness appears to hide a stammer. And he glowers at me again.

'We were your father's neighbours,' he says, and nods across the way in the direction of the burnt-out shell of the chalet next door. I sit down on the chair opposite him.

'When your father came here, he was wandering, he was lost. He had a demon.' He nods again to the burnt-out shell, the charred planks of wood poking out of the breeze-block base. 'Good came out of evil. We were saved.' He leans close to me and spits out words as if they were tiny arrows designed to pin my ears back.

And then there's this tap on the glass. We both look round. A young dark-haired woman appears at the door, heavily pregnant, wearing a short yellow cotton maternity dress. She pokes her head in through the open door.

'Hello?'

Feet on a lower step, what she lacks in size she makes up for in vitality. And she's very pregnant, a burden that fills her smock, nearly as big as herself.

'I see you've already met my husband. Mind if I come in?'

She tilts her head on one side, then back, nervously.

'Hadn't got as far as introductions,' I say.

'We live next door,' she says. 'I'm so sorry to hear about your father, really.'

'But I didn't really understand what you meant,' I say, looking at the bearded giant.

'He's not been bothering you with this Bible code of his, has he?' she asks, as if it is as normal as a new lawnmower. She's as chirpy as he's dour, with big brown eyes like a cartoon character. 'Do you mind if I sit down?' She pats her bulging stomach, laughing. 'Only I'm dead tired with the little one – so active, praise be.'

'Praise be,' a deep echo from her partner.

So I say, 'Come in.'

And when I glance at him he's changed, his gloom gone. He's gaping at her lovingly as she plumps herself down beside him with a sigh.

'I was busy with the washing when John said he was coming over to see you – hands in the twin-tub. A woman's work, you know.' And then she hesitates before she says: 'Has John told you?'

'Has he told me what?

'The good news?'

'No,' I say, 'I've just had the scripture lesson.'

She looks at me oddly for a moment, then giggles. 'He's studying the scriptures. He memorises it so easily, praise be. It's a gift.'

'Praise the Lord!' comes the echo.

'I'm miles behind in my Bible Study. But then I've got other things on my mind,' she adds, and points to her belly as if she wants me to say something about it.

I nod. 'So you're my father's neighbours?'

'Yes. I'm Lena and this is John. Hope you don't mind us intruding, you must have plenty on your mind, only we felt we had to, you see, after what happened. Your father was ...' and she hesitates again.

'Your husband said he was a demon.'

At that she frowns at him as if he'd said something he shouldn't have. 'Well, that's what one of the Elders said. But no, he wasn't possessed, I don't believe that. He had sort of gone astray. But then so had we all. Before the fire.'

Husband glowers again, like a Holy Ghost: 'We were plucked from the gaping mouth of Hell. Rescued. Saved by His Grace. Sinners plucked from the flames, praise the Lord.'

'Praise the Lord!'

'The fire?'

'Oh, it was awful. We lost everything,' she says.

She looks at him and he looks at her. She speaks. 'Shame on us, we brought it on ourselves. We were with sin and the Lord punished us. He saw the evil that was in us, and punished us.' Her gaze falls, ashamed, to the floor.

'You see, we'd bought this Bible,' he starts.

I ask the obvious: 'God punished you for buying a Bible?'

He smiles patronisingly. 'No, you don't understand. It wasn't just any Bible.'

They glance at each other like the very words might call up something horrible to punish them. She's flapping her eyelashes and he's sticking out his lower jaw and scratching his balding head, both of them studying the other, hoping they have the cue.

'It wasn't an ordinary Bible,' he grunts.

'It had the Devil's mark on it,' she whispers. 'We bought it because ...'

They look at each other as if the words about to be spoken might bring a bolt of lightning down from the heavens and tear the chalet in two.

'Because we were Satanists,' she says finally, almost so quietly that I don't hear.

'Satanists?'

He nods: 'Students of the occult. The Black Arts. Followers of the Dark Prince.'

'But praise the Lord, we were saved!' she bounces in.

'Praise the Lord!' he echoes, and hallelujahs follow.

I shift myself in my seat and consider. 'I'm not quite following this,' I say.

She whispers again: 'The Bible had the Devil's mark on it.'

'What exactly did this mark look like?'

'There was a thumbprint on every page,' he grunts.

'Right through the whole book,' she whispers.

His bulging eyes open wide as the saucer-eyed dog's in that fairy tale. 'When I saw it in the bookshop I knew, I said, see, it's the Master's mark. A sign.'

'We were terrible sinners,' she says. 'You wouldn't believe it now, to see us so full of joy and Christian happiness, praise the Lord, but only a few months ago we were sinners. We succumbed to temptation.' Her voice is still low, but hopeful, the joy is returning to her life from a very distant place, she's enacting the course of her salvation in front of me right now. She checks with John and leans forward towards me.

'I went with men,' she tells me. 'Not just one or two, but many.' And as she stares at the floor, blushing. How young she is, hardly more than twenty, about to burst with a bairn, cursed with a troubled past and trying to erase it. John lays a hand on her shoulder, gently.

'So what has this Bible with a mark like a thumbprint in it to do with the fire?' I ask.

He turns to me. 'Not any thumbprint, it was his thumbprint. The Black Master's.' The way he says it, in that chillingly slow voice, I could almost believe him.

She looks up, blush gone. 'It was the Saturday before Easter. Not that we cared anything for that then, in our depraved state. But every Saturday we'd go to town, you know, to do our shopping, on the bus. We went to the bookshop because, God spare us, John wanted to buy a Bible. He said it would help us with that thing I told you about. We could read it backwards, memorise bits you said, John, didn't you? And the very first one he picked up had the thumbprint in it ...'

'We didn't know what we were doing.'

I think, no, you did not.

She gives a horrified shiver at the thought of it, looks at him, sitting there with a fond smile on his face, changed by her presence.

'What happened?'

'Well, we came back here on the five o'clock bus and in to see your father. Colin was here too, wasn't he, John? We used to buy your father whisky from the off-licence in town. He was drinking heavily then, we all were ... anyway, we were sitting in here, us, your father and Colin ...'

'Who's Colin?' I interrupt.

'Colin who used to live in our chalet, the one we're in now. He was a cook on a fishing boat.'

'I'm confused,' I say.

'He left after the fire. We moved into his chalet. I think the fire frightened him.'

'The awesome power of the Lord's vengeance.'

'We tried to help him see the true path, but he moved ...'

She nods her head, flutters her eyelashes. 'Anyway, we were all sitting in here drinking, your father, Colin, me and John. John was telling your father about the Bible we'd bought. Then suddenly Colin said, "Does anybody else smell burning?" and your father went and looked to see if the cooker had been left on, or if there was a heater on in the bedroom, or a cigarette burning or something.'

She turns to him, and it seems as if John can't wait to get on with his lines. I've got the feeling that this story's been told many times to the folk round about, the church congregation, that it's well rehearsed now.

'Then Lena saw this light outside ...'

'And, dear God protect us, it was flickering on the curtains ...'

'Flaring up just like the fires of Hell ...' As he speaks, her brown eyes open, a look of terror on her innocent face. 'The fires of Hell,' he repeats. 'Consuming our old lives ...'

'The very next day,' she beams. 'It was Easter Sunday. I went to the church up the road ...'

' ... and asked Jesus to come into her life.'

'The minister was so kind, even though I was brought up a Catholic and called him "Father" a couple of times. He took me into his house and we talked about everything, how I was frightened and everything like that. And he gave me a Bible, a perfect one this time, praise the Lord!'

'Praise the Lord!'

'Saved from the little fire and the Great One,' she laughs, nervously, as if maybe she still can't quite believe her lucky escape.

'"The fire that shall never be quenched. Where the worm dieth not, and the fire is not quenched": Isaiah 66 24,' he says, and she claps her hands in sheer delight.

Saved they surely are. And I sit there amazed, trying to imagine that pendulum swing, that Easter rebirth, the sudden switch of allegiance from darkness to light.

'Satanism?'

'Yes, though it shames me to admit it. We used the Black Arts to take control of the minds of others,' she says, 'but praise the Lord, He has washed away our sins.'

'Praise the Lord!'

So hard to believe. Even he looks sweet now, childish and awe-filled, as if they want me to pat them on the head and give them a lump of sugar. I'm still trying to puzzle it, this odd couple, old and young, big and small. Then she gives John a peck on the cheek and flutters her eyelashes fast, a signal. He shakes himself and speaks.

'We have come with a message for you. Although your father was intemperate he was not evil. Evil possessed him.' He stops and glances at her, whose face has blushed again. She takes his hand, real gentle like, and gives it a squeeze.

'Fret not thyself because of evildoers,' he says to her quietly, then turns back to me, to carry on with his sermon. But she blurts out, pink and ashamed, 'I sinned with your father before we were saved.'

'Sinned with him?'

'You know …' she says, in a sharp whispering voice, then ducks her face out of sight again.

I shudder. Could it be true? But there they sit in front of me, a testimony unchallenged.

'You're shocked,' she says, quietly.

'Yes.'

'You see now how full of sin we were? You see, the Lord had to send that fire.' Now she takes his hand and pats it. He's getting heated and she calms him, by stroking him. He looks at her, all soft and sweet. They seem like two one-legged folk, like cards leaning against each other, supporting each other. If one moved away, the other would collapse.

I take a gulp of air, get up and walk to the rear of the chalet. I feel them watching me, these strange reborn creatures, but when I turn to face them they're still sitting staring into each other's eyes, metamorphosed into heavenly peace. She looks at him and he looks at her, and they both look at me. I know something's coming. At last she takes a deep breath and turns it into words.

'So we've come to tell you that your father has gone to find the Lord.'

'What?'

'The last time I saw him, that's what he said.'

'What?' I can't believe it.

'It was the last time anyone saw him,' John adds.

'When?'

'Last week. What day was it again?'

'Thursday.' John volunteers.

'Are you sure? What exactly did he say?'

'Let me see now,' she starts. 'I met him outside the chalets. He seemed happy, in fact I thought he might have been drunk. But then he said, 'I'm going to see the Lord, Lena. The Lord has called me.' I was so happy for him. That he'd seen the light at last.'

I can't picture it, not my father, saved – but then maybe I didn't know him any more. Maybe, living in this place, anything was possible.

'Praise the Lord,' she says. 'We had tried to help him see the light, ever since the fire. Not that we'd pushed him. But if you let your joy radiate outwards, then people can see how happy you are and after a while, they start to wonder, maybe I could be that happy myself.'

'And what else did he say?'

'That was all.'

She looks satisfied, as if that's obviously the end of the story. What more could be added? What more could I want? What could come after such a joyous moment, without it being an anticlimax?

'It's because of that we know that he's all right. He's with the Lord. Wherever he is, he's all right. He's with the Lord. Praise be!'

'Praise be!'

I'm disturbed by how unconcerned they seem. 'But did he have a bag with him, a suitcase or anything?'

She just looks at me blankly. 'I'm not sure. I was only hanging out the washing.'

And then John chimes in, 'At first, when we didn't see him we thought maybe he'd gone away for a while, to be alone with God. I went away by myself when the Lord called me. After Lena was saved … before I was. She said that if I didn't come to know the Lord, then she would have to choose between Him and me. And I knew which one she'd pick.'

They both laugh. I just can't credit this Christian openness. It's truly disarming.

'So I went off on my own for a few days, to stay in a friend's caravan in the north of the island, to ask the Lord to come into my life.'

'And he did! Praise be!' Her eyes melt into tears of joy.

'Praise be!' echoes the ghost.

The words 'Seek and ye shall find, knock and the door shall be opened' come to my mind. Though I can't quote chapter and verse, the thought doesn't surprise me. My head is full, from my childhood, of all these Biblical fragments, lying there like seeds waiting for a drop of faith to wet them, to set them sprouting. But my father. That sham! For years he pretended he was the perfect Christian pillar of the community in Perth, before the truth came out. Did he really repent?

'I must go in a minute,' she says, 'But before I go I want to tell you, we knew you'd come here.' Lena peeks at John, proudly. 'The Lord showed me in a dream. In the dream I saw you coming here,' she croons, then with a downturn in her voice, 'Only it was in a red car, and you didn't, you came with Dr Hart.'

'But we knew you'd come. The Lord spake unto Lena in a dream.'

'We knew you would come seeking your father.'

'Yes!'

And they laugh, yes, laugh heartily, these joyous Christian folk, these saved souls, sure of their righteousness. Never seen it so close up before, but it's something, that blissful childlike quality, that I-was-lost-and-now-I'm-found, that blind-but-now-I-see routine.

She stirs herself. 'Well, we just wanted to give you that message. To bring hope to you. The Lord knows you're suffering right now, He knows and He has chosen me as his messenger, to tell you not to worry, because your father is safe with Him.' And she smiles a sugar-cane smile, then struggles to her feet, happy as a Christmas carol.

'I have to go back now. Six days shalt thou labour ... and the day after tomorrow's the Lord's Day. We have a special meeting on Sunday afternoon. Maybe you'd like to come along? I'm making a banner. It's going to say "The Lord preserveth them that love Him".' And she laughs as she juggles her burden down the steps, humming a praisesong, somehow like a Disney bunny, going home to her burrow in the Jesus theme park.

I look at the husband, who's slowly getting up, stiff and old compared with her. Old enough to be her father, almost, beaming after her, totally infatuated with that incredible bubble of life force, that holy charm. He stretches upright and the look of misery spreads over his face now she's gone, like the sun has gone in and he's back out in the rain. Against the door, he's the same black shadow that first came in and spooked me. Now his sunbeam's gone, his eyes bulge out. And then he leans in close to me again.

'You need not suffer on account of your father,' he grunts. 'In the Bible it says that "Fathers shall not be put to death for the children, neither shall the children be put to death for the fathers. Every man shall be put to death for his own sin." Deuteronomy 24:16.'

Then he leans closer, till I smell his breath. 'But you know, There is a Bible within the Bible, and there's a code above the law.'

And then, with surprising speed, he's gone. The light floods back. What was my father doing, hanging out among these these hallelujahs, burning chalets and Devil's thumbprints?

I blow out a heavy sigh, a great long breath. My heart's beating fast.

I look around the chalet, trying to remember what it was I was doing before they came in. I was thinking about something, what was it? Think! But it's no use, I can't remember. So I sit for a moment, staring at the faded Renoir print, trying to calm myself. But there's no peace in here, just the nagging that there's something far wrong

something bad

smelling

CHAPTER ONE (CONT.)

I have said that I but recently came to this knowledge of Zetland, and it is true that until a matter of some eight months ago I neither understood its geographical position, the extent of the country, nor its strategic nature. I realise that my early perusal of maps had not aided this, as the archipelago rarely appeared in its true position or comparable scale in such documents, presumably as it spoiled the composition of the frame, being simply too far north and too far east to fit neatly.

I was surprised to learn that, in acreage, the Zetland archipelago is larger than the county of Fife by some ten per cent; and that because of its long narrow shape, were it to be laid over a map of Scotland with its northernmost isle at Aberdeen, the southernmost would appear somewhere on the latitude of Peebles to the south of the capital. I had not realised either that it shared latitude with Bergen and Oslo, with Stockholm and Helsinki, with St Petersburg – indeed, the southern tip of Greenland. Its strategic position in the north Atlantic, with deep-sheltered anchorages, meant that it was a crucial haven for all sea-borne traffic – a factor that would become still more prominent after the so-called discovery of America by Columbus.

I imagine that my ignorance of Zetland is not dissimilar to that which must have prevailed generally in Scotland, when it first acquired its northern outpost in 1469. In these years, before charts or maps, it can only have been a vague notion, this 'Ultima Thule', a place where Vikings and pirates might congregate, or where a rival prince might shelter his navy. And in the early years of the sixteenth century, with Scotland struggling to protect its independence against the English, that state of ignorance appears not to have been greatly enlightened.

However, we might assume that the people of Zetland became ever more acquainted with the deeds of those to the south – for instance, the tragic loss of the flower of Scotland at the battle of Flodden in 1513, so poignantly captured in Mrs Cockburn's famous song, included the

Lord Sinclair of the period and many of his men. News of this would no doubt have carried to our parish, indeed, some men may have gone with their lord to die. The emergence of our great 'turbulent priest', his excommunication in 1520, the peasants' revolt in Germany of 1524, these tales too must have been carried across the North Sea by the Hanseatic traders to island ears. They would surely have heard, too, that Frederick of Denmark had proclaimed the right of every man to choose his own religion in 1527, and that Henry VIII of England had proclaimed himself Supreme Head of his own church in England seven years later. With all this change around, it may have seemed that an era was indeed ending, when the Hanseatic League was broken up in 1535.

Scotland would not avoid this upheaval for long. The days of the great Reformation were not far off. Henry would soon invite James V of Scotland to York, in an attempt to persuade him to thrust off the yoke of Rome as he himself had done. James, hesitating, failing to keep the dictated appointment, would invite his own doom. His army at Solway Moss he would give to the command of his favourite, Oliver Sinclair. The army would refuse to follow him, and the great Sinclair influence ended in the ignominy of defeat. After which, James V took to his bed, depressed, to die weeks later of a broken heart – or, as John Knox would seem to suggest later, poisoned by his wife Mary of Guise.

The English invasion of Scotland, involving the capture of Edinburgh and Leith in 1544, sent the child heiress, Mary's daughter Mary, off to France for safety – and the turmoil that follows is well documented: the burning of the martyr, George Wishart; the killing of Beaton; the siege of St Andrews, Knox's imprisonment and exile – these I assume as common knowledge, so prominent are they in the annals of our nation, as with the events that follow Knox's return in 1559, leading to the Reformation of 1560, the return of Mary to the throne of Scotland in 1561, and the struggles of the following decade – all these are legend.

But it is at this point that the distant parish in question begins to feature in the story of our nation, in a minor role, just as it is at this point that the Scots begin to fundamentally affect the life of the Zetlanders. Major players on the Royal Mile of Edinburgh have hands in both, for the coming of the churchmen, engaged in carrying out the work of the

Reformation, is the first substantial act of Scotticisation – and Mary, in granting her illegitimate half-brother Robert the Earldom of the Orcades and the Lordship of Zetland, instigates what is now known as the 'Stewart tyranny' in these places. It is about this time too that Mary's third husband, the rash Bothwell, makes his brief appearance on the Zetlandic scene – an incident recorded in his 'confession':

Thus I embarked somewhere in the North of Scotland, as mentioned above, having decided to follow this advice. And passing by the Orcades I went ashore in Zetland, where I encountered some ships from Bremen and Hamburg, and negotiated with the boatswains what I would give them per month as long as they would serve me.

Some of my enemies found out that I was ashore at the house of the Receiver, and separated my ships as I will explain. The above-named rebels had gathered four well armed ships and fitted out with soldiers and artillery, whose leaders were the said Lord of Grange and Tullibardine, who at the break of dawn entered a harbour of the said island called Bressay Sound, where four of my vessels were moored; and as the boatswains caught sight of them, my Captains and soldiers being ashore, they cut loose the tow ropes of their ships and moved to another harbour to the north of the said country, called Onst. However, their main ship, which was pursuing us, was closely observing one of my vessels which had the slowest sail and to which they gave chase. My ship went ahead while the other followed behind. But it so happened that the enemy ship (which was chasing my slow one) and my own hit an open rock concealed under the sea, so that their said ship, which was the better one and served as flagship, remained there while mine, although somewhat damaged, escaped. When I heard that my enemies intended to go ashore and pursue my people, I embarked suddenly with them at the said harbour of Onst, where my intention was not to stay but only to confront my said enemies, but these three ships caught me so much by surprise and exerted such pressure (as they had previously done), that I could not put up any resistance and was obliged to set sail, and ordered one of my ships (the one in which was the remainder of my silverware, clothes and furniture which I had brought from Edinburgh Castle) to go to another harbour called Skallvaa, and there to convene with the said Hamburgers, and catch up with me on my way to Denmark, as had been previously decided, and as he had promised the rest of my people whom I had left behind in the said island. The said rebels pursued me with such intensity that we fought for three whole hours and by a strike of the canon, they snapped the great mast of my best ship. At the same moment, a storm coming from the south-west broke out, which was of such strength that I could not continue my said journey, and was pushed towards the Norwegian coast, where I had to repair my vessels and replenish their supplies as, due to my hurried departure these had not been properly provisioned. The day after I left Zetland, I arrived somewhere on the coast of Norway called Karmesund, where I was taken to a ship from Rostock, which had been following us that night, to lead us in daylight to the said harbour, because my pilots did not know it: which he did and lent us his ship to carry one of our towropes ashore.

In the meantime arrived Christen Aalborg, the Captain of one of the King of Denmark's ships named *The Bear*, and asked us where we were coming from and where we wanted to go; to which the boatswain of my ship answered that we were Scotch gentlemen wishing to go to Denmark to serve his Majesty. I ordered that he be honoured according to the customs at sea and the jurisdiction of foreign Princes ...

But we must leave these 'foreign Princes' to their great adventures now, noting, as we pass, the picture Bothwell's narrative provides of Zetland as a frontierland with ships of different flags in port available for hire at the right price; with, we may assume, smuggling the norm and pirates not unfamiliar. We may imagine with horror the vile evils that prevailed in such lawless havens, and turn in admiration to the work of Bothwell's uncle, the Bishop of the Orcades, and Jeremy Cheyne in Zetland, in establishing our great Protestant church in such barbaric times, which was apparently efficient and swift; Cheyne settled himself and his family in Zetland, as did other men of the faith, and in time these families acquired land from the old 'Lairds of Norrowa'. In the case of Cheyne, one of his offspring, Robert, obtained the lease of the lands that comprise the parish we are concerned with in 1576, from the Norse owner, and he was charged by James VI 'to build ane hous and fortice upoun the saidis landis of Valay for sauftie thairof fra the hiland men, perattis and otheris invasionis', as Valay controlled access to the best harbour on the west of the islands and so is a strategic holding.

It would appear that this fortification was part of a grand plan to secure the Zetland archipelago, as at the same time Stewart had his half-brother Laurence Bruce build a secure foothold in similar manner in the northern part of the islands, while Lord Robert himself made a base at the southern end of the group, closest to his main stronghold in the Orcades, at the place which Sir Walter Scott would later give the Romantic name 'Jarlshof' in his 1822 novel, *The Pirate*.

---

22 June 2000 – Norbie

I straighten out the papers more or less as they'd been, wash the cup I've used, and generally sort the place out. The things I'm going to take I put in my rucksack and sling it over my shoulder. I shut the glass door with a sense of relief, yes, relief, and lock it with the key that Dr Hart gave me. I walk down past the burnt chalet and the born-agains' chalet, glance up and see him sitting with his back to me, bent over, maybe reading the great black book.

Then I head down towards the shore where the old stone arch is, the remains of that old church. My mother's steps. The shore draws me. There's something about that curve, the shape of the beach, a perfect arc. I jump over a ditch, climb a couple of fences, striding now. There's a burn to be crossed, and I look for the best place to jump the stream. Everywhere's sheep and lambs, nuzzling at the grass, though there's precious little left for them to eat. They look up as I go, stare at me before deciding whether to make a break for it or stand their ground. The burnbanks are strewn with sheep-shit, great clumps of thistles the only thing not eaten, thriving with the lack of competition from other plants, purple puffs of bloom brightening dull colours. And there's not a tree to be seen save those in laird's garden in the distance and a couple of withered willows growing at the side of the burn.

Down at the shore, the flat land's marked by a line of dried up seaweed from an extravagantly high tide, then a fence plastered with bits of weed and plastic, frayed rope and stuff from the sea. Plastic bottles and shredded black bags. At the head of the beach are the biggest stones, big smooth ocean-worn ones, that have been rolling and grinding in currents and tides for centuries before they got pushed up here in some cataclysmic storm. A strip of these boulders runs right round from one side of the curve to the other. Below that there's shingle, smaller stones and pebbles, more moveable. And lower down, the mica-sand that changes with every tide. The waders are running around, in and out of the water. Oyster catchers. Sandpipers. Terns. This place is alive. Despite the rubbish collected there, despite the bare peathills and the lack of vegetation, it's alive with birds like I've never seen before.

I take a pack of trail mix from the store in my rucksack and chew and watch and chew and watch the birds. They don't bother about me. The sound of the waves rushes in, drags back over the sand, then rush, then drag and rush, and drag. I'm calmed by it, getting a perspective on things again, on why I'm here in this strange place, back in my father's life.

Satanists? I shiver.

The wind is cold, but I have the gear to keep it out.

At the water's edge, I stop, lift a round flat chuckie-stane as Martin and me called them in Perth, position it between my forefinger and thumb, and send it skimming out over the flat water behind the waves. It bounces along once, twice, three times, then skips another three or four, and sinks. I lift another and send it out, spinning. This time it hits a wave as it rises, and goes nowhere. I pick up another but instead of throwing it, I just weigh it in my hand, juggling it for a while. I walk along the beach slowly, examining the sand in detail. Among the sea-junk there's things I've never seen before, clearly organic, natural, but I don't know what they are. A little square pouch, maybe some sort of eggsac, with a curled wisp at every corner. And there's a fine black-tipped feather. I put them in my rucksack, for my son.

Wonder how he'll grow without Christianity. Maybe I should give him a taste of it, take him along to church sometimes while he's still young, so that the mystery's exploded. Or maybe I should try to talk about it, explain it to him? About the destruction of native cultures by evangelicals intent on doing God's work. The wiping out of whole peoples, supposedly ignorant heathens who couldn't see they were wrong in their beliefs. That terrible ugliness of the self-righteous.

And yet I know it wasn't always like that. The Culdees, those who sought out the quiet places in the first millennium of Christianity, they were inspired, some of them. The early saints, the voyagers, like Brendan. I know some Christians are truly good people whose religion is a private and a personal strength, something that they never push on others. Like our mother.

And that has to be good, that depth of faith, that belief. If the theory and the practice are united, if the hypocrisy that comes from saying one thing and doing another is quashed. Our mother, she was like that. She was quietly religious, a good Christian woman, a lay preacher going round the parish, delivering sermons. Praying quietly. Inspiring love. Consoling. Or was that my idealised notion of her? Was she really on some kind of egotrip?

Now would be a good moment for a white dove to land on the old arch, for her spirit to come and give me a sign, while I'm wavering. Instead, two crows are fluttering around, above a hummock of heather just beyond the churchyard. They're stirring up a steuch, flapping and carrying on. Big black corbies, their beaks like tapered metal punches, sharpened to perfection. I've got to admire them, the species, the way they've evolved into such a perfect survival machine. Crows are the real kings of birds, like rats are the kings of the rodents, as *Homo sapiens* are kings of the primates. It's that eat-anything adaptability. The corbies are crowing, flapping around. I get up and walk over to the broken down dyke to see what the commotion is. I see them circle and settle on the hummock, and a creature prostrate by a stone.

It's a lamb, newborn. And then I notice on the other side of the stone there's a ewe. It moves closer, looking down at the lamb pitifully. The lamb doesn't move. It's dead. Stone dead. The crows stalk nearer, hopping two-footed forwards, heads turning jerkily about, watching all directions. The ewe darts forward, scatters them. They lift into the air. One flies low, swoops close to the ewe. It turns and tries to chase the crow away. The other corbie lands, jouks forward, settles on the lamb and digs its black talons into the wool of its neck. The crow's black beak shoots like a spear to the eye of the lamb. The beak jabs again, again, then opens and takes hold of the eyeball. It pulls, gets a better grip and pulls again, the eyeball coming whole from the socket, red veins trailing.

I leap forward, waving my arms and shouting, running over towards the scene, leaping the fence into the park. The crows flap their shiny black wings and lift from the heather hillside. The eyeball drops from beak to the ground. The mother ewe stares accusingly at me as if it was my fault, pawing the ground like a bull, the futile effort of a parent trying to protect a dead bairn from the black corbies, from my black shadow, from the blackness. The sharp beak that wants the eye for sweetmeat.

I'm breathing deeply, chest pounding. I can see the organ on the heather, the eye watching nothing, removed from its casing. The lamb lies still, short curls of wool tight over its warm body. It lies on the heather, peaceful, blind. The mother'll stay with it till it's cold. Then the crows'll eat, the ants'll clean the evidence away. Only a few bones a child might pick up and admire, might take home to identify. A few wisps of wool in nearby nests. A clue caught on a barbed wire spike.

I turn my head away. I'm on the other side of the fence. It's not my lamb, my bairn. But my stare goes back to the eyeball lying there looking up at the sky, the clouds moving, at heaven. It's perfectly formed. Something entices me to lift it up, some desire to take it back to the socket and see if I can't fit it back in. It's like an amazingly beautiful jewel, but soft, delicate. It's incredible, really, the design. I tentatively pick it up.

But dead is dead. Dead as a doornail, as my father would say. Nothing anybody can do. Let the corbies come, let the corbies scavenge. That's their purpose. I could sit here all night and they'd just wait, they'd wait till morning and I've fallen asleep and then they'd come down to do their useful work, of sorting out the mess.

Up away, up over the hill, I keep walking, keep moving till I hardly see it now. It's just a speck of white on the heather with two specks of black above it, yin and yan, swirling, transforming, changing, one into the other. Just moving lines. I can't switch it off. Nature is love and birth, and violence and death.

I walk up over a wet heath covered with flowers. Tiny flowers that barely reach above the heather. Milkwort, tormentil. Bog cotton in that wet bit there. Purple and white orchids, spotted beautifully. At the summit of the hill, I look out along the long finger of land, the cliffs running all the way to the point and watch the sea. A boat is moving among the misty islands. A long ship lies out on the horizon, a tanker maybe carrying oil, an energy-bomb ready to dump on the world. I stand a while and dream of being elsewhere. And on the horizon, drifting in and out of form, that three-stepped island hovers again – Thulay, the outermost.

There, maybe.

For now it's time to go back to Dr Hart's. The police might be there. What can I do that they can't? But I'm intrigued now, those born-agains, that fire. I'm carrying my father's secret notebook. And there's this feeling I can't just go.

I descend the hill towards the beach and the old church again. By the fence at the turning place is a small green van, with its driver stretched over the bonnet. Dressed in dungarees, with a flat cap on his head, wearing scuffed old wellies, it's the old man who offered me a lift. He seems as native as the dockens, grown in this place and rooted here. He's standing a little in front of the archway, leaning on a fencepost, then looks up, pipe in mouth. The black and white collie is at his side, tongue out, watching me approach.

'Aye aye, fine day,' he says.

'Yes, it's nice,' I answer, looking up.

'Just visiting, are you?'

'Yes, just a couple of days.'

'At the laird's?'

'Dr Hart,' looking at the tall house.

He nods. In the field between us and the sea, there's a flock of ewes with their lambs.

'They look healthy,' I say. 'Are they yours?'

'Ya, mine. Dey're no bad. But you always lose some. I found one this morning, eyes oot.'

He shakes his head, takes the pipe from his mouth, and spits a jet of saliva into the soil. The dog sniffs at it and lies down, still panting.

'Up in the hill there.'

And he points towards the place. I don't know whether to say what I'd seen or not. But somehow the fact that he cared binds me to him.

'What did you do with it?' I ask.

'Oh, just buried it. Good and deep, like. Poor peerie ting.'

And he spits again. I wonder what his feelings are for all these sheep of his.

'Do you have many?'

'Many?'

'Many sheep?'

'Oh hunders, hunders, up in the hills …'

'How do you know which ones are yours?'

'Well, they're marked, of course.' He nods slowly and looks at me as if I have just asked the stupidest question imaginable. 'All marked.' The leathery skin wrinkles on his forehead and he stares at me, faintly smiling, not unkindly, but as if I were a child, hardly able to walk or talk or do anything for myself. It's such a penetrating look that I have to break free of it, yet I don't really want to get away. There's something warm about his company. Natural. So I bend down and speak to the dog. It seems to cower backwards, then rolls on its back and exposes its throat.

'It's all right. You can clap her. She doesna bite.'

I stroke her gently at first and then more firmly, ending with a couple of pats. And then I stand up and smile and say I best get back, and he says 'Cheerio,' and leans again upon the fencepost, to watch his sheep. The dog sits upright and alert at his side.

I'm unable to put my finger on the source of the feeling, but a sense of déjà vu descends. Just a momentary thing, but a feeling that I've walked this way before. As if in other shoes, maybe another body, I'd seen the curves of this bay before. The great green breakers roaring in, tearing in off the Atlantic winds and ripping up the seaweed from the rocks.

And I realise I forgot to ask the old man about the graveyard

the old church

the arch

Perth

Dear Mr Scot

Thank you for your reply. The information you sent is helpful to me, but I still do not quite see all the connections.

Regarding the notebooks, I can't say exactly what they are or why they were written. They are incomplete, it seems, and the order of the various episodes uncertain. The man who called himself a pilgrim, who stood barefooted at the door of the manse with his father's brogues in his hand, a man I now know to be a child I baptised, David Cunninghame, left them in my study along with the envelope containing your letter and the copy of Gabrielsen's history, various family documents and the like.

I wonder at his motivation. Surely he would have noticed that he'd left it behind and come back for it? I feel it is all a test of my stewardship of my flock, sent by the Lord. I'm still no closer to finding David, but I feel I understand why he appeared at my door that day. It is most remarkable to think that he was wandering around in Norbie Hall, in the house of his ancestors, unaware of it, if that is indeed the implication.

I expect, unless your son-in-law is successful in tracking him down by means of his computer or he returns to collect the papers he left, then the mystery will remain – and I will continue to wonder.

The Lord's ways are manifold and mysterious indeed.

Yours faithfully
Archibald Nicol (Rev)

PS – I continue to edit Gabrielsen.

CHAPTER ONE (CONT.)

One might wonder at the sudden interest in the islands by the southron, after years of disregard, yet the Scots had long coveted the Dutch domination in fishing around the islands, though they had allowed the trade to continue at a price. The Dutch fleet was substantial – one writer reports fifteen hundred fishing boats, or 'busses', four hundred support vessels and twenty gunships all operating around the coasts of Zetland. Others reckon, on occasions two thousand two hundred fishing vessels alone.

Fish was the one great resource the islands offered, and the Scotch 'land-grabs' of the period were spurred by a further aim, beyond the paltry soil, to control the harvest of the sea rather than the land, for the rich fishing trade would have then to pass through their hands, and they would thus be able to control it.

It is wrong to suggest, as some have done, that the Church was wholly complicit in this assertive Scotch move, and that it acted as an arm of the new rulers. Though there were perhaps some who performed the will of the tyrant Robert Stewart, there were others of the ministry who supported the claims of the maltreated peasantry and helped to bring charges against the despotism of Lawrence Bruce in 1577, which, though successful, did little to alter the general course of action. Lord Robert's son Patrick Stewart was no better than his father in pressing the natives and imposing his hated mark upon the islands. He oversaw the building of Skallvaa Castle by forced labour, and earned for himself the soubriquet 'Black Patie', while Bruce fortified the north at Muness, Onst, in the Scotch style.

By 1603, when the death of the virgin queen Elizabeth opened the throne of England to Mary Queen of Scots' son, James the VI of Scotland, Earl Patrick Stewart had established such a stronghold in the north that he allowed himself the hubris, it appears, of fancying himself as ruler of the northern kingdom. He was, after all, the grandson of a king, albeit by an illegitimate father.

I find that I have been seduced by great men, dates and history, the illusion of coherence lost in digression – and I am no closer to my aim. As yet, the parish we are concerned with has only briefly featured, and besides the possibility of plague and the loss of menfolk, fighting either for Norse king or Sinclair Earl, nothing in our broad sweep has touched upon it. Perhaps, in terms of life as lived from sunrise to sunset, the ephemera of the everyday, nothing much has changed in the last however many hundred years, except the weather. Mortality, illness, the search for spiritual transcendence of a rugged, miserable physical life, all these no doubt went on as regularly and routine as planting and harvest, as the spinning of the millwheel or the drudgery of looking after the beasts – and amongst all that, the little joys of life and birth, the fruit of love, side by side with the back-breaking tillage, the life-endangering fishing; all the human dramas enacted in the same little huddle of houses unchanged in centuries; back to back against the prevailing elements, sharing celebration and consolation, belief in God; watching as shoots grow, praying they will not be frosted or eaten, but will flourish, desperate for sunshine and rain, with the blessing of heaven.

As the planets orbit according to the ineffable hand of the Lord of Creation, it appears all things are in some way cyclic, as if time were a great millwheel grinding on and humanity the riverwater that passes through, turning and being turned, forced to divert and disperse. Yet that perhaps is but the product my own situation, in these twilight years, with my dear Margaret gone, my ministry behind me. Like an old hermit, I have retreated here to my library, wrapped in tweed blankets and study, seeking what? This lost sheep? Or wisdom? The milk of human kindness dries around me, parched as my skin, withdrawn, while the tumour grows. I tremble and avert my eyes as I pass the mirror, my disfigurement has grown so terrible. I wonder, was I a vain man, and am I being punished now for that? Did those careful glances in the mirror before leaving the vestry for the pulpit always contain an element of pride? I dread to recall how Margaret looked at me in those last month's of her life, how ugly I must have seemed to her. I think of the last look she gave me, how I turned slightly aside, as if to hide my ugliness, and how she sighed so deeply. As if resigned.

~~And I think back to the moment when David the barefooted pilgrim came to the manse, how balanced and happy our lives still were then. David who had abandoned everything and was the living embodiment of 'consider the lilies' beatific purity, who looked around the fine manse I lived in and saw that I was not~~

~~I find this morning I had written too much last night, had digressed into matters personal, which have no part in this task. I will therefore obliterate them and beg the reader's indulgence. Once, some years ago, I was offered, by a parishioner, an invention called an 'Apple'; which I was told would simplify my writing and enable me to correct any mistakes I might make before anything whatsoever was printed. I refused, partly because of the ominous name, but also because, as I told my kind-hearted would-be donor, I trust myself to write by hand exactly as mind dictated. I was a thoughtful writer who would only commit to paper once ideation was complete. My pen is no longer so assured. It seems have become somewhat prolix as I have aged. Forgive me.~~

~~What is this~~

Earl Patrick was hung, as he deserved to be. The old Lawbook of Hjaltaland was swallowed in his labyrythine plottings, or confined to his infernal dungeon. 'Zetland' was taken as a Crown possession, as James VI, soon to be James I of Great Britain, determined to secure his far spread lands, just as James I of Scotland had attempted centuries before.

Though the hated Stewart Earls were gone, Zetland was changed forever more. James I did not reconstitute Norse Law, nor knock down the Scotch castles, nor return appropriated land to the former owners. The methods of Laurence Bruce and his ilk may have been officially censurable, but their purpose had achieved exactly what the Crown desired.

So at the beginning of the seventeenth century, our remote parishioners found themselves in changed circumstance, with a reformed Church of Scotland, Scotch lairds, Scotch Law and ever-increasingly, a Scotch tongue around them. Undoubtedly there must have been some Scotch spoken in the islands previously for commerce alone, along with Dutch or Danish or German, but the Zetlander's own primary tongue had remained the old

Norse speech, with its great store of legend and superstition – yet by 1600 it was no longer the language of power.

So we find a Zetlander, in a Norn rhyme of the period, telling with pride to the listener that his son has been to Catness and has learned to call things by their Scots names: 'It was in a good hour that my son went to Catness: He can call rossa, mare ... big, bere ... eld, fire ... klovandi, taings.'

Soon would follow the English language, with the glorious publication of the Holy Bible of 1611, the 'Authorised Version' known as 'The King James'. God's word in the English language without admixture ~~which the wandering pilgrim who visited me rejected, when I offered him The Word in a little traveller's volume to take with him on his way, placing his hand on his heart and saying, 'The Word is within me'. How diminished I felt at his generous smile, when he had nothing to give and every reason to take from~~

James's patronage gave unto the nation The Holy Word in the language of the common people, though we may imagine our remote parishioners questioned which 'people' they were, when so confronted with the English.

A further grand reach of the monarch took the nation unto himself in a different fashion, with his sponsorship of Timothy Pont's mapping of Scotland. Pont, an obscure figure whose devotion to his task led him among robbers repeatedly, was commissioned as early as 1592 to conduct a mineralogical survey of Zetland, and it is his sketch of the archipelago which first outlines the shape and true scale of the isles for the human eye. After Pont's death in 1614, his maps were acquired by Sir James Balfour of Denmyln in Fife, an antiquarian appointed Lord Lyon of Scotland in 1630, and by means of Balfour's friend and fellow Fifeman, Sir John Scot of Scotstarvet, who had connection with the printers Blaeu in Holland, Pont's maps were finally printed in an atlas, in Amsterdam, 1654.

The alert reader will have noted that I have at last introduced into this narrative a character whose name corresponds with that of the family whose history I had promised at the outset – and it is indeed from the said Sir John Scot of Scotstarvet that our remote parish's Scots descend. But at the time of Sir John, the family line was as yet far from Zetland, as far as

Pont's map was from a true recording of Zetland's outline.

It would take two further generations before the first John Scot settled in our parish in 1696, as the husband of Girzel Michell, heiress of Valay, Thulay and Norbie; before he became proprietor of the fortice of Valay. In the interim, this John's elder brother George married the Countess of Stormont, and was appointed Steward Depute of the Orcades and Zetland in 1670.

Before that, too, blowing to the Zetland shores in the 1630s, came famine, Covenanters, plague; and in the 1650s, Cromwell's soldiers, to capture the Dutch fleet and build a garrisoned fort, above the sheltered harbour where the Dutch fleet had anchored since the 13th century, on the other side of the main island from the Scotch base of Skallvaa, where Earl Patrick's hated castle stood. This east-coast harbour would gradually become the main port of the Zetland group, and develop into the town of Larvik.

George Scot of Gibbleston landed in a war zone when he became Deputy Steward for Zetland, in command of this fort in Larvik, a growing centre for trade, illicit and otherwise, thanks to the 'Dutchies'.

The Dutch had made much of 'The Great Fishery' around Zetland; in 1651, they outlined its operation in their parliament, at that time worth a third of the exchequer, so that the news of its richness and importance further aroused jealous interest. The English sent spies north to Zetland, who reported back to London that they estimated the Dutch owed two and a half million sterling of arrears for their fishing, a tax unpaid since the days of the Stewart Earls. The Dutch responded by burning the fort and part of the town of Larvik – and so the dispute might have rumbled on, had William of Orange not been invited to restore liberties in Great Britain. It was in the settled state following that happy succession, that John Scot, a grandson of Scot of Scotstarvet who had published Pont's maps, younger brother of the Depute Steward, married a Zetlandic heiress. The losses suffered by the family at the Scotch debacle of Darien meant that he must seek his fortune, and this northern colony, though perhaps cold and depressingly barren, was at least was free of Spaniards and tropical disease.

The estate of Valay with its dramatic cliffs and the supreme isolation of the fabled isle of Thulay no doubt made an immediate impression on the young Scot. He perhaps understood that here in the north, opportunity existed. The rich trade in fish could be his to profit by, along with his fellow landowners, once it was wrested from the hands of the Dutch. The prize was certainly substantial, as estimates reckoned that the Dutch economy gained by some £3,000,000 each year. By owning the beaches on which the fish was dried, by imposing a tax on salt so making the curing too costly, the new Scotch land-owners would gradually take control.

Had John Scot and his like any regret at leaving the warmth of their neuk in Fife, or whatever southron county they exited, we must not underestimate the importance of human greed in overcoming reluctance to endure even the least hospitable of climes.

We cannot blame any person from seeking to profit by their labour, nor their organisation of labour, yet I cannot escape the facts that lie before me – the Scotch churchmen acquired land and power in Zetland and were a major cause in establishing a race of lairds described by Tudor as 'greedy, gripping, Scotch donatories, who looked upon the islands as a milch cow, to be squeezed for their own especial benefit'. I am reminded of the wisdom of Solomon:

My son, if sinners entice thee, consent thou not. If they say, Come with us, let us wait for blood, let us lurk privily for the innocent without cause: Let us swallow them up alive as the grave; and whole, as those that go down to the pit: We shall find all precious substance, we shall fill our houses with spoil: Cast in thy lot among us; let us all have one purse: My son, walk not thou in the way with them; refrain thy foot from their path: For their feet run to evil, and make haste to shed blood. Surely in vain the net is spread in the sight of any bird. And they lay in wait for their own blood; they lurk privily for their own lives. So are the ways of every one that is greedy of gain; which taketh away the life of the owners thereof.

Proverbs 1: 10–19

22 June 2000 – Norbie

I ring the front door bell of Norbie Hall and wait, expecting to hear the dogs burst out barking. I wait. Nothing happens, so I ring again. Still nothing. Try the porch door but it's locked. I swing the rucksack from my shoulder, set it down on the doorstep and sit beside it. I wait, scrutinising the trees in the laird's garden. Only a few and none of them bigger than the shelter afforded by the house and the walls of the garden. But at least there are trees. A couple of larches. A yew. A sycamore. And a few elders. This fact alone marks it as different from the landscape round about, never mind the garden walls, the expanse of lawn and the gravel path that runs up to the front door. I think of the old laird living here on his own, lonely, five storeys of damp rooms all to himself and I think of the born-agains cramped into that tiny chalet, expecting a baby.

Then I hear a dog barking in the distance. It seems to be coming from the back of the house and so I follow the path round. There's a greenhouse built on to the back, the glass cracked and missing here and there. Inside, I can see the laird moving around among the greenery. One of the corgis comes running out barking at me. Dr Hart looks up, sees me and gestures, mouthing, 'Go round to the door.'

The place is full of tomato plants, with a good crop of fruit beginning to ripen. It's hot inside and the dog-pack's lying panting. He looks at me slightly suspiciously.

'I called round to see you at the chalet, but you weren't there.'

'I went for a walk. After I'd had a look round the place, I wanted to think.'

He nods. 'I believe you met the Stouts.'

'Stouts?'

'The people in the other chalet.'

He shakes his head ruefully. 'They're really very upset by what's happened, you know.'

'Are they now? Can't say I noticed.'

'But she's so nice. Jolly nice.'

'It was him – the man. He's strange.'

He looks at me as if I'm stupid or heartless or something.

'He's an invalid. Some kind of motorneurone disease.'

'Ah,' I say, faintly embarrassed, 'That would explain it. I just …'

He's taking a seedling out of its pot, carefully tipping it upside down, gently opening the root-ball out slightly, so that it'll shoot into the new compost, and then transferring it into a bigger pot. He works quickly but without hurrying, expert at it. I hadn't reckoned him for a gardener, tending plants so fragile.

'I'll be finished here in a short while. Why don't you go and get yourself something to eat from the kitchen? Mrs Mitchell left a cold plate for you in the fridge. Then you can tell me if you've thought of anything.'

'Thanks. I'm hungry, right enough. But the front door was locked.'

'Back is open. Just round the corner there. Keep the front locked because of the wind.'

So I go in through the back door, and it leads into the kitchen. I see the fridge and open it. There's a big dinner plate, a huge salad, covered in cling-film. I sit down on the pine bench, at the table in the alcove. There's no cutlery visible, but I'm not bothered. I just wash my hands under the kitchen tap. And eat.

Dr Hart comes in. He looks at my empty plate and smiles, goes to the sink and washes his hands. Then he pours himself a glass of something from a jug in the fridge and sits down in a chair, at an angle to me.

'So, tell me. Did you come up with anything?'

'There's a couple of things.'

'Oh?'

'Well, his gun. In a letter to me a while back, he had he mentioned a gun.'

'Yes. A .22.'

'But it's not there anywhere, is it?'

'No. It's here, upstairs in the gun cupboard. Quite safe.'

He nods. Then I ask about his dog. He'd mentioned a dog to me as well. Surely the dog wouldn't have disappeared, even if something terrible had happened to him?

'Ah, the dog. His dog, as he liked to call her. Though she wasn't really his. He'd just adopted her.'

'But would he have had it with him?'

'Probably. She was mine, you see,' says Dr Hart, sadly. 'One of my corgis, a bitch, seemed to take a shine to him. So I let him look after her. If she wasn't with him, she'd be with me.'

'But she isn't with you, so she could be with my father?'

'Yes, wherever he is.' He stands up and goes to one of the small windows, looking out front.

'He liked to walk along the ness. Every day when the weather was fair, he went there. He might have had the dog on a leash, because of the sheep.'

'The ness?'

'On the other side of the bay. I think the police should organise a search. Six days are six days,' he says.

I'm not convinced. My father could be anywhere, visiting friends, or just travelling.

'I want to make a few phone calls, check a few things out.'

He shrugs. 'Of course. You could put together a list of friends he might have been in touch with? To give to the police when they arrive. That would narrow the search down.'

Dr Hart doesn't try to hide his scepticism. I sense he believes my father has gone over the edge somewhere, taking the dog with him.

'What was the dog's name?' I ask.

He looks surprised. 'What difference does that make?'

I shrug this time.

'I called her Lakshmi. But everyone else called her Lucky.'

The thought strikes me – Lucky the corgi pulled down to its death by a stumbling old man. I imagine the two of them falling, connected by the leash, spinning round and around, like bolas, the collar choking the dog as it's pulled downwards, my father gripping the leash as if it might save his life, then the dog spinning round, all in an arc the radius of the leash, then lower than the body of the man, beginning to pull him down. Equilibrium in that moment between when they're balanced, in perfect free-fall, then falling, pulling tight till they hit the rocks in sequence, dead, dead.

But I won't admit this is more than one possibility. Why should he not have taken his dog, his lucky corgi, with him on his travels? Not to Australia, obviously, but then he wasn't likely to be going there. But to

Perth, to Edinburgh or Glasgow. Or somewhere on the island?

Dr Hart is dubious. But I'd seen the kennels on the ferry. It's possible, as plausible as the bolas flashing down to the sea below, surely?

Dr Hart smiles fondly, but with a deep gloom over his brow.

'You need to understand: this is very serious; this is an island. No one leaves without their name appearing somewhere on the lists of aircraft or ferry passengers. Your father's name isn't on those lists.' He takes a breath, and carries on: 'He left no message with anyone to say that he was going away. Local radio broadcast an appeal for two nights running, asking him to contact the police, or anyone knowing of his whereabouts to do so. There's a slim chance that he may have left some other way. Or that he may be somewhere on the island and doesn't know people are looking for him. But it's a slim chance. I appreciate you want to keep your hopes up, but we must be realistic.'

So he gives me a sheet of paper and I start to make a list of all the folk my father might have been in contact with. Of some of them, I can only remember names, others I've got addresses in my head. Then he brings me the phone, plugs it into a socket in the kitchen, and goes out, leaving me to use it. But even so, it doesn't feel private.

In the drawing room upstairs, I've stood a while and looked into Dr Hart's gilt-framed antique mirror with ram's head ornaments round the edge and seen how, as I get older, lines emerge on my face that I seem to recognise from having looked at my father's face. My face merges into his. Or it emerges from his. And hers. And then I feel the little brass key I found at my father's and pull it out of my pocket. I look at it a while, and all that while it looks familiar. But then they all look alike to me, keys.

'I have the key here,' I say, when he comes in. 'And I found this on the window ledge while I was there. Does it open some lock in the caravan?'

He corrects me by saying, 'chalet, not caravan', then reaches over holding out his hand to take the keys from me. He turns the strange one over and over in his palm, like a connoisseur. I half-expect him to pull an eyepiece from his waistcoat pocket, to give a valuation. But instead he just gets up.

'Excuse me one moment,' he says.

I wait. Dr Hart comes back carrying something. I recognise it immediately. An old wooden casket, made of a red wood, maybe mahogany, about two feet long by eighteen inches wide, a foot deep. The panels are plain, no ornamental carving or anything. I remember my grandmother giving it to him, on his fortieth birthday. 'The family kist', she called it.

Dr Hart sets it down on the table. 'He asked me to look after this for him. Said it had certain documents in it. Your key fits.'

Dr Hart hesitates a moment, then lifts a glass and hands it over to me. I put it down and lift the kist up. It's heavy. The key is sticking out of the lock. I turn it. The mechanism's smooth.

'Yes, you're right. It fits,' I say.

'Well well well.'

I sit there with the casket on my knees. Dr Hart waits expectantly for me to open it. But this is my business, family business, what's it got to do with him? I'll take this with me, up the narrow staircase to the room at the top he's given me.

I close the door behind me and lay the kist on the bed, then sit down beside it. Now that I've got the casket, I have a strong sense of Rod Cunninghame. As if I'm closer to him than I've been yet. This family heirloom, the kist of ages, I hadn't thought of it in twelve years. Now it feels like it's mine, and I'm the keeper of the secrets. Or the teller of the tales.

Count to ten ... I open the lid. Papers, neatly folded.

Birth certificates. Hers, Ella Margaret Walker. 29th May 1934. 6lb 4oz. His, Rod James Daniel Cunninghame. August 22nd 1933. 9lb 13oz. Marriage certificate, my father and mother's. Rod to Ella. St Leonard's in the Fields, Perth. June 3rd 1964. Then more certificates.

Life assurance policies: Allied and Prudential, Assured Life. All neatly folded away. In a hundred years that's all anybody will care about. Who married who when, what kids did they have. What their occupation was. Cause of death. Time, date, place. Spirits reduced to statistics, the human frame of life ground down.

And then I see it. I pull it from the box and run the pages through my fingers. They tremble. And in the low lamplight of the attic room, I lie back on the damp feather quilt and gawp at it. That book. That terrible book, that bringer of childhood nightmares. I'm being transported, transmigrated. The memory tape loops back as I pick it up. Its shadowy cover, the hollow dome of the temple, just the skeleton remaining, the sky dark with clouds that could be the remnants of the atomic mushroom. And that single word, printed white on black cloud in the top left hand corner.

I lift it up and turn it over. Imagine him putting it in here with all the family papers like that! Then I open the book. A postcard falls out. On one side, there's this map of the city 'showing extent of damages'. The explosion centre, in the middle of a triangle of marked places, Aioibashi, Kamiyacho and Shiyakusho. Then a thick red line, captioned, LED LINE ... BURNT OUT AREA, a thinner red line, captioned LED LINE ... COMPLETELY DESTROYED AREA, and a thin one: LED LINE ... HALF DESTROYED AREA. Below that, PLACE OF PINK MOST DENSELY POPULATED AREA PRIOR TO BOMBARDMENT.

I stare at this card for a while, struck by how the system of rivers looks like a human hand. Then I flick it over and read the text.

Aug. 6, 1945 – 8.15 a.m. That was the instant of the sudden turn of world history. 'A flash of the century, over the skies of Hiroshima.' From one B-29 superfortress, the first atomic bomb exploded at an altitude of 570 meters. The hot rays radiated for a radius of 3,000 meters, and in an instant, 69% of the whole city was left in ashes. There were more than 200,000 casualties. When the smoke faded from the great delta, Hiroshima, it was changed to a 'rubble city', and the remains of the brick buildings, stood like a ghosts.

'Death city, Hiroshima' – The city which instantly turned to a burning dungeon: the victims 'wandered' like a somnambulist, and was wrapped in desolate death.

It was called the 'atomic desert', and that only vultures dwell, and would be barren for 70 years. This, was only a rumor. Grass began to grow, and the trees burst out in the burnt desert, and people increased gradually. With the blessings of

the great nature, and by the citizen's sturdy will; the campaign
for No More Hiroshimas is expanding throughout the world,
and have started to establish a new 'City of Peace'.

PUBLISHED BY JAPAN TRAVEL BUREAU

I was never sure exactly what it meant to him, this book, how he felt about it, but I know it meant a lot. I knew he'd bought it in the early fifties in Hiroshima when he was a young seaman, just twenty years old.

The book is in two sections. The first has maps I studied as a child. Pictures of the atomic devastation, a text in Japanese and what approximates to English. Then the second section is a kind of tourist guide, 'picture guide book', with photos of the rebuilding of the city that took place afterwards. I flick through the pages. There's the hollow dome again, behind a cherry tree in blossom, with a banner hanging from it, the word RESTFUL at the top and a Japanese script below.

He had carried the book to his new home in Scotland, where his mother came from, years before I was born. But I can remember him telling me about it. The horror of it, a bomb that could destroy a fair city like Perth in an instant, just like that.

And all those early attempts at indoctrination, they'd worked. I grew up hating war, till I learnt about its necessity later on in the playground, the hard school of tarmac and skinned knuckles. Now I'm the keeper of this terrible treasure, this book of death. A thing come halfway round the world from its place of origin. When I look at it, I think of the hollowness of that dome. A great black void that draws me into the text, to read: *City of peace, city of the seven rivers, the city of death, the phoenix of a city … Hiroshima.*

But the truth is that I have never even come close. Not even close to understanding why my father kept this picture book. I remember him showing it to me, reading the skewed English text to me: *By and by, unexpectedly, on the sixth of August in 1945 the world's first atomic assault utterly devastated this city.*

I open the book at random, at a fold-out page with the title CITY OF DEATH. It's a black and white picture of rubble, with a line of hills in the distance. The only identifiable objects are four trees, completely stripped of leaves and twigs, one block of flats and a few telegraph poles. Everything else is like the surface of the moon.

> *Atomic Blast: the blast was severe, and caused a whirlwind at the same time. All the wooden houses, big tombstones, and a tall camphor tree measuring three stretches of a man's arms, located within three kilometers from the explosion were blown down.*
>
> *On a bridge which was located a kilometer and a half from the explosion center, men were blown up while crossing it, and a child who had been in its mothers arms was snatched away from its mothers' embrace by the blast.*

Now the pages are marked. The card covers, tied with a silvery cord through the punch-holes, are torn here and there. The paper binding's burst. But the photos still seem timeless images of the void.

After he left Perth, and sold the house, he had nothing much in the way of possessions. He didn't gather any moss, as he used say. But this book, this he kept hold of. He must have carried it with him, maybe because it reminded him of his early days. This he'd hung on to. Put it in the box in a treasured safe place, wherever that might have been in the rooms he rented.

This kist must have been a kind of constant in his shiftlessness when he left Perth, when he moved to Edinburgh. It was like he had to follow, to follow his bairns out there, into the world. As if he didn't want to be left behind, to wizen, grow old and die. He couldn't let us go after our mother died, he needed to be around us.

Hiroshima ... city of death, city of peace, city of the phoenix.

A young Aussie deck-hand, not long in the Merchant Navy, sailing into the delta of the River Ota. On shoreleave he buys this book and a few weeks later in Amsterdam, he and another lad jumped ship. I never really knew what he did after that. There was a gap of a few years between those years at sea and the batch of stories that filled the next space, his beatnik years, on the Aldermaston marches, and time he spent in Languedoc and Paris. These things were never really dated or fixed in my mind, somehow.

Nor did they last all that long, though in his memory they were endless. Somewhere along the line he got swept up in that post-war idealism. Before ending up in Perth. Before settling there.

They say over the city looked chaotic with things soaring high up. A windspout sprang up in the direction of Hiroshima station. Drums; wagons; lumbers; durning wood, etc were seen soaring; 'Man!' cried someone. Looking up I saw a figure or two flying up, while in the direction of the Asano Sentei, the limbs of a man swept up were distinctly visible …

I remember the last time I saw him, two years ago, in early September, just before he left for the north. By that time the drink had taken over – he turned up at my flat in Edinburgh in the middle of the night, looking terrible. We were in bed asleep. He kept ringing the bell. For some reason I had a feeling it would be him. It was as if I'd been dreaming that he'd come.

I took him into the kitchen, shushing and trying to stop him falling against the bathroom door and crashing through the glass panel. He leant against our tall fridge and knocked the whole thing over, spilt the milk, and the eggs cracked on the lino, and him on top, grinning. Naomi came through and swore at him in German.

In those days, I didn't know what to do with him. He'd changed so much in such a short time. Into this lush. When the pubs closed and he'd run out of listeners for his stories, he'd descend on Martin or myself, always repentant, looking for a bit of sympathy. Martin lived on his own and he used to put up with it. He said he was in mourning, mourning our mother, this was his way of dealing with it, and he'd stop drinking when he was over it.

But what it was he was trying to prove, I didn't know. Maybe it was just a way to get attention. There were moments when he'd be flaked out, lying there on the couch and I'd be talking to Naomi about something, and he'd open an eye without moving his head and watch. Deliberate, so I'd see him and stop talking. Like a little boy, almost.

He was always the performer. When he was still in Perth and in the favour of the town, when he'd had the right amount to drink, he was outstanding. He'd take the stage at local gatherings and he'd really sparkle. Then everyone loved Rod. He'd be spouting his Burns. And when he was doing his poetry, his Scottish accent was perfect. It was his party piece. His way of showing he belonged.

Later on, after the family break-up, the act hackneyed. He'd start his recitations, didn't matter where it was, in the pool-room of whatever pub he happened to have chosen, wherever. Nobody applauded then. They'd only tolerate him for so long, before the bar staff told him where to go. Not that he was ever a troublemaker. But, with his tongue, he'd wind folk up. He looked like he was trouble. The same dirty old suit.

This was my father, later. Hard to believe the state he was in, after our mother died, after they'd retired him from the paper and he'd sold the house, and he turned up in Edinburgh. After it emerged he'd been married in Australia. That was a revelation all right. But there was more to follow. There was Tanya.

For years we didn't know about her, till one morning when he was sobering up, sitting at the kitchen table with his pen and his notebook, writing, and he looked up and said suddenly that his daughter was coming to meet him that day. He blurted it out, like it would choke him if he didn't. I just couldn't believe it. She was thirty-five now, he said, and had written to him two years ago from Sydney. Wanted to make contact. That was all the information he volunteered. I asked him questions but he wouldn't answer. He just got up and left. But thirty-five meant she was nearly ten years older than me.

So when I saw him next, I asked him, how come? How come he'd kept this a secret all these years? She was our sister, surely we had a right to meet her. He'd shrugged. Said it was our mother, he just couldn't tell her. Just couldn't face her. The marriage only lasted a very short while. They'd been young, she was pregnant, they thought they should get married. But it was a mistake. The whole thing. A disaster. It was then he left Australia, went to sea, and made his way to Europe.

Then, a few years later when he was in London, before he'd even met our mother, she'd written, this first wife, and said that she was getting married again and wanted a divorce. Said she'd rather not keep in touch.

It was her decision. She wanted a clean start, he said.

I was mad, really mad about that. Considering Martin and what had happened then. The way he'd behaved. It must have seemed to him like history was repeating itself. No wonder he'd said he'd take care of that. But not once had he mentioned this marriage. Not once. And he'd lived all those years with our mother as a total hypocrite. Almost as if he was a bigamist. I told him I wanted to meet her. But he acted as if he didn't hear, said it was up to her how much contact she wanted with the family. He stomped out of the flat. Then he was gone. He packed up and left his bedsit. Left Edinburgh as unexpectedly as he'd appeared.

I lay the Hiroshima book down, on top of the certificates. In the kist, below where it had been, I see a pile of photos. There's a wedding photo, him and our mother. She's in her white flowing dress, near-hidden under the virginal bloom; he's fat-faced and young, standing tall and smiling, a quiff of black hair falling down over his forehead. Underneath that, there's a colour snap of the family, all of us, taken in about, what, 1969 in Princes Street Gardens, under the shadow of Edinburgh Castle. He'd stopped a passer-by to get everyone in.

I can recall it clear as can be, the yellow coat our mother's wearing, the short corduroy trousers Martin's wearing, and him in his houndstooth sports jacket. Me and Martin are screwing up our eyes, heads cocked over on one side. Our mother looks proud, arms round each. Him, he stands off to one side a bit, as if he was just about to turn and walk away. As if one second later, he'd be out of shot.

Under that again is a photo I've not seen, an old one, another wedding photo. It looks like my gran's face, but I've never seen the photo before. I know that she removed all the pictures of her husband, our grandfather, from the house soon after he was killed in the first year of the Second World War. *The* war, as she calls it. My father said she'd said she didn't want to be reminded. So she got rid of all evidence of him. No wonder he used to say he didn't know his father, when I asked about him, if he just became a silence after he was killed. And maybe that explains the Hiroshima book, his CND membership in the early days, him hating war so much. And here in the kist, there's photos too, of our old house in Perth, in Abbot Street, the one we lived in right through our growing up, the house I loved, and the house I hated to see sold. Our extended womb.

And another photo of a house, this time with a verandah. An Australian house, my father's first home. I flick it over to see if there's anything written on the back, but there's nothing, nothing but a serial number.

Below the photos in the box, there's an old exercise book, a jotter, a red jotter, with '1938' written on its cover. At first I think it might have been his, when he was young, five years old, a first school-book. But when I open it I see it's filled with a perfect copperplate handwriting, very grown-up. It's a journal or a diary. The first page seems to be some sort of quotation.

> *Creativeness needs purification; needs the purifying fire. In a civilised world creativeness becomes so degenerate that it calls forth a moral reaction against it, and a desire for ascetic renunciation and escape from the world. We find such degeneration in many tendencies of modern art and literature; in which the spirit of eternity is surrendered to the polluted spirit of the time. We find it in political and social life where the struggle for gain and power destroys the creative desire for social justice. In every sphere the lust of life damps the creative burning of the spirit. It is the direct opposite of creativeness. Creativeness is the victory over lust of life. That lust is overcome through humility and through creativeness.*

And then a name: Berdyayev. Then following, on the next page …

> *January 1st—The time is fast approaching when one must decide on a course of action and hold to it. Few can be in any doubt as to the intentions of the National Socialists in Germany, nor the Fascisti in Italy. Yet we must continue to work for peace.*
>
> *I begin this year by resolving to stand by what I now hold to be the only truly moral position. As a Christian, as a creative spirit, I can neither partake in any armed struggle, nor*

undertake non-combatant duties. I find myself, as Berdyayev writes, moving towards a desire for ascetic renunciation and escape from the world: yet I know I must not weaken. Attitudes towards me among my friends and colleagues are rapidly hardening. At Bill's Hogmanay party last night I got into a furious argument with two young socialists one of whom claimed to have been in Spain, fighting Franco. No doubt under the influence somewhat, he was bragging about having shot a dozen Nationalists. I asked him pointedly if he thought himself a better man for having done so, at which juncture Bill laughed and said they would have to excuse me as the local Pacifist. The way he said it hurt me deeply, though I suppose that this is the kind of contretemps I must expect to occur ever more frequently over the coming months. If it comes to war, as many believe it must, then I will have to face the full fury of patriotic man.

January 2nd—Today the Nationalists bombed Barcelona with forty-nine killed. It hurt me deeply to think of civilians being punished for the intransigence of their leaders. I cannot help feeling that if it were only possible for the average citizens of nations to come together, they could between them yet avert the doom which hangs over Europe. What is required is a revolution; not of Marxist intellectuals or proletarians but of peace-loving Christian people everywhere; truly a revolution of the spirit.

I run through the pages, looking to see if I can find who the writer is. It can't have been my father. Could it be my grandfather? I know so little about him, it's hard to decide. It might be. But then he went to war, did he not? So maybe he set out with a New Year's resolution and found himself abandoning it? The dates of the entries get less regular as the year goes on. I try to think of 1938. The little I know about it, trying to come up with some crucial date that might give something away. A point of contact between my ignorance and this journal – September! Munich,

Chamberlain's peace in our time speech. That was 1938, was it not? I flick through the pages, line after line of perfect handwriting. February March April May June July August September.

Here's something ...

> *September 29th—Herr Hitler has invited Chamberlain to take part in a conference in Munich tomorrow; along with Daladier and Mussolini, after Roosevelt appealed to him for the maintenance of world peace. The dictator has spoken and the others will obey.*
>
> *My position at the Academy is now untenable. Several of the pupils went home yesterday and told their parents they believed I was a German spy – simply because I had tried to explain to them that not all Germans were Nazis; and to intimate how the Treaty of Versailles had led to the present destabilisation. Rector Alexander understood the mistake – at least he said he did – nevertheless I was firmly warned against any further such lessons.*
>
> *Soon the neighbours will be demanding a ban on my Wagner recordings!*

I lay the jotter down. Is this grandfather's handiwork? I thought that he was an insurance clerk, not a teacher. At least as far as I know, he was. But then folk changed jobs, even back then. I feel guilty, knowing so little about these people. My life is speeding past and I know so little of my family.

All I can think of are the saved, the Satanists – fire, burning a baby's crib, and the Lord's

vengeance

Letter from Philippa Gabrielsen
to Rev. Archibald Nicol
November 3rd 2000

Bon Hoga
Serrafir
Tokumua

Dear Archibald

I'm enclosing the transcription of an interview I did with Miss Mimie
Jeromsen last month. As I told you in my earlier letter, she was a maid
in the service of the Cunninghame family in New Zetland for some forty
years, from 1920, when she came out, till Robina died in 1964. After
that she went to live with her brother in Serrafir.

There's a problem with the interview – despite the fact that she's
lived most of her life over here she has never lost her native Zetlandic
dialect. Indeed, if she ever did speak English or Tokumuan, she seems to
have forgotten them. I would guess her whole life was lived within the
closed ethnic community and, as she explains, one of the reasons her
mistress employed her was because she was from the same village and
spoke the same dialect, and the mistress wanted to keep that and other
traditions alive with her children.

Now I have acquired an understanding of 'Alroki', as the pidgin of
Tokumua is called, but the original dialect of Zetland is very different.
So I don't pretend to understand everything I've written down and may
in some places have misrepresented her. I have simply tried to be true to
the sound of her voice. The version of 'Alroki' which she speaks is older
and denser than anything I've ever heard, and there's no one of her age
or particular pedigree here who can help me to decode it further.

So I am asking you a favour in the hope that as a Scotsman and
a scholar you may be able to assist me in this. I know that there are
many similarities between the Scotch language and that of the Zetland
archipelago. In fact, it would be a favour to the whole Zetlandic

community here, were you able to assist me with this, as we are trying to gather as much of the history of the Zetlandic settlers for a new community website.

Aa da best

Philippa

PS – I include a description of the local creole, for your interest – if it *is* of interest. Just ignore it, if not.

MISS MIMIE JEROMSEN: 1ST INTERVIEW

(TAPE ON) *So I've come here today to the Ilesburg Huse in Serrafir, Tokumua, to talk with the oldest member of the Zetlandic community, Miss Mimie Jeromsen, a well-known personality to folk in the colony since she arrived here as a young woman from the Aald Rock. Miss Jeromsen, or Mimie, if I may, perhaps you'd like to tell us yourself just how old you are.*
A'm a hundir year aald, me lass. Ja, wan hundrit year. Whit tinks du a'dat dan?

Remarkable and many congrats. And still in good health?
Ja, dat I im. No sae ill ava. Tho I dunna dance muckle noo (LAUGHS).

I'll bet you were a dancer in your day, though?
Oh dat dat, ja, dat I wis, nae doot.

The dances from the Old Rock?
Ja ja, dem. Da Aald Rock. Zetlan. Aye.

And what dances did you use to do, Mimie?
Oh, da Thula reels, Quhid reels, aa dat. Ja ja. Laek whan I wis a lass an dat. Ja, back atill da aald days, in Zetlan.

Do you miss those days, Mimie?
Och weel ja, bit du sees, du manna, fir d'ir naen a'dat fokk ta da foar ony maer, nor dat wye a life. An d'ir noght, du sees, ta tink lang fir, firby joost da time hitsel. Hit's aa diffrint nooadays, ja. Or so dey tell me. Dis oil'at dey fan, du kens, aa aroond Zetlan, most affil deep, oot ati'da very depts, awa frammir as da far haaf. Ja ... hit's aa a lifetime sine.

The world's a different place all over, I guess?
Ja ja, dat dat. Hit's nothin noo ta gjing fleein aa ower, ta dis young aens. Aa da wye here an back ta da Aald Rock as if hit wis joost naethin. Bit eensadays du kens hit wis da ends a'da Eart. Whan we wid set oot. Even in 1920, we kent little. Bit fir da first a'dem'at cam quhit tinks du saa dey whan first da ship med laand?

(PAUSE TAPE AS MISS JEROMSEN SEEMED TO DRIFT OFF, MAY BE A LITTLE TIRED. I WONDER HOW FIT SHE IS FOR THIS. THE NURSE ASKS IF SHE WANTS TO STOP, BUT THIS IDEA SEEMS TO REVITALISE HER AND SHE BRIGHTENS.)

Na lass, lat wis gjing on. Whar wis I noo? Ja dat wis wis dan, set oot fir da very ends a'da very Eart, wi nae idea really whar it wis we wir gjaain. Hit myght is weel a'been da Mune, fir aa we kent. Hit wis kynda da promised laand in mony wyes, da Happie Laand across da sea, apo da very idder side a'da wirld. A lokk a'fokk toght hit wid be laek Heevin.

How well informed were people about what lay ahead?
Da fokk hed nae real idea a'whit lay afore dem, na naa. Dey coodna really hae.

And you came here after the First World War?
Ja, eftir da First Waar. I cam oot in 1920, just a slip o a lass, an wis in service ta a Zetlan couple at hed settled here, da Cunninghames, as dey caa'd demsels dan. But I kent da family fyn, as dey wir been da laird an his wife ati'wir parish no dat lang afoar I wis boarn – Scots, dey wir, bit dey changed dir name, fir dey fell oot most aafil wi his middir an sisters. Me ain middir hed been a maid ta da leddy whan dey bed in Zetlan and

dey wir come ta be braalie guid frieends, du sees. An it wis me middir'at fixed me up wi dis 'graand opportunity' ta sail ta New Zetland an mak mesel a new life oot dere.

But you wanted to come out here then?
Weel du sees, lass, dey wirna muckle option fir a lass danadays an da Gret Waar hed taen a most aafil toll apo da menfokk. Dey wir an aafil a'dem killt an woondit an dem as med it hem, weel du kens dey wir mony a'dem never da sam ever eftir. An dat wis joost da wye a'it. I never toght no ta gjing …

(MISS JEROMSEN APPEARS TO BECOME EMOTIONAL, SO I SUGGEST WE SUSPEND THE INTERVIEW TILL SHE FEELS BETTER. I WAIT FOR A WHILE IN THE VESTIBULE, BUT A NURSE COMES TO TELL ME THAT SHE ISN'T ABLE TO CARRY ON THAT DAY.)

ALROKI — VIKIPEDIA, THE FREE ENCYCLOPEDIA

Alroki is a creole language, one of the official languages of Tokumua. It is the first language of many 'Urban ni-Tokumua' (those who live in Serrafir and environs), and the second language of the rest of the country's residents. The Tokumuan national anthem is in Alroki. More than 75% of Alroki words are of English or Scotch dialect origin; the remainder combines a few dozen words from Italian, with vocabulary inherited from various languages of Tokumua, mostly limited to flora and fauna terminology. While the influence of these vernacular languages is low on the vocabulary side, it is very high in the morphosyntax. Essentially, Alroki can be described as a language with an English vocabulary and an Austronesian grammar.

Tokumua was first settled by Melanesian people speaking Oceanic languages several thousand years ago, but the first substantial contact with Europeans was not until around 1800, when a whaling station was established. In the 1870s and 80s, many Ni-Tokumua (as people from Tokumua call themselves) were recruited to work on newly established plantations. These multilingual situations resulted in the formation of a pidgin, which has evolved over the last hundred years or so to become the language that is spoken today. The name given to the language derives from the term 'Old Rock', the affectionate name for their former home brought by the Zetlanders who settled there in the 1870s.

ATTITUDES AND CURRENT USE

Alroki is the common language that is used by most of the people of Tokumua. There are many separate languages belonging to the Oceanic subgroup of the larger Austronesian family spoken in Tokumua, but almost everybody also speaks Alroki as a second language. Most of the younger people living in the town of Serrafir speak Alroki as their first language.

Alroki is a variety of Melanesian pidgin, declared by the constitution to be the national language, a situation which arose as a kind of compromise to allow local politicians to avoid a politically divisive choice between English or Tokumuan, both of which were used as languages of government prior to independence in 1980.

Alroki is the language of debate in the national parliament, as well as of politics generally. It is the medium of the radio station that broadcasts nationally. Many public notices, as well as items in the local newspapers, are written in Alroki. The largest single document that is written in Alroki is the partially completed translation of the Holy Bible.

Most children attend at least six years of primary school, where education is offered through the medium of either English or Tokumuan. Alroki is now formally incorporated into the school curriculum. The same has been true of local vernaculars, through recent moves to incorporate these into early primary education.

VOCABULARY

The major lexifier for Alroki is English, with words such as 'brij' for 'bridge' and buluk for 'cow', from 'bullock'. Some words of English origin in Alroki are archaic, belonging to the unique dialect brought by the first European settlers from their native Zetland in the far north of Scotland, e.g. 'piri' for 'small' or 'hansil' for 'gift'. Others are more general in origin e.g. 'masket' for 'rifle' (from 'musket') or 'giaman' for 'tell lies' (from 'gammon'), or stylistically restricted, e.g. 'puskit' for 'cat' (from 'pussy cat') or 'bruk' for 'ruined' (from 'buggered up').

Some words of English origin have meanings which are modelled more on what is found in local Oceanic languages, such as 'han', which means both 'hand' and 'arm', while 'leg' means both 'foot' and 'leg'. However, there are a number of common words of Italian origin in Alroki as well, such as 'boncompila' ('happy birthday celebration' from 'boun compleanno'), 'pago' ('you're welcome' from 'prego') and 'bajo' ('to express affection' from 'bacio' (kiss)).

There are also a number of words derived from local dialects, most commonly referring to local culture, flora or fauna, e.g. 'nakamal' (meeting house), 'nabanga' (banyan tree) or 'nasiviru' (parrot). It is usually difficult to assign a particular language of origin for such forms because those local words which are most likely to be incorporated into the Alroki vocabulary are those which are most widely distributed in the languages of the country.

SOUNDS

While many words in Alroki are recognisable from their English (and sometimes Italian) origins, the language is not pronounced at all like English (or Italian). At the same time, because Alroki is spoken by most people in addition to their own local vernacular, there is a tendency for some sounds to be pronounced in ways that show influence of the local languages.

The consonants we find in most people's Alroki are: p t k b d g m n ng f v s h l r y w. Also, the sound that we write as 'ch' in English is found in Alroki, though it is written as 'j'. Words in Alroki are often pronounced with consonants dropped or vowels inserted between consonants when they come from English words that contain sequences of consonants together, e.g. 'district' becomes 'distrik', 'electric' becomes 'letrik', 'school' becomes 'sukul', 'six' becomes 'sikis'. Sounds in English that are not found in Alroki are also usually adapted to the nearest equivalent sound in Alroki, e.g. 'th' becomes 't' as in 'Matthew', which becomes 'Matyu'; 'z' and 'sh' both become 's' as in 'sip' ('ship')

There are only five vowels in Alroki: i e a o u. Other vowels in English are generally adapted to the nearest equivalent vowel in Alroki, so a word like 'burn' in English is pronounced as 'bon'. Distinctions such as that between the vowels in 'kill' and 'keel' are not made in Alroki, and both of these words come out simply as 'kil', which means either 'injury' (from 'kill') or 'keel'. The so-called front-rounded vowels of Italian in words such as 'légume', 'vegetable' loses its rounding to become plain front vowels. The word for 'vegetable' in Alroki is therefore 'legim'. In addition to these pure vowels, Alroki has a number of diphthongs, and the practice is to write these as 'ae' (corresponding to the sound in English 'eye'), 'oe' (as in 'boy'), 'ao' (as in 'cow').

Nobody has tried seriously to study the intonation pattern of Alroki, but it certainly seems to have a unique melody involving an unusual rise and fall of the voice while speaking. Although there are plenty of differences of vocabulary and grammar between Alroki and both Pijin and Tok Pisin, one of the more immediately noticeable characteristics of Alroki is its distinctive intonation.

GRAMMAR
Basic sentences
When you want to say that something (or somebody) is something else, there is no verb meaning 'be' in Alroki, and the words describing the two things are simply placed one after the other, as in:

'Mi domini' – 'I am a teacher.'

'Du fantin' – 'You are hungry.'

When the first part of the sentence is a noun or a pronoun other than 'mi' or 'du', the second part of the sentence will usually be separated from the first part by the small word 'i', as in:

'Tomson i fantin' – 'Thompson is hungry.'

'Mifeloo i bos' – 'We are the bosses.'

To indicate that an action is being performed, a verb follows a pronoun or a noun, with the word 'i' coming between the two as described above. Thus:

'Tomson i kukum raes' – 'Thompson cooks the rice.'

'Mifeloo i ridim buk' – 'We read the book.'

However, if the first noun is plural rather than singular, the word 'i' is replaced by 'oli':

'Ol man oli kukum raes' – 'The men cook rice.'

'Ol skolla oli ridim buk' – 'The students read the book.'

'Ol bos oli fantin' – 'The bosses are hungry.'

TENSE AND ASPECT

Verbs in Alroki do not have endings to express meanings like present continuous or past tense in English. A verb can appear on its own, as in the examples just given, where it can have any tense depending on the context. But if you need to indicate the tense, this can be done by placing a special auxiliary between the word 'i' (or 'oli') and the verb. Other meanings can also be expressed by words of this kind, e.g.

'Tomson i bin ridim buk' – 'Thompson read the book.'

'Tomson i stap ridim buk' – 'Thompson is reading the book.'

'Tomson i save kukum raes' – 'Thompson can cook the rice.'

'Ol skolla oli man ridim buk' – 'The students must read the book.'

There are two exceptions. Firstly, the future tense is expressed by the form 'mibae', which is not placed between 'i' (or 'oli') and the verb at all, but it appears either before the word 'i' (or 'oli'), or before at the beginning of the sentence, e.g.

'Mibae Tomson i ridim buk' – 'Thompson will read the book.'

'Ol skolla mibae oli ridim buk' – 'The students will read the book.'

Secondly, if you want to indicate that something has already happened, you do this by placing 'fenes' after the verb, e.g.

'Ol skolla oli ridim buk fenes' – 'The students have already read the book.'

'Tomson i fantin fenes' – 'Thompson is already hungry.'

NEGATIVES

To make a statement negative in Alroki, all you have to do is put the word 'no' between the word 'i' (or 'oli') and the verb, e.g.

'Tomson i no kukum raes' – 'Thompson does not cook rice.'

'Ol skolla oli no ridim buk' – 'The students do not read books.'

It is possible to place 'no' before any of the other words that express tense or aspect (except 'bai'), as in:

'Tomson no binabil salem hoos' – 'Thompson did not sell the house.'

'Ol bos oli mann no ridim buk' – 'The bosses must not read the book.'

'Mibae ol man oli no kukum raes' – 'The men will not cook rice.'

TRANSITIVE VERBS

Verbs that have objects in Alroki generally have a special ending to indicate this. So, compare the following:

'Sera i stap rid' – 'Sarah is reading.'

'Sera i stap ridim buk' – 'Sarah is reading the book.'

This ending is sometimes '-im', sometimes '-um', and sometimes '-em'. When the last vowel in the verb is 'i' or 'u', then the vowel of the ending will be the same, but when there is any other vowel in the verb, the ending will always be '-em'. That is why we say:

'Sera is bin kuk' – 'Sarah cooked.'

'Sera is bin kukum raes' – 'Sarah cooked the rice.'

Also:

'Hus mibae i low' – 'The house will burn.'

'Lulu mibae i lowem hus' – 'Lulu will burn the house.'

PREPOSITIONS

There are four main prepositions in Alroki:

lang – 'in', 'on', 'at' or 'with'

blang – 'of' or 'for'

wedim – 'along with'

seko – 'sake of', meaning 'because'

Hence:

'Mi stap slip lang hoos' – 'I am sleeping in the house.'

'Ol skolla oli save swim lang da bon – 'The students can swim in the river.'

'Mibae mi kuk blang du' – 'I will cook for you (sing.)'

'Mibae mi kam wedim du' – 'I will come with you (sing.)'
'Mi bin kam seko ol skolla' – 'I came because of the students.'

The preposition blang is also used to indicate possession, e.g.
'hoos blang mi' – 'my house'
'ol skolla blang domini' – 'the teacher's students'
'domini blang ol skolla' – 'the students' teacher'

A FEW ALROKI WORDS AND PHRASES

Yes – Ya
No – Na
Hello – Ay-ay
Nice to meet you – Fyn seko di ken
How are you? – Fu blang du?
Thank you, I'm well – Di tak, nae si il
What is your name? – Di blang ka?
My name is – Mi blang ka
Goodbye – Chiri
Please/You're welcome – Mi wilikim?/Di wilikim
Thank you – Tak blang di
Excuse me – Maes blang mi
I'm sorry – Firigi seko mi
You're welcome – Pago di
I like you – Di piri chul
I can't speak [much] Alroki – Mi no save spaek (mukil) Alroki
Do you speak English? – Di spaek Ingilis?
Is there someone here who speaks English? – Feloo spaek Ingilis blang herabut?
Never mind – No lit (pron. 'leet')
Look out! – Waatch di!
Good morning – Bon moarn
Good night – Bon nut
I don't understand – Mi no ken

Where is the toilet? – Bug blang abut?

Leave me alone! – Lat mi laen!

Don't touch me! – Di mana rek mi!

I need your help – Di mi man elip

It's an emergency! – Seko maesit serio!

I need a doctor – Mi sik (pron. 'seek')

Can I use your phone? – Mi di ring-ring?

23rd June 2000 – Norbie

I wake up shaking, gripping myself tight for a moment till I'm sure that I'm alive. I'd been slipping down something in my dream, as if I was being swallowed, or sucked in some giant throat. I'm sweating and my heart is pounding. My pillow is wet. But it's okay, I'm alive. I lie awake for a while, calming, calming. Then I look at my alarm. It's 2.23. But the sky outside is bright, like dawn. And then I click this is midsummer. No, it's the night after midsummer's night. The 23rd of June.

I get off the bed, go to the window and stare out at the sea below the laird's house, agitated by the dream, that dream of death I had. The light is strong up here in the north at this time of year. In the east, above the finger of land at the far side of the bay, the sky is pink with dawn already. Or do sunset and sunrise just flow one into the other?

I put my boots on. The sky is brightening already, and I feel a pull, a strong pull to walk those silver sands on this midsummer night. As if there he'll be alive, not in these tatty old papers in the kist, this twisted tale made up of marks on trees. But this midsummer night is not a dream. I want to walk, I need to get out and walk, to walk the strange dream off. I open the bedroom door and slip quietly down the stone stairs. One of the sleeping corgis growls but doesn't wake, as I tiptoe past the drawing room. Through the open door Dr Hart is sleeping in his chair, still wearing his jacket and all clothes on, a glass of whisky on the table at his side. A gentle drunken sleep.

I pass by quickly, wanting nothing and nobody to break the heavy silence that I creep through. The door is locked but the key is on the inside. I turn it, pull the heavy handle, feel the night chill hit my face. I walk out past the walled garden, down on to the road that leads to the beach below. Everything's quiet, except the gentle slapping of the waves along the sand. There's no wind. The dawn light glistens in a perfect arc. Already I love the curve of this beach, this natural shape. I admire the ocean's craft to carve the land, to throw up sand and stones into these patterns.

Ahead the sands stretch, striped by the waves. Comforting, somehow. This is a still place. I cross to shelter by the dunes. I lie and watch as in the easternmost sky, the rising sun shines down so wanly that I can't feel the touch of warmth upon my cheek. But it warms me just by being there, the light alone's enough, this midsummer's night. The voice inside me rests. My quest for peace is done, in the time it's taken to leap the threshold from the summer night to the summer dawn. Summer, the time we never fully realise till it's gone, when the winter hurricane blows. An echo comes to mind, what was it learned for, was it the Higher exam? Aye, that song. *Full fathom five thy father lies, Of his bones are coral made, Those are pearls that were his eyes, Nothing of him that doth fade, But doth suffer a sea-change, Into something rich and strange.*

The words have stuck, these years, till now they've new meaning. Five fathoms deep. Bones are coral. Pearls, Nothing fades, but suffers change, to something strange. A chain.

I look down. A hundred feet maybe. I see the shape of seals, round and solid, lying on water-circled rocks, their bristly chins moving, singing their barking calls. And then I notice something lying in among the rocks, a lighter grey against the dark grey-brown of the stones. I look closer, try to zoom in on it, to make it out. It's looks like something lying huddled between rocks, like a sheep maybe. But why would a sheep be down there among the stones, why would it be lying so still? And is it not too big for a sheep, is it not more the size of a man?

Suddenly panicked, I run along towards the cliff edge, down over the grass for a better view, till I see a grassy pathway heading down the slope to the rocky shore below. More a sheep track than a path, no more than a boot's width. It cuts at an acute angle across the sharp slope, then hairpins and goes back in the other direction, to about halfway down. After that

I can't see where it goes. But it must go somewhere. I look around for another route, but no. Only one way down. The drop is near sheer in other places.

The task looks hard, but tentatively I begin, leaning in against the grassy bank, away from the drop. In the early morning gloom it's hard to see where to put my feet, and my head is spinning, my heart racing though I try to calm myself, and go cannily down.

Slowly, slowly.

Trust my feet.

Lean into the bank.

I reach the hairpin and twist my body round. I stop, breathing heavily. The wind whistles in my ears, as it meets the land's end and rises sharply up towards the cliff-top. Then I go on, holding on to the grass tufts for safety. On down, until I come to the place that I couldn't see beyond from the top.

I'm about twenty feet above the shore now. The wind's blowing cold spray in my face. The huddled shape on the shoreline still doesn't seem to move. Still I can't see exactly what it is. I look at the path ahead of me. Here it goes sharply down. The grassy bank is gone. There's a bit of a ledge about three feet below me, where I could stop myself if I slip. A tiny corrie in the face I could fall into safely. So I throw myself towards it, right foot hits the ledge, begins to slip, I grab towards a tuft of grass growing among the rock and manage to get a hold. I pull myself back up. The grass threatens to come away, then comes loose, just as I get my balance and fall into the safe place. A lash of spray hits my face and shoulders. Heart pounding.

I stand there, leaning back against the rock, peering back up at where I've come from. I've got no choice but to carry on down. I get my feet into the crack and feel my way along, edging my way, foot by foot, gripping the wet rock ridge with cold hands.

Four or five feet away, the crack opens out into a cranny, a crevice in the rock that flattens as it slopes towards the shore. If I can just get over into that, there's only about fifteen feet to go. I swing my left leg over to catch a ledge, and stand there for a moment, fully stretched between two safe places, facing into the cliff. Christ! My foot slips out of the cranny.

I feel myself fall backwards, entering the emptiness endless open space air winding me, my side thumps against the cliff face, I seem to bounce bounce, and I feel the sea wind lift me from the land, slithering down the rock face on my backside. I feel something pierce my side and then I'm lying at the bottom of the cliff staring up at a birl

   a cloudless

      fly

         Martin

A History of Zetland with particular attention
to the Parish of Norbie, Valay and Thulay:

CHAPTER TWO

'THE JOHN SCOTS'

Herrings are commonly most plentiful here and are very near
the shoar, and here the Dutch & c. dispose their Nets begin
Fishing the 24 of Iune: and generally leave of in August or
September. 2,000 busses have been Fishing in this Sound
in one Summer. This Fishing Trade is very Beneficial to the
Inhabitants, who have Provisions and Necessaries imported
to their Doors: and Imployment for all their People, who
by their Fishing, and selling the various Products of the
Country, bring a considerable sum of Mony yearley. The
violence of the Tides and Tempestuous Seas deprives the
Inhabitants of all foreign Correspondance from October till
April, and often, till May.

H Moll, Cartographer, 1685

We have seen how the Scots acquired Zetland, and how they subsequently
arrived on the great steed that was the Reformation. We note, also, the
similarities between the land grabs of the northern Stewart era and the
roughly contemporary Irish plantations. Yet the incomers soon became
native and the first John Scot to be born a Zetlander came into this world
at Norbie in the year 1700, the firstborn son of John Scot, formerly of
Gobbilstun, and Girzel Mitchel, heiress of Valay, some of whose letters
survive in a family archive.

The towerhouse on the isle of Valay was finally completed in 1696,
yet Girzel chose to have her child in the cosier old laird's house, or Aald
Haa, at Norbie on the Zetland mainland. Valay, though spectacularly
beautiful, 'seemes isolated even by Zetlandic standards, quhile Norbie has
a populatuon of six hundred sowles, a busy pier with a shoppe and a
few reputable families wha, tho' they ocupie landes that are within estate

boundaries, hae had freeholde since Norse times.'

Norbie had the advantage of a social life over Valay and perhaps there may have been one or two ladies of comparable standing with whom Girzel might have felt at liberty to share her worries over childbirth.

The Scotch towerhouse, though far more impressive than the old 'Huis' of Norbie, was a cold exposed place, and Valay was designed more as a lookout post for a military force than a family. It became John Scot's retreat away from wife and children where he, with his militia, 'watched the sea and the traffic thereupon, as it passes into the sheltered harbour that is Vass'. From there, he conducted his arrest of the fishing from the Dutch, and created his trading empire, organising his newly acquired tenants to his will.

But perhaps, before we proceed to consider this John Scot (the third generation after Sir John of Scotstarvet) further, it is necessary to meditate on the name before us for a moment. It occurred to me upon finishing the preceding draft of the first chapter that some readers may assume I have invented the name 'John Scot', for the purpose of suggesting a representative quality, as if this figure may stand for all Scots in Zetland, the part for the whole. I must state clearly that this is not so – the name is as history gives it, with no modification. However, there is some value in this idea. There is no doubt that the actions of our highly individual individual do in fact represent a general trend throughout Zetland in the early eighteenth century.

So 'John Scot' may be considered as might 'Jan Norris', 'Ian Gael' or 'John English', in their own narratives, to be to some extent a generic name in this story. It is interesting to note that these names are normally only applied by others when the family has been exiled from that country, or where, as in the case of the Border Scotts, affiliation may require to be stated in a debated land. So the Israelites only truly become Israelites in Egypt.

Further, I might note that the name 'John Scot' calls to my mind, as a churchman, the heretic John Duns Scotus, who

The Scots of Norbie, like so many of the colonising 'Suddrons', were a Fife family. Indeed, Zetland was at this point sometimes referred to, jokingly, as 'New Fife', in imitation of 'discovered' lands such as 'New Caledonia' and the like. One might wonder at the Fife connection at first, yet it is no great surprise that the native of this county should be quick to grasp the northern opportunity – for a few fishermen of Fife had long cast their nets in those waters, and others had equally as long desired to take over the Dutch monopoly. Besides which, of course, the Fife folk had access to Timothy Pont's map.

The Scots of Norbie were not the only family by that name to buy land in Zetland. In fact, there were a number of other Scotts in Zetland, though Norbie were the only ones to use the distinctive single 't' spelling, notably in the north at Mukkilnev, and at Melbie also. One of these, the offspring of Sir Hector Scott of Scotchhall (which locally became 'Scotch-it-all', due to his habit of eradicating signs of 'Norseness' wherever he found it) established itself in the old capital, Skallvaa, where his grandson Sir Walter was doubly eminent as High Judge and Chief Chastiser. His career ended badly when he was found guilty of beating to death, with his walking stick, for no apparent reason, an old beggarman he met on the shore at Skallvaa – 'He had the temerity to ask me for money' is all the criminal would say in defence of his actions. Although his trial caused a scandal at the time, and proved that even the gentry could not escape the law, his demise did nothing to affect the fortunes of the family.

These Skallvaa Scotts were from the Borders, and were related to the forebears of Sir Walter, the great Scotch writer. As the Scots of Norbie were not related directly to the great Scott family of the Borders, they and the Scotts of Skallvaa intermarried closely over a number of generations. The 9th laird of Norbie's parents and grandparents were exclusively a combination of these two families.

But let me return to John Scot III, as we shall call him, at his towerhouse in the early 1700s. Girzel, young John the first native-born and their daughter Barbara joined him there, for foreign sailors had brought with them a plague, the dreaded smallpox, which would scar Zetland's children for the next seventy years – 'the pox has no mercie for beautie nor wealth,' as Girzel was wont to say in her letters. Valay, in its isolation, became 'the preferred residence', and the desire for society 'less urgent'.

This withdrawal unto the safety of the wilderness came at a time when the state of Scotland was in great flux, with the end of the Stuart line upon the death of Queen Anne, and the so-called Jacobite rebellions, yet these tectonic shifts had little impact on our parish or the proprietors of this estate. John Scot III would not join the rebels. He had no time for sentimental excursions into the past. He was a descendant of 'a man of the future', a man who had helped map the nation, Scot of Scotstarvit.

Of more interest was the Union of Parliaments in 1707, because it opened up the Atlantic trade to Scotland and increased traffic past the Zetlandic shores, with American-bound ships often calling in at Vass for supplies, or to wait out a gale. Sometimes, disaster overtook them. The wrecking of the *Batchelor* on Valay's southern coast saw a number of poor souls make their way ashore who never reached further than Zetland, but many more were lost on the rocks. Girzel's account of the survivors, though brief, is heart-rending: 'I never saw such poor wretches as those drookled and battered sowls who crawled ashore and chittered those twartree nights in the byre'.

As it was, John Scot III and his ilk were about to benefit from a piece of legislation which would finally reward them with the riches of the Zetlandic waters. Along with his peers, John Scot had long realised that, with land in Zetland being comparatively valueless, he must gather the sea's harvest for profit. The Scotch landowners knew that to their Zetlandic tenant-fishermen, the possession of a croft with its accompanying rights of hill-pasture, was the *sine qua non* of their existence, but that there was no profit there. Scot had control of a wide expanse of moorland, it was true, but it was for little use other than as rough pasture or peat workings, as there were no roads into this forbidding hinterland of vapours and mists, and nothing would grow there. What good farmland there was lay mainly in Norbie itself. So John Scot III subdivided the crofts there and increased the overall rental on his estate by creating more tenancies. He encouraged large families for this reason, though the land itself was ever more hard pressed and famine not uncommon.

More importantly, he had a number of stony ocean beaches perfect for laying out fish to dry, and harbours for fishing stations. So when, with the imposition of a tax on foreign salt in 1712, the Dutch stranglehold was finally broken, he set himself up in business as fishing magnate and fish-curer. In his tenants he had people dependent upon him for their very existence, and because he required men to crew the boats, he made that a condition of tenancy.

Scot took control of everything and expected total devotion in return, making it a condition of tenancy that each should furnish and fit out the fourth share of a fishing boat – but as the boats were all six-oared, they had to find two extra boys to complete the crew at their own expense.

Whatever catch the boats brought in, John Scot 'bought' from the men – or rather, Scot's hireling gave them goods from out of his shop. The operation was a very effective local monopoly, and the tenants found that their account with the shop was never cleared, no matter how productive they were.

Then, with the catch of fish secured, Scot organised the curing of it, so that each tenant was obliged to provide 'beach boys'. If any of these boys left the estate, his father would have to pay 'liberty money'.

By these means, Scot turned our isolated parish into a successful venture – at least from his point of view. The population still suffered from the pox, the infant death-rate was high from a variety of causes, but with large families encouraged the number of workers was kept at an efficient level.

Scot's methods were in many ways condemnable, yet he was also keen on certain improvements, and he saw to the provision of a small school for the prodigious among his workers at Norbie in 1713, with a teacher supplied by the Scottish Society for the Promotion of Christian Knowledge. He introduced that 'strange fruit of the Earth from South America, the potato', found that it grew 'tolerably well' where the soil was best, and so cultivation spread.

But then a new source of employment began to open up, after 1731, when the first Dundee whaler bound for Greenland called at Vass, looking for able seamen to complete the crew. Scot of Valay 'was not well pleased that three men went. He tooke his gun and went out shooting tille he had killed three great blackback sea-maws by Aald Mina's Whole', Girzel tells her cousin, 'and has now taen his bed in a mad fit.'

There is no further correspondence between Girzel and this cousin, unfortunately. Though his death is unrecorded, it would appear that John

Scot III, having established his little empire, did not live to see it flourish, as in 1736 Girzel conferred the estates of Valay, Thulay, and Norbie on her son, the first native-born John Scot, the IV, on the occasion of his marriage to a younger cousin of hers, Elizabeth Mitchel. The marriage was blessed with the issue the following year, again at Norbie, of John Scot V.

The mid-years of the eighteenth century saw a major schism in the parish, which had the result of forever after separating the inhabitants of the mysterious isle of Thulay from their neighbours, when in 1752 the calendar changed from Julian to Gregorian. The long-suffering and God-fearing Thulay folk, thought to be descendants of Irish settlers from pre-Norse times, would not hear of such a thing, suggesting in one of their famous 'mailboxes' (~~merely a bottle thrown into the sea so that it will arrive, hopefully, on the western shores of the Mainland~~) that 'Mankind would be as wyse trying to flee from the great Kame (1,400 ft. high) as disturbing heavenly mechanics'. They informed the world that they had gathered 'The Parlie Men' at the traditional place, 'The Ting' as they called it, and agreed to appoint one among them to be 'The Keeper of the True Day', whose task it would be to remember each day at sunrise the old date, and write it down in their Great Book of Days. And then, for insurance, they appointed a 'Keeper of the Keeper', whose job it would be to visit the Keeper each day in case he fell ill, or died, and forgot to mark the book. To this day, the Thulay folk still celebrate Old Christmas and Old New Year, just as their forebears have always done, though the roles of Keeper and Keeper's Keeper are no longer filled.

John Scot V of Valay married Jane Henry, a landowner's daughter from Vass and had an heir, John Scott VI of Valay, born 1760. He indulged a passion for climbing and the collecting of birds' eggs from boyhood, which brought about his literal downfall in 1765, when attempting to reach a Sea Eagle's nest on an isolated cliff. This tragic end passed into local legend – and gave its name to a precipice, The Laird's Faa – and seems to have brought the romance of Valay to an end, for the following year the dead climber's father, John Scott IV, also died, of heartbreak (according to Gabrielsen), and his widow removed the children to the aald Huis of Norbie, as John Scott VI later explains, 'for the steeps o' Valay aye pat me in mynd o' the Laird's Faa.'

Smallpox was waning in the archipelago by this time. The world beyond Valay, indeed Zetland, was no longer so threatening, and the islands were becoming ever more British. A regular sailing now brought mails six times a year from Leith to Skallvaa. The port of Larvik, that former haunt of pirates and Dutchies, became quite a metropolis, and a new class of gentry arose there – the not-quite landed merchants and military men from the British fort, lawyers and excisemen. The success of the harbour, deeper and larger and more sheltered than Skallvaa's, meant the new town was soon challenging the old capital's supremacy, and the history of strife between the new power and old included mutual raids and burnings.

Elsewhere, in the north of Zetland, a laird named Bruce pioneered new fish-curing methods, and sought out new markets for the result in Spain and Italy. Others lairds began to experiment with industrial ventures: a mill and weavers at Katfirt, for instance, and an extensive copper mine and other sundry diggings at Konigsburg. John Scot VI attempted, like many, to exploit the kelp that grew in abundance around the shores, and a number of great kilns arrived, scattered along the shorefront at Norbie.

The first *Statistical Account of Zetland*, compiled by one of the old Sinclair family, was published in 1790, the same year as the first proper road was built from Larvik to Tingval. This was a major boost to the new port in its growth, as it made the carting of produce from the harbour to the central valley of the main island, and vice versa, possible for the first time, further threatening the old Stewart capital's dominance. Larvik and Tingval had previously been separated by a steep-sided valley impassable by horse and cart.

Vastness Hill, the great mass of barren peat-moor at the heart of the Scot estates, stood a long distance from either of the warring seaports, though the allegiance of the westside always lay with the old capital, which had the advantage of being closer. So it was that when John Scot VI, the heir born in 1760, attained majority, he married one of the Skallvaa Scotts, Catherine, a cousin through previous marriage between the families, and the daughter of Sir Hector. They began to erect a grand, three-storey house a little way along the shoreline from what became known then as the 'Aald Huis', but the labour was long and troubled by poor workmen, so Norbie Hall was not completed for twenty years, until the preparation for the welcoming home, or 'hamefarin', of their son John Scot VII and his bride Margaret Nicolaesen, after their honeymoon in the year 1800.

A magnificent setting it provided, being in its day the most modern of all the 'big houses' of Zetland, and the little harbour became a favourite place for the yachts of the gentry to anchor, with an assured welcome ashore. The couple, too, were perfectly modern; they are recorded as sophisticated, keen to travel, and they spent seasons in Edinburgh and London, as well as making lengthy journeys to the continent. Both he and she had been beautiful apart. Together they were doubly glamorous. She, the delicate Margaret, finished abroad, the daughter of a Lord Admiral Nicolaesen who had acquired a large estate in the north of Zetland – while John Scot VII was handsome, a dashing young man, his father's favourite, who had taken The Tour, and was desired by every eligible landowners daughter and servant girl alike. He was proud of the extent of his property, which placed him among the leading landowners in Scotland by acreage, though the land itself was dismally unproductive. Unlike his father, John Scot VII had been educated in the south in addition to the private tutors brought north for the purpose of preparation; he knew exactly what the fashion was and how to please a fine young lady in furnishing a dwelling-house.

These two John Scots, who became known as the Elder and the Younger, were very close, according to Gabrielsen, but John Scot the younger was fully 'North British' in a way his father had not been, for that culture took some time to reach these remote shores. He took over the task of appointing the new Hall and finished it with exquisite style, employing a small team of Venetian house-painters to create, in the drawing room, colourful scenes of rustic happiness along the lines of Ramsay's *Gentle Shepherd*. These foreigners had come to Skallvaa for one job, at Scottshall, but then found themselves in demand at all the big houses in Zetland. They guarded the secrets of their trade most vehemently, even insisting no one should observe the mixing of their paints. In Norbie they worked feverishly as the wedding day approached. The last highlights on the maidens' tresses were hardly dry by the time the flutter of confetti began to fall. And nine months later, born in London to John Scot the younger and Margaret (née Nicolaesen), came a son, John Scot of Norbie, the eighth by that name.

Of course, in the great world beyond, these were troubled times, with revolution on everyone's lips, and Boney on the march. Even far distant Norbie was affected. For one thing, John Scot's younger brother James set off to join the Royal Navy in 1803, and for another, there was the coming of the Press Gangs to carry off young men, so even the remotest corner of our remote parish felt the effects of war. Seventeen men were taken from Norbie in all, on three different occasions, before the conflict was over. The familiar phrase 'lost at sea' haunted Norbie Hall and all the lands around it. War levelled laird and peasant as all feared the same loss.

James Scot, RN, had joined the 46 gun HMS *Fisgard* under Captain Kerr. He saw action with Nelson at Porto Severa in 1804, became a ship's surgeon, served on HMS *Rose* and was heroic at Trafalgar. Norbie Hall was jubilant when the mail packet came, with the news of his deeds. Though other households mourned, the laird's was spared and the John Scots, Elder and Younger, toasted the prodigious exile.

Yet death was not far from the door of the Hall. Weeks later, the delicate Margaret, the 'Flower of the North' as Gabrielsen records her being described to him once, took a fever from which she never recovered. John Scot the younger was distraught. With two young children to care for, he inquired of a Skallvaa cousin, Barbara Scott, whether she might care to act as governess and when, with the passing of the months, he found himself drawn to her gentile ways, he proposed. She, not as young as she was, nor indeed he, accepted and though at first the bed was cold – some said visited by the spirit of the dead wife – in time it warmed, and this second marriage was also blessed with issue.

Cousin Barbara proved a good wife in every way. The elegant faint presence of Margaret, too delicate to age, was replaced by a stiffer, better defined femininity, which believed in 'the Good Book and Education'. During these years, Barbara often condemned the new frivolity that was abroad, especially in time of war. A very literary woman, she devoted that skill entirely to the service of the Lord God, penning essays on aspects of theology and the Gospel which she then posted to the Minister of

Quharv, a long-time acquaintance and a man she often remarked was 'an inspiration'. It was to him that she confessed her sense that the childish exhortations of her Larvik cousin, Dorothea Primrose Campbell, the 'childe poetess', when she had them printed and bound at Inverness, 'display all the selfish affectatioun of a soul taen up with itself'. And it was to him that she confessed that she thought her husband John was far too concerned with his voyaging here and there 'in respeck of his affairs to tak proper tent of his ain bairns' spiritual welfare'.

Alas, she would not have long to wait before his voyaging came to a watery and tragic end, before John Scot VII, the Younger of Norbie sank in the *Doris* off the Aberdeenshire coast at Cruden Bay. This act of God tested the faith of Barbara Scot to its limits, yet she was confirmed in her faith by her divine friend in Quharv, who advised her simply: 'Consecrate yourself, Barbara.'

Letter from Peter A Scot
to Rev. Archibald Nicol,
November 26th 2000

Miami

Dear Reverend Archibald

I forgot to answer your question in my earlier letter – yes, the history is incomplete. I believe Gabrielsen was a schoolmaster in the village, and something of a Norse scholar, but he died before he carried through his intention. He reaches his own place in history, ie. the founding of his school and the coming of the Crofting Commissioners, but goes no further. Some of the 'Chapters' seem little more than sketches, and the last is just a title. But still the document has value, even as fragments.

I realise also that you may not know who Albert and Robina are, as what you won't get from Gabrielsen is, of course, the story of what befell the house of the Scots in Norbie, Zetland, in the 1890s, once the outcome of the investigations of the Land Commission was decided. So much back rent was due that, when it was wiped away by the Commission and the rents forced down, the estate hit serious financial difficulties. My great-grandfather, the previous laird, Doctor Scot, had been borrowing against what he anticipated he would receive in these debts, and had been building up the estate, new houses, a new field plan and a drainage scheme, but the Commission suddenly pulled the rug from under all that. Not that he lived to see the outcome himself.

His son, Albert, my grand-uncle, was in his minority when his father died and an unscrupulous factor attempted to prise the estate away from him. He put up a bit of a fight, but really his interest was elsewhere. He was fascinated by the invention of the automobile and desperately wanted to escape the responsibilities of managing land, a task to which he was not at all suited.

The end came in a rather messy manner, with court cases and the like, which I believe to be the reason for the split between the two sides of the family. As I understand it, ultimately grand-uncle Albert emerged with sufficient capital to begin a garage business when they finally arrived in New Zealand. At this time, for some reason he began trading under his mother's maiden name of Cunninghame.

The story is yet more complicated, of course, by the fact that Albert had gone very much against his widowed mother's desire, in marrying. The woman he chose was a poor crofter's daughter, who was also eight years older than he. He was only nineteen when they married and the scandal was huge.

But the story of the love between Albert and the beautiful lace-maker, Robina must wait for another day.

Yours in faith
Peter A Scot

23rd June 2000 – Norbie

There's a lump on the left side of my head, some blood clotted in my hair and my side feels like it's been speared. I push myself upright, sit a while, rubbing my lumpy head. It's bleeding a bit. No bones snapped, at least. Just a whacking great graze on my side. I'm alive.

Martin, I'm still alive.

Somehow. I don't deserve to be, no

And the shape on the shore I saw? Slowly, painfully, half-feart by what I'll see, I look. But it's a sheep, wool scattered around it, eyes pecked out.

I lie there, just staring at the thing that is not my father, thinking Christ, I nearly got myself killed for a dead sheep!

I sit down on a rock and put my head in my hands. The waves are crashing in around me, spraying me, waves of salty water splashing me.

Jesus!

Then I hear a whistling noise. Not a bird sound, a human one. And when I glance up, I see someone is walking along the shore towards me. A boy, maybe eight or nine. A Huckleberry Finn type, in wellies, with a fishing rod, an old jacket and a hat. And as he gets closer, I see him stop and stare at me, surprised, annoyed maybe, that somebody else is out as early as him, invading the solitude. His face.

Martin.

I start to hobble down to the shore towards him, slipping on wet stones as I go, my body clumsy, injured. 'Hey! Wait a moment!' I shout.

Out on the shore in the new daylight, with the waves running in and striking the rocks behind him, he turns and looks at me. For a moment he's one of the seals, hesitant, waiting to see which way to go to get away, like one of the sheep. But then he doesn't. He turns to face me. As if he recognises I'm no threat. He waits, as I scramble through the stones towards him. I'm breathing heavily, my side is sore where I banged it, my left elbow, head too. There seems to be a little blood. I can barely speak when I reach where he's standing, a few feet from the wavebreak.

'You all right?' he says. 'I saw you coming down.'

In agony, I neither shake nor nod my head but something intermediate.

'Yeah. I just wanted to … to speak to you,' I manage to say.

He squats down beside me, holding his fishing rod. 'Sure you're okay?'

'Just slipped coming down the cliff, winded myself.'

I point up above, at the place where I fell and he traces the line of my arm to where I've indicated.

'I saw you falling. Sure you're all right?'

'Yes,' I say, and laugh, almost proud of the misadventure.

Then he lifts his arm in the direction he's come from. 'But you could just have walked around the point,' he says. 'The tide's right out.'

I blink at him as I try to take in what he's told me.

'Aye,' he says again. 'You could've just walked round the ness.'

It is ridiculous, really.

'You're Rod's son, aren't you? Did you want something?' he asks.

I catch my breath. What did I want? To say something wonderful, something about taking care, not risking himself on the cliff face, not letting bullying fathers drive them over the edge. But then he knows more than me, he knows the tide is out anyway.

So all I say, all I can think to say is: 'Do you live around here?'

The lad nods, pokes his hat up with the end of his fishing rod and looks at me.

'Over there. Innertoon. So, d'you reckon he's dead, like?' he says. Beautiful. So straightforward, this youth.

I shrug. 'Nobody's sure.'

Then he lifts his head and gazes out to sea. 'My dad's dead,' he says, and I'm suddenly sobered and saddened, my own hurt forgotten. 'Car crash. That's why we left where we were stayin. My maw wanted to make a fresh start. Somewhere different. Got a job running the pub here.'

He lays the fishing rod at his side and takes a bottle of Coke from the bag across his shoulder. He offers me a drink. I take a swig and hand it back. And he holds out this thin bony hand to take the bottle, half-smiling. He starts poking at the stones with his boot.

I feel like I should be able to say something wise and wonderful, but I just can't. There's this sharp pain in my side where I banged it on the rock. We just sit there, like bairns together. The boy looks up, stares out across the water towards the far shore, the long brown hills now turning rosy in the dawn. Then after a moment, he says, 'When he was killed, I couldn't even bear to think of him. But now it's okay. It's good to mind him. Things we used to do together.'

I nod. I can't talk. He's the wise one, letting me know how it'll feel.

'I used to think of him as this guy … well it's daft, but there was this story, William Tell, it was like … our story. When I was wee, he used to tell me it, ken?'

The boy glances at me. I smile, nod. He flicks his hair away from his face and sniffs. 'That's a cool wee dug he had. Your dad. That wee Lucky. Used to let me take it out walks.'

He puts the Coke bottle back in his bag and sits there staring out to sea. I can't help thinking that he's grown up in a way I haven't yet, that's he's taken something choking inside himself at an age when I hadn't a worry in my head. Again I'm struggling for words. He stands up, picks up his fishing rod. 'I better go,' he says. 'Hope you find him.'

As quick as that, he's gone, hopping away over the shoreline stones like a little wader, carrying his hopeful rod as if it was a pilgrim's staff. I trudge slowly round the point and make my way back towards the beach, and the old stone arch, over the rocky shoreline where the tide's ebbed out, sore all over now, and cold with it. The walk's a trial, an agony. I keep slipping on wet stones, but round the point, and see again the bulk of Norbie Haa across the bay.

Back at the beach, I find a warm spot out of the wind and sit for a while, watching the morning sun come up over the eastern hills and light the land. The birdlife's breakfasting, a constant flap of wings, landings, take-offs. Terns. Sandpipers. Oystercatchers. I'd no idea of the variety of species. No idea so many feathered creatures lived along these northern shores.

And then out of the water about thirty metres away, something rounded appears. It looks like a head. I screw my eyes up. It looks like a head. But no, I won't get fooled again. Yes, it's a head and it's attached to a body. A head that bobs up and down with the waves. A head, bobbing in the water, right enough.

Rounded, with eyes like a dog's, it's a seal, a sentry maybe come to see who I am, what I'm doing there. But it's not

human

It's not my father's body, though that might yet float in. Though it might be lying somewhere, waiting for the search party, for the police net to trawl it out. Yes, that might happen.

Walking up the road, the bang on my head is pulsing, my side's sore, the lack of sleep's psychoactive. I have to remember senses are no longer trustworthy. Passing the old church, the solitary archway standing solid against the sky, I tell myself that if I should hear noises, glimpse apparitions, if I should feel as if there's someone lurking there, watching, I'll remember

that dream of falling

I traipse into the walled gardens, the sun now warm on my injured head, the terrible pain where I bashed against the rock, just where the ribcage ends on my right side. I hold the sore place with my left hand, my arm crossed over my chest as I go, crunching over the gravel towards the big house. His corgis are awake, snapping and barking at each other while Dr Hart sits on a bench, watching them with benign countenance. He turns to me as I approach. I feel so bad, I'm really glad to see him, pleased to see his moustache. A wild joy at reaching haven overcomes me.

'Good morning. You must have been up early,' he says.

I let go the tight hold on my injury and carefully sit down beside him, exhausted, nearly too tired to be hungry. But my guts are rumbling like an underground river, churning up, frothing.

'I woke up,' I say. 'I couldn't sleep. Went for a walk. In fact, I haven't really been to bed at all. I fell …'

Dr Hart raises thick eyebrows. 'Are you all right?'

'It was nothing, just a bang on the head. I'm all right.'

'Are you sure? But you must be tired? Hungry?'

Then he peers at me so close, I smell dogbreath.

'God, you don't look at all well,' he says. 'Let's get you fed and then I'll take a look at you properly.'

Letter from Philippa Gabrielsen
to Rev. Archibald Nicol,
December 5th 2000

Bon Hoga

Dear Archibald

I am enclosing a brief history freshly written by one of our key members, which I think you will find interesting. It sheds light on the story I told you in an earlier letter, which I now realise wasn't the true story.

The author John Inkstir is by blood part-Zetlander and part-Murikavi, a brilliant young scholar who graduated with 1st Class Honours from the University in Christchurch. He has recently taken up the post of Archivist with the Tokomuan government at 'Da Hus a'Myndins', as our little museum is known. He is proving invaluable to our project and we look forward to more from him in due course.

I hope life in Scotland is treating you not so badly, and that you are keep (sic) your health. My very best wishes to you for a Happy Christmas and for the year 2001. There is something quite sci-fi about the very idea!

Aa da bestist, as we say here

Philippa

CAPTAIN JAKE KULINESS & THE COMING OF EUROPEANS TO TOKUMUA (NEW ZETLAND)

It was on the second of his three voyages to New Zealand that the English explorer Captain James Cook first recorded the existence of the island group we now call Tokumua. He found the islands to be sparsely populated by Polynesians. Oral history tells us they had settled there about 1500 and, living in isolation, had become known as the Murikavi people. Their exact origin remains a matter of dispute and their number is uncertain, though again oral history records that the Murikavi population was about

2,000 at the time of the coming of the Europeans around 1800.

The Murikavi lived as hunter-gatherers, taking food from the sea and from native flora. Cook found them notable because war had been outlawed after generations of fighting, suggesting they may have a similar origin to the Moriori of the Chatham Islands who similarly abandoned warfare as uncivilised. Arguments were solved by consensus or by single combat, but at the drawing of blood, the fight ended.

Cook's first voyage in 1770 had confirmed that New Zealand was not a vast southern continent as Joseph Banks, the naturalist aboard the *Endeavour*, recorded. The rounding of Stewart Island's South Cape demolished 'our aerial fabrick called "Continent"', Yet the vast unexplored ocean to the east remained, where a great continent might yet lie, and on his second voyage (1772–75), Cook used New Zealand as a base for probes south and east, which finally proved there was no such landmass.

Sealers and whalers began hunting the surrounding ocean around 1800. Shore-based whaling started in New Zealand around thirty years later, when the Greenland right whale fishery collapsed, making New Zealand whaling competitive. Additionally, sealers found that there were few seals left and were keen to transfer their energy and capital to a new venture, and the number of sperm whales fell, increasing the demand for the less valuable oil of right whales, which were caught close to shore.

Shore-based whaling was considerably cheaper than sea-bound, with its attendant supply ships. It was also safer and the oil kept better. So the first substantial station in Tokumua was established in 1830. It is estimated that around 20 per cent of the indigenous Murikavi population soon died from diseases introduced by these foreigners. The sealing and whaling industries ceased activities about 1860, while fishing remains as a major economic activity today.

The first important figure in the European era of Tokumuan history is Jake Kulinis or Kuliness, a Scotch sea captain from Zetland who first arrived in the islands of Tokumua in 1830. His father was a schoolteacher in Sellafirt, Zetland. His great-grandfather had escaped from the Battle of Culloden, where he had fought for the rebel Scotch against the English army.

Young John was the oldest of eleven children and his father, with a salary of only £10 per annum, found it hard to make ends meet. So, like many Zetlanders of that period, Kulinis took to the sea. It was for Greenland that he first embarked, when a whaler on a five-year voyage lost many of her crew to a Press Gang ship seeking sailors for the Napoleonic Wars, and put into Sellafirt in the hope of finding local replacements. Jake and his brother both embarked, aged 12 and 13 respectively. Though his brother was drowned, Jake proved to be a lucky whaler and further voyages to the Baltic, China and the South Seas followed.

However, Kulinis's luck changed rather dramatically when he was 'shanghaied' aboard an American whaler, along with with four men, in San Francisco. When the vessel that had captured them was on the latitude of Samoa, the five attempted to escape in an open whaleboat, hoping to make landfall there, but instead the boat drifted for over a month and two thousand miles, before being driven ashore on a coast shunned by mariners of the time – one of the islands known in those days as the 'Cannibal Isles' – today, Malaita. Three of his emaciated companions died in the wreck, and the fourth was clubbed to death by natives on the beach and later eaten, but Kulinis fought so bravely that he was allowed to live, although stripped of his clothes.

The tribe, known as the 'Salt-water Folk', lived on a tiny, artificial island built centuries ago to escape the malarial jungles that infested the principal island of Malaita. They were perpetually at war with the 'Bush Folk' who inhabited this main island. Kulinis was accepted into male society and lived in the men's longhouse. By passing on skills he had learned as a child in Zetland, he gradually won the respect of his captors. In battle he was particularly successful, and apparently killed over seventy of the 'Bush Folk' in various encounters and, by his own admission, took their heads as trophies. His warrior prowess and closeness to the 'Salt-water' chief, Kabu, led to the 'Bush Folk' putting a bounty on his head, so that when he went to the tribe's favourite natural swimming place on the main island, he always took an armed guard to protect him.

In time, Kulinis became the chief's most valued advisor and he was adopted as his 'firstborn son', and made heir to the kingdom. Even today, to the Malaitans he is a hero who helped prepare them for the inevitable collision with white 'civilisation'. But after eight years of living among them, in a state of more or less perpetual war, he grasped a rare opportunity for freedom. A British ship anchored offshore and Kulinis persuaded Kabou to allow him to contact the crew, saying that from them he could obtain certain items that would amaze his chief. He wrote a message in charcoal on a piece of driftwood: 'I am John Kulinis – a shipwrecked captive. Please take me home to Britain.' The message was taken out to the ship by a canoe of islanders and is now in the National Library of Australia.

Kulinis's wish was granted and he left, promising to return soon with various wonders from the white world. Malaitan oral history has it that Kulinis was picked up by his uncle, Kapimori. In fact, it was a Scotch ship's captain called Murray.

When Kulinis arrived back in Australia he became an instant celebrity, and was the subject of much newspaper coverage. By the time he had sailed to Britain, he was already a national hero. With the help of a journalist, he published a pamphlet about his experiences, which sold in great quantity throughout Britain, and amazed contemporary society with the account of eight years in 'the most savage place on Earth'.

But the sanitised version Kulinis gave of his adventure has been challenged as a result of a Malaitan oral history project, which reveals a more gruesome truth: Kulinis survived only by partaking in cannibalism and the 'taking of heads'.

Throughout the years of his absence, Kulinis's father had always believed that young Jack was alive and made several attempts to trace him. His disappearance was well-known locally, and the young Kulinis's return to Zetland was a triumph, involving local dignitaries, and the event is commemorated in the museum. But once the fuss of his return was over, he could not adjust to the cold northern climate and longed for the South Seas. In particular, exhausted after his experience of total war in Malaita, he had set his mind upon the archipelago of Tokumua, a place he knew to be essentially pacifist in nature, as he had worked a few seasons at the whaling station there before his captivity, and had picked up something of the Murikavi tongue. He decided to make himself a permanent home there.

Kulinis set off for London once again, where he fell in with an old English trader by the name of Burke, who had befriended him years before. Burke gave him command of a brig carrying convicts to Australia. Burke's 'out-east' partner, Alexander Hare, a merchant who once had been the British Resident in Borneo, was a shady character who kept a harem and was a slave-trader. When the Dutch took over Java, Hare was banned from residence in Netherlands Indies.

It was two years before Kulinis could return to Tokumua, with a cargo including sheets of iron roofing, axes, hammers, barrels of nails and a host of other wonders, such as a grindstone that continued in use up until the 1960s, only to discover that Hare had settled there with his harem of Malay women and an entourage of slaves. Kulinis made his base on another island, at Serrafir, and a state of enmity developed between the two.

In the early days Kulinis made his wealth by exploiting the island's rich phosphate deposits. He employed a number of labourers from the Murikavi and set them to work building his fine house, which he named 'Oceania'. This is now the Tokumuan Prime Minister's residence. Hare's encampment failed to thrive, and was finally abandoned in 1851.

The system of rule Kulinis established bore considerable resemblance to the one he had known as a youth in Zetland. Kulinis paid his workers with tokens redeemable only at his store, which he called Da Truck Hoos, in imitation of the method he knew from Zetland. When a British seafarer visited Tokumua in 1855, he observed 'The Tokumuans are nominally in a state of freedom, but they are considered as slaves.' Kulinis however did provide makeshift houses and little vegetable gardens for each family, a concession which was met with great joy by the natives who, despite his autocratic ways, loved their master.

In the 1860s, Kulinis, still a folk-hero in Australia after his sojourn in 'The Cannibal Islands', was hired by the Queensland government to regulate so-called 'blackbirding', the sickening human trade that had recently become the scourge of the South Seas. It was during this period of his life that Kulinis met the fate he had avoided twenty years earlier, when in 1868 his ship arrived at Aoba in the New Hebrides, en route to Australia, and Kulinis took a party ashore for fresh water. When they failed to return, others went to investigate. They found the bodies of their captain and his companions, minus their heads.

When the news finally reached Tokumua, the people were furious.

For the first time in many generations, they were stirred to fight. They formed a war party and demanded that the remaining Europeans should take them to the New Hebrides to wipe out the perpetrators, not realising just how far away this was. This is a measure of the esteem that Kulinis was held in and still is, although by today's morality his colonial life-story is deeply troublesome. Yet his name lives on in the folklore of both the Tokumuan and the Malaitan people, as the man who brought them into the modern era.

When the Tokumuan House of Memory representatives visited the paramount chief of the 'Saltwater Folk' in Malaita in 1999, they discovered a huge blown-up photographic portrait of Kulinis in his hut, which must be one of the earliest photographs in the archipelago.

As the representatives looked on, one old woman reached out her hand to touch it, murmuring 'Yaki, Yaki, Kapiyaki – mi luv'. She is the mother of the current chief.

The spear Kulinis brought back to Zetland still has pride of place in the local museum, while his gruesome necklace of human teeth can be seen in the National Museum of Scotland, Edinburgh.

John Inkstir
Archivist, 'Da Hus a'Mydins/ The House of Memories', Tokumua

23rd June 2000 – Norbie

I have decided not to shave when the laird's voice resonates through the white-painted wood-panelled door. 'Are you awake?'

Just about.

'I'm sorry to disturb you when you aren't well, but there's a police officer downstairs and she wants to interview you.'

I sit up. 'I'll be down in ten minutes.'

'Very well, I'll tell her. We're in the drawing room. Shall I get Mrs Mitchell to make some coffee?'

'Please. Thanks.'

So I ease myself up from the bed, my clothes still damp, a coldness in me. I take off my jersey, open my shirt, lift up my clothes and look at the place that's hurt. There's a sizeable bruise on my side, a big broad graze, and underneath a very tender spot on my ribs. And then I look at my left arm, below the elbow. Bruised, but it's okay. Pain's bearable now.

Downstairs in the laird's drawing room, they're waiting for me. Dr Hart gets up when I open the door. He's put on a green tweed suit and a bright yellow tie for the occasion, and he stands to attention, extending a hospitable tweedy host's arm in my direction as I walk slowly in. The policewoman stands up and holds her hand out, she's friendly, she's sympathetic to my predicament, she says. I watch her carefully, as she watches me. She's young and handsome, blonde hair tied back in a short ponytail.

'I'm WPC Waugh,' she says. She has a soft Invernessian accent. I shake her hand. It's icy cold. She asks me to sit down, she has her notebook out and is preparing to write.

'You've come all the way up here from Edinburgh, I believe.'

'Yesterday. When I heard. I had a few days off due. Well, I spoke to my grandmother and she suggested it. She was worried, and wanted me to come.' I bend painfully to sit, trying not to let the pain show. WPC Waugh glances at Dr Hart, who's hovering behind the sofa where I'm sitting.

'Oh, I'm sorry. Would you rather I left you two alone?' he says.

She shakes her head. 'Not on my account,' she says. 'In fact, I think it might be useful to have you here, seeing as you were one of the last people to actually talk to the missing man, Dr Hart.'

Then she turns to me. 'It's some time since you last saw your father, isn't it?'

'Yes, it's two years since I saw him, two years since he left the south and started on this odyssey northwards.'

'Two years.' She writes. 'In that case, it might be useful for Dr Hart to remain, and perhaps between what the two of you can tell me, I'll be able to build up a picture of your father's state of mind.'

'Would you mind?'

'No,' I say. What difference would it make? There is something about her, something about the way she sorts us out, into our proper places. Something I feel I can trust.

'So let me ask you, first of all, about yourself?'

So I give her all the details.

'Now, about your father. How exactly did he come to be here, if that's not too hard a question?'

I hesitate. It's hard to find a beginning to the story. 'I've only heard fragments,' I say.

'Well, let's try something different,' she says coolly. 'You've no idea what might have happened to your father, have you?'

I think of that holy ghost.

'No, except … there was that fire. And the people in the place next door, that born-again couple.'

'What could they have to do with your father's disappearance?' she asks me, blue eyes piercing. Then she writes something in her notebook. I try to see what it is but I can't. She keeps the cover held at an angle to shield it from me.

'I think he might have threatened me.'

wpc Waugh is interested. 'Might have? What exactly did he say?'

'Well, it wasn't really a threat as such, he just quoted this thing from the Bible, Deuteronomy somewhere, about putting people to death. About fathers being put to death.'

Dr Hart laughs. 'That sounds like John,' he says. 'But you mustn't attach too much significance to his biblical outpourings.'

'Is your father the kind of man to just up and leave like this?' the wpc asks.

I laugh, thinking back. 'If he'd just wandered off, it wouldn't surprise me. He's done it before,' I say.

'You mean this isn't the first time?' the WPC asks. I nod.

'No.'

'Can you give details? I mean, about the last time.'

'It's a couple of times. Since my mother died.' She looks at me again, that stare, that cold stare. I feel the shiver, the dampness in my bones from the ocean's penetration. And then Mrs Mitchell comes in with the coffee and a plate of biscuits, and I love her for just that simple act.

'You mean he just went off without any warning?'

'Yes. Without any warning.' And she writes again, something, something in shorthand.

'Where did he go?'

'He just moved on.'

'Moved house?'

'He didn't have a house,' I say. 'He sold our house, that is, the family house. After that he just rented rooms.'

'And this was where?'

'In Edinburgh, first, then Glasgow.'

'But the family house was in …?'

'Perth.' She writes again in her notebook, her hand jerking around, making mysterious hieroglyphic strokes on the paper. My father's secret language. Then she pins me down with that look of hers, that cool blue look, the water depth in her eyes.

'So when you say he sold the family house, he realised quite a sum then, did he? Enough to keep him comfortably?'

'Why?'

'Well, it's just that someone who's travelling about like that, moving all the time, sometimes there's a reason. Debts, or perhaps they've made an enemy or …?'

Exasperated, I say: 'Listen, I'll tell you about him, and what happened. We'll save a lot of time that way, instead of this question and answer, I'll tell you …'

She mellows and smiles just a bit, just the slightest upturning of the corners of her thin-lipped mouth.

'If you want. But really, I just wanted to ask a few questions at this stage, to try to get a picture of his movements.'

She flicks back a page in her notebook, determined to follow her thread through the labyrinth, no distractions. 'Perth?' she says. 'He was a journalist there, wasn't he? When did that come to an end?'

'1992. He took early retirement as they put it. In fact he was sacked.'

'Dismissed?'

'Sacked over a story he was working on. He fell foul of one or two powerful folk in the town.' She seems interested in this, her hand lifts from the writing position and it points the pencil towards me. 'Oh? And who was that?'

'Politicians. Local politicians. It was over the travelling folk. What they used to call the tinkers,' I say. 'You see, there was always a lot of travellers in the area, right back, way back through the centuries.' She nods her head. I twist, turn on the seat to try and quell the pain from the spear wound in my side. I take a breath. 'My father used to say they were the original metal workers to the clans, and that they'd travelled around selling the weapons and jewelry they made. But after the Jacobite rebellion, that was the end of the trade in weapons, because of Hanoverian oppression, and the tinkers, the travellers, they ended up with only the pots and pans and that left. So they turned their hand to whatever they could, casual work on the farms. The horse trade. Anyhow, there was a camp a few miles outside the town, near Perth, a traditional camp where they'd wintered for centuries, until the land was bought, and the new owner wanted them off. And so they went to the local councillor with their case and it turned into a real stink locally. The camp was cleared and the travellers, to make a protest, moved right into the centre of the town and set up a camp on a bit a wasteland that had lain empty for years. Right in the middle of the town. There was no sanitation, nothing like that. I don't know all the details, but my father, he wrote stuff, printed stuff in the local paper. He threw in all this stuff about the clearing of Jewish ghettos in the Second World War, about how the outsiders are always the scapegoat, the ones with no rights. That made him a lot of enemies. And finally the paper's owner suggested this early retirement. It couldn't have come at a worse time for him.'

She sits writing, then looks up sharply up when I stop telling my tale.

'Why was that?'

Ach, how to say it, how to begin to say all the things that lurk there, back in that time, that time when our family imploded.

I turn on the seat. 'Our mother was getting chemotherapy for cancer. She was dying. And then in the middle of all this, this woman turned up, an Australian, claiming to be my father's daughter from a first marriage. My mother found out. Just before she died, she knew all about it.' It killed her, I think, but I don't say it. 'Afterwards he sold the house in Perth and moved away, at first to Edinburgh, to be near me and my brother, and then, when that wasn't working out, mainly because of his drinking, he moved to Glasgow. But that was only for a few months. The first I knew of him heading north was a postcard, about a year ago. He was in Caithness for a while, then in Orkney and finally he ended up here.'

She's taking notes, frowning, then she smiles. 'I'm not sure I've got all this,' she says. 'You're going faster than my shorthand.'

'My father was really fast – shorthand, I mean.'

She glances at me, flicks the pages back and starts to read it through silently. I see her eyes twitching left to right, as if she was watching the barrel on a typewriter move along. Finally, she looks up. 'There's quite a story in there. And can I ask you, how did he take this ... all these changes?'

I say, 'Badly. He took it all badly. It was like he'd been weakening without anybody noticing, then after the funeral he snapped. He'd been drinking heavily for a while, but keeping it a secret, managing to hold everything together, just about. But after the funeral, the barriers came down. He just got drunk. All the time.'

And then it became every day.

'And what sort of an effect did that have on the family, I mean the rest of you? And your grandmother, you mentioned she was still alive?' she asks me.

'Martin, my brother, he was at university then. Our grandmother, she took it all in her stride. She couldn't see it.'

'Or she wouldn't?' Dr Hart asks.

'And the rest of us tried to shield her from the full extent of the trouble because of her age, though she knew something was wrong.'

Dr Hart takes a breath, like he's going to speak again, then hesitates.

Then he says, 'I wonder, didn't she know about this other family, this early marriage of your father's anyway? As I understand it, she lived in Australia herself, so wouldn't she have known that your father had been married there?'

I let this pass without comment. Of course, he's right.

When she has heard enough silence, WPC Waugh says, 'We'll look into every possibility, of course. We're checking out these people you've suggested we contact, and we're trying to trace the last steps your father took. At the moment we're not sure if he actually left this district or not. We have no sighting of him. We're still checking to find out if he left the island. The airport and the ferry terminal have given us nothing. And we'll set about organising a search for tomorrow or the following day, focusing firstly on the coast around here. Dr Hart told me he liked to walk along the ness. If there's any possibility that you've overlooked in this list, then please do contact me at the station.' She stands, picks up her hat. 'Now, if you'll excuse me, I'm going over to your father's chalet to meet my colleague, to see if he's found anything. I can offer you a lift, if you'd like to come with me?'

'No,' I say, 'I'm not feeling too good. I think I'm catching a cold. I'm going to lie down.' And that pain in my side again, sharp as a dirk, digs as she leaves.

Dr Hart sees her out, down the stairs past the barking corgis, and they stop in the hallway by the back door. I catch fragments, floating up the stairs.

'Well, goodbye. I'll call if there's anything else.'

'Thanks. I'll pop in before we leave, with the key.'

'Goodbye, then, Caroline.'

'Bye.' The door scrapes closed, then open again.

'Oh, by the way.'

'Yes?'

'Don't say anything to the Stouts. No need to worry them just now. I'll talk to them. They shouldn't have interfered.'

The back door clicks shut. Then old Dr Hart is fondling his dogs, and promising to feed them. I don't want to see him, so I go quickly back up spiral stairs to the bedroom and close the door. I lie on the bed, aching.

Touch my side. I turn, trying to find a position that's pain-free.

I'm worried by the intimacy between the policewoman and the laird, somehow. First-name terms. But why should they not know each other, all of them indeed? It's a small island, and the church and the village hall belongs to all, all classes, all professions. But in the drawing room, they'd made out as if they were total strangers, I didn't like that sense of being kept on the outside like that. Though maybe they had to, maybe they thought I'd expect it, that if they were too friendly, I'd suspect ... what? I'm from a small town myself. I know how it works, the pretending that it's bigger than it really is, the use of formal address, so that everybody gets to feel important, everybody with some public role to perform. My father played that part, for years. He liked to be Mr Cunninghame, the assistant editor of the *Advertiser*. He liked that. Dressing up, putting on the tie, the formal voice, the whole performance. And when he wasn't that anymore, when he didn't have that social function, he fell apart. The secrets he'd kept covered by that formal title, his bad habits, they just oozed out. Like he'd been flayed and the beast within couldn't be contained.

I lie on the bed, the ordeal over, my side aching. Under the T-shirt, the graze is weeping a bit. But the wound is clean, there's no dirt in it. I take the medicine bag from my rucksack and carefully paste the healing cream on, rubbing it in. My jacket must have protected me from the worst. I lift it up from the chair and look at it, the place where the impact was. There's a tear in the waterproofing, and the white padding is poking through. But it's repairable. I rub my sore right arm and roll my sleeve up. The bruise is turning blue quickly, the redness fading into purple. It's a tattoo now. A tattoo the shape of an armband, the way it curves round my bicep. A black and blue armband.

But I've survived, the wiser for it happening. I'm ready now to accept the worst, that fathers die, that his body could be there at the cliffs somewhere, or out in the sea, afloat. That he might have fallen,

like Martin

    like

    me

A History of Zetland with particular attention
to the Parish of Norbie, Valay and Thulay:

CHAPTER THREE

'THE WRECK OF THE DORIS'

Wild o'er the hollow-groaning main
Flies furious the Spirit of the storm;
Tempests and howling blasts compose his hideous train,
And clouds of darkness wrap his giant form.
The billows heaving to the skies,
Then tumbling low as many fathoms deep –
Mix'd with the horrid roar the drowning seaman's cries,
As down he sinks to everlasting sleep!
Be still, my heart – methinks I hear
The shriek of anguish on the moaning gale;
And frightful, dismal scenes of pain and death appear,
Struggles for parting life, and breathless corses pale!
Oh! wretched she, whose arms no more
Shall clasp her son – oh! more than wretched wife,
That widow'd long shalt live in anguish to deplore
The fate of him far dearer than thy life!
Ye lovely babes! now wrapp'd in sleep,
Peaceful and calm, while howls the passing storm!
Ah! little do ye dream that the tempestuous deep,
Rolls o'er your late fond father's lifeless form.

> Dorothea Primrose Campbell,
> 'Lines Written on a Stormy Night', 1813

The wreck of the *Doris* is one of the defining moments in Zetlandic history, coming when local confidence was high and Britain was asserting its full naval power on the oceans. Aboard were a number of the most prominent islandmen, and their loss affected many of the leading families throughout the archipelago. That none escaped the tempest served only to hammer home the finality of the blow.

The incident, so dramatic, so widely reported throughout the country, had the effect, as disasters do, of focusing the eyes of the wider world on the area concerned. It was, for many denizens of the south, their first awareness of Zetland, and it lent further support to the movement petitioning for a proper system of lighthouses and lifeboats around the British coasts.

Inadvertently this would result in the arrival on Zetlandic shores of Walter Scott, Bart, in 1814, whose experience provided the first popular glimpse of Zetlandic life, in *The Pirate*.

But let us return now to Barbara Scot of Norbie, the second wife and widow of John Scot the Younger. She was 'glad to receive' her cousin's lines on the loss of the *Doris*, and suspected that she had been 'too harsh in judging Dorothea Primrose's early efforts at verse'. There was 'a genuine sentiment' in these new lines, a maturity which pleased Barbara, who had been consecrating herself for months, as the minister had advised her, by the time the manuscript arrived. But she softened as she read:

Ah! never more th' expecting friend
Shall greet the luckless *Doris*' distant sail;
Each cherish'd hope, alas! and boding fear must end,
As time confirms the melancholy tale.
And thou, oh, Norbie! art thou gone –
In life's meridian snatch'd so soon away!
For thee, but all in vain, love, wealth and pleasure shone,
Nor could th' appointed hour one moment stay.

But she would not play 'the wretched wife' that her cousin suggested she might be. She had children to look after, and her work lay before her. She would 'see to their education, and prepare them for the highest vocations, impress of them the virtues we true Christians aspire to', as she wrote to her friend in Quharv.

She determined she would leave Norbie for Skallvaa, where her sister remained, taking her boys with her – and leave the beautiful new Hall of

Norbie to the old man and his heir, John Scot VI – the Elder – grieving into his whisky, and the son of the delicate Margaret, John Scot VIII, whose father had drowned. She would be closer in Skallvaa to the support she required – closer to her family, and to her dear divine. She might even visit Larvik, to 'exchange views with this literary prodigy of a cousin of mine', who intrigued her so, 'once the year of mourning is over'. And she had heard, too, that her much more illustrious literary cousin, Sir Walter of Edinburgh, was planning a voyage to Zetland, which would bring him to visit his relatives in Skallvaa.

~~Zetlanders have always declared that Scott's *Pirate* gave no true picture of Zetland life; but the most intimate and diversifed knowledge of Zetland life has never inspired a book worthy of an instant's comparison with *The Pirate*.~~

It was when the fate of his first novel, *Waverley*, was hanging in the balance that Walter Scott set out on his 'voyage in the lighthouse yacht to Nova Zembla and the Lord knows where'. This voyage, undertaken, Gabrielsen tells us, with great zest and in highly convivial company, took six weeks, one of which was spent at Zetland. Scott sailed from Leith on July 29th 1814, along with Robert Hamilton, Sheriff of Lanarkshire; William Erskine, Sheriff of the Orcades and Zetland; Adam Duff, Sheriff of Forfarshire; David Marjoribanks, son of the Provost of Edinburgh; and the Reverend Turnbull, minister of Tingvallie in Zetland. In charge of the party was Mr Robert Stevenson, the great engineer and designer of lighthouses, the grandfather of the author RL Stevenson. He was 'surveyor-viceroy over the Commissioners', and so had charge of the whole party, and is the figure most often referred to in Scott's diary.

The yacht sailed northwards along the Scotch coast, passing latterly Cruden Bay, the scene of the wreck of the *Doris* and thereafter sailed directly to Zetland. When they had been at sea three days, and there was still no sight of land, Scott laughingly advised Erskine, Sheriff of their mysterious destination, 'to issue a meditatione fugae warrant against his fleeting territories', but just then a Dundee whaler they encountered told them the port of Larvik was a mere twenty miles distant, and they dropped anchor there on the night of August 3rd.

Scott took great pleasure in avowing he had not been seasick, as that dog James Hogg had predicted he would to Byron. The prediction had seemed quite safe at the time, as they had sailed in a gale, and the area of sea just off the southern tip of Zetland, known as 'Da Rowst', had a reputation as a terribly turbulent tide-race.

They arrived in Larvik just at the time of year when the Greenland whalers were returning the Zetlandic portion of their crews. Scott reckoned that around a thousand of them disembarked, and he remarked how the town of Larvik was aflame all night with drunk and riotous sailors, though they appeared to be the English portion of the whaling crews. He was informed that they got drunk at the expense of the Zetlanders, who were honour-bound to treat their guests at whatever cost, having bragged of their homeland and its hospitality throughout the voyage – while they themselves largely remained sober. The temper of that night grew so wild that Sheriff Erskine felt obliged to mobilise his militia to arrest several of the Englishmen.

The following day, Robert Stevenson set off on a voyage to the northern reach of the archipelago, and the ultimate extremity of Britain, where a lighthouse was thought to be necessary, though in fact it would not be erected until 1854, by his two sons.

Scott remained in the port. He made his way to the fort, garrisoned at that time by two companies of veterans, 'jolly dogs' as he called them, and there made friends with the officers, so that one of them walked with him to the ancient 'broch' at Klikimin, then in a far superior state of preservation.

Walking on further, Scott noticed how patchy the Zetlandic agriculture was, and felt deeply the depressing effect of the sweeping moorland without trees. He saw the first Zetland sheep, 'a miserable looking, hairy-legged creature, of all colours, even sky blue'. The ancient watermills amused him, and he remarked to his companion that such a primitive contraption must have required great patience. On the rough road back to the harbour, his companion explained to him the complexity of local land tenure, which he recalls baffled him.

The following morning, the great author turned his careful eye to the natives. They were, he observed, 'strong; clear-complexioned, handsome men; and the women very pretty', but he turned the ferocity of his quill on the local habit of making women carry everything: 'I strongly disapprove of the invincible native habit of making the gentle sex burden-bearers, when there are perfectly good ponies in the field.'

Scott found, in conversation with Mr Collector Ross, that abstemious Zetland, with its 22,000 inhabitants, annually imported £20,000 worth of spirits, tea, coffee, tobacoo, snuff, and sugar. Scott regarded this importation of foreign luxury as quite monstrous, and he was 'aggrieved to find porridge as a food, quite exploded'.

Word had spread from the fort, and now the great author's presence was the talk of the town, and certain of the notables sent boys to beg his presence. One, a Mr Mowat, was an old friend of his father's and had seen Walter as a boy. So he dined with the Mowats, in the company of a Dr Edmonston, who had recently published the first substantial history of Zetland. Edmondston was an authority on ornithology and, the two men getting along so well, they arranged a voyage to the nearby bird island of Nouss. Here Scott found the scenery was 'tremendous' and 'sublime', and the white mass of solan geese studding the cliff in the sunlight quite amazed him. The party then went on to the famed Cradle Holm, a rocky stack to which, in 1633, a cradle was strung from ropes connecting it with the Holm of Noss. At first this gave islanders access to gulls' eggs, but later a larger basket provided carriage for up to twelve sheep. The cradle operated for over two hundred years and numerous sketches and narratives were made by visitors and passing mariners.

The following day he took up another invitation, this time to call on one of the Scott families, landowners in Brassay, where he heard much of the laird's difficulties in introducing improvements among the old-fashioned and antiquated Zetlanders, whose 'barbarous habits' seem to have furnished material for most of the evening's conversation.

On the Sunday, Scott rode with Duff to the Tingvallie where he breakfasted with 'friend Parson Turnbull, who came over in our yacht'. It was four miles there and the rough road 'ended in a bog', but Scott liked Tingvallie. 'The land in the interior much resembles the Pel Heights, near Ashestiel,' he wrote, meaning the house near Selkirk where he had moved in 1804, where he wrote the works which brought him fame as a poet, which is immortalised in the epistles which preface the six cantos of 'Marmion', wherein Scott describes the effects of the changing seasons upon its scenery. He observed that 'Parson Turnbull is a Jedburgh man' and that his 'prayers were exceptionally good', following the service, and with such familiar reminiscence, Scott endeared 'Wild Zetland' to himself.

From here, the great author rode south through Da Ting Vallie, passing the site of old Norse Lawting, set on a small holm in the middle of Tingvallie Loch, a long narrow jewel of opaline. From here it was a matter of a couple of miles to Skallvaa, where he was expected to dine at the residence of his cousins, the Scott family of Scottshall, though they had located northwards some three generations before.

First, he saw the scene of the Stewart tyranny and wondered at the iron ring from which 'Black Patie' had hung his hapless victims. He supposed that the stubborn natives described to him by Scott of Brassay had good reason not to trust their rulers, and felt 'a shudder of dread'.

The mansionhouse of Scottshall made for a far more pleasant environment and he was pleased to note that 'two young ladies, daughters of Mr Scott's, dined with us – they were both Mrs Scott, having married two brothers. The husband of one was lost in the unfortunate *Doris*. They were pleasant, intelligent women, and exceedingly obliging.' These ladies were, as the alert reader will have noted, Scots and not Scotts, for they were, in turn, Catherine the wife of James RN, the hero of Trafalgar, and Barbara, John the Younger of Norbie's widow.

As these ladies are the only ones mentioned in Walter Scott's diary, it has often been claimed for them that they were the originals of Minna and Brenda, the sisters who feature in *The Pirate*. Whatever the truth, the great author – whose fame was still uncertain at that time and based upon his poetry – records that it was the lady widowed by the loss of the *Doris* who procured for him the description of the Papay Sword Dance which appears in the notes to the novel.

Riding back to Larvik that night on his 'miniscule steed' through the 'Simmer Dim', as he had learned to call the summer twilight of this advanced latitude, he was struck with the thought that he would write a tale of Zetland if, when he returned to Edina, the verdict on his *Waverley* was found to be one of approbation. And much of what Scott used in his depiction of Zetland in *The Pirate* was gleaned that night at his northern cousins' dining table.

Barbara, widow Scot, also records her memories of this famous encounter, to her correspondent in Quharv. Her southern cousin had impressed her with his 'rapier wit' and 'sincere sympathy for the condition of the people of Zetland. He also listened to all I had to say and never once showed signs of boredom,' she wrote.

The effect on her was immediate, for having conversed with the single most eminent Scotch author of the time, her self-esteem was boosted and she found that she too could write poetry, which she offered later, with a note of humblest apology, to 'The Wizard of the North' and her cousin Dorothea Primrose Campbell, the poetess, alike. Miss Campbell was delighted to hear from her 'fellow northern poetess and dear cousin.' She invited her to visit, so they might 'exchange views of Cousin Walter's latest work,' meaning *Waverley*, and so that Barbara might see the piano which had been shipped north to Miss Campbell's schoolroom in Larvik, as a gift from the great man.

Barbara was 'slightly surprised to read of this'. She wasn't aware that Miss Campbell, whose father had ended his life in debt, was 'of such close acquaintance with Cousin Walter'. She hoped to visit, yes, but couldn't see a time. When no letter came from the south, to thank her for her packet, no opinion on the quality of the poetry, she sank back into her maternal duties. Though she continued to write, the subject of her verse became more introspective and, finally, the cry of an aggrieved heart for love. She hesitated to send it, but finally did, to the one person who would be sure to reply – to take seriously the outpouring of sentiment her heart had thrown up from that wreck off the Aberdeenshire coast. To her surprise, by return, he sent a poem penned by himself, attesting his love for the 'dear heart so sadlie troubled', and within the year they were wed. The minister of Quharv became stepfather to John Scot the Younger's two sons, a week before the schooner from Leith brought cousin Walter's polite but late reply, with many thanks for the description of the Sword Dance and some platitudes about the 'interesting verse' she had sent to him.

The great author explained that his path homeward from that night at Skallvaa had taken till midnight in a downpour of rain. He was 'never so pleased to see a straw mat in his life'. By morning the rain had passed, leaving a sharp clear air, and he wandered with 'kind old Mr Mowat'. He went on to tell her that the yacht left the wild whaling port and sailed southwards to the island of Mussay, where the finest example of an ancient 'Pictish Burg' still in existence was situated. Scott and his fellows went ashore and speculated, in a baffled sort of way, on its mysterious builders. From there the yacht sailed round the southern headland, and into Quhendil Bay, where the party was brought ashore and welcomed by the local proprietor, Mr Grierson. After a substantial repast they climbed the nearby headland, where Stevenson intended to establish a lighthouse, at Zumburg.

Here, above any other place in Zetland, Scott found his muse: 'It would have been a fine situation to have written or spoken madness of any kind in poetry or prose.' As it was he did neither, but spent a while pushing large masses of 'sand-flag' from the brow of the cliff, watching as they thundered down the rocks, cracking and showering splinters into the sea. His companions left him to his thoughts, and returned to the old house, where Grierson was furnishing gin and water.

Left alone, the great author sat on his rear and slid his way to the bottom of the landward slope, then set off to clamber his way back to Grierson's mansion along the coast. On the way he came upon 'a picturesque old ruin', and he felt the spirit of the Viking era, though it would not be until excavations more than a century later that his intuition would be proved true.

Scott was only a few hours at this southern extremity of Zetland, yet the great rock headlands of Zumburg and Quhytefell, separated by the perfect curve of numerous shell-sand beaches 'rich in mica', made a great impression. So it was that he decided, high on the sublime headland he would establish his barbarian prophetess, 'Norna', withdrawn from the world. And at the ruined house, he would site his 'Jarlshof'.

Here the romance of *The Pirate* would drape itself across the landscape, his invented names would be made actual in time, just as Stevenson's lighthouse would forever mark the coast. And as the Lighthouse Commissioners' yacht sailed off to the south, Zetland had one last impression for Walter Scott's journal, when that stretch of water with hideous reputation showed why it had gained such notoriety. James Hogg's prediction came true – the great writer was sick as a dog.

Yet even this experience he turned to good account, with his vivid imagination creating for the reader the picture of Da Rowst in a storm, and the horrid plight of a vessel caught in it, for *The Pirate* eight years later. And in his composition of his 'Song of the Zetland Fisherman', he paid tribute to the men of the sea.

It would be wrong to overstate the role of Scott's voyage in creating widespread interest in Zetland, as his arrival there was symptom as well as cause. Already Sinclair's *Statistical Account* and Edmondston's *History* had forged a literary path, had brought to the printed page something of the culture and condition of the place, and created an interest among the 'Suddrons', regarding this isolated province. Yet there is no doubt that Scott's novel, when it met the light of day, helped to foster a desire among the general public to see the 'towering precipices' for themselves, and taste something of the exotic flavour described.

Nor was 'Cousin Walter' the first to describe the islands in a novel – that fell to the young poetess of Larvik, Dorothea Primrose Campbell, whose *Harley Reddington* appeared in London the year before Scott's *Pirate*. This was a lively tale of a man born in London society to a Zetlandic beauty who has hidden her poor origin from all, till her son is shipwrecked there. On the shores of Larvik, Harley is rescued by strange troglodytic creatures who speak a coarse tongue he cannot understand. He is horrified to learn they are his near cousins! Miss Campbell's career did not match that of her famous cousin, sadly, and she died forgotten in an Asylum for Retired Governesses in Camden Town.

Years later, in 1829, Scott records fond memories of the northernmost point of his northern voyage: 'I have an agreeable recollection of the kindness and hospitality of these remote isles. I have a real wish to hear of Zetland's advantage. I often think of its long isles, its towering precipices, its capes covered with seafowl of every class and description that ornithology can find names for, its deep caves, its smoked geese, and its sour sillocks. I would like to see it again.'

~~This morning I find I have varied from the true path of my history again~~

last night. I have ignored our parish and distant events. Therefore I will attempt to summarise the state of Norbie in the year 1815, when Napoleon meets his Waterloo, and the

INVENTORY OF JOHN SCOT THE YOUNGER'S ESTATE
AS RECORDED IN THE COURT BOOK OF ZETLAND

Inventory of the Personal Estate of John Scot the Younger of Norbie who died on the 20th Febry. 1813:

> At Larvik the seventeenth day of March One thousand Eighteen hundred and Fifteen John Scot Senior Esquire of Norbie who gave in the inventory underwritten desiring that same might be recorded in the Commisary Court Books of Zetland conform to law, which desire the said Commissary depute found to be reasonable and ordained the same to be done accordingly – the tenor description follows –

	£		
1st Principal Sum due on current account by Sir William Forbes and Coy. Bankers in Edin. Of State date the 31st day of December 1812	484	5	3
2nd Interest due to the 20th July 1813	2	7	9 ¾
3rd The Deceased's Household Furniture, farm stocking, implements of husbandry, sold by auction at his Hall of Norbie October 1814	186	13	4
4th His Bed and Sable Linen & Books sold by auction at Larvik Sept. 1814	71	2	4
5th Sundry pieces of silver plate weighing together 130 ounces appraised by Henry Robertson, Appraiser	52	10	
6th Debts due to the deceased by Mr John Harrison	2	12	7
Mr Alistr. Nicol, Merch.	1	7	9
	800	19	0 ¾

> In presence of Andrew Duncan Esquire, Commissionary
> Depute of Zetland appeared John Scot Esquire of Norbie
> Senior, father of the deceased John Scot of Norbie Junior
> who being solemnly sworn and examined dipones that
> the said John Scot Junior died upon the twentieth day of
> February one thousand eighteen hundred and thirteen and the
> deponent has entered upon the possession and management
> of the deceased's personal estate as trustee for his widow and
> children who are in infancy. That this deponent knows of no
> settlement or other writing left by the deceased relative to
> the disposal of his personal estate or effects or any part of
> these. That the foregoing inventory which is subscribed by
> the deponent and the said Commissary as relative hereto is a
> full and complete Inventory of the personal Estate and effects
> of the said deceased, wherever situated and belonging, or due
> beneficially to the Deceased at the time of his death in so far as
> the Deceased come to the Diponent's knowledge ... &c.

Two and half years after the drowning of his dear lamented son, John
Scot the Elder was glad to sign this document, for it finally meant that
his affairs were in order. He had cared so little in life for legal papers, and
took such a cavalier approach to fiscal matters – so the absence of a will
was 'no great surprise'. With the inventory, the situation of his widow and
children could be settled.

The old man would not remain at Norbie Hall, nor would his ward
and heir, John Scott VIII, his grandson by his dead son's late first wife, the
delicate Margaret Nicolaesen. Together they retreated from tragedy to
the old towerhouse on the island of Valay, which had always held a place
in the affections of the male Scots. Norbie Hall lay for a while, empty,
then the servants were sent away, and the windows were boarded up. The
romantically carved gates with their twin dolphin motif were chained,
along with the memory of the beautiful young couple who had designed
the house, both brought home early to heavenly paradise with the Lord.

The estate lands, but recently the scene of intense attempts at
'improvement', slid into a mournful torpor.

Yet despite the attempts to wring more from the land, little had really changed in terms of method in the previous hundred years, since John Scot the III first organised the fishing to his advantage, and the Greenland whaling began. The people still lived as they had done, under the laird's rule, though the Napoleonic wars had taken many men from the islands, and few were left to fish or till the land.

The estate accounts no longer looked so pleasing. The debts owed by tenants to the shop for their provisions soared. But change was sailing home then, somewhat scarred and toughened by the Navy and the experience of war, with coin in purse. Thousands of Zetlanders had served – they had seen other places, other ways of life. They had become British heroes, and expected a fitting welcome.

23rd June 2000 – Norbie

I will not look, but get up and walk away. Up over the big stones, to the grass at the beachhead, to the burn. Over the fence I go, in among the sheep and the thistles, and round the burn's curves, up towards the hill behind, where the chalets are cut into the slope. I glance back. I follow the curves of the burn till I come to the narrow bit I'd jumped the day before. I leap the burn and now I'm on the chalet side. My head is thumping. My side aches.

Up the grassy bank I go, panting, a grue growing inside me. From the top I look back, trying to see where the minister is, but I can't. He's not where he was, at the beachhead. And then I think I glimpse him, coming through the burn course, coming after me. Through the dusk, through the midsummer dusk, I jog now, up the steep hill towards the chalets. Every so often I look back to see if I can spot him, but he hasn't crossed.

I'm nearing the chalets, panting hard. The pain is thumping sore again. There's a stitch sharp as a dirk in my left side, so I stop at the fence and bend down, gasping, hands on my knees. I stand there a while till the stitch has passed, till I've got my poise back, my breath. There's no sign of the black crow on my trail. I survey the chalets, one with a light on behind the drawn curtains, the one in the middle that is just a burnt-out shell, then my father's in darkness. In the fading light the feeling's eerie, the darkening moorland hill behind with only a washing-line breaking the horizon. I picture the born-again couple sitting with the Bible out, praying. I've a good mind to go and chap the door. A sudden urge, despite the hour, it's not that late, to climb the steps and chap the door, to ask them

CODE WILL SAVE

Instead I go up the steps to the darkened chalet and try the door. It's locked, as I expected. My father's life is locked to me. But round the back the windows are ajar to help get rid of the smell still lingering. I jam my hand inside and feel around for the catch. I can bend it no bother, release the glass frame, and swing it full open. I grip the sill and pull myself up, then in I go, head first, scrambling through the narrow space, my wounds aching as the sill scrapes me.

On the other side there's nothing to hold onto, so I just fall forward, my feet sticking outside. Then I feel something soft below and drop down softly, onto my father's bed. The blankets are damp. I roll off the bed and stand up, go out into living area. Everything seems as if it's been disturbed by the police. I sit down in the glasshouse, avoiding the broken strap on the chair.

The tiny sliver of moon is rising over the
      finger of land
           that points

Bon Hoga
Serrafir
Tokumua
NZ

Dear Archibald

Many thanks for the Christmas card and those photocopies of the history. It was good to read your letter. I'm glad to hear that you are finding some solace in this work since your wife died. She must be such a dreadful loss, after so many years together.

It will take me some time to digest everything, but we are very glad of the work you've done in transcribing this. Would it be possible, do you think, for you to give me the address of the man who you obtained the original copy from, as we would very much want to have it included in our museum here.

Speaking of the museum, I am enclosing another essay by our young archivist, John Inkstir, which tells the story of the Zetland settlers who arrived in the late nineteenth century, and of the fishing industry they established here. I expect some of it will not mean a great deal to you, but nevertheless you may find it interesting in parts.

Aa da best fae a weet Tokumua,

Philippa

THE COMING OF THE ZETLANDERS

BY JOHN INKSTIR

Among the many thousands of Scots who arrived in New Zealand in the
1860s were a substantial number from the Zetland archipelago, far to the
north of Scotland. Some of them settled on the West Coast, at Charleston
and Nine-mile Beach, while others mined for gold in Otago. One of the
earliest emigrants was Robert Stoot, a native of Larvik who had trained
as a surveyor and hoped to find work in the goldfields. As an eighteen-
year-old, he came out in the winter of 1863 aboard the *Lady Milton*, a
voyage that took 128 days. In December, while the ship was off Madeira,
he found himself up aloft helping to bend a sail, and so impressed the
captain that when he came down, the master asked him how long he'd
been a sailor. Stoot laughed and replied that he came from Zetland where
everybody, men and women alike, knew how to handle a boat.

Stoot settled in Dunedin, and on failing to find his desired post,
embarked on a career in teaching, law and politics. Like many Scots, his
political beliefs were radical and he was a key figure in the drawing up
of many of New Zealand's earliest 'acts'. He became Prime Minister in
1884, but gave up party politics, latterly serving as chief justice of the
Supreme Court between 1899 and 1926, and he played a significant role
in fostering tertiary education in New Zealand.

Proud of his Zetlandic heritage and anxious to help his people, Stoot
encouraged others from his homeland to come to New Zealand. This
was a time when traditional living conditions back home had become
unsustainable due to overpopulation created by the improved general
health of the islanders; from the late 1700s up to 1881, the Zetland
population had increased to over 31,000. Emigration to other parts of the
globe became an ever more attractive proposition. Fishermen and seamen
from Zetland arrived in significant numbers between 1871 to 1888, with
the offer of 'assisted passages' to New Zealand.

As noted, Zetlandic men are renowned for their seamanship and were
frequently the target of the Royal Navy Press Gangs, so it is not surprising
that a large number of those who settled in Wellington ended up working
for various shipping companies, the Harbour Board, as 'watersiders' and

stevedores, or as fishermen working out of Island Bay. The Zetlandic population concentrated in Wellington, where a society was formed in 1922.

Some settled elsewhere, persuaded by the opportunity to purchase cheap land; a colony was established at Port William on Stewart Island, another at Karamea on the West Coast, though neither was to thrive. In 1904, when assisted passages were resumed, a group of Zetlanders even made an unsuccessful effort to farm the bleak and forbidding Macdonald Island, but had to admit defeat after four terrible years.

One of the many tiny Zetlandic colonies attempted was in the isolated archipelago of Tokumua, or 'New Zetland' as the colonists named it. The connection with Zetland was already established through the fabled exploits of a native of the northern isles, the complex character of 'Kapiyaki', or Captain Jake Kulinis (various spellings), by the time the ships arrived from the 'Old Rock', bringing the ninety-nine settlers and their little Zetland sheep, all led by their minister Reverend Thorwald Gabrielsen.

Once the site of an old whaling station, Serrafir was chosen by the early Zetlanders partly because of its proximity to the fishing grounds in Bloomil Straight. The bay was reasonably protected from the prevailing northwesterlies and the mountainous hills of Delting Island gave some shelter from the southerlies, depending on their severity.

The only other Europeans to settle there was a group of Italian fishermen from Genoa, who came out from Wellington in the 1890s to establish a fishing station because the waters around the isles were proving so profitable.

The weather and sea conditions in Bloomil Strait would have been more familiar to the Zetlanders than the Italians, who hadn't had to contend with strong tides and rips in the Mediterranean. They were net rather than line fishermen and the Zetlanders taught them the technique of long-line fishing. They did not have much experience of tidal variation. The Zetlanders also introduced canvas buoys capable of withstanding tidal conditions. Made in six panels sewn together leaving a hole for inflation, the canvas was soaked inside and out with linseed oil, then painted with red lead and tar to make it waterproof. These were much more reliable than the barrels or drums used by the Italians, as they could not withstand the water pressure and would implode with the loss of any attached fishing gear.

Oilskins could be bought ready-made in New Zealand but the Zetland fishermen preferred their 'smookies', which the Zetland women made out of canvas, lined with calico. They too were oiled with linseed and hung out to dry, which might take weeks. Most fishermen wore two of these garments as they were not completely waterproof.

There were about 250 Zetlanders in New Zetland in 1909, with a number of substantial families well established in Serrafir, including the Gabrielsens, the Arthurs, the Bruces, the Dungkins, the Huntirs, the Inkstirs, the Irvins, the Isbistirs, the Johnsens and the Pottingirs. The Bruces lived in Melbie Street, the Dungkins, Johnsens and Teits in Norbie Street, and Inkstirs, Isbistirs and Arthurs in Bousta Street.

The former laird of the Norbie Estate in Zetland from where the bulk of them had come was also resident there, having emigrated with his family and entourage in 1904. His family, the Cunninghame-Scots, built a large bungalow at the top of the hill, overlooking the harbour and the original house of Serrafir, built by the legendary 'Kapiyaki' (Captain Jake Kuliness).

The best-known fishing family in New Zetland were the three Teit brothers – Erasmuss, who arrived here about 1893, and his younger siblings Jake and Patie. Jake was the first Serrafir fisherman to be given the honorary title, indicating mastery: 'Mr Bloomil Strait'.

The Zetland and Italian communities cooperated together but seldom socialised, although the Tokumua football team of 1921, which sailed to New Zealand to compete in an all NZ competition, was made up of both Italians and Zetlanders. The Zetlanders in Serrafir also formed the South Thule Tennis Club, which was located on the corner of Bigton Street and The Esplanade.

The Zetlanders were almost one large extended family, married to and working for each other, but destiny was against them. The 1930s Depression saw prices for fish drop drastically, and this led to the establishment of the Serrafir Fishermen's Cooperative Ltd, with both Zetland and Italian fishermen participating. The Cooperative stabilised the market by purchasing, preparing and selling the catch to retailers and to fulfil New Zealand government contracts. They paid a minimum wage to their members. The Cooperative was successful until 1963, when internal divisions led to its demise.

The downturn in the fishing industry led to many Zetland fishing families leaving Serrafir for more lucrative markets. The Inkstirs, Dungkins, Pottingirs and Mouats went to the Chathams. The Teit brothers moved to Napier, where Jake's son Peter eventually became mayor and was subsequently knighted.

A History of Zetland with particular attention
to the Parish of Norbie, Valay and Thulay:

CHAPTER FOUR

'TO ZETLAND'S ADVANTAGE'

I have an agreeable recollection of the kindness and
hospitality of these remote isles. I have a real wish to hear
of Zetland's advantage. I often think of its long isles, its
towering precipices, its capes covered with seafowl of every
class and description that ornithology can find names for, its
deep caves, its smoked geese, and its sour sillocks. I would
like to see it again.

Sir Walter Scott, *Journal*

Of the many Zetlanders who fought in the Napoleonic Wars, there
are three who particularly interest our parish. The first is the surgeon,
James Scot of Norbie, hero of Trafalgar, and the younger brother of John
Scot VII; the second, an acquaintance of his from rather less elevated a
background, who rose to be the great hero of Zetland in the nineteenth
century; and third, a more minor figure in history who nonetheless begins
to fill the vacuum of power left by the wreck of the *Doris* on the west side
of Zetland. All three stories will intertwine in time.

Let us begin with James Scot, the second son of John Scot VI of Norbie,
Thulay and Valay, born 6th March 1785. After his heroics at Trafalgar,
James joined the *Banterer* as surgeon; when the ship was lost on the St
Lawrence River, he suffered extreme hardship among the ice. Eventually
returning to Britain, he married in 1810 his sweetheart, a distant cousin,
Catherine, daughter of John Scott of Skallvaa; she is said to have been the
model for Sir Walter Scott's Brenda.

James Scot was subsequently appointed to HMS *Euralys* under the
command of Admiral Dundas, whose cousin had acquired both the
Orcades and Zetland for the sum of £60,000 in 1766. He was part of the

Scheldt expedition, and served aboard three other vessels before the peace of 1815, after which he went on half-pay to study medicine in Paris, from where he begins a correspondence with his father in Valay, so providing a source for much of what follows.

After graduation, Scot was appointed surgeon aboard the HMS *Brittania* and then, in 1826, selected as lecturer to the Royal Naval Hospital and curator of the museum at Haslar; in 1830 he was made Director to the Mental Asylum, where he 'brought about many improvements'. He left this post in 1838, and went to Portsmouth as Deputy Inspector General of the King's Fleets, but suffered a serious injury in a carriage accident which in time forced him to give up his profession. After his retirement, he lived in Musselburgh near Edinburgh.

James Scot first became acquainted with his slightly younger fellow Zetlander Anders Arthursen in London during the 1820s. Like Scot, Arthursen had left the islands at an early age to join the Navy, and made his career furth of the shores of the 'Aald Rock'. Both were patriotic Zetlanders, but unlike Scot Arthursen was of peasant stock and formerly a 'beach boy' charged with curing fish landed at Brassay – though admittedly, his father, as manager of the fishing station, was a mite elevated. He had some education from Rev. Turnbull of Tingvallie, the 'Jedburgh man' of Walter Scott's acquaintance.

The Press Gang visited Brassay and took away two boys. Young Arthursen only managed to avoid their clutches due to the fortunate personal intervention of Thomas Bolt, agent to Lord Dundas, who explained that the lad was a valuable employee and 'to take him would be to incur the wrath of the potentate'. In due course, Arthursen volunteered at the end of his apprenticeship in 1808 which was, as he later said, 'typical of a Zetlander to refuse to be told to do anything, and then to do it of his own free will, and do it well'.

Arthursen distinguished himself in the Navy and, with Boney safe in Elba, he landed at Portsmouth, with very little to his name. From here he set out on the long hopeful road to London on foot, where he hung about the docks and survived as he could – he thought about going back to sea, or going home to Zetland, but he had a hankering to stay and try his fortune in the great seaport. During this difficult time, he records that his 'daily diet was a tuppenny loaf, a pennyworth of cheese, and a glass of porter every other day'.

Arthursen's fortunes turned when he found employment as a clerk in a ship-brokers. The master, a Mr Welch, took a shine to his scrupulence and 'the lad from the far north', as he called him, was made a partner. He recalls in his memoirs that 'the firm was not such a great concern at this point – our first ventures were limited in scope and it was only through the acquisition of an American schooner that had run aground at Dover, which we then fitted with guns and used to run cargo to Portugal, that we entered the ship-owning business'.

When Maria II of Portugal's troops required guns for an insurrection, Arthursen provided them, travelling incognito as a courier for her supporters – and when her cause succeeded, he found himself feted in Portugal: 'With the monarch's blessing, the firm went on to establish a successful steam route between London and Liverpool, Falmouth, Vigo, Oporto, Lisbon, Cadiz, Gibraltar and Malaga. Thus, the Peninsular Company was formed.'

To this network of trade, Arthursen wished to add, to extend into the rest of the Mediterranean. He was a visionary of a kind and even dreamt of carrying on trade beyond Alexandria, overland to the Red Sea, and then the far Orient. At this point in its evolution, the relatively new steamship had never been tried east of Suez, and sailing ships were limited by their dependence on the monsoon winds, which dictated only one voyage per year. Yet Arthursen felt sure that steam could defeat the steady southwesterly from May to September, and the steady northeasterly from October till April – it was simply engineering, to build an efficient and powerful engine to make headway against them.

All the while, in his mind, he had another idea – that of 'a canal at Suez which would allow shipping to pass from "Med to Red".'

Arthursen's career as co-founder of the line has been well documented and it is not my aim to relate it at length. What matters here is that, at the peak of his powers, he turned his entrepreneurial skills to the benefit of his fellow Zetlanders, and continued to do charitable work on their behalf throughout the rest of his life.

One of his earliest good deeds involves his friend James Scot, the naval surgeon of Norbie, and impinges directly on our parish. But before traducing that venture, I shall introduce to the reader the third of the Napoleonic veterans I promised at the outset of the chapter, namely James Berrick of Roovik.

Unlike the aforementioned Scot and Arthursen, Berrick did not distinguish himself particularly in service of his nation – at least there is no record of this. Press-ganged in the second round of the activity, for the American War of 1812, he only reappears in the islands in 1820, when he establishes himself as a merchant and fish-curer at Roovik. He married an older woman, Margaret Greig, the grand-daughter of a minister at Vass, and daughter of the merchant on Papay. As she was a widow of a small proprietor based in fertile Roovick, Berrick appears to have married well, and into a business with Margaret, for she was a strong woman known to have more than a full part in the running of affairs.

After Berrick's early death she continued to run the concern till her sons were of an age to inherit. Maggie Greig was, by all accounts, a hard woman to please, whether by client, husband or son: 'There's naethin maks her grin but siller, an she girns at aathin ither,' it was said.

Under the strong auspices of her determination to survive, twice bereaved or not, from the 1830s Berrick & Co were to become a powerful economic force on the west side of Zetland over the next century, and Maggie and James' younger son would find his fate entwined with that of Norbie, when he became factor.

Let us return to the remote parish at this time. The chained gates of Norbie Hall have been opened, and the grown-up John Scot VIII uses it for the season, though he lives the greater part of the year in Edinburgh near his uncle James, the naval surgeon, now retired due to a carriage accident. The young heir is married now, to an heiress of modest fortune in Edinburgh property but no land, and they live well in Gayfield Square, but the union has not yet been blessed by the heir that is expected – the son who will be John Scot IX.

The towerhouse of Valay, now called the Aald Haa, or Old Hall, has been the home of John Scot IV, the Elder, in his later years.

Barbara Scot, the model of 'cousin Walter's' Minna, now the wife of the Minister of Quharv, has seen to the education of her two sons, with the help of her 'dear divine'. The eldest, Charles, has become Master of the Customs House in Larvik, and is a dashing figure, the scourge of smugglers in his speedy Customs vessel. The youngest, Robert, has followed his uncle James and apprenticed himself to the surgeon's art under his supervision in Edinburgh.

Here Robert has tasted society and met his venerable cousin Sir Walter in his last years. His mother, alone with her minister at last, begs him to 'write more of your meetings with the great folk of our capital,' as 'our days here at the manse are not so coloured with learning and conversation as in the former times'.

Our Barbara, whose letters have provided so many insights, is now a mature woman of middle age living in a changed world. The background is of a Zetland transformed when the veterans of the Royal Navy returned, and found the old fishing no longer satisfactory. Forty miles to the 'Far Aff' grounds no longer seemed such a distance, to men who had rounded the great capes and sailed the vastness of the oceans. 'Even the shapes of the boates seem different,' she observes to Robert, and she was right.

Larger decked boats had begun to appear, 'smacks that can reach as far as Faroe, two hundred miles to the northwest, or Iceland beyond that again, even Rockall'. The beaches of the islands are such calamitous scenes these days, 'such industrious places full of strangers' that she feels 'quite isolated.'

And then, in 1832, there came what Zetlanders later called, with typical understatement, 'The Bad Day'. On Martinmas Day, or July 16th, a hurricane burst upon the fishing fleet as it lay at the 'Far Haaf', with the result that by midnight, sixty boats were lost and some three hundred fishermen with them. Though some appeared later, the effect was disastrous. The tale was told in the national press. Zetland's 'Bad Day' won great sympathy and brought charitable contributions from many sources.

Anders Arthursen coordinated the appeal. It may be ventured that this awoke the benefactor in him, as from this time onward he intervenes in the life of Zetland regularly from his London base. In 1836 he published, entirely at his own expense and mostly written by himself, the first newspaper in Zetlandic history, the *Zetland Press Journal*, which aimed to inform his countrymen in the north of what was happening in the wider world. In the first issue he placed certain dummy advertisements to take up vacant column inches, and sell the idea of advertising to interested parties.

One of these was another of his dreams, for a mythical steamship voyage to show the adventurous tourist the wild west coast of Zetland, where our parish lies, which he poetically titled 'The Red Coast', in recognition of its marvellous red sandstone steeps; he eulogised on the 'mountainous slopes of Wild Thulay, the most remote of Brittania's isles with the sole except of St Kilda, where the natives still live according to the calendar of the previous age; by means of the ancient art of fowling, which enables their survival in the very midst of the Atlantic. From here we will sail north to the Faeroe Islands and to Iceland unto the Setting Sun.' The idea – that of using steam for tourist cruises – was unique, but even had they a vessel capable of steaming in these seas, the likelihood of finding passengers willing to undertake such an excursion for pleasure seemed unpromising. Yet nine years later, the Peninsular Line took up the idea, not in the far north but in the Mediterranean. Arthursen, aware of the value of the press, sent a free ticket to the great writer Thackeray, who was very sick, but felt obliged to write a book about it – though he had his revenge by refusing to have his name used.

I digress here, but it is perhaps useful in that it shows Arthursen's remarkable capacity to not only imagine but enact the previously unimagined. In the next scene, the reader will see how this affects 'The Red Coast'.

But first, it was with sadness that the news of the death of the wife of John Scot the Elder at Valay arrived in 1837. It was a time of trial for all the people, with poor crops and worse fishing. The old laird felt powerless to help his tenants and wondered now if he had done too little in his life to try to 'improve' as had his first son. The worry compounded his mood, and he withered perceptibly in a few months. He signed over the estate to his grandson, the still childless John Scot VIII.

Barbara wrote to James, 'at a loss as to what we should do'. James had the solution. Inseparable in life, after her death John Scot the Elder left his wife on the island of Valay and moved, at James' encouragement, to live with him in Edinburgh. Here he fretted over the intermittent news from Zetland, and when letters came deploring the state of things there, with such waves of famine and emigration and a plague upon all the livestock, the old man wished he might do something. James, a man of healing after all, agreed. They should do what they could for Norbie and the people there. But what?

Arthursen provided an idea – ideas were his business after all, though he had also proved he could deliver upon them. For a hundred years and more, the fishing had been entirely in the hands of the lairds, as we have seen, and Arthursen believed this provided little incentive for the fishermen, trapped in continual debt to the landlord's monopoly. What if they were to found a free fishing station, where the men had everything to gain from its success? Would that not inspire them?

Arthursen knew exactly the place – the island John Scot the Elder had just vacated: Valay. If only Scot would lease the land, Arthursen would do the rest. And so, in 1838, to the amazement of the other proprietors in the archipelago, the Zetland Free Fishery Company opened for business with a flourish, despite predictions of gloom, and ran successfully for many seasons.

The Zetland Free Fishery was one of many ventures Arthursen made on behalf of his countrymen and women. In 1838, he provided the funds for the first steamboat connection with Leith; he made a presentation of some fine examples of Zetlandic lace knitwear to Queen Victoria, and as a result influenced Edward Standing to subsequently promote the unique skills of Zetland's women, as demonstrated in their crafts, by the establishment of a cooperative exporting directly to his shop in London. By so doing, Arthursen again created an outlet beyond the laird's shop, where previously the women's handiwork had been bartered for goods, as had the fish catch, and the farm produce.

Sadly, not even the work of Arthursen and his ally James Scot, RN, could stand against the forces arrayed in opposition to Zetland's advantage at that time, for the Lord in his wisdom deemed it necessary to send among the people an even worse pest than the pox. For overpopulation was now a serious concern; since the conquest of smallpox the number of souls had doubled, and poor harvests from land and sea over repeated seasons made this unsustainable. And when the one industry which had shown a little promise failed in 'The Great Herring Crash of 1842', famine set in.

In 1843, a Poor Law enquiry was held but the outcome was slow, while people starved. A letter to *The Scotsman* of 10th June 1846 reported:

DESTITUTION IN ZETLAND – From a communication, dated 'Larvik, 25th May' in the *John O'Groats Journal* of Friday last, it appears that famine is spreading rapidly among the Zetlanders. The following is part of the communication alluded to:–

Want and misery are now written on many a face, where till now, such had not been seen, and, if not promptly relieved in some way or other, there is great reason to fear that during the summer, and before the crops can come on so far as to be made available, even in a half-ripe state, for the pressing wants of the population, cases of death from actual starvation, will neither be few nor rare. At this moment individuals are known to the writer of this, who have not tasted bread for a whole week, and others who have neither tasted bread nor meal in any shape for periods varying from ten to fifteen days, who when they had scraped together the sum necessary, had to take their bags under their arms, and to travel distances of from six to eighteen miles – Zetland miles too – before they could procure the small quantity of meal which they were able to purchase, and that, too, at a most exorbitant price. The breakfast of shell-fish has to be gathered in the morning, at the sea-side, among the rocks, before the cravings of hunger can be satisfied; then the next meal, consisting of fish, with perhaps a few potatoes; and if they have a little meal, fish, and bread, or else fish and potatoes again, before going to bed comprises all that they can afford, fish and potatoes being the chief, almost the only articles of diet, and bread being used more like a luxury than as the staple article of food. These are not cases of rare occurrence.

Driven by the need for immediate action, Arthursen himself stood for parliament the following year and called at all the harbours of the islands, aboard his steam-powered yacht, canvassing support in the company of his agent, the equally eloquent and charismatic James Scot, RN. In his speeches, he made it clear that he was standing as the first candidate drawn from the mass of the people, not from the ranks of the gentry: 'The seat has been passed between two rival aristocratic families for centuries, as if it were their own to share. The monopoly of the lairds will be broken.'

In Arthursen's case, the pretender had the support of the son of a laird, the 'Hero of Trafalgar' at that, and this alliance seemed to suggest a new dawn. Perhaps the ruling classes were at last coming to their Christian senses? On a vast wave of public hope, swelled by desperation as well as belief, Arthursen was carried to Westminster. But greater challenges than the aristocratic hold on political power followed, with potato blight in 1848 adding to the parlous state of the people.

The government's solution was to be a programme of public works, intended to both feed the immediate hunger by the payment of workmen in flour, while at the same time creating something which would be to Zetland's future advantage. So the people began the building of the 'Meal Roads', so called because workers were paid in 'meal', or flour; and over the coming years they would engender a transformation in the Zetlandic way of life.

Zetlanders had always been boat people – men, women and children alike knew how to handle oars or sail as a matter of necessity. It was by far the easiest of transports between settlements, for the hills were wild and barren, offered no shelter, and were full of peat bogs. Many superstitious tales were told about the hidden dangers and the creatures that lurked there, among the peat clefts and the heather brows. Murders happened there too, and folk disappeared.

The Meal Roads of the mid-1800s instigated a change, which led in time to the motor car, and the end of the boat as the essential tool; and gradually followed the abandonment of many settlements no longer convenient in the new road-based transport system.

Change, too, came in the hills of the Wesidill Vallie, where the landlord was intent on turning his whole estate over to sheep, and was clearing tenants before the flock with the point of a pitchfork and a firebrand.

Scot the Elder of Norbie was not that kind of landlord. He was, in his old age, showing compassion – just in time, as some said, for he died in the summer of 1850. John Scot VIII, the childless Edinburgh socialite, inherited. But only six months later he too was dead, tragically, from a heart attack in a box at the Royal Lyceum. The double bereavement sent a bolt of lightning through the parish. With old John and his idle grandson, the folk at least knew what they were getting. Now, suddenly, the estate passed to the only remaining son of John Scot of the *Doris*, Robert the surgeon, the second born of Barbara Scot – the first of their sons, Charles of the Custom House, having died in his youth.

So the nephew and protégé of the surgeon who had followed his uncle's path by joining the Royal Navy, became the Laird of Norbie, Valay and Thulay. He was at the time of his succession the Superintendent of Hospitals at Portsmouth, as far from Zetland as the coast of Britain stretched.

Robert was the first 'Scot of Norbie' not to be named John and he came north to look over his domain in the summer of 1851. He had not visited since leaving seventeen years before, nor seriously considered this eventuality, as there had been two siblings with a more mature claim.

The conditions of the people in Norbie appalled him. Though I have found no specific description of Zetlandic dwellings as they existed at that time in Norbie, Valay or Thulay, we might imagine their repair not so different from the general impression given twenty years later in the second Truck Commission report by William Guthrie:

> The Zetland cottage or hut is of the rudest description. It is usually built of undressed stone, with a cement of clay or turf. Over the rafters is laid a covering of pones, divots, or flaas, and above this again a thatch of straw, bound down with ropes of heather, weighted at the ends with stones, as a protection against the high winds which are so prevalent. Chimneys and windows are rarely to be seen. One or more holes in the roof permit the escape of the smoke, and at the same time admit light. Open doors, the thatched roof, and loose joinings everywhere, ensure a certain ventilation,

without which the dwellings would often be more unhealthy than many in the lanes of our large cities. To this, there is no doubt, we must attribute the comparative absence of fever, the occasional presence of which, I think, is greatly due to that violation of the plainest law of nature, the box-bed. This evil is often intensified in Zetland by having the beds arranged in tiers one above the other, in ship fashion, with the apertures of access reduced to the smallest possible size.

Drainage is wholly unattended to, and the dunghill, or midden, is invariably found at the very door. As the house is entered, the visitor first comes upon that part allotted to the cattle, which in summer are out night and day, but in winter are chiefly within doors. Their dung is frequently allowed to accumulate about them; and I was told that this part of the house is sometimes used by the family in winter as a privy. Passing through the byre, the human habitation is reached. The separation between it and the part for the cattle is ingeniously effected by an arrangement of the furniture, the bed chiefly serving for this purpose. The floor is of clay, and the fire is nearly always in the middle of it ...

23rd June 2000 – Norbie

I wake up suddenly, heart pumping. Still here in the night, the glass chalet night. The moon has moved higher, further round to the south. There's a rhyme in my head, God knows where it comes from, but there it is in my head

> Just as I am, without one plea,
> But that Thy blood was shed for me.
> And that Thou bidst me come to Thee
> O LAMB OF GOD I come.

Buried since childhood ... and then I see somebody's moving around outside in the half-light, a big shadow moving slow, the Holy Ghost. I duck down out of sight and watch him shamble around. It seems as if he's looking for something in the grass, his head bent low as he goes. Seeing him trudging about, I realise I could project onto him every bad feeling, every suspicion I've got, turn him into the villain. My father's murderer. I could make him the scapegoat for all my misery. That would be easy. Simple, with his strange slow ways. And then he turns, is gone.

I sit there a while longer, feeling a calm come over me. Thinking about them out here in the middle of nowhere, about to bring a child into that cheap and inadequate dwelling. I feel sorry for them, despite their newborn joys.

Then I get up and go back out the way I came in, struggling through the opening and closing the catch, feeling the bruise on my sore side. The light is on in the born-again chalet, but the curtains are drawn across the glass front. There's music playing, a choir singing, jangling tambourines. I listen a while before I chap the glass. It takes a repeated knock before the curtains are drawn apart and the door opens.

It's her. Lena.

'Oh,' she says, 'it's you,' disappointed.

'I'm sorry,' I say. 'Sorry to come so late.'

She stares at me a moment. Her face is blotched and her eyes all tearful, like she's been crying. She steps back inside, into the warmth.

'Maybe I should just go, come back in the morning?'

She glances up, tries to smile. 'No, no, it's okay.' All Christian, never turn away a stranger.

'Are you sure?'

'Come in, sit down, please. Really. Can I make you some cocoa?'

'No, no thanks. It was just, I was thinking ... thinking about what you'd said the other day, about my father. There's something bothering me.'

And she gets all flustered, flapping her arms while the belly burden jiggles under her baggy jumper. She turns away from the door. I hesitate on the threshold, unsure what to do. It looks cosy inside with the stove going. Then I see, lying stretched across the floor, this strip of white linen, two long bamboo sticks at either end stapled into a fold, and it's painted with a slogan.

THE LORD PRESERVETH THOSE WHO LO

The writing starts off big and then gets smaller and more cramped, till it runs out of space. A pot of paint with a brush sticking out of it sits on a sheet of newspaper. But there's no sign of him anywhere, the Holy Ghost. Maybe he's another night-roamer, maybe these light summer nights are disrupting everybody's sleep patterns?

'Please come in,' she repeats, like she means it this time, stepping back and opening the door fully. 'I didn't mean to be so unwelcoming.'

I sit down on their couch. Above the fast-burning stove, there's a poster, a pretty painted picture with the title 'The Broad Way and the Narrow Way'. I've seen it before. In it, there's two roads. One is like a wide street, running through the centre of a valley with lots of folk milling about on it enjoying themselves. That goes towards an abyss where flames wait. And the other is a narrow mountain path that winds all the way up the right side, till it reaches Heaven.

'I thought you were John,' she says.

'Is he out then?' I ask.

She flushes. 'Yes. He went out for a little. We had an argument, a real barney, I'm ashamed to say.'

And then all of a sudden she bursts into tears, right there in front of me. She flops down onto the couch, keels over to the side, and howls a moment, leaning on the wooden arm. Then she turns her head, face buried under wild dark hair, and squints down at the white painted sheet on the floor.

'I was painting the banner for Sunday and it went all wrong. Look, I haven't even got enough room for the LOVE, never mind the HIM! She points at the letters, then she sniffs, sniffs back the weeping, to smile at me, looking for some encouragement. And cries some more.

'Could you not do the extra letters round on the other side?' I say.

'But that's no good!' She's annoyed. 'And the paint's running out!'

'I was only joking,' I say.

She looks surprised, then laughs. As I watch her sitting there studying her wayward lettering, I just can't imagine my father having an affair with her. And yet she'd said it had happened, and she should know.

She lifts her head up. 'I'm so ashamed for crying like this in front of you. But it's John. He's been out drinking again. And then he gets so …' She clears her throat with a cough, coming to herself again. 'Oh, he reads the Bible,' she says. 'And I'm sure he really wants to change. But inside he hasn't, not really. He's doing it for me, you see, he wants to make me happy. But I can see through that, and that makes me even more unhappy.'

'But he loves you,' I say. 'Anybody can see that.'

Then she pulls herself together a bit, sits up straight. Still her eyes are fixed on the wayward letters. 'But why can't he stop drinking then?' she says, more to the banner than to me. 'He goes to the pub and gets drunk and comes back here … I know it's none of your business, and you probably don't care, and I don't want to trouble you. But I need to talk to somebody. I mean, I've nobody, nobody but him. John.' And she bursts out with 'I wish my mother was here.'

I feel sorry for her, so far from home, from things familiar. And she starts to cry again, really sobbing. The sweet lass I'd met yesterday, so open and full of joy, is now just a mess of hair and tears. And carrying this burden, this great belly burden.

'I hate it here,' she wails. 'I hate having to send John into town shopping, because I dread him coming back. I know he'll come back drunk and start criticising me. But I can't go now, now that I'm near my time. I just can't take the bus journey anymore. I hate this place.'

She looks at me, expecting a response.

Then, when I don't speak, she sniffs. 'I'm sorry,' she says. 'I'm not normally like this. I'm very emotional just now. The slightest little thing sets me off. Really, the argument was nothing, I'm over-reacting probably.'

I feel like I should say something. Something wise. 'Folk don't always change sudden like that,' I say. 'Like you said you did immediately after the fire happened. Sometimes it takes a while, it's a slow process. And John's older, maybe more set in his ways. But I'm sure he's genuine about it.'

And she brightens up then. 'I'm hope you're right,' she says, then adds,

'Did want to talk to us about something? You've come all the way over here. Go on, tell me, what was it? I want to help, really. I do understand what you must be going through and here I am mithering away about my own problems.'

This is bad timing. 'Eh no, it was nothing really. It was just that, something came to mind, about my father, and I wanted to ask your husband. But it doesn't really matter right now.'

But she says, 'No, it's all right. I'm okay. What was it you wanted to know?'

I can't tell her. So I say, 'He didn't just mean he was going to see the landlord, did he, that day you saw him?'

'Oh,' she says, 'I hadn't thought of that.' But then she shakes her head. 'No, I'm sure he definitely said the Lord. At least I think so. I had my hands full with a basket of wet clothes. Anyway he didn't call Dr Hart the landlord, just Peter. They were quite friendly, you know.'

And then she bursts out into tears again, crying afresh, fresh salt water. I can do nothing, my hands are rubbery and hopeless, my sense of timing obviously terrible. I know I should go, but she starts speaking again, before I make a move.

'You've been talking to John, haven't you?' She's almost glaring at me. 'He's got it into his mind that your father and me were sneaking around behind his back. But we weren't, it was only one night, one night when John was away in town drinking and I went in to see him. I was just looking for a little love. For someone to talk to. But before I knew it, we were kissing and …'

And she buries her head again, under the hair.

'Did he take advantage of you, then? When you were upset?' I ask.

'Oh, I don't know,' she says angrily. 'It just happened, all right? I told you before what I was like then, didn't I? Now, praise be, I know I was a sinner, I know that now. But it was the way I was then. Before I was saved, I didn't value myself, my body, I thought sex was love. I was a stupid, sinful woman. Even though I didn't mean anything to happen that night. And now I wish to God that it had never happened. But it did, and after the chalet burnt down and I saw the light, I had to tell John, I had to confess. There wasn't any way I could have lived here and kept that secret to myself. Not when I'd asked Jesus to come into my life. But since then, since the chalet burned down, and Colin left, and your father disappeared, it's all gone wrong. It's so lonely. If it wasn't for Jesus coming into my life, I wouldn't have got through it. Everything's been so ...'

And she howls again.

'So there was really nothing to it, then? With my father?'

'One time. One night. One stupid night. That was all. I've said so over and over. Why won't you believe me?' she says, like it wasn't really addressed to me at all. 'One night, when I was drunk, may the Lord forgive me! But if you really want the truth, I'll tell you. John's convinced the baby's isn't his. That's what we were fighting about. It wasn't the banner, but your father!' She looks at me fiercely, shakes her head furiously, then hides her face away, a dark eye staring through tousled hair. And momentarily I see Martin's 'mistake', back then, with her dark hair, angry and crying that night in my father's car.

'But it can't be anybody but John's,' she moans. 'I know it's his. It's John's. But it doesn't seem to matter how often I tell him, he won't believe me. Oh, he says he does when he's sober, but when he's drunk it all comes out.' She's wringing her hands, as if she wants to wash them. Then she starts again, blurting out. 'I can't stop thinking that I'm about to bring a child into the middle of all this. It's all a terrible mistake.'

Words spew from her lips, then she lets out a deep breath. 'Oh God forgive me for saying it.' And she lays her hand on the child inside. 'Forgive me, little one. Oh Jesus, help me!'

'Here, now,' I say. 'You shouldn't punish yourself,' I say. 'Things'll get better. Maybe John's feeling the tension of expectation too. Maybe he's drinking because of that, because of the stress.'

'Do you really think so?' she says, a little pacified. But she turns to face the wall, long dark hair down her back. I reach to stroke it, kindly, but she jerks the shoulder that I've touched, the bairn inside her, safe out of sight.

But then she turns around and gives me a smile. 'Thanks,' she says, 'You're right, I'm being silly. The Lord will take care of us. I just have to trust in Him.'

I want to comfort her. 'That baby will change everything for you,' I say. 'Your man won't leave the house. He'll forget all about this and just sit doting on it. And you'll be away off to the town shopping yourself again.'

She peers up at me sitting there, as if she's realising I'm a stranger. 'You'd best go,' she says, 'in case he comes back and finds you here. Really, you'd best go.'

'Will you be all right?'

'I'll be fine. Don't worry, he won't hurt me. You're right, he loves me. But you'd better go now. He might not be so pleased to see us together.'

So I do what she says. At the door she whispers, 'God bless you,' and I feel a strange clandestine pleasure as we say goodnight. I slip down the steps, half-expecting John to spring out of the shadows, a fist raised to strike me down. And then I think of my father old and lonely, years since a woman had come near him, and maybe thinking it'd never happen again. A last taste of youth. Easy maybe, just to blank out the damage that it might do, forget all the difference, just to act, not to think. Just to feel her warmth, her softness, her skin, pliable, supple. Her mouth opening, reaching to meet his.

But then they were among the demons then, according to her. Or demons were among them, tempting them with pleasures irresistible. If that was how they saw it, if they were serving the Devil as they'd said, if they thought they were born to sin, then maybe it was my father who was the victim, caught up in their trauma.

I come to the top of the hill above the chalets, where the road bends sharply in a hairpin back around the bay towards the laird's house, with the other proper tarmac road branching off, over the hill and on out of the village. At this junction there's another road, a track of two gravel lines with a green turf strip in the middle, heading up the hill. Against the darkening western sky, I can see it goes to a church. Not the old church, the ruined one by the shore that's just an archway, but another one that's obviously still used. There's a sign, set back from the verge a bit. In the dark I can just make out the name of the incumbent, Rev. S Pirie.

It's a plain building for a church, more like a granite barn, sitting at an angle to the road. Around it there's a dry-stone dyke, the tops of gravestones just visible above it. I see the corbelled gable's single arch window, and a bell tower at its height against the midsummer night sky. A long strip of cloud hangs above the roof, tinged with grey-pink. Behind that again is a heavy serge blue.

As the night comes in, I turn off the route back to the laird's, towards the church. My feet are just going there themselves, no decision made. Reversing the chase, now I'm on the minister's trail. My boots crunch the gravel, a coarse grinding sound in the quiet, and I step onto the grass so my steps will be silent. The tang of the sea blows up from the beach below, catches my nostrils. The wind's changed, now it's blowing towards the land.

As I approach, I see there's another building behind the church, a dwelling-house. It's the manse, separated from the church by a dyke. A solid two-storey house with a front porch and a light on. And there's a light on in a downstairs room too, no curtains drawn. As I get closer, I can see straight in, to bookcases, a reading lamp, a mantelpiece with an open fire burning in the grate below. And a couch, two folk sitting there, the tops of heads visible.

It's him, the minister Pirie, and the man from the chalets. He's got his back to me but I can tell it's him, he's so big, and that long hair down his back is unmistakable. I watch for a while from behind the dyke. I hear the mumble of voices, but I can't make out what they're saying. And then they stand up. They disappear out of sight, like they're going out the room, as if John is leaving. I step into the semi-dark at the side of the church. The front porch door opens. The sound of their voices carries through the stillness. I step further back into the shadow. John speaks, says something I can't make out. But then I hear him grunt, 'Goodnight then.'

The minister answers, his barking pulpit voice ringing against the stone walls of the steading. 'Now you mustn't worry, I'm sure everything will turn out all right. Put this Bible code out of your mind. Trust the Lord. It's a difficult time for everyone, and with a baby on the way and all that, no wonder you're feeling apocalyptic. But I'm sure it will pass. Remember the lesson of Job.'

John laughs.

'Man is of a few days and full of trouble?' he says slowly.

The minister tuts at him. 'Now, now. You know perfectly well what I mean. Patience.'

But John isn't cowed. 'Patience isn't mentioned in Job. That's an old wives' tale.' He's sure of his learning, even with the minister. And the minister doesn't contradict him. All he says is: 'But the lesson, the lesson is just that, isn't it? You mustn't weaken now, John: "For I know that my redeemer liveth, and that he shall stand at the latter day upon the earth".'

The porch door closes with a final goodnight and John comes down the path and through the iron gate, out along by the wall of the churchyard. His giant bent shape approaches, looking at the ground in front of him. He's talking to himself, muttering away like earlier on outside the chalet, muttering something I don't catch. Then he raises his head, his face strained with agony.

'And I have heard many such things … miserable comforters are ye all. Shall vain words have an end?' he calls out.

The sound bounces off the walls of the church. I'm hiding in the shadows as he approaches, pressed against the stone. He's going to pass close to me, a few metres away. For a second, I have an urge to duck and run. I could outrun him easy, but I don't. I feel I've got to stand and watch, hope he'll pass and not see me. He steps nearer, closer, slowly, over the crunching gravel. His head's bowed to the ground again, he's not looking in my direction, he's mumbling away to himself. Then he lifts his head and cries out, 'Ye are forgers of lies, ye are all physicians of no value. But I am not inferior to you. Will ye speak wickedly for God and talk deceitfully for him?'

Suddenly he stops, looks right at me. I don't move. He stares at where I'm standing, his mouth open, peering through his long hair as if he doesn't know whether he sees me or not. As if he's trying to adjust his eyes to the dark.

'Who's there?' he asks.

Stand still. Say nothing. Wait.

'Who is it?' he says in a low voice. I stand still, holding my breath in case it makes a cloud and gives me away.

Then after a minute or so, he seems to visibly shake, starting with his head, then his hands and arms, and he drops down onto his knees, onto the gravel path. Still, I stand absolutely still. His big hands come up to cover his eyes, his head drops right down to the grass and the soil.

'Forgive me. Forgive me,' he says, his body and voice quaking. He's gibbering strange words, a language I've never heard. Or is it tongues? Is he speaking in tongues? 'Abba ... abba ... abba ... abba,' he's grunting. 'Strack omage silerian', it sounds like. 'Aff ate tress erack omage strack, abba, abba.'

I feel a chill pass over me. A cold, cold hand on the back of my neck. But he's not looking at where I'm hiding. I've got to stand my ground, wait and see what happens. Then he digs his hands down into the soil, lifts up a handful of earth and glowers at it.

He speaks again. It sounds like 'Breet trass az omage strack, abba.' He slowly raises the earth to his mouth and begins to eat it, his hair hanging down across his face. Although it's dark, I can see that his mouth is opening and closing, that strands of the long hair from his head are in his mouth, that he's chewing on hair and earth together, his face set in trial, as if he is doing a penance. Then he looks up. 'Az omage, abba!' he cries.

'Abba?' he says again, like it is a question demanding an answer. Then, quite shyly. 'Is that you, Abba?' He's staring into the darkness, but not at where I'm standing.

I slip away around the gable of the church. Abba is gone, over the dyke at the side of the manse, where I crouch down. There's a terrible chill on my skin, as if I've blasphemed or something, like maybe a block of stone from the church will topple from the roof and kill me. As if I've taken the name of this Abba in vain.

I peep over the wall till I find a vantage point. He trudges down the gravel road, past the sign and on towards the chalets, shaking his head from side to side as he goes.

The omnipotent glow passes as I walk down the track to the sign. Mortal again, with the pain from the wound in my side nipping, I have a growing feeling that somehow I've interfered when it wasn't my place. But by the time I get to the laird's house, I've justified it to myself. This place is driving me crazy. I came here sane and look at me now, impersonating strange deities in a churchyard at midnight.

The lights are out in the laird's house and a panic hits that it'll be locked and I'll need to go back to the chalet and spend the night. But when I get there, it's all right. Though the lights are out, the back door's open. Though the dogs growl, and one of the corgis barks behind a closed door, I make my passage.

In my room, the travel alarm says 12.13. I lie down on the bed, bodily exhausted, but my mind is churning. And my side's aching after the walk. I stare at the flaky paint for a while, thinking. There's still no real clue. Just strangeness everywhere. Still I haven't solved the puzzle. And so I reach for the bundle of papers at the bedside, where my family's life waits for me to piece the broken fragments back together.

And I close my eyes. But Abba runs through my mind

      a word

          for

~~'Time's Chariot'~~

~~5.30 on the morning of March 30th, 2001. More importantly it is Sunday, and I will not go to church again today. After seventy-five years of regular attendance, I wonder that no one comes to look for me? Is there none left to do so? Am I the last living member of the glorious congregation that surrounded me in my prime?~~

~~It is the sixth week of writing this history. I have surprised myself, far surpassing what I thought I was capable of. I have not written so much so quickly since my early days in the ministry, when the flow of ideas for sermons, and the habit of writing essays I learned while studying divinity, caused me to spend every day aside from Sunday filling notebook after notebook. The habit dwindled as the years passed. I had my sermons already written, my ideas established, and only texts to recycle. And of course there came Margaret, who filled my evenings. Margaret! How she would laugh to see how much I had written, how she loved to pull the pages from my typewriter and admire my turn of phrase. If she could only read this. But then, had she been here, I would have told the story to her,~~

~~would have discussed it, till it was clearly defined and understood – and I would have committed none of it to paper.~~

~~Today I am driven by the sense that I may not have tomorrow the health I have today. At any moment, I feel my illness may take such determined hold, that I may not be able to sit at my desk to write again. Today, I still rise from my bed unaided, to find my way along the passage to my study. Now it strikes me – this must be the day in the year when the clocks change. If t ...~~

24th June 2000 – Norbie

Light dull grey. Thick fog at the window. I look at the clock: 7.30. No sound in the house. I get out of bed and open the window. The waves are still breaking. Somewhere out there in the mist I can hear the gentle rushing, then the dragging back over the pebbles. I listen. Even the birds seem quiet, everything subdued. In the soft damp air, I get cold so quickly, I leap back in under the covers and lie there staring up at the blotched ceiling, the flaking paint that's hanging above my head. The morning light creeps slowly in.

The shower washes away the chill that's been getting into my bones. Suddenly I'm feeling good, the pain's eased, and the sore is healing. I rub some of the cream on it before I dress.

Downstairs in the kitchen, Mrs Mitchell is cooking bacon and egg. She looks up. 'Good morning to you, my dear. A bit misty today,' she says, then: 'What can I make you for breakfast?'

'Porridge, if that's all right?'

She's bonny when she smiles, so confident here in her kitchen.

'Fine. But it'll take awhile. Dr Hart's upstairs, in the living room. Go on up if you want. I'll shout you when it's ready.'

He's sitting in his studded leather armchair reading the paper, with half-specs on. The local paper, the equivalent of the *Perth Advertiser*. 'Good morning,' he says, all friendly. 'You look well.'

'Thanks. Yes. I feel better.'

'There's a piece in the paper.' And he taps his finger at a column on the front page:

MAN MISSING ON WEST SIDE

Police are growing concerned for the safety of a man missing from his home on the west side. Rod Cunninghame (68) was last seen on the morning of the 16th of June. Cunninghame, a retired journalist from Perth, moved to the island in 1998. Anyone with information on his whereabouts is requested to contact the police station.

Reading damps my mood. The laird looks at me. 'There was an announcement on local radio again this morning. And the police are planning to search the ness today.' He looks out the window at the white bank of fog pressing against the glass. 'That's if they can see anything in this damn mist. At the minute, I can hardly see the driveway. It's a curse, this weather. Hate it intensely. The way it narrows everything down. All too regular an occurrence, I'm afraid.'

I sit down on the seat opposite him. He's staring out the window, waits for me to speak, but I don't. He shakes the paper out and pushes his glasses up his nose a fraction. Then as if remembering, 'Oh by the way,' he says, 'Reverend Pirie went looking for you last night, but he couldn't find you.'

CODE WILL SAVE

Like I've done something wrong, something unspecified, I'm guilty.

'I went for a walk. Did he want something?'

'No, no, nothing urgent.'

And then Mrs Mitchell calls 'Breakfast!' and we troop downstairs to the kitchen.

I begin my porridge.

'Did my father attend Reverend Pirie's services?'

As he sits down to his plate of bacon, sausage and eggs, Dr Hart looks up at me and says: 'Yes. Sometimes. I think he went along more in order that he could argue over the content of the sermon later.'

I nod, not really surprised after everything I've discovered about his life here. Or the minister's strange ideas. But I want to ask something. A sort of a religious question.

'Religious?' he says, hesitating with the fork at his lips.

'Well, I'm not really sure if it is or not, but the word 'abba', have you ever heard that word used, to do with the church?'

He's chewing away on his bacon and egg, frowning, and won't speak with his mouth full. Well, of course. I wait. 'Strange you should bring that up. Reverend Pirie used that very word in his sermon last Sunday. The first time I'd ever heard it.' And he looks at me suspiciously, as if I'm digging into something and he doesn't know why.

'What did he say?'

'He drew attention to the closeness between Jesus and God, and used the word "abba" to illustrate his point. Abba is almost like a pet-name, he said, as it is used by Jesus, in I think St Mark's Gospel. If I remember correctly, he said the modern-day equivalent might be "papa". Reverend Pirie used it to show that Jesus really did have a son's relationship with God. And he mentioned the parable of the Prodigal Son as an example of that compassionate, paternal love which Jesus attributed to God. He does have some rather odd notions, I'll admit. Not quite what I thought I was getting when we interviewed him.'

He eats again for a while, watching me out of the side of his eye. Then, 'Why?' he asks.

'Nothing,' I say. And he stares at me, again expecting explanation.

I can see he's wondering what I'm on about, that he thinks I'm a bit disturbed. But I don't let on. I let him have his mystery and go back to my room.

Outside, down in the driveway, there's a scrunch of stones and the rough purr of a vehicle approaching. The dogs start barking downstairs. I jump to the window. Out of the fog, a police Land Rover appears, then a squad car, and another. Doors swing open. Five men get out of the Land Rover, dressed for the sea, in oilskins and rubbers. One man sits on the step and starts climbing inside, then pulls out a wetsuit and zips it up. A couple more are taking equipment off the roof-rack. They're obviously here for the search.

My heart is thumping. Pounding again. The laird comes out with his Barbour jacket on. The dogs are running about, sniffing the strangers. Dr Hart starts talking to one of them. He points down towards the beach, towards the pier and the old stone arch concealed by the fog. I open the window to listen, try to catch what they're saying.

'Cliffs,' I hear … then the name 'John', between the dogs yapping and grunting. But mostly it's just low rumbles and I can't distinguish individual sounds.

The laird's talking to one of them, pointing this way and that. The men are playing with the dogs, laughing and joking. And for no particular reason I can think of, I recall that Sunday School song, spelling out the word happy.

I'm H A P P Y, I'm itch ay pee pee waee …

I know I am I'm sure I am I'm H A P P Y.

Convincing ourselves, even if we were standing there with snot running out of our noses and our throats burning. 'I'm itch ay pee pee waee,' we sang, and so we were supposed to be.

And then the laird turns and points up, to where I'm peering from the window, and the policeman lifts his eyes and looks. I duck back behind the curtain. What's he saying about me? What's he pointing up here for?

I peep out again. The arm's still pointing vaguely towards me but the heads have turned away. They're gazing back in the direction of the sea, towards the finger of land that's no longer visible. Just plain grey.

Ach, let them look. Let them stand and stare and do whatever it is they have to. Let the laird go out and act the lord and master, let him describe his estate, his barren empire, let him talk about me if he wants. I don't care. Norbie Hall means nothing to me.

But despite myself, there's a grue growing again, the thought that this might be it, the moment I've been dreading. When I came here I'd no idea why, except that she'd asked – Gran, unrefusable. And at first I'd thought that it was my job to search, that I'd be the detective who would solve the mystery, I'd find him dead or alive, and carry the body home.

I no longer trust myself. My certainties are no longer sure. Everything here in Zetland is

transformed

I have crossed out my errors, and am annoyed with myself. My mind wanders, my copybook is blotted, as Margaret would have said, and I have no time left to repeat, to write afresh. I should continue with my history, even unto its conclusion, for I am now but a week or two away from completion, and from understanding everything. Yet how paltry one's research appears when strung together like beads on the string of pages, how little you see of the many cul-de-sacs, the breakthroughs, the sudden insights experienced.

I will have my say after all. I will not obliterate these words. I have been troubled, sorely troubled, yes, by all that has befallen this manse. For these things I weep; mine eye, mine eye runneth down with water, because the comforter that should relieve my soul is far from me: my children are desolate, because the enemy prevailed.

There are things I must say. I have my own story to tell. It will act as a primer for what follows. It was the summer of 2000, I can't say now what date. The encounter seemed less meaningful then. But I recall it was a Friday, because we were having fish. When the doorbell rang I looked at Margaret and we both, wordlessly, considered, then I rose with a sigh and ambled down the hall to the front door. When I opened it, on the other side there stood before me a bearded young man, who held in his left hand a pair of leather brogues. I looked at his feet, and saw they were bare, and what is more, red and painfully blistered. I took him in, for he was a poor fellow in need of help, a lost soul whom the Lord had sent to us. He explained he was recently bereaved, subsequently had passed through a religious experience and felt he was 'born again'. I took him in and Margaret allowed him to bathe his injured feet.

His attitude was oddly detached and other-worldly. I considered calling the doctor, but decided to wait.

David, for that was his name, shared our dinner. I gleaned that he had recently arrived in Perth from Blair Atholl on foot, where he had lived for nine days at the house of his recently deceased grandmother. The brogues were his grandfather's, which he had set out wearing, walking towards Perth, only to have to remove them due to the painful blisters he had showed me. His behaviour was most peculiar. Margaret thought he might have been taking drugs.

I pressed him for his name but he would not tell me; rather, he said 'I am a nameless pilgrim.' I asked where he lived and he replied he had walked away from his former life and would not go back, that he was a pilgrim intent on doing the Lord's work, wherever the Lord's path may now take him. I questioned him further on his conversion, and he began to tell me in very fragmented manner, of a voyage to the north in search of his lost father. I thought at first he was referring to Our Father in Heaven, but he insisted that it was his real father he had sought there, because he had disappeared without trace around midsummer and had later been found dead.

Margaret and I did not quite know what to make of it all. In our forty-five years of marriage and ministry, we had encountered our share of troubled souls, those who had 'wandered as blind men in the streets, have polluted themselves with blood, so that men could not touch their garments.' Although he seemed a little unbalanced to us, and was certainly traumatised, yet there appeared from within him such a gentle sense of certainty that I found his stare disconcertingly direct and his company strangely pleasant. I found myself offering him a bed for as long as he required it, though Margaret found him impossible and his presence in the manse caused some dispute that night, and in the following days. This was a very rare thing between us, indeed, I thought it very out of character for her to turn anyone away, and told her so. I believe she suspected he was sent from the Devil and would bring us harm.

24th June 2000 – Norbie

In the window the glass is wet, lined grey-white by the damp air. Foggy inside as it is out. My fingers rub a circle, like the bottom of a bottle, water droplets swirling into tiny streams that run. I look out. Maybe it has cleared a bit. The shapes of a few trees in the garden below are maybe more distinct than they were. But the beach is well out of sight.

And this place is now a different world from the one I saw when I came here. Then it was completely open, nothing breaking the view, no barriers to vision, no trees, no buildings, not even darkness. The naked land where I wandered the other night when I slipped and fell is gone, that open brightness, that midsummer light. In a single night it's changed, it's closed right in, become oppressive.

Yet strangely it somehow feels easier to be in. That openness made me want to walk, to explore, to get out and search. It filled me with a kind of nervous madness.

Now it's changed, it's a place to be still in. A room in the middle of a thick fog, a little cube of clarity. I think back over all the things that have happened. First the phone call from Dr Hart, then talking to Gran, and her insisting I should come here. The minister's Bible code. Then the born-agains. The cliff fall. It seems like something that has happened to somebody else, or to myself in some adjacent world, some parallel life

CODE WILL SAVE

and then I feel like I want them to find him. I want that police launch to come back with the body – his body. I want my father back, dead or alive.

Breathe in, out, in, calm. It will resolve itself. All will be righted. And yes, maybe I've got to face these things. Maybe before I can go forward, I've got to go through this process. And so I go on. I have to go on. I pick up the bundle of papers, then sigh.

But there's a voice. A pleasant musical voice, echoing up the winding stair from below, coming between me and the hollow box. It's Mrs Mitchell. I hear her getting closer, calling my name. For a second I feel threatened by the intrusion, then picturing her, warm and somehow real, I call back.

When I open the door, she's a step below, peeping up, her grey hair over her forehead. She smiles, makes a kind of 'do you really want this?' face, then says: 'There's someone here who says he has to talk to you. John, from the chalets.' Her face is offering me the option of having her make an excuse on my behalf, but I want to see him, I want to hear what he has to tell me.

'Could we talk in the kitchen with you, Mrs Mitchell?'

'Of course,' she answers. 'And my name's Mary.'

Downstairs, John's waiting, with his Bible. On the table his lumpen fingers link in a loose form of prayer, as he sits sideways to me, staring straight ahead. He seems less menacing, less strange, here in the kitchen in daylight. I feel sorry for him, for the weakness last night. When he sees me coming in, he smiles at me, kindly, and stands up. He's wearing a brown three-piece suit, short in the arms, and as he stretches to shake my hand, the sleeves of a royal blue shirt rush out. His hair looks combed, fixed down, and I seem to see a warmth in his eye. Or do I? There's an eagerness, an urgency to see me, to make me sit down with him, to talk, that's clear. And he doesn't fire Biblical quotations at me, he just speaks straight, though very slowly.

'I have to see you, because I have heard the voice of God. Last night.'

Mrs Mitchell's over by the window, with a bottle of cleaner and a cloth, wiping down the surfaces and generally buffing up. She peeks at me and winks, suddenly Mary, an ally.

'I was told to come.'

'By this voice?' Mrs Mitchell, now Mary, asks. He is shocked by her intervention, screws round in his chair and fixes his eye on her, as if trying to make her feel uncomfortable. But this is Mary's kitchen. Nowhere could she be more comfortable, so he turns back to face me, even though he answers her question.

'Yes.' He seems nervous, panicky, despite the slow drawl. Without any warning, he moves with a speed I didn't think him capable of, and throws himself before me on the floor. As if he just abandoned himself to gravity. 'I'm not the avenger,' he says, to my boots. It is an impressive prostration as prostration goes. And I'm inclined to want to believe him.

'Get up,' I say. 'That's not really necessary.' But he doesn't move. He just stays there, his backside sticking up in the air, his face at my feet. And he begins to mutter something, in that strange tongues-talk. Somehow I just can't bring myself to move. As if I'm frozen, spellbound. Then there's a swipe and a swish and he's leaping up, and Mary's there with her broom. I realise what's she's done and laugh. The prostrated man is shocked, really shocked, but Mary's beaming all over her beautiful face and he's so taken aback, that after a second he just smiles. Then he actually laughs. We all laugh.

'Oh I'm sorry, John,' she splutters between gasps for breath, 'I was just sweeping up the crumbs from the breakfast table and I didn't have my glasses on.' She winks at me as she says it. 'I wasn't expecting to find a great big arse under my kitchen table.'

'John,' I say, for I feel that we are now on first-name terms: 'Please, sit down and talk to me. Tell me anything you want to.'

Then he's at ease, it seems. Between me and the end of Mary's broomstick, we've put him there. He sits back down in his chair. But he doesn't break into confession. He sits, eyes closed, as if in prayer. In awful prayer

CODE WILL SAVE

'Look,' I say, after a while, 'There's really only one thing that's bothering me, and that is this … just how much did you fill my father's head with this stuff about demons and fire?' He doesn't answer, but looks at me cannily. I go on: 'I'm not suggesting you had any motive other than to evangelise. I just caught myself wondering if maybe you hadn't been pressurising him …'

'No, no,' he starts up in protest, 'No, we never put any pressure on him or anything like that. No. Whenever we spoke about God to him, it was because he wanted us to.'

Mary pitches in from behind. 'And how often would you talk to him about God?' She's put her broom down but from the look of apprehension on his face at the sound of her voice, John won't be doing any more acrobatics today.

'I don't know really,' frowning.

Mary prompts: 'What, once a week, once a day, or …'

'Maybe two or three times.' The Holy Ghost looks at us like we can't add up. 'A day.'

Mary looks at me. 'For the love of God,' she says.

'We'd just pop in to see him, you know, a cup of tea and see how he was. We were being good neighbours. Lena, mostly.'

'Pfff!' Mary's non-verbal, but clear enough. She throws her cloth into the sink and begins to run the hot tap. Clouds of steam rise in an already condensation-fogged room.

'Good neighbours, with Bibles,' I say.

'And tracts,' he adds.

So there is a picture forming in the fog, of regular visits through the fog, with words of threatened damnation, and all the time the thought of what had happened that one dark night between the lass and the old man. It's quiet. Nobody speaks for a while.

'I know what you're thinking,' he says to me.

'What am I thinking?'

'You're thinking I drove him to topping himself.' He's speaking slowly now, calm again. I try to weigh the tone, to analyse it.

'That's not what I was thinking,' I say. 'Your conscience is clear, so why worry?'

I watch his expression, carefully, as he considers.

'Yes,' he says. 'That's true.'

A minute or so more passes, as he breathes deeply in and out, composing himself. He seems relieved and I feel relieved too. I don't want to add to this man's misery, not by tricks, not by mockery. So the Holy Ghost stands up slowly, looking straight in front of him.

'I need to pray now,' he says, and without word of farewell, trudges out the back door.

Mary looks at me and shakes her head.

'What was that all about?'

I watch him stride away into the mist past the outhouses, in his brown suit, the jacket all lopsided because of the weight of a heavy square bulge in his left pocket.

We both laugh. But I can't laugh as much as she can. When she realises I've stopped, she gazes at me kindly, that same pitying look she gave me when we first met, and offers a nice cup of tea.

'Thanks,' I say. 'I'd like that.'

She goes to the sink and fills the kettle through the spout, sets it on the stove.

'How well do you know him?' I ask.

'Ach, he comes here every so often to see Peter ... Dr Hart. Whenever he's paying the rent. Or sometimes he comes and plays chess. But he never seems to win. He's a queer bird, if you know what I mean.'

Mary brings a teapot and two mugs to the table. She puts a cosy on top of the pot, with a picture of a sailing ship on it. 'The Tea Clipper *Norman Court* built in Glasgow, 1869', it says. Then she fetches her cigarettes and lighter, sits down. She leans in close, ready to divulge.

'No, but he's strange, whether he's ill or not. I mean he has this disease apparently, but he's never been to see the doctor once. He's not on invalid benefit. They're just getting the ordinary dole, same as anybody else would. My sister,' Mary says, 'she works in the Post Office. Not that I should be telling you this, of course.'

She leans closer to. I am against one wall, she against another. They meet in the corner. Both of us lean towards that meeting. She rests her head against the stone, then turns to face me. 'I'll pour the tea then. Before it gets stewed. I don't like a strong tea, me.'

'Me neither,' I say, though truly I don't mind. But there is something about Mrs Mitchell makes me want to agree with what she says. A warm broom-wielding protectiveness, a good-humoured, big-smiling toughness, even if she is a gossip.

'Sugar?' she asks.

In my mind, drifting the day through the fog, thick at the window, where the brown-suited man walks by, lopsided by the Bible in his pocket.

'Do you want sugar, dear?'

'No, thanks.'

'The fog's really thick,' I say. 'Do you think they'll be able to see anything out there?' Meaning the search. But she doesn't make the connection, as if she misheard me.

'Terrible,' she says. 'I'll hardly see to drive home.'

So I follow her. 'Do you live far away?'

'No, a couple of miles. With my mother.'

I sip the warm tea. 'Funny, the only place I ever drink tea with sugar is at Gran's. She got it into her head that I took sugar. I did when I was young, and nothing can shift an idea once it has taken root.'

She lights a cigarette. 'My mother's like that,' she says.

Again I follow. 'You said she was wasn't well?'

'Och, she's not so bad. More frail than ill. She just needs someone there on a daily basis. I'm not so trapped.'

'Do you miss the mainland?'

'Miss it? Oh yes, I miss it. The movies. The dancing. The pubs. The men,' she laughs, a wheezy fag laugh. But even through tobacco and perfume, I smell her, she's close, leaning now against the painted plaster wall. Some little drizzle of condensation has gathered in a whorl upon the wall, where her head touches and her hair sticks.

'But it is beautiful here, even I can see that,' I say.

'That's true, this time of year. Try winter.'

Then she laughs again. 'Ach, but even then, every so often there's a day that makes me glad I live here. But you see, I never really liked it, growing up. Couldn't get away fast enough, me. I was on that ferry and away from here before anybody could ask where I was going.'

'And where were you going?'

'Oh, the city! Glasgow. I had cousins there. And didn't I think it the grandest place on earth! And that was before they started cleaning up all the old buildings. Kelvinside, I do love it there.'

Then she looks at me and smiles, that pitying smile. 'But why am I talking about me?'

'I've always been a good listener,' I say.

She smiles: 'But you've got your own worries, my dear. I shouldn't be sitting here blethering about my nonsense when you're in such a predicament. Do you want to talk at all?'

I think I do, but don't at that moment. 'In a way it's relief to be discussing something else. I'm not sure. I don't know how I'll feel about anything till I know … you know, what's happened. At the moment it's like I'm in the middle of this fog in a strange place, with a lot of strange people.'

'You are,' she laughs.

'How serious about being a Christian is he?' I nod in the direction of John's exit.

'I don't know. To tell the truth, he gives me the creeps.' Mary drags on her cigarette, then coughs. 'It's one thing to walk the walk, as they say.' She's laughing. 'But I learned to clear the awkward customers in Glasgow. The office was always gathering them. Certain times of the month, usually when the moon was full.' She's laughing again, and sucking on her Silk Cut, and coughing a little, but this time I can't laugh along, because a thought suddenly strikes me.

'Mary, can you read shorthand?'

Puzzled, she stops wheezing and answers straight. 'Shorthand? Of course.'

I decide to trust her. 'I've got this notebook of my father's and it's all in shorthand. I never did learn, though he tried often enough to teach me. I seemed to have a block or something.'

She lays her hand gently on my shoulder. 'Never fear. Just you bring me the notebook here. If I can help I will.'

CODE WILL SAVE

So I go up the winding stairs and find the little notebook in my rucksack. The pain in my side's bearable, but I pull up my fleece and my T-shirt and check. It's fine.

Out the window the mist has lifted a little. I can see the little pier, where the search HQ has made its base. There's two policemen playing with the dogs and the whine of an engine somewhere out there in the moisture-heavy air. The Land Rover has been joined by a patrol-car and there's one tall figure draped against its rear.

And on the bed there's the box, the book, the hollow dome. Those reminders of absence.

But for now it's enough to be going down the cold stone stairs through the inner mists of the laird's house, to see my ally, the whistling cook.

Press *Rewind*, *Stop* and *Play*, to our mother whistling hymn tunes as she worked in the kitchen, cooking, cleaning, quietly desperate. Gran working in the kitchen, cooking, cleaning, with that firm Presbyterian urge for cleanliness to be next to Godliness. And our father coming, the lord in his manor, taking off his tweed jacket, his cap, sitting down to eat the food she'd prepared, exactly on time. His bluff tone, his stories of the day at the newspaper office he worked in. His Australian vowels and stresses.

'Here it is,' I say, from the bottom of the staircase.

And I hold it up for her to see, never thinking once that she's a stranger. She doesn't feel like one. She takes the notebook from me and puts on a pair of reading glasses, from a case on a shelf behind the table. Everything in its place, a place for everything.

'Let me see … well, he's got a messy hand, your father.'

'He was so fast,' I add, involuntarily, seeing his hand dart across my imagination. She frowns, lifts her glasses up and down, peering, and I realise that she doesn't see very well, that maybe her broomstick work was an accident after all. She flicks through the pages.

'Well I can read it, just about, most of it, anyway.'

'Will you, then?'

'What, you want me to read this whole book to you now?'

'Of course, no, I didn't really expect that. But it's just that I'm eager to know, in case there might be anything there that's important.'

And she looks at me as if she's asking herself, well if this is so important, why does he have it and not the police? But she doesn't say it, no, she just nods.

'All right. I have to go home shortly to see to Mam, but I'll be back at three o'clock. Come and see me then and I'll tell you what I've discovered. Help yourself to lunch from the fridge. It's all ready.'

I'm not too sure about letting the notebook out of my sight, somehow, but it's Mary, I tell myself. Mary of the Judicious Broom. We have already seen one battle together.

And it's lonely having the big house, this Norbie Hall, to myself when she's gone, driving off in her battered Fiesta over the bumpy road.

It's strange wandering through it without fear of coming across anybody. As if it was mine.

I could go into any room I liked and as long as I didn't disturb anything, no one would know. As if it was really my house.

And it feels odd, to be the laird of it, to feel it as the laird would feel it, as his.

So I do venture a distance, along the corridor on the third floor. There's a door open. His bedroom, unmistakeable by the smell of dogs and old man. An office or study too, home to a large desk strewn with papers and book cases to the ceiling. A large bathroom, comfortably fitted. And a cupboard. The cupboard is locked. The gun cupboard he mentioned, at a guess.

Where my father's gun is.

The gun that hasn't blown his head off.

On the spacious landing of the third floor, where the door to the narrow stairs up to the attic floor where my closet is, there's a statue, a Buddha in beaten copper. A great big thing, beautifully embellished. And there's a painting of a woman hanging in an alcove, a spotlight above it, but it isn't on. I can't see it properly in the poor light so I search till I find a switch.

But the bulb doesn't work. Nothing comes, no light on the lovely young woman wearing a lowcut dress, displaying cleavage of tropical proportions, the jungle flower in her hair. The former Mrs Hart, maybe? I run my fingers over the canvas. It's filthy with dust. Mary's broom doesn't reach this far, it seems.

Wandering through the empty halls of Dr and the absent Mrs Hart, the hollow dome of Hiroshima seems to swallow me. I'm struck with a terrible sense of gloom. The mists have fallen again, as thick as first thing. The air is damp, penetratingly cold. I want to be hopeful, restful. But I can't. All the mad dashing around, all the labour, activity. For what? So that your portrait lies gathering dust, while none but your ancient husband knows it's there, let alone who it's of? So I wander back to his study. I don't go in, but stand with one foot either side of the threshold, looking along the titles of the books on his shelves, reading them in clumps: *Empire & the English Character*, *The House that Sugar Built*, *God's Chinese Son*, *The Teller of Tales*, *British Empire and Commonwealth*, *Imperial Commonwealth*, *The Offshore Islanders*, *The Land of the Great Image*, *Great Navigators and Discoveries*, *Foreign Mud*, *Lives of the Indian Princes*, *The Oxford Book of the Sea*, *Along the Clipper Way*, *Plain Tales from the Hills*, *Robert Morrison*, *Mary Slessor the White Queen*, *David Livingstone*, *Rudyard Kipling*, *Sixty Poems*, *The British Empire*, *Wild Life on the Equator*, *Outposts of Empire*, *The Principal Voyages of the English Nations*, *Hakluyt* Vols. 1–7.

So it goes, on round the walls and up to the ceiling. Stacks of them. And there's one I recognise. It was my father's. Or rather, my mother's. *Poems of Henry Lawson*. Had he loaned it to the laird? I go into the room and take it from the shelf. There it is, 'selected by Walter Stone, illustrated by Pro Hart'.

Yes, it is my mother's book. Or it was. A gift from one of my mother's many church involvements, the BRF. I remember it well; 'The Bible Reading Fellowship'. The meetings, the collections, the 'socials'. And I remember my father's delight when they sent her this book from Australia as a thank-you. He'd grabbed it up. Not that she was bothered. After she read the introduction, about how Lawson ended up drunk and dissolute, she didn't think it a fit present for one BRF branch to be sending another, no matter how much he might be Australia's bard. Too coarse by far for Perth's chiselled morality.

And by it there's another, a book I don't know, but one that catches my eye. It's the name. That name, 'Bendigo'. That magical word from childhood. 'Meshack, Shedrack and to Bendigo,' I used to say to myself, a rhyme I had in my head, as I skipped along Abbott Street, maybe to the corner shop for a sweetie, maybe to the swings. It was a word that explained how we were different, our family, how we were Australian as well as Scottish. 'To Bendigo, we go!'

I take the book from the shelf. *Bendigo and Eastern Goldfields Sketchbook*, drawings by Unk White, text by John Bechervaise. And it falls open at pages 18 and 19:

Most of the coaching inns have disappeared, yet, here and there, as at Gaffney's Creek, where work goes on, and the stream is milky from the washing of the crushed ore, still the traveller may pause and hear heroic tales. At the bar he imbibes the added refreshment of optimism ... that soon, with cheap electric power, the water will be pumped from Dempsey's and the Rose of Denmark, and prosperity will return. The Ai Consolidated Mine is into its second century. 'The water defeated them,' we are told sadly. 'Everyone nearly wept when they had to put the lid on the workings'.

The region is still regarded as possessing considerable potential, though further economic reef-mining anywhere must depend on the price of gold, which has been stationary at about $30 per ounce through many years of spiralling costs.

There must be time to talk in such places, and to receive advice. 'Don't buy shares when the stream's running white,' advises our hostess, who once assisted Paddy Mcveigh, Out from Warburton ... where one of her customers became known throughout Victoria by the brewery advertisement captioned: 'I allus 'as one at eleven!' 'Wait,' she continues, 'until the water's grey ... there's always a streak of grey rock with the gold!'

At Knockwood the streams flow together as the Goulburn, and, at Kevington, eighty miles as the roads wind from Walhalla, the river is broad and beautiful, running down to Jamieson and Lake Eildon, a splendour which the old diggers might have woven with their dreams of Eldorado. Though it is with reluctance – especially in good weather – that one completes the crossing of the Divide, Jamieson is a rewarding, gentle place today. A century ago, it was a bustling provisioning centre for the eastern goldfields, with pack-trains trudging into the Beechworth area as far as Wandiligong and the Ovens Valley, and the fields of the Mitta Mitta.

All those Scottish names, next to native.

I sit down in the laird's study, stunned by this. Why has it taken me so long to realise that this is important? Was it because I hated it for being the thing that marked us out as different from all the others on Abbott Street? Except the Singhs, of course. And there it is, clearly framed, what we and the Singhs shared. Products of Empire, of the Great British adventure, both our families. Of emigration and exile.

Here it is then, the Old Courthouse. Unk's sketch. That place I've never been to, but I've heard about since I was a child. And I begin to flash the pages through my hands, looking at the other drawings. Maybe I will go there someday. To Bendigo. So I go upstairs, back to the family kist, back to my closet with the Bendigo book in my hand. I don't care how I'll explain it to the laird. I just have to have it for now.

It's part of the quest
        a clue

A History of Zetland with particular attention
to the Parish of Norbie, Valay and Thulay:

CHAPTER FIVE

'A GOOD MASTER'

And oh! Ye Zetland lairds be kind,
And shield th'industrious poor
From hard oppression's iron rod,
And tyranny of pow'r.

Oh! Think how noble 'tis to smooth
The couch of want and care;
To bid the honest tenant smile
And sweet contentment share.

Oh! think what fond and fervent zeal
Shall sanctify your cause,
When never forc'd by pining want
To break your rigid laws.

How sweet the meed of conscious worth,
More dear than public fame!
How sweet the blessings that repose
Upon a good man's name!

Then rule with mercy – so shall Heav'n
Your fondest wishes speed;
And joy, and peace, and plenty reign
From from Scaw to Sumburghead.

Dorothea Primrose Campbell,
from 'An Address to Zetland'

'It is perhaps too much,' writes Dr Robert Scot, the incoming laird, 'to expect the folk of Norbie to lose the habit of thinking of the laird as "Master John" lightly, after there have been so many of them.' For as the new laird rode the marches and set about a structural examination of each dwelling in Norbie during the summer of 1851, he was more than once wrongly addressed as 'Mestir John' by the factor and tenants.

Not that Dr Scot cared what they called him, as long as they had respect – and he realised, as a relative stranger, 'remembered only as a small boy who had played along the beaches of Norbie a very long time ago,' he would have to win that from them.

As a Christian and as a medical man, carefully tutored by the Minister of Quharv in boyhood and by his Uncle James in adulthood, his first concern was for the condition of the people's wellbeing, and that meant, primarily, their dwellings.

Although a few properties had been improved variously by tenants, in certain cases housing was pitiful – rudimentary assemblies of stone that a beast would not be happy to live in, though many of them did 'share their houses in some fashion, with the cattle and the stray pet sheep, the collies, the hens, cats and vermin'. He determined to invest the revenue of the estate in its stones and mortar, to begin a transformation at a fundamental level; and from that, happier tenants would live healthier lives, so work harder, and be able to pay their rent. If he were to encourage their initiatives as Arthursen had done in Valay, it would be to everyone's profit. As a single man on a good naval salary, he had 'no need to squeeze the estate like a milchcow'.

Dr Robert Scot's first act, once he had inspected the estate in the summer of 1851, was to appoint a new firm as factors. The current management had 'creaked along in increasingly decrepid fashion' and was insufficent to his progressive needs, for he had no intention of giving up his naval career and knew that his visits would be but few. It was vital that he should have a man, indeed men, on the ground in Norbie to attend to all the things he had determined to do as laird, to carry out his wishes as instructed.

Dr Scot looked around, consulted, and selected Berrick's of Roovik. The leading partner was a young man of thirty, but the firm, though young itself, was not without pedigree, Berrick's mother, Aald Maggie Greig, as she was still known, having been the daughter of the merchant in Papay whom Scot had known in his early youth at Norbie, before his mother carried him off to Quharv. This James Greig was a decent and educated fellow, himself a son of the manse, so that this Maggie came to be the granddaughter of a well-loved minister in Vass.

The family firm of Berrick & Co started out as fish-curers. It was begun by the energy of his father James, a Napoleonic veteran, and carried to commercial stability by the gritty determination of his mother, after James died young. Dr Scot had heard the tale that Maggie Greig 'wirked him inanundir da aert', as one old fellow put it.

Lewis Berrick was protégé to this infamous mother's driving ambition and by her connections through her father's family in the south, he had attended Dollar Academy. He was very bright, the dominie had said, and would do great things – an energetic, some said avaricious merchant who was carrying the Roovik business to new heights and new harbours, challenging even the supremacy of established firms in the old westside capital of Skallvaa.

To Berrick, the factoring of the estates of Valay, Thulay and Norbie was a rich prize that could extend his influence far beyond the current westmost reach of Vass. The fishing around Thulay was particularly good and had him rubbing his hands, we may assume, at the prospect of acquiring control. He was prepared to establish his younger brother in the old Haa house there and have him administer the shop and the estate directly, 'under my closest personal supervision'.

From a letter to this brother in the Berrick & Co archive, it would appear that Lewis Berrick was less interested in Dr Scot's programme of good works, however. He could, as an educated man and a Christian, 'understand the point of view', while at the same time seeing the world as 'not a wholly Christian place, where barbarians often have to be dealt with as barbarians'. But these views appear to have remained confidential to the occasional letters he sent his younger brother and junior partner, James. Lewis Berrick was well aware that they would not find an agreeable reception with the good doctor.

James Berrick, a less driven soul than his older brother, protested in his reply, and commended Dr Scot for his 'fellow feeling'. Nonetheless, Lewis decided to appoint James to the refurbishment of the Norbie estates. As his younger brother had 'such sympathy for the work Scot wishes to carry out'. He himself would concentrate on the 'prosecuting the fishing'.

The Norbie estate was soon experiencing the beneficence of 'Doctor Scot', as he subsequently became known, often prefixed by the word 'guid', and a number of boys born during his period of influence bear his name in tribute, as thanks for the new house into which the suckling child has been born. 'Robert Scot' something becomes a popular appellation in a number of tenant families from that time on. One family even included the title, christening their son 'Doctor Robert Scot Jarmsen' (known in later life as 'Docksie Jarmsen,' noted by Gabrielsen as 'latterly famous as a streetsweeper in Larvik').

Let me hesitate a moment here to acknowledge again that the story of the coming forty-two years, and much of what has preceded, comes directly from an unfinished manuscript written by the local schoolmaster in his latter years, during the 1890s, which remained in family archive, till that was given to the Zetland Museum. This work has furnished much, and my debt to James Gabrielsen is great, for it was his handwritten account that provided the key information in my quest.

I have discovered from my researches that Gabrielsen was born in 1825 in Norbie, the son of a man from Vassness, who had married a Norbie lass and come to live there, after the Napoleonic upheavals. Gabrielsen was afflicted by polio as a youth and so unable to follow the normal course for a boy, fishing and so forth. He proved studious and displayed a natural genius remarked upon by anyone who chanced to exchange words with him as a child. He had, it appeared, an adult perception and an insatiable curiosity that soon won him the mentorship of the parish minister. His parents, God-fearing folk, found he had a natural memory for large quotations from the Holy Word and the minister of Vass recognised in him 'a future stalwart of the church'.

Before he was seventeen, James Gabrielsen found himself in Edinburgh at the Church of Scotland Training College, where he met with a large social circle and held forth with professors. Gabrielsen realised he did not wish to become a minister. He set his aim on bringing 'enlightenment' to his own people – for he was truly of peasant stock – and after training he returned to Zetland to work as a schoolteacher and missionary in Quharv, where he met the then elderly Barbara Scot, 'model of Brinna', and wife of the Minster there – and now the matron of the new laird of Norbie, the mother of Dr Scot.

When they realised their common Norbie origins, friendship was sealed, and when Gabrielsen confessed that his deepest ambition was to return to Norbie as a teacher, Barbara wrote to her son advising him that she had found the perfect man for the parish school. She too had been caught up by the new laird's enthusiasm for improvement, and felt that her son's venture was the fruition of her Christian dedication, in teaching the Gospel message to him so avidly when he was a boy.

Gabrielsen kept a journal in addition to writing his memorial of the history of the parish, and records there, on his arrival at the old parish school of Norbie in 1858, that 'Doctor Scot is, the folk say, the best laird they have ever had and he is never here – whether they equate the two, we can only but surmise.'

According to Gabrielsen, Doctor Scot had left Berrick & Co a list of houses he wished to see improved, and in what way, and a list of those to be demolished, with new dwellings to replace them. James, who was kinder by nature than his brother Lewis, was glad to see those instructions made actual. The Berricks were not proprietors of old like the Scots, and they were not uniquely a combination of the old landed families as the Norbies were.

The father of Lewis and James, James, the founder of the firm, had been 'of the people, a poor man who married well and through his efforts in partnership, some would say junior, accumulated wealth and status'. It was said that he was jealous of the lairds and knew he was not seen by them as one of their number – his wife, whose background as granddaughter of a Scotch minister, was more elevated and she never stopped reminding him of that fact.

So the Berrick family contained both the old gentry's disdain for the 'barbarian Zetlanders' from the mother and an element of the peasant's envious distaste from the father, to put it mildly, for all things 'Scotch' – most of all the lairds themselves, which was so deeply ingrained in Zetlandic peasant culture as to be crucial to its definition.

Doctor Scot's goodwill faced up to centuries of mistrust and maltreatment – 'A good laird is better than a bad wan, but they're aa still lairds,' as one old expression phrased it.

The brothers Lewis and James seemed to embody these two attitudes respectively. James's sympathies lay with his dead father, for the people and against the laird, and so he was glad to be the agent and angel of good fortune, able to record in his day-book that the estate had 'settled the sum of £34 on the new dwelling house at Snouster, tenant J. Herculsen'.

James liked to be liked, and spent as much time as possible in Norbie, supervising the workmen, some said to his neglect of his accounts. He found occasion to stay in Norbie Hall, where none now lived bar the retainer. At times, we know from his letters, the estate felt almost his.

Gabrielsen recounts that the unexpected arrival of Lewis, who had become curious regarding James's lengthy silences in Norbie, brought him back to fiscal reality. When Lewis examined the accounts in detail, he found that James had allowed far too much debt to accrue. He was instructed to demand payment under threat of stopping all credit, which, as the estate shop that Berrick's operated was the only source of luxury in the village, meant severe sanctions.

James protested that it would do no good as 'they are all poor folk and have not a brass farthing to pay with!' But Lewis insisted under penalty of removal from his 'fief' in Norbie, so James agreed. To his surprise a number of accounts were, if not fully settled, then at least brought into the realms of acceptibility. But even so, he recalls in a letter to his mother 'the feeling that I had asked them for every groat they had saved, and that I had bled them dry by so doing'.

Gabrielsen records that Dr Scot was well pleased, when he returned two years later, with the progress that had been made in the renewal of housing. 'The Guid Doctor' was given a rousing welcome by the tenants of Norbie and Valay , and was intending to visit his lands on the isle of Thulay for the first time, had the mists not come down quite entirely.

So while his voyage had not taken him quite as far as he hoped and intended, what he saw of progress elsewhere gladdened his heart. He liked the young factor, James Berrick, and although he had initially worried when Lewis wrote to explain that his younger brother would in fact be taking control of the Norbie project, under Lewis's supervision, the hierarchy seemed effective.

Doctor Scot also liked his new schoolmaster, Gabrielsen, the fellow selected by his mother, and was greatly impressed by the classes he inspected. His mother's choice had been a sound one, as he knew it would. He felt satisfied, as he wrote to her, that 'in truth, Norbie was in a state of positive revolution by comparison with certain other estates in Zetland'. Doctor Scot, with his independent income, felt he was 'showing the way to other lairds. Sheep are not the only alternative, nor emigration. People may live well here, given incentive and assistance.' His 'wealth and knowledge could be dispensed for the common good'.

And then, Gabrielsen suggests, something began to nag at the Laird for the first time, the sense that he should have an heir, to carry all this work of his on. He was by then forty-two years old and had never been particularly close to marriage, having spent most of his mature years at sea. Though he had romantic encounters scattered through his student years in Edinburgh – in particular, the daughter of a professor from St Andrews – he had never seriously considered himself in need of a wife.

However, now that he had Norbie, Valay and Thulay, all seemed changed. In his quiet moments, Scot grew broody, and that summer he openly expressed to Gabrielsen his wish for a son to leave this wonderful and curious place, these 'dear quaint people' who so loved him when all he had really done was the decent thing, in bringing their world a little closer to one fit to live in.

As he was returning to his post at Portsmouth, he stopped a few days with his uncle James in Musselburgh, to break the journey and bring him up to date with Zetland and Norbie, as he found it. Uncle James had arranged a dinner party, at which the forty-two-year-old Doctor Scot by some great fortune met the sixteen-year-old daughter of an old friend of his uncle's, recently returned from Poland where, it turned out, the girl had been born. Her father, Albert Cunninghame, was an engineer who had worked for the Bank of Poland overseeing the construction of their headquarters in Warsaw, through a connection with the Sobieski Stuart family. Her mother was Polish, and she had about her, according to Gabrielsen, a rather exotic beauty which he termed 'Slavic'.

Agnes, as she was called, spoke both Polish and English perfectly, though her English had the faintest hint of her continental youth, as well as being quite fluent in French and Italian – and for someone so young, she carried herself with a grace and maturity that was quite remarkably well defined. Her dress and hair, he wrote to his mother, 'seemed to remind me of an earlier style', worn in London years before but still quite the thing in Poland, obviously. She seemed 'somehow more feminine than the British girl of today'.

Dr Scot, charmed, found himself expansive in her company regarding his career as a surgeon in the navy and his benefactoring stewardship of the vast estate of Norbie, Valay and Thulay. Agnes seemed herself quite impressed by this eminent gentleman, who seemed to have so taken a shine to her. When he wrote to her from Portsmouth afterwards, sending the letter care of his uncle in Musselburgh, to be delivered personally by him to her hand in confidence, she was flattered, and replied. Besides everything else, he was a good-hearted individual, and as she was lonely in Edinburgh, living quietly with her father and his off-putting manner where suitors were concerned, she welcomed Scot's letters and was disappointed when his work prevented them.

The odd couple learned, as missives went 'painfully slowly' north and south between Abercrombie Place and his naval quarters at Portsmouth, that despite the age difference they agreed on many things and 'held the same essential values'. Scot was amazed. Could it be that, at his advanced age, he had 'truly come to know love for the first time?' But could he 'genuinely expect a woman twenty-six years the younger to consider a proposal?'

The answer to the first question seemed obvious. The second he puzzled over as the years passed and she grew to be 'the most dazzling creature' he had ever seen.

This we know from their correspondence and the letters that passed less frequently as time went on, between Doctor Scot and his mother. Yet the fine details of their romance are lost. Where they were when he proposed to her, how he phrased it, whether she hesitated in shock or smiled in gratified anticipation, we know not. But the 'Guid Doctor got his young wife, and wed before he was fifty', in 1859.

After that, their letters cease. But from birth records we find a daughter Agnes, 1861, then a second, Florence, 1863, and then, third in age but first in line to Norbie, Valay and Thulay, Albert John Scot, born at Portsmouth in 1865.

24th June 2000 – Norbie

It's cold, so I take off my boots and slip under the heavy feather quilt. I open the kist again. It's so hard to settle to this. As if it is a kind of final act, that if I once engage with all these papers, then it will precipitate the end, that the launch will bring the sealman ashore and I'll be faced with the terror of identification.

Then the crunch of gravel growing louder interrupts and I go to the window. There's no distant boat motor whining, but the sound of a car, the police car, slowly materialising out of the fog. It's Dr Hart with one of the policemen driving. He pulls up outside.

'You're sure your men wouldn't rather have their flasks in the warmth?' Dr Hart asks him, getting out.

'No, really, no need,' says the policeman. 'We're all equipped. But I'd appreciate the use of your toilet.' He puts on his cap. Then they both pass out of my sight, around to the back of the house. I open the door of my room, so the sound from below will echo up. I hear them coming into the kitchen, go down a distance, down to the main hall, in my bare feet. Stay out of sight. After the flush, and the snap of the door opening, voices.

'So you think you should call it off?' Dr Hart asks.

'I think we have to. Till the mist lifts.'

'I suppose you're right. It's pointless in this weather.'

'The way I see it, if we haven't found the body around the cliffs to the west or the east of the ness, then he didn't fall there. There's too much rock between the cliff face and the shore. He wouldn't have fallen into the sea, so the body would still be there among the rocks, above the tideline.'

'But if he fell off the south face, he'd have gone straight into open water and the tide might have carried him anywhere.'

'Depending on exactly when he fell and which way the current was moving.'

'So we may have to search the whole network of waters before we find him. I'll organise the helicopter as soon as the mist lifts.'

'Do you think there's any point in waiting here today to see if conditions improve?'

'The forecast is bad. More of the same.'

'Yes, I know.'

'I'll think we'll withdraw forces till tomorrow.'

'Probably wisest.'

'Yes.'

Quickly and silently, I go back upstairs. So there's no sunken-eyed sealman coming ashore today. Is it relief I feel, or just familiarity based on known suspense, more waiting? It's not welcome, really. More of this powerful surge of emotion

   overleaping

         me

Lying awake on my bed, I think about Australia, and all the other bits of the British Empire that used to so dominate the map of the world in my primary school classrooms. Huge areas of pink, denoting the dominions and territories. Protectorates.

And thinking about this old laird who has brought the artefacts and the attitudes of imperialism to this northern island, I realise again just how huge a part of the history of this small country the British Empire has been. How emigration and immigration, departure and arrival, have been the pattern whereby so many of the rich folk of this country have captured or consolidated their estates. And the victims, those whose journeys led nowhere but the bottom of the sea. Yes, houses were built of sugar, like the title of that book, or of cotton, or jute, or tobacco. Or slaves. Yes, slaves too. Like the Portuguese, the Scots were quick to take to the seas and, under the flag of union, to grab what they could. At any price, often enough, like Angus MacMillan in Gippsland, down Bendigo way. My father told me about him, this man from Skye who persuaded an aboriginal to guide him to the southern coast, then claimed the land for himself and hunted the natives down like vermin when they complained. The Scots were colonisers as much as colonised. Whip-crackers for the Imperial will. It's a realisation that hits suddenly when confronted by the evidence, like with my friend Andy who went out to Western Australia as part of a theatre group, believing all the world loved a Scotsman, to find himself the subject of serious mistrust among the native Australians in the goldfields. But if you spent your life in Perth, conforming to the traditions, of course you'll think the world loves you. Because you'll only be surrounded by those who believe the same myth as you do, that all the world loves a Scotsman.

No, it may be true to say that in all parts of the world a Scotsman may be loved by somebody, but usually it will be by descendants of those Scots who made that part of the world theirs, by force of hard work and personality – and often, violence. And it's not so strange, then, to think of this place in the wastes of southern Australia, where Gran had gone, taking her only child, my father, only for him to come back, and then to bring her back, from Bendigo. A widow with a son, determined to make a new life, to leave the darkness of the death behind her.

He'd rejected that, he'd committed a folly and had left. An indiscretion, getting a girlfriend pregnant, just as Martin did, but then marrying, then disappearing, running off to sea. It's hard to believe how much the diffident exterior of that little old woman in Blair disguises.

I'm surprised by how much I really want to know about this now. But the laird's souvenir picture book is not the source. There's names and places, but none of my people. And it is my people I'm seeking. I'll have to ask Gran and hear from her just how it all happened. I asked her once, 'Why Bendigo, of all places?' 'Because my cousin was there,' she said. 'Simple as that. No choice. Like walking a tightrope.'

Yet there is something that keeps me from my family papers. I don't know what it is. Some kind of force holds my hand back from lifting it all and beginning to read. It's only paper with inky marks on it. Why should it be so hard to pick up?

Lying back on the bed, I close my eyes.

The fog's inside Norbie Hall and out. In the distance I hear the sound of lambs and ewes bleating, forlorn cries of 'Where am I?' and 'Where are you?' I hope the shepherd is there, to keep the corbies away.

The sheer waste of it. All those years of compromising and where did it get him? Just made him bitter against everybody. Against his own son. I know he resented Martin for being the high achiever, for doing things that life had denied him. University and all that. He was envious. All those years working for the burghers and he ends up here, in the back of beyond. But then that was where he came from, long ago. Bendigo, the back of beyond in the abandoned South Australian goldfields. Yet he carried around this 'we are better than everybody else' attitude. I didn't want to be better than anybody. I just wanted to fit in. I spoke their language – Scots.

But it was shaming for him, the literary man, for his child to be speaking that way. He hated that. He had no sense of Perth as itself, for itself, in itself. What it was to be interior to it, or Scottishness. Independence was a dirty word, as nationalism was forever a dirty word, tainted by the Nazis. To be a socialist and to want an independent Scotland was to him to be National Socialist. I'd argued with him many times over that.

I went on the marches. After the election on April 9th in 1992, I went to Calton Hill in Edinburgh, I joined the Vigil, I wanted to see that flame burn until Scotland was free. I was among the thousands that thronged in George Square, Glasgow. Scotland United! Not because I hated the English. Not because I believed that Scots were different, a race apart, but because I loved that map and its unique traditions. That shape like a prehistoric beast, its head up in the wilds of Sutherland, its shoulders stretching from Buchan Ness to Torridon, its guts the industrious Lowlands, and the Borders its powerful haunches. But the legs were gripped in a rugby tackle by England. They were trapped in the Union. Where England kept Scotland sitting on its shoulders so that it looked bigger to the rest of the world, but lost its own distinctive head in the outline, its sense of itself, Scotland's legs, the very thing that would let it move independently, were trapped.

Ach, that's all nonsense. Now I see it differently. Since my mother's death, since Martin's death, all that political rhetoric is harder to mouth. Or stomach. But back then, because I'd believed Scotland was a separate country with a distinctive culture and I recognised that politically it was meaningless without a parliament, I marched. I protested. I argued with him that I wasn't a nationalist, because the word 'nation' laid the emphasis on nativity, on birth, on the people. While I loved the land, the country, the tradition. I told him I was a Terra-ist, not a terrorist and definitely not a stormtrooper. But he couldn't see it. And now I understand that coming back from Australia when he was a young man maybe meant he didn't feel it was his place, his language. He was a child of Empire. For all his right-on politics, the language of the Empire was what he spoke. The local tongue, my Scots tongue, that was just slang. Bad language, to be erased.

I lie a while, emptying the mind, till at last there's peace. I drift into the stillness, absorbing nothingness, the still fog

that is
choking

CHAPTER SIX

'A CRY FROM ZETLAND'

My pupils were often forced to sit with pools of water under
their bare feet, and the rain pouring in on them through the
roof; so that some make little boxes to keep their books and
copies from being destroyed by wet; and that in winter they
sit shivering on the forms, their hands being so cold that they
can use neither pen nor pencil.

James Gabrielsen

At the time of the census in 1861, the population of the Zetlandic
archipelago reached 31,000 souls, having climbed steadily from a low of
15,000 after smallpox scourged the people in the eighteenth century.

Severely pressed, the prospect of emigration grew ever more attractive
to the poor folk and, as Gabrielsen tells us, 'Australia and New Zealand
were already well known when advertisements began to appear in the
newly founded *Zetland Courier* of 1862, offering "Free and Assisted
Passages to Queensland and South Australia for Single Female Domestic
Servants, Married Couples having no more than three children under ten
years of age, etc. etc."'

From this point onwards, the drift of hungry folk steadily increased,
families old and young, to a barren patch of earth on the margins of the
Empire, many of them to the south island of New Zealand, some to crew
the ships of the world and settle in a foreign harbour, some to establish
trading posts in the north of Canada with the Hudson's Bay Company,
which advertised the same columns for: 'Labourers at £22 per annum,
£23 for sloopers – five years engagement, free passages both ways, good
rations.'

Certain destinations were less distant – many left the islands to join
relatives in one of the little Zetlandic communities that had grown up in

Aberdeen, Leith, South Shields and a few other seaports where Zetland sailors had made their home. According to Gabrielsen, almost 5,000 departed in the 1870s alone, and in total 8,000, more than a quarter of the population, in the twenty years after that zenith of 1861.

The year 1862 saw another of Anders Arthursen's beneficent schemes come to fruition, with the establishment of the first secondary school in the archipelago, at Larvik, the place of his birth. For long a Dutch anchorage and a lawless haven, the eastern town was by then firmly established, secured by a British fort, rather than a Scotch castle, as with the old capital. Larvik had become the capital in everything, leaving Skallvaa outstripped, and Arthursen's fine school capped its predominance. His aim was to provide an 'educational institute such that from it the youth of Zetland could proceed to any university'.

This was a radical vision. Generally, even primary education played only a small part in the life of the islands at this time, though it was open to all. As fees were charged, only some could afford to send their children, when 'even small hands might take a fish or knit a stocking', as Gabrielsen has it. He recalls that his own Christian Society salary of £30 was augmented by these fees – 'three shillings for each term of reading, writing and arithmetic'. The first term of the year began after harvest was home, and ran till New Year's Day. Christmas, not being greatly celebrated at that time in the isles, was not a holiday. The second term began directly after that, and ran until it was time for the 'voar wark', as the spring-time tilling and sowing was known.

As the folk cultivated the ground by means of their little Zetlandic spades and not with ploughs, all able hands were required to assist, and Gabrielsen describes with some pride the graceful speed of 'a team of four delvers, working together like well-drilled soldiers'.

The number of terms any student might attend was few – two or three were normal. For those prodigies who showed some gift, they 'might join the tutorial team as a pupil teacher, and thus further their own education through continued contact with their master'. In some cases, as with James Gabrielsen himself, a few select individuals – 'the native genius which springs up everywhere, however little encouraged – would progress to further study on the Scotch mainland'.

Groomed by the local minister as a future member of the clergy, after studying in Edinburgh, Gabrielsen returned to Zetland fired with zeal to educate his countryfolk. As noted, at first he found a post at Quharv where he met the mother of the new laird of Norbie – Gabrielsen's home. From his obituary in 1899, we learn that through her he came into the circle of one Robert Lang, schoolmaster at Glubbavik. Lang, himself an important figure in Zetland's history, besides teaching the basic curriculum, was expert in land-surveying and navigation, and would take capable students under his wing in order to advance those arts among the population. One of those was James Angus Stoot, later to become the best-loved of the nineteenth century Zetlandic poets.

As Stoot had done before him, Gabrielsen apprenticed himself to Lang informally, around 1850. For two years, he walked over the bare hill from Quharv to Glubbavik to learn all he could from him – particularly navigation, as it was not a topic his Church of Scotland education in Edinburgh had addressed, and he was keen that he should be able to give all his pupils the kind of practical skills that would better equip them for their lives. As time passed, Gabrielsen tells us, there developed an additional reason for his 'faithful trips to the Lang household', and within a couple of years, prior to his appointment to the post in Norbie, he married Catherine – Katie – eldest daughter of Robert Lang, herself a capable and experienced educator who had taught for a decade in her father's school.

No doubt, for his bride, the long sea route round the west ness of Zetland was a journey into the uncivilised provinces, and a long way from the jolly intellectual circles of British Larvik or Scotch Skallvaa. Yet she passionately shared in her husband's dream of educational improvement and so plunged herself into the work of tutoring the children of the parish, alongside her young husband, that the people said they had 'gotten twa dominies fir ae feein'.

The task facing the educational pioneers was not an easy one. Gabrielsen himself states that, on their arrival, 'few missionaries ever opened the door of a school whose prospects were less cheering'. But shared evangelical zeal for the work inspired both Jimmy and Katie – labour that both believed not merely important, but vital to the development of their own people; without it, even when grown to adulthood, they were as children in the world.

The young couple began their married life in the humblest of conditions at Norbie. The old school was reportedly 'little more than a lambhouse' and the picture Gabrielsen paints is pitiful indeed, as we shall shortly see. Their dwelling-house was a modicum better and had the advantage of a more sheltered situation, but it was still bitterly cold in winter.

After the comparatively palatial schoolhouse at Glubbavik, James felt for his wife's condition, and when their first child was born in November of 1862, they struggled to keep him warm, and worried till summer. He was 'completely bald when born and it took a long time for his little pate to cover with downy hair. Yet with tender care he grew stronger, and became in time every inch "peerie Jimmy".'

Other children followed, one every two years, till by 1868 four little Gabrielsens curled up in two little box beds in the tumbledown schoolhouse at Norbie. Gabrielsen writes that 'they helped each to keep the other warm, like whalps'.

Life for the 'Guid Doctor' in Portsmouth during that time must have been similarly taken up with expectation and the accommodation of a swelling family, as Dr and Mrs Scot's three children were all born between 1860 and 1864. I have no record, but it is safe to assume that their circumstances were easier and their accommodation more convenient than that of the Gabrielsens. Dr Scot was less enthusiastic in his improvements to the estate than he had been before his marriage; and with his wife pregnant, they could not countenance the sea-voyage. Besides, the laird had had an unexpected shock in 1864 when he was informed by Berrick the factor that the Minister of Vass, Magnus Thompson, had persuaded the presbytery to back his petition for the building of a new manse. Consequently, the estate had to furnish a sum of £2,200 for its building.

For some time, revenues from rent had slumped. During those 'hungry 40s' and the almost as desperate 1850s, more and more tenants fell into debt, and with the unexpected cost of building the manse added to that of the new houses Dr Scot had insisted upon since he inherited, the accounts suddenly made unpleasant reading.

Happily, all that was forgotten by the time the whole family visited on the first occasion in the summer of 1865 – even the infant heir was in the party. The people of Norbie 'feted the Dr Scots as if they were Queen Victoria and Prince Albert themselves. Wherever they went across the limited tracks that connected one part of the parish to another – there was no connection by road to the rest of the islands – in John Scot the Elder's ancient carriage, people in the fields stopped work, then cheered and waved their sharp little hoes or rickety hayrakes at them. Those nearest the track came over to the dyke, ready to speak should the laird deign to delay – and he often did, introducing his wife, if she had accompanied him.' Then his 'ting a'Polish wife', as she was referred to at first, would lean over and greet them gracefully, 'raising her neatly gloved hand and smiling. And they had such handsome, such fine English-speaking children! It was more than the folk of Norbie could comprehend, after so many years – what was it a score, without a laird? To have the gentry among them again was strangely marvellous, like an honour long denied them,' writes Gabrielsen, who goes on to explain that the laird's choice of wife was immediately popular. It was agreed, as 'the speak o the rigs' carried impressions across dykes from one group of haymakers to the next, that she 'had the air of a queen about her; that she was a fitting figure to rule the roost in Norbie Hall, whatever her age'.

The new 'queen' was amused to learn that among her 'subjects' were a family whose surname was Pole, presumably in remembrance of a forebear from the land of her birth, who had washed up in Zetland somehow. 'Silly though it was,' she wrote to her sister in Fettes Row, 'yet it made me feel not quite so much the stranger.'

Mrs Agnes Scot liked Norbie, she confessed in this letter, particularly that she was the only one of her class in the area, and therefore 'unchallenged'. In Edinburgh, Portsmouth and London, among the drawing rooms, restaurants and church halls of her class, she was simply 'one of many – and if truth be told, being twenty-six years younger than my husband means I am often in company all of a generation older than myself' – which, while it meant she was sometimes indulged because of her youth, seemed in her opinion 'to mitigate against a mature regard of my true qualities on their part'.

While in Zetland that summer, 'da ting a'Polish wife' planned a grand dinner at Norbie Hall and, with Berrick the factor's advice, invited the appropriate functionaries and parties in the parish. The evening ran 'like clockwork'. She had thought of 'absolutely everything'. Crockery that had been polished repeatedly during the house's dormancy without ever being used came out of the creaking cabinets in the kitchen, steam and smoke rose again from the great black ranges and the hall was warm with the marvellous aromas of the dishes she had personally supervised, 'rehearsing thrice', of the game her husband and guests had taken from the estate.

Among those who dressed in their best that fine July evening we find 'Mr and Mrs J Gabrielsen of the Schoolhouse'. Somewhat to the surprise of all, it was these two, the humble guests, who 'sparkled with sophistication' in the rarified atmosphere of the great hall, and not the local gentry. It was the conversation of the schoolmaster and his wife that was sought by the laird, their views that were admired, their goodnight that was the most regretted, when the time came for the non-resident company to make their way home through the 'simmirdim'.

Before leaving, the Gabrielsens had not missed their opportunity to outline the dreadful conditions they continued to work in, and the pressing need for new premises, if their work was not to be impossibly difficult and constrained. It was clear that they had awakened a great desire for learning in the place, by offering practical knowledge, such as navigation and geography that the young sailors could use, alongside the basic subjects and Bible Study.

The growing appetite for learning must be nourished – in feeding that native hunger for knowledge, the laird would be improving not merely the land, but the capacities of those who would work both it and the sea.

So advised, the 'Guid Doctor' Robert Scot, in view of all assembled, agreed that something must be done.

This being their 'Farewell to Norbie' dinner, the summer idyll came to an end soon after, and when the steamer from Skallvaa anchored next in the bay by the 'Haa', the family got into a 'flit-boat' with their large quantities of luggage, and sailed off southwards again, waving goodbye to their 'many good new friends – the dear children had many fond memories to take away with them. Indeed, it has been a summer to remember, blessed with two good voyages, from Leith to Larvik, and the return passage.'

Norbie Hall returned to slumber. The great kitchen cabinets creaked shut and the ranges cooled. Sheets were drawn over furniture and staff reverted to 'skeleton crew'. But the life had returned to it now, and the house was aglow with promise. The twin dolphins that John Scot the younger and his delicate Margaret had selected for the gates in 1799 were 'painted white, and now came to embody the new couple's love'.

Back home at Portsmouth, the Scots felt it hard to settle down again, as Agnes told her sister in Fettes Row: 'Life seems very dreary and ordinary afterwards to the children. Robert and I have been particularly impressed, nay inspired, by the Gabrielsens and the marvellous work they are doing. The young schoolmaster is an omnivorous reader, and is collecting a library to which the people around him have free access, while his wife is a delightful person for a companion.'

The Scots agreed they should help the Gabrielsens as far as was possible. He was apparently a great scholar of all things Scandinavian, and a passionate recorder of all that was in danger of being lost to the general public regarding the old customs, the folklore and history of Zetland. He had begun contributing articles on these subjects to magazines and newspapers such as *The Scotsman* in the south. 'Indeed,' Mrs Scot writes, 'Gabrielsen is a very remarkable and agreeable man. His talk is full of information, anecdote and humour. His wife too is a splendid woman, and every bit her husband's ideal helpmeet.' On this, she assures us, both the 'Guid Doctor' and his 'ting a'Polish wife' were perfectly in agreement.

What impressed the Scots most of all, however, was the absolute trust that the people of the parish had clearly placed in the person of the schoolmaster. He was one of them, but educated to a high degree, indeed, far beyond the level required of a parish teacher. They went to him for help with all their difficulties, and he thoroughly understood them. With such a powerful figure, such a will for good at his shoulder, Dr Scot felt heartened in his desire for 'improvement', and Agnes with him. The appeal of the place increased for them. A 'nostalgia had been born, for our own land, our own place'.

Practicalities remained paramount, however, so the Scots discussed matters reasonably afterwards and agreed that while Norbie was a magical place where they could be happy together in retirement, and where the people needed them, there were serious financial considerations. But soon the pull of the north became too strong, and Dr Scot began lengthy negotiations to take a pension from the Navy, and they began to plan to move their family to Norbie on a permanent basis. Once satisfied the terms were right, and he was assured he would have full benefits, so that they could enjoy life while continuing to do the good work of improvement among 'these dear people' fate had entrusted to them, he set the date for action as 1869.

Agnes made plans to begin shipping their developing collection of foreign curios and items of antiquarian interest northwards slowly, cataloguing, wrapping and casing. But when, a few weeks after sending the first detachment, she received a letter from Katie Gabrielsen pleading with her to intercede with her husband for the new premises adverted to, she was hesitant.

Dr Scot replied, and was forced to explain the estate was 'not presently in a sufficiently well balanced fiscal state for great outlay, having as yet not defrayed the cost of the new manse in Vass, and the construction of the new dwelling-houses built since 1850.' In future years, he assured Gabrielsen, there would be better opportunity for such a venture. But in order to show the proprietor's great goodwill to their brave and valuable work, the estate would happily grant to Gabrielsen any plot of available land he chose, as the site for the new school. And when finance was forthcoming, he could construct there a schoolhouse with schoolroom, with peat and crofting rights attached.

It did not take the Gabrielsens long to decide. They had kept in mind a particular location all along, in the hope they might get it, and had already surveyed it, using skills learned from Robert Lang, her father. They had decided upon it as the most central position in the area; no pupil should have to walk more than a mile and a half to get there; it was well above the floodlands and it had the best possible outlook, over the green meadow fields of Norbie to the two freshwater lochs; to the north, the beach beyond and the ridge of cliffs that faced St Magnus Bay, with the pretty low green isle of Papay on the horizon. And on a clear day, the majesty of Thulay's steeps could be seen on the western horizon. It was a view to inspire both teacher and pupil. There would be a brand new boiler stove capable of heating the premises, and the children would bring sufficient peats among them to keep it burning, as in the old premises. The flue-system was designed to burn longer on less fuel and the full round shape was such that it would radiate heat throughout the whole room most efficiently. It was the latest such design. This was the stuff of their dreams, Gabrielsen records.

The schoolmaster wrote to Dr Scot with his choice of land and found it blessed, by return of post, two months later. The dream now had ground on which to grow at least, and they sketched draft after draft of their ideal premises – not only the new schoolroom, but a schoolhouse attached, the future home to their growing family. It was 'their great hope'.

Meanwhile the good work in the old Norbie school went on among the many draughts, leaks and puddles. Word of the Gabrielsens' successes spread and, as class numbers grew sharply, they began to formulate a plan. The numbers now enrolling were far too many for the 'old lambhoose'.

So James Gabrielsen obtained a list of all the schoolmasters in Scotland from the Board in Edinburgh and wrote individually to each, explaining their predicament, asking that each schoolmaster might subscribe one shilling for the building of the new Norbie school.

News of his scheme travelled, and the novelty of it and its situation brought the attention of the press. The following letter was published in *The Scotsman*, outlining his case:

'A Cry from Zetland'

Society Schoolhouse, Norbie
Zetland, February 24, 1869

Sir,
I am engaged in soliciting a subscription of one shilling from each of the parochial schoolmasters of Scotland to assist in rebuilding my dwelling-house, which has fallen into such a state of disrepair as to be no longer habitable, and beg through the medium of your columns to tender my grateful thanks to the undermentioned schoolmasters, who have so

promptly and generously responded to the letter I lately addressed to them.

Will you allow me, for the information of those gentlemen who have not only sent me what I asked, but in many cases more, and whose friendly notes have cheered me, and those from whom I still hope to hear, to give a fuller statement of our situation and circumstances?

A school under the Society in Scotland for Propagating Christian Knowledge was established in the parish sometime about 1780, but the school premises never were good, and it always has been with us 'the pursuit of knowledge under difficulties'. On my appointment in 1858, I found education at the lowest possible ebb. The attendance for several years previous had been very small and very irregular. Few could write, and fewer still could cipher. All the young men were common sailors, but, for want of education, not one of them ever rose or thought of rising in his profession. Few teachers ever opened school whose prospects were less cheering.

I have, I think, succeeded in awakening at least a desire for instruction. Books and newspapers are now in demand. The attendance at school during the last few years has been largely on the increase. Sixty-three scholars have been enrolled during the current half year, the highest number since the school was first established. Several of my pupils have passed their examinations creditably, and are now officers in the merchant service, and the Society's inspector has on every case reported favourably of us.

I fear, however, that if the house be not rebuilt soon the salary will be withdrawn, and the people will be deprived of the means of education at the time they are beginning to appreciate its value. And when I tell you that my house is very bad, and has been very uncomfortable for long, that I estimate the cost of rebuilding it at £150, and am without funds, and that the distance to the nearest school is six miles, without a road, and across one of the bleakest moors in Zetland, I have said enough to elicit the sympathy of everyone engaged in the arduous work of education.

There are, I know, numerous demands on the liberality of the people of the South, and nothing but dire necessity would ever have induced me to make this appeal. But I cannot think of the people among whom I have lived so long being deprived of the school without my doing everything in my power to aid them, and would fain hope that there are several among your numerous readers who will assist me in rebuilding the schoolhouse and thus secure to the people of this remote parish the blessings of education.

My school is equally as uncomfortable as my dwelling-house, but I have a better prospect of getting it rebuilt. If the children attending warm, well-lighted, well-ventilated schools in the south knew that my pupils were often forced to sit with pools of water under their bare feet, and the rain pouring in on them through the roof; that some of them make little boxes to keep their books and copies from being destroyed by wet; and that in winter they sit shivering on the forms, their hands being so cold that they can use neither pen nor pencil – they would, I am sure, follow the example of the excellent children attending the parochial school of Clochean, Aberdeenshire; and each of them would give their teacher a half-penny to send to me to help me to build a comfortable schoolroom. I shall be happy to acknowledge the smallest trifle I may receive.

James Gabrielsen, Esq.
Schoolmaster

He then proceeds to list all the subscribers and their donations, ranging from 'The Earl of Zetland' himself at the head of the social scale, to 'Mrs McM of Morningside' of the middle, to 'Scholars attending Donibristle Colliery School' at the earthier end. He concludes with the following postscript:

I shudder to think of having to pass another winter in my present premises, and am, therefore, anxious to commence the building of my house and school in May. Should any more of your readers feel inclined to assist us, their subscriptions will be thankfully received and acknowledged, by John T Reid Esq, artist, 2 George Place, Leith Walk, or by myself. As many schoolmasters and others have been at a loss how to send their collections, I may mention that a Post Office order on Larvik, payable to me, will reach me easily.

When we read in Gabrielsen's memorial history of the parish, that the winter of 1869 seemed 'to begin even before the harvest was in, when snow fell in September and lay so long that the crofters had to take the ears from the stalks where they poked out of the snowdrifts', then the plaintive appeal seems all the more pressing.

The readers of the national press were kind, as we can see from the long list of subscribers that grew steadily from this point onwards, and his fellow schoolmasters did not let him down, yet with the call on charity made by the Crimean War, the sums raised were not enough. Although the Gabrielsens had wasted no time in beginning work as soon as they could, buying materials and organising the team of local volunteers that came forward to construct foundations, the completion of the project remained impossible for lack of money.

As time went on funds continued to trickle in, but progress was slow. Gabrielsen found himself in the unfortunate position whereby he could find the money only to complete the building either of the schoolmaster's house or of the schoolroom itself. He confesses himself to be 'sorely tested, as to motivations, whether social or personal – and what alloy of the two I must employ to make them fuse as strong as one inseparable material'.

Let us leave our westward parish for a brief diversion into a contemporaneous narrative, offering a different view of life in Zetland in the summer of 1869, for contrast's sake. It is compiled from the letters of the author Robert Louis Stevenson who that year voyaged north, as had the wizard Sir Walter Scott forty-five years before, aboard the Lighthouse Commission's yacht.

Stevenson was nineteen years old, and far from the sophisticated author of future years. He appears here as filial son accompanying father, still attached to his 'Dear Mamma' in Edinburgh by a stream of correspondence. Yet a writer he undoubtedly was, even at this tender age, as we shall see.

Stevenson's party arrived in Larvik just prior to midsummer of that year, after having sailed north via the Ness of Cat and the Orcades. They landed about eight o'clock in the evening and on arriving ashore 'saw many people on a gravel spit at the corner, drying fish on the baked white stones'. Stevenson notes how the houses 'present their one gable to the water, which leaves their foundations, and their other to the main street, which runs parallel to the line of the shore'.

The town was alive with folk when they alighted there, and Stevenson notes a resemblance to a village of the Riviera, heightened by 'narrow side-lanes, which climb the hillside on long flights of ruinous steps between high houses on either hand.' The party then went up to Cromwell's fort, he observing with his writer's eye how it 'overhangs the water with a circuit of heavy grass-grown walls, backed by mounds, supported by ruinous buttresses and pierced by some four-arched gateways', and that 'sea-pink blooms thickly among the lightened crevices of the old stonework.'

Generally the fort made a rather melancholy impression on the young Stevenson – he was told the story of a recent prisoner, a young man sentenced to forty-five days' imprisonment for shooting ducks at Onst, who had hanged himself 'behind the midmost of these blank windows before the first night had come ...'

After having the full tour of Fort Charlot, four of its gentlemen came out with them to 'take grog on board. Among these was Captain McKinnon of the *Eaglet*, a Revenue cutter, who told him about the smuggling, which the Faroe fishing so encouraged. Apparently on their first voyage of the season to Faroe, they never smuggle; for should they be caught, they would be detained too long to get away again; but on their second they bring home as much as they can get, for they fear not apprehension. McKinnon said they did not think themselves dishonest, because the Zetlanders believed that smuggling was their right – yet they gave the customs no little trouble by their disguise of it.

'In these bright nights of the north, he cannot get near them before they have thrown everything overboard; but on some occasions he manages to catch them napping,' Stevenson writes. 'One foggy night last summer, for example, he left the cutter behind an islet and took a circuit with his gig. They did not observe him till he was close at hand; but when they did they lost no time. He saw them tumbling tobacco overboard out of a great big sack; and when he boarded, the scuppers were awash with brandy and a man below was still staving in the casks.'

The captain then told the visiting party the habits of one character, called 'Preaching Peter', who, whenever he came back from the Faroe fishing, sent word around to announce he was going on a 'missionary tour', and travelled about preaching in all the hamlets. After he gave the benediction, the congregation would crowd round. 'There were no more Biblical pronouncements – instead of 'Peace go with you,' it was 'How many do you want?' So he improved the people's souls while he filled his own purse.

Stevenson learned from Dr Campbell that the famed writer George MacDonald, author of many tales including *Phantastes* and *The Princess and Curdie,* had passed through Zetland bound for Norway in a yacht a short time before, and that he had treated MacDonald for an inflammation of the knee. He went on to explain that leprosy and lazar houses had 'lingered into last century in this *Ultima Thule* of the ancients; and was succeeded by smallpox so violent that it swept away one-third of the population'.

On the distant isle of Thulay, he said that out of two hundred souls there were but six men left to bury the dead. They 'tried inoculation in its more violent early form, but it killed one out of every four or five patients. But there was one local man, Joannie Notions, a jack-of-all trades – a wig-maker, tailor, shoemaker, fish-curer, and haphazard "doctor" – who thought of weakening the matter introduced. He dried the pus on glass plates, mixed it with camphor, hung it for long enough in peat smoke, and finally buried it for years. When this long ceremony was at an end, he used it and, out of three or four thousand, lost not one life; but his useful discovery was eclipsed by general vaccination which followed shortly after.'

Closing his letter to 'Dear Mamma', the young Stevenson allows himself some of the poetic licence he would become so famous for:

'Four-bells – midnight – has rung some time ago. Upstairs it is perfectly calm, the sky very dark with mottling of white and gray cirrus, and the yellow moon half out, half in the clouds above the houses of the town

– the whole thing mirrored to perfection in the water of the Sound. Some fishermen are singing on the shore, probably in imitation of Italy; for they please themselves by calling Larvik the northern Venice.'

The Zetlandic sixareen boats he describes as 'crook-backed, with high stem and bow', and the appearance of this fleet upon 'the still, bright waters' was like that of 'Indian canoes. It verily required the faint scent of peat smoke to remind you you were still in Scotland.'

The following day, the lighthouse yacht party went ashore to Reverend Sanders of the Established Church, who gave a most excellent sermon, 'swarming with epigrams'. As instances, Stevenson quotes: 'The Bible required the gloss of the great teacher: the book of Moses had to be set up in the gospel type.' 'Yes, my friends, we find the devil in the narrow way as an angel of light – as a preacher extolling the righteousness of the everlasting God,' and 'Men's consciences may be elastic; but Heaven's gate is not.'

In the afternoon, they went again to the church to hear Rev. Sanders and were surprised to see that the congregation had doubled in size, because 'the people, lured by the long clear night, sit up to all hours and do not rise till nine or ten'. After church, the visitors went for a walk behind the town 'to see a Pict's house … From a sandy point, on which the little ripple lays curves of strange-looking emerald slime, there stretches out a causeway of rough stones … The whole islet, thus joined to the mainland, is buried in stones and stone ramparts, with many unroofed underground chambers; and the centre is occupied by a hollow round tower not unlike to a lime-kiln. In the thickness of its walls are passages along which I had to creep on all-fours, stairs with steps three inches wide, round chambers buried in perfect darkness, and small doorways, like coal-hatches in a modern house, which seems to have led by covered ways to the outlying subterranean rooms.'

Clearly the young writer's imagination was fired by the burg of Klikimin, and not in altogether pleasant ways. The idea that the people who built and occupied it may have been no more than three feet high he finds 'singularly disgusting … I fancied the place swarming with little dirty devils talking outlandish jargon and brandishing their flint-head axes; and, with the natural human hatred for swarms of minute life, I confess that I brought myself to share in the horror of these old "Peghts" which is felt in the Orcades and Zetland to this day.'

The visitors then walked up the road, into a valley with a small stream. The lowlands Stevenson found inland were cultivated 'after a skimble-skamble fashion: ruinous walls ran here and there, sometimes wandering aimlessly into the middle of the fields and there ending with as little show of reason, sometimes gathering into gross heaps of loose stones, more like an abortive cairn than an honest dry-stone dyke; for crop, it seemed that docken and the yellow wild mustard, which made bright patches every here and there, were much more plentiful than turnip or corn. Mixed up with this unwholesome-looking wilderness were thatched cottages bearing every sign of desertion and decay, except the curl of smoke from the place where the chimney should be and was not; and in some cases presenting bare gables and roofless walls to the bitter ocean breeze. The uplands were a sere yellow-brown, with rich, full coloured streaks of peat and gray stretches of outcropping rock. The whole place looks dreary and wretched; for here nature, as Hawthorne would have said, has not sufficient power to take back to herself what the idleness and absence of man has let go. There is no ivy for the ruined cottage; no thorn or bramble for the waste wayside.'

They then returned to the Larvik foreshore, and went down to the waterstair, where their boat awaited. Before embarking, Stevenson recalls how they had 'waved a handkerchief for the gig, a romantic action which made me remember many old daydreams when it was my only wish to be a pirate or a smuggler'.

The islands of Zetland held a certain fascination for the young Stevenson, clearly, and when, years later, he came to write his *Treasure Island*, the map which he drew of that distant rock bore a remarkable similarity to that of the most northerly Zetlandic isle of Onst, which he visited on the northmost leg of their voyage.

From there the Lighthouse yacht sailed for the southern headland at Zumburg, where a substantial lighthouse, first lit in 1821, had been built by 'Grandfather Stevenson' following his voyage with Sir Walter Scott.

This, the southern most point of Zetland, as Onst is the most northerly, is joined to the mainland by a narrow isthmus of low sand-hills and thin grass. There is shallow tidal water to one hand, and the sea batters the other. Inshore of this isthmus, the land is high and bare, with the huge crags of Quhytefell Head jutting out into the wild ocean a few miles off.

Anchoring in the shoal pool, they 'rowed to a small slip on the beach with some gray houses at its head, one of which purported to sell "Tea and Tobacco" with blotches where "Spirits and Ale" had been painted out – a silent commentary on the success of the Scotch temperance league among the people'. They had then two miles to walk up to the narrow headland, 'which rises in precipitous cliffs to the east and on the west, from whence it stretches down to the sea in a gentle sweep of spring turf. However, the voes run in on either hand with a rush of water and a screaming of gulls, and leave but a neck of land three hundred feet above the surf. The spray flies over it in clouds.' Down in these voes, they saw white gulls sitting on their eggs and the young ones beginning to walk about, before they visited the light. 'The light's setting is thus a splendid one, and is itself three hundred feet high.'

Among the sand-hills by Zumburg Head, on a grassy mound stand some low and ruinous house-walls, which are all that remains of Jarlshof, so often mentioned in *The Pirate*. Stevenson appears from his letters not to have realised that the house itself, as it appears in Scott's fiction, was the product of the older novelist's fancy in all but these evocative ruins.

A little way above this, they came to an elegant new house built by the proprietor Mr Bruce of Zumburg. Bruce welcomed the visitors and toured them around the premises, which were rather Gothic in appearance despite their lack of years. During its erection, he explained there was much disturbance among the masons; the Aberdeen men, who were members of one Trade Union, refused point blank to work with Zetland men who were not. The people, Stevenson notes, called this new house of the laird, with picturesque simplicity worthy of a primitive country, and 'verily refreshing after miles of Laurel Groves and Ivy Lodges', 'the New Building of Zumburg' – which he called 'a hollow boom as it were of bursting surf'.

They took dinner with Bruce and went on board again, passing easily through a jabble of short cresting waves which, in spring tides and heavy gales, becomes the fatal Zumburg Roost which caused Scott discomfort.

From there they headed west, to the remotest isle of the archipelago, the famed rock fortress of Thulay. Here the need for a lighthouse was still unmet. The coast of Thulay was the wildest and most unpitying they had yet seen. 'Continuous cliffs face the sailor who would make landfall, from one to fourteen hundred feet high, torn by huge voes and echoing caverns. They line the bare downs with scarcely a cove of sand or a practicable cleft in the belt of precipice. The harbour is but the merest mouth of the merest stream. At intervals, the steep coast runs out into strange peninsulas, square bluff headlands, crooked heads and feet, and plumb faces of stone. Every feature was once named in the ancient Thulay tongue, but after the plague many meanings were forgotten – only the sounds remain, as puzzling to the native as to the visitor. Everywhere,' Stevenson notes, is 'tinged with the faint green of some sort of lichen.'

Close by their landfall was the long, bleak shore onto which the Duke of Medonia's vessel, the flagship of the great Armada, was driven in a storm, as the ragged tail of the sea force attempted to make its way back to Spain around the north of Britain. It was strange to the visitors, 'to think of the great old ship with its gilded castle of a stern, its scrollwork and emblazonry, and with a Duke of Spain on board, beating her brains out on the coast of Thulay.'

As they pulled into the tiny cove, a tall thin man, with a small ragged boy running along at his heels like a dog, came down to the shore as if to meet them. The man said he was only four days old in Thulay, and on their asking after his name and position, replied: 'My name is not important, gentlemen. I am a servant of the Lord Jesus Christ, and have come here to preach His word.' They learned later that he had been sent over in Mr Berrick of Roovik's sloop, and occupied the room which that gentleman to whom the island belongs keeps for himself in the minister's house. Stevenson continues thus: 'To this he showed us the way; and the minister himself, Mr Macfarlane, led us to see whatever was interesting. The appearance from the landing-place is very picturesque; for the land, sloping gradually upward, ends in the clear-cut, sharp and singularly wild and savage outline of the cliffs. It was toward this farther side, that Mr Macfarlane escorted us. We first saw the schoolhouse, a dark, damp apartment, wet with rain droppings, and half-roofed with wreck-timber thrown across the rafters: it required the "tawse" and the ragged school-books to remind you where you were.

'On our way thence to some strange holes in the land, we heard that our first friend was one Lord Teynham – the family name, Curzon. It was strange to find a nineteenth-century nobleman preaching the gospel in desolate Thulay. Here as nowhere else they have set their faces against change – and nowhere are the natives more tight-lipped about the past. For instance, the people are very unwilling, Mr Macfarlane mentioned, to speak about the Armada sailors – indeed, almost the only fact they will communicate is that, when hand in hand, the shipwrecked Spaniards reached right across the island. Their reason for this is easily understood: they believe it throws discredit on their ancestors; for it was said many of these unfortunate foreign seamen were murdered and eaten; the Spaniards having been unfortunate enough to come ashore in midst of a famine. With so many extra mouths to fill, and no prospect of finding food for even the natives, it appears that men became as beasts. But there can be little question that the Duke himself must have consented to the deed; for how could the unarmed islanders – even now only three hundred in number – have kept head against Medonia and his sailors and soldiers? And again, if such were the case, how did so many escape, by way of Kirkcaldy, to their own country?

'The Armada seem to have left little trace in Thulay now, beyond a bayonet and the like, with the exception of the coloured woollen work which they are said to have taught to the islanders. It must have been a strange sight – all these southerners, fresh from the oranges of Seville, living in filthy cottages on the wildest island of our northern archipelago: very rusty, I doubt not, were their cuirasses, and very ragged the lace, and ruffle, and sash of the Spanish grandee officers, ere they had done creeping among the gios and caverns of the immense coastline. What kind of fatal hunt went on among that rocky terrain, man pursuing man for food? Were the chased given sporting chance, or secretly dispatched?

'Before this horror tale was heard, we had reached what we had come to see. The land, as I said, slopes almost continuously from the low shore on the Zetland side of the island to the cliff top at the other; but in two places, the ground suddenly leaves your feet and you see a huge rocky tank, some seventy feet deep, with a great arched doorway into the ocean, right through the hill-side: the noise of a stone dropped in reverberates with a hollow boom and splash up the rough sides on either hand. Close by there lay a fine, graceful curve of exposed beach, surrounded by steep red cliffs, and strangely marked by a great red stack or isolated pillar, standing among the heaped brown sea-weed on the sweep of the bay. We were told this western coast of Zetland was known as "The Red Coast".

'On our return we entered the church, a cottage set with plain unvarnished wooden benches and a ditto pulpit – neat and tidy, however, and seating for two hundred and fifty. It was surprising to see such regularity in so rugged a land, where nothing seems to obey any pattern.

'Outside was a small graveyard, with headstones consisting of rough slates about a foot high thrust into the ground. On two alone are there any letters, and these two are made of wood and cut by a man in the island. They were two of the oldest men that had ever died in the place, and yet the ages were but sixty-one and sixty-four respectively. Intermarriage and bad homes make them a weak lot; and almost none of the women, as I hear, have good eyes. One of these inscriptions I had the curiosity to copy, by reason of the error it contains. "In memorium of T Wilson. Born January 5th, 1801. Died January 13th 1865, aged sixty-four years and eight days. Time flies." My father took out his knife to alter the mistake; but Mr Macfarlane stopped him, as the people would have looked on it as insulting the dead. Apropos of tombstones, the same gentleman told us that there were some lettered stones on the hill-top, but what the inscriptions meant he was unable to tell us. They believed them to be holy relics left by the Papas, the original settlers of the eighth century or thereabouts, from whom the early faith was handed down untouched by Reformation until the 1700s. Sadly a plague had wiped out much of the ancient knowledge, as it was a purely oral tradition.

'From the church we proceeded to the store, where tea, teapots, linen and blankets are sold to the inhabitants; and where the inhabitants expose, on the other hand, their quaint-patterned, parti-coloured, knitted socks, gloves, and mittens.

'During our absence his lordship had been taking Mr Curry about among the sick folk; and he said that of all the miserable people he had ever seen, they were the worst. Two twin old women of six-and-eighty years, literal skeletons, lived in misery and sickness in a wretched den waited on by the daughter of one of them, now well up in years herself. One of these had burnt her foot the day before, and the cloth she had wrapped about it was no finer than ordinary sacking. Their twin wailing was a dreadful sound; they seemed to complete each other's utterances as if they had but one mind; their only hope, they said, was in death.

'Such more or less seems the condition of the people. Beyond reach of all communication, receiving such stray letters as may come not once in six long months, with diseased bodies, and wretched homes, they drag out their lives in the wildest and most barren island of the North. Their crops, raised with often hard labour from a cold and stony soil, can only support them for three months out of the twelve. Indeed, their only life is from the sea. It is the sea that brings the fish to their nets: it is the sea that strews their shore with the spoils of wrecked vessels. (Thus we saw in the minister's house a huge German musical box saved from the wreck of the *Lessing*.)

'In Scrabster Roads, Tuesday 22nd. This letter goes tonight; hoping all are well, believe me your ever affectionate, RL Stevenson.'

It is Sunday morning again, early. Habit has me awake, ready to preach. A week ago I felt close to completion of this historical sketch but I have not made the progress I hoped. I find it more difficult than I had imagined, to weave the many threads together. Around my study, books and papers are scattered, my normal fastidiousness forgotten; these are now filleted of their importance and their particular interest.

Ahead of me still lie three bundles, clipped together, the papers ordered chronologically. Photocopies: one, schoolmaster Gabrielsen's unfinished history of the parish; the second, papers on the Scots of Norbie; and the third, relevant passages I have culled from various Government reports conducted on the 1870s and '80s on the precarious state of life in the archipelago. Underneath these on my desk, the barefooted pilgrim's story, the cause of all this.

This man's appearance in my life marked the beginning of the end of everything I had taken for granted prior – my happy marriage, my work in the ministry, my choice to serve God and care for His children rather than have a family of my own. Dear Margaret agreed. Or did she? Even this now seems something I took for granted, without her smiling reassurance at hand. She always said she agreed. But were there wistful moments maybe, when she thought about children? Missed having them? I still cannot believe she has finally gone. I still expect a little knock on the study door, her cheery greeting, the offer of a cup of tea. If only she would peep into my study again, as she used too. All those years, my close companion, at my shoulder.

How brief a life! No more than a year, begun in the dark and the mists of midwinter, ended there too, and in between the rising sap of spring, the fruitful days of mature growth, the storms of leaf-fall, the eternal illusion of hope till winter's snows, and finally new birth in Christ

Zetland's affairs were much in the public arena, and under national scrutiny, during the late nineteeth century. The work of Anders Arthursen, and the many tales of famine and deprivation, had gained sympathy. This, coupled with the success of Zetland crafts spurred by the gift of a much-discussed 'work of art' in the form of a great 'lace hap' or shawl to Queen Victoria, gave the isles a prominence in the consciousness of Britain they had not known before.

Gabrielsen's imaginative scheme towards building a new school 'had fired interest in our parish in particular, and so Norbie too enjoyed a brief fame hardly worthy of its size or situation'.

Since Arthursen's first attempt to break the landowner's stranglehold on the fish trade on Valay, there had been increasing disapprobation voiced regarding the landlords and their methods. Truck had been illegal in Britain since 1831, but the law had proved difficult to enforce. In 1871 a government appointed commission investigated, 'although at a safe distance from the facts'. As the report made clear, 'Time would not allow of a local inquiry at Zetland, nor can an inquiry be adequately conducted into the Truck which is alleged to prevail there otherwise than upon the spot. No opinion accordingly is offered either as to the extent of, or the remedy for, the alleged evils; but the necessity of some investigation by Her Majesty's Government into the condition of these islands seems made out.'

And so a Second Truck Commission was proposed, which would travel to the islands concerned and hear testimony of all parties. Having been appointed by a warrant dated December 23rd 1871, one of the Commissioners, William Guthrie, was directed to proceed to Zetland and institute an inquiry there under that Act. Gabrielsen, in attendance, records the following.

'Guthrie, a man from a farming family from Kyle, had studied Law at Glasgow University and thereafter devoted himself to the literary aspect of the Scottish legal system. From 1866 to 1871 he acted as law reporter for *The Scotsman* and *The Glasgow Herald*; from 1867 to 1873, he edited the *Journal of Jurisprudence*, and championed the cause of the Established Church, intelligently enough, in a pamphlet *The Democratic View of the Church Question*. As first official recognition of these services he was appointed one of the authorised reporters of the Court of Session in 1871, when he was also appointed a Commissioner under the Truck Act, and he went on to make an elaborate and highly literary report on the fishing and knitting industries of Zetland, based on 16,887 questions he had put to various witnesses:

> I went to Zetland at the beginning of the year, a time when the seafaring people of the country are generally at their homes, and at once began to take evidence with regard to the system of barter or truck which prevails in various trades and industries in these islands. Evidence was taken respecting the hosiery or knitting trade, in which a very large proportion of the women of the country are engaged. Evidence was also taken with regard to the fishing trade, which in its different branches affords employment for part of the year to the whole of the male population, with few exceptions ... It appears to be quite possible that fishermen should receive the whole of their earnings in shop goods, and I understand that the truth of the allegation that most of the men actually are so paid, and that they have no option but to take goods for their fish,

at prices fixed by the merchant, was intended to be the main subject of this inquiry ...

The only cases in which fishermen came forward voluntarily for the purpose of stating grievances, on hearing of the Commission, were those in which they are bound by their tenure to deliver their fish to the proprietor of the ground, or his tacksman. As in all these cases they are also supplied with goods from the landlord's or tacksman's shop, it was necessary to hear fully what the men had to say, even although their complaints appeared to involve a question as to the tenure of land, as well as the payment of wages.

At the public enquiry in the old Toll House of Larvik, the benches and the gallery were full to overflowing with many nominated representatives from all the parishes of the archipelago, who had all converged on the little capital, bearing the testimonials and wishes of their electorate. Gabrielsen tells us the town 'was alive with a vital energy, as if something hitherto unimaginable might be about to become actual', and that the atmosphere was charged with a 'sense of the epochal'.

Gabrielsen, who as we know was greatly taken up with the cause of his people, had travelled by land and sea all the way from Norbie in the far west, in order to record these historic events, and notes that at the outset 'complaints about fishing tenures were made by tenants on the estates of Zumburg and Quhendal, and on the island of Bura. It was also clear to the Commissioners, from the evidence cited, that an obligation to fish for the laird existed and was enforced on a number of the estates. On some others, tenants were nominally free, although how far they were able to exercise choice was doubtful.'

At first Guthrie addressed the assembled company as one, and enquired of whoever would speak, 'Are you not at liberty to make your own bargain about the land, the same as any other tenant in Scotland is?' To which a voice from high in the gallery called out in reply, 'We are no awar o that.'

Guthrie made a note and continued: 'Suppose you were to object to making this bargain, could you not get a holding elsewhere?' From the crowd below, on the benches this time, another voice answered him: 'It is not likely we would get a holding elsewhere.'

When Leonard, one of Guthrie's fellows, asked why, then a third voice arose: 'We wid very likely be deprecated as no being legal subjects, an the heritors would all ken that we were not convenient parties to give land to.' Another voice added: 'That is one reason; and another reason is, that holdings are sometimes not very easily to be gotten.'

'And do the same conditions exist elsewhere in Zetland?' the questioner continued.

'So far as I know, they prevail all over the country, or nearly so,' said the informant.

'You think that, if you were trying to move, you would not get free of a condition of that sort?' asked Guthrie.

'We might get free of it for a time, but by next year the parties to whose ground we had removed would bind us down to the same thing.'

'But supposing all the men were united in refusing to agree to such conditions, there could be no compulsion upon them?'

'They have not the courage, I expect, to make such an agreement among themselves,' said the main spokesman again, a heavily bearded fellow from the north of the main island, who Gabrielsen identifies as Erasmus Rattar.

Guthrie leafed through the papers in front of him, and gazing at a sheet he then selected, said: 'It is proper to call attention here to the fact that in agricultural subjects held from Martinmas to Martinmas on a yearly tack, the forty days' warning to remove, which is held sufficient by the law of Scotland, is objected to, with some reason, as too short.'

Rattar, in response, made the following statement: 'The forty days' warning given before Martinmas may be well enough for tenants in a town like Larvik, who have nothing except a room to live in and can flit without a thought, but it is very disagreeable for a tenant holding a small piece of land and livestock as we do. As soon as our crop is taken in, we maun start work immediately, and make ready the rigs for next season. We have to manure, collect peats, and prepare for thatching our houses, and maybe by Martinmas have expended as muckle as six pounds' worth of labour and stuff on our crofts. It is a hard fate then to be turned off our holdings, receiving only forty days' notice, and perhaps only getting £1 or £2 for all that labour.'

'Do you think you would be more at liberty to dispose of your fish, and to deal at any shop you pleased, if you were entitled to longer warning?' asked Leonard.

'I don't think the warning would alter anything of that, but if I kent that I was to be turned out at Martinmas, I would start to the fishing earlier, and get a muckler price for my efforts, instead of working upon my land.'

A general hum of agreement passed through the company. Rattar nodded in response, looking around at those who applauded his sentiments, and receiving their looks of gratitude with grace.

A number of tenants came forward to speak and the Truck Commissioners then took evidence from certain merchants who had been summoned to advance argument in justification of continuance of the system. Notable among those was Lewis Berrick, leading partner in the firm factoring Dr Scot's estates.

The elder Berrick brother was a man of natural authority, well-educated, tall and aristocratic in his bearing, who although at this stage 'not yet in full command of his own destiny, having not acquired the capital necessary to fulfil his ambition, nonetheless behaved as if he were already a duke,' as Gabrielsen tells us. Guthrie and fellows noted the awe, if not outright fear, he appeared to inspire among the peasantry that had previously been forthcoming in freedom of speech.

When invited to comment in explanation of the system, Berrick said that it had long been accepted that 'the man whose farm cannot keep his family until settlement comes, as a matter of course, to the fish-curer's store for assistance, and even the most thriving and prosperous man with money in the bank almost invariably has an account at the shop. There is a mutual understanding that when a merchant buys a man's fish, he ought in fairness to take at least a part of his goods at that merchant's shop.'

Guthrie then asked of him, 'Do you think a man would stand permanently in arrears with the shop if he had money in the bank?'

Berrick answered, 'No, but in many cases, if I settled with him in January, I believe he would deposit a £10 note from that year's settlement and begin a new account with me, get a new boat, and let it stand on the shop's account until the following year.'

'Is it a common thing for men to deposit some of their money in bank and begin a new account with you?' Leonard asked.

Berrick nodded at this. 'Yes, I believe they do that every single year they can. They would be great fools if they did not keep their passbook with the shop, and get interest on their money. Plenty of the Faroe fishermen are able to live on their own resources, but still they come for supplies on the passbook. The system has obtained so long, of fishermen taking advances, they cannot understand why they should use their own money to buy necessary supplies before they proceed to the fishing.'

Guthrie then asked: 'Does not this system of long settlements induce people to be careless of their money, even improvident?'

Berrick's reply was thus: 'I think we all know there is a certain class who, if they have money, will simply spend it. That class is very well looked after by the fish-curer and are only allowed small advances such as will enable them to get through the year, and so to be as little in arrears as possible at settlement. If these same folk had money in their own hands, I am certain it would not last them so long.'

'So he will only allow a certain amount of supplies from the shop?'

'Yes, so much a week or a fortnight.'

'Or cash if they want it, to a limited extent?'

'Yes, cash would be given to a free man.'

'But not to a bound fisherman?'

'Not unless it was for a necessary purpose, to purchase something, for instance, which the merchant cannot supply.'

Berrick's performance in the Toll House was admired by all who witnessed it, and news travelled. While by then a well-known figure in the west of Zetland, he had still not created his grand profile in the broader consciousness. In the future, according to Gabrielsen, 'he would become "ertkent", when his empire stretched to take in the old capital of Skallvaa'.

Nonetheless, Berrick's theories, or perhaps the slightly arrogant manner in which he advanced them, seemed to alert the Commissioners to his business's *modus operandi* and so we find that the distant isle of Thulay

– where the Berricks' power had been unchallenged – comes under their special scrutiny, as evidenced in a note to the effect that, as Lewis Berrick is the only source of information about it, there is a sense of dubiety over the state of affairs on Thulay. I quote from their report:

> This island is situated eighteen miles from the nearest point on the west side of the Mainland. It is three miles long, and two miles broad, yet its hills or precipices are very lofty, the highest point being estimated as 1,369 feet above the sea. In 1861, the population was 233. It is the property of Dr Scot, Esq. of Norbie. The fishing and the shop are entirely in the hands of Messrs Berrick & Co, who are factors for the proprietor. No other shop is allowed, and no other traders have attempted for some time to trade with the people at the island. I did not hear, directly or indirectly, that any complaints are made by the people with regard to the business arrangements of Mr Berrick, but the Commissioner heard no representative of the people of Thulay. It is said, indeed, that the people are trucked; but current rumour in Zetland, even among the opponents of truck, does not allege that any gross abuses exist in the island. The island is difficult of access, and the only evidence with regard to it is that of Mr Berrick himself.

Guthrie summarised the general situation thus:

> Fishermen, as Adam Smith remarks, have been poor since the days of Theocritus; and it would seem that in Zetland the Truck system begins whenever the farm fails to support the family, and the tenant finds it necessary to obtain supplies or advances before the time of settlement, or a boat, fishing materials and provisions, to enable him to prosecute his calling. It would seem that in Zetland the merchant needs to use no influence or compulsion to bring the fisherman to his shop. As the laws against Truck do not apply to him, he scarcely ever seeks to conceal that the earnings of his employees are paid in

goods, and he is even prepared with arguments in defence and indication of the practice.

...

It thus appears to be quite possible that fishermen should receive the whole of their earnings in shop goods, and I understand that the truth of the allegation that most of the men actually are so paid, and that they have no option but to take goods for their fish, at prices fixed by the merchant, was intended to be the main subject of this inquiry ...

...

[Yet] the only cases in which fishermen came forward voluntarily for the purpose of stating grievances, on hearing of the Commission, were those in which they are bound by their tenure to deliver their fish to the proprietor of the ground, or his tacksman. As in all these cases they are also supplied with goods from the landlord's or tacksman's shop, it was necessary to hear fully what the men had to say, even although their complaints appeared to involve a question as to the tenure of land, as well as the payment of wages.

What Lewis Berrick made of their investigation is not recorded, but when nothing came of it, no legislation or reprimand, he probably considered that he had performed well in his appearance. But the Report, when published, seemed to identify a deeper seated set of abuses than Truck.

Following his investigations into the practices of the fishing curers, Guthrie also questioned merchants in relation to the hosiery trade, as it was then known, although since the work of Arthursen and Standing in advertising the finer knitwear, such as the lacework shawls and veils, in the 1840s, the articles bought and sold included a broader range than simple socks, which had been the most common article of manufacture in the seventeenth century, when the great fair was held annually on the occasion of the visit of the Dutch fishing fleet to Brassay Sound.

The Reverend Brand, an early traveller in the region, records in his *Brief Description of the Orcades, Zetland, Peghtland Firth and Catness* (1701) that:

The Hollanders repair to these isles in June, as hath been said, for their herring fishing; but they cannot be said so properly to trade with the countrey as to fish upon their coasts, and they use to bring all sorts of provisions necessary with them, save some fresh victuals, as sheep, lambs, hens, etc., which they buy on shore. Stockins also are brought by the countrey people from all quarters to Larvik, and sold to these fishers; for sometimes many thousands of them will be ashore at one time, and ordinary it is with them to buy stockins to themselves; and some likewise do so to their wives and children, which is very beneficial to the inhabitants, for so money is brought into the countrey, there is a vent for the wooll, and the poor are employed ... These (Hamburg and Bremen) merchants seek nothing better in exchange for their commodities than to truck with the countrey for their fishes, which when the fishers engage to, the merchants will give them either money or ware, which they please.

The work, or 'makkin', as it was known in the dialect of Zetland, was firstly carried out solely by women knitting with yarn spun from wool grown by their own flocks, or those of their neighbours, and they bartered their handiwork to merchants. Guthrie notes the practice 'is so thoroughly interwoven with the habits of the people, that the question has never been raised in the local courts, and it does not even appear to have occurred to merchants that they might be held to infringe the law'.

One of the women interviewed was a Margaret Wylimsen, a native to the parish of Norbie, Valay and Thulay. Gabrielsen's transcript runs thus:

'Do you always get goods for your knitting?'

'Yes, I get goods, because I can get nothing else.'

'Do you want to get money?'

'I hardly ever ask for money. I asked for a penny the last time out of 35 shillings, and they refused to give it to me. I got all the goods I could use out of the work I had taken in, and when it came to the last penny I asked for it in money, but they would not give it.'

'What did he say he would give it in: sweeties?'

'No, they would not keep any sweeties for fear of having to give them.'

'What did they give you?'

'They gave me the penny at length, but they said we must always take goods.'

The investigators also interviewed various merchants who were involved in the trade of hosiery, including the keeper of the factor's shop at Norbie, a Mr St Clair, who told the following story:

'Three girls came into my shop, each of them having a shawl to sell, worth £1. At that time the noise had come up about cash payments, and I said to them, "Now, what would you take for these in money? I am not saying that I will give you money, but what would you take for them in money?" One of them said, "I ken you will just be going to give us money." I said "Why? Don't you think the goods you get cost us money?" She said, "I ken that fine. I will give my 20s. shawl for 18s. 6d." I said, I could not give her 18s. 6d. for it, and asked her if she would take 17s. She said, "No," and that it would be most unconscionable to take 3s. off the price of a shawl. I said, "I don't think it, because when I sell the shawl again, I can only get 20s. for it, and then there is a discount of 5 per cent taken off."'

Guthrie's response was, 'I suppose that bit of trading came to nothing: they did not take money?'

'No,' the merchant answered, 'they did not take money; but another one said, "I would not sell my shawl for 18s. 6d. or 19s. either, for I see a plaid in your shop that I want for my shawl; and what good would it do me to sell you the shawl for 17s., and then take 3s. out of my pocket to pay you in addition, when you are willing to give me the plaid in exchange for the shawl?" That was her answer to me.'

In 1840, Catherine St Clair, an Edinburgh author of Zetlandic parentage, wrote thus about the 'marvellous excess' of tea-drinking she encountered while in Zetland thus: 'The indulgence amounts to an absolute vice!' She recounted the story of 'a poor man in the parish of Brassay, who had the expensive affliction of a tea-drinking wife, and was cheated by her secretly selling his goods to obtain tea.'

The merchants of Zetland used tea as the currency women were paid in for their fine hosiery and shawls, and hand-knitters were forced to turn this payment into items they needed by bartering with farmers, neighbours and friends for their essential supplies. One of those interviewed, a woman from Norbie who had accompanied Gabrielsen on the long journey to Larvik, a knitter named Mary Coutts, explained to Guthrie and his fellows what the custom was.

'We give the tea to the crofters, and we get meal and potatoes for it. We have sometimes to go to travel all over the west side to dispose of it, even to Papay and Thulay. Our aunt, Elizabeth Coutts, has done that many a time, for our own house, not for other people. She took the tea there and got the meal and potatoes in exchange.'

Leonard inquired of her, 'Did she get the full price for your tea from the farmers?'

'I could not say. They did not weigh out the meal and potatoes which they gave in exchange, merely gave a little for the tea which my aunt gave them.'

'Have you often had to barter your goods for less than they were worth?'

'Yes, often.'

Guthrie then asked of her: 'Do you support yourself entirely by knitting?'

'Yes,' she answered, 'For I cannot work at anything else. I knit fine shawls and veils and I have been paid in goods by Mr St Clair. I never asked any money from him, because we knew that it was the rule that we would not get it. I wanted it for many purposes; but I would not have got it even though I had asked it.'

'But you could not get on without some money, I suppose?'

'No. I sent some shawls and veils south to a woman in London, for money to pay my rent.'

'Did you get enough money from them for all that you wanted?'

'I was often at a loss for money, and then I had to sell the tea and other things which I had got in Larvik for my hosiery. I sold tea and soft goods.'

'How much goods did you sell in that way?'

'If I sold a shawl for about 18s. I would get 18s. worth of goods, and of that a good deal was tea – perhaps one pound or a pound and a half.'

'Would you sell all that tea?'

'Yes. Finally.'

'Did you always bring home some tea from Larvik in order to sell it?'

'Yes.'

'And did you always find some of your neighbours ready to buy it?'

'Yes, there were always some of them kind enough to buy it from me.'

'You did that very often, because you had no other way of getting money?'

'Yes.'

'Would you rather have money than be paid for your work in the way you have mentioned?'

'Yes, I would rather have money, but we all knew that we would not get it, and therefore we never asked it.'

'Do you think you could make a better use of the money than you do of the goods?'

'Yes, a great deal better. We would not have to traik around the country trying to find someone to buy the tea.'

During Guthrie's lengthy investigations, many Zetland women spoke forth of the tyranny of the knitting trade, and the effects of payment in tea. But when the Truck Report was published in 1872, Guthrie seemed less than condemnatory of the practice, even to the point of defending the merchants and their interests.

While Gabrielsen found time to follow the political events of the period, he and Katie had been far from idle in pursuit of their dream. By the time of the Truck Commissioners visit, the school at Norbie had taken shape to the extent that he was able to make a woodcut of the premises, which he then published in *The Scotsman* in the hope of securing the last funds required, to equip the schoolroom with the boiler they hoped would keep the pupils warm even in the heart of winter.

Letter to *The Scotsman* from James Gabrielsen

Norbie, Zetland,
10th January 1871

Dear Sir

The Schoolhouse and School which, through the liberality of Clergymen, Schoolmasters, and other friends of education in the South, I have nearly succeeded in erecting in this locality is a plain, neat, and substantial building, well lighted and ventilated. It is on a piece of ground granted by the landlord to the School for ever, and will, I hope, prove a blessing to the poor people of the district for generations to come.

The district benefited by the School is situated on the north-west of the Mainland of Zetland, contains a population of 606, is distant 10 miles from the Parochial School, and the School attendance has of late years increased from 30 to 70 Scholars.

The old School buildings, which were built in 1790, and were at best of an inferior description, had fallen into such a ruinous condition as to become uninhabitable, and they either had to be rebuilt or the salary would be withdrawn.

The general poverty of the people was such that they could do nothing, and I could not think of their losing their School without my doing everything in my power to help them. It has been a hard struggle, has occupied every spare moment of my time for upwards of two years; and had the appeals on behalf of the sick and wounded soldiers not seriously interfered with my scheme, I believe I would have succeeded in raising funds to complete my buildings in a satisfactory manner; but I am sorry to say that I am still £35 short of the sum necessary to finish the Schoolroom.

The School is open to all, and is attended by the children of every denomination in the district; and as I have no sympathy with the advocates of a secular system of education, I have done my utmost to secure that the Bible shall always be taught in the School.

I am sorry to trouble you, but I am anxious to finish my Schoolroom so as to enable my Scholars to pursue their studies in comfort; and if you will be kind enough to favour me with a small subscription, or bring my case under the notice of any lady or gentleman whom you think might sympathise with me, you will exceedingly oblige,

Your obedient Servant,
James Gabrielsen

His appeal was successful and the work completed, so that when the Education Scotland Act 1872 made it law that all children between the age of five and fifteen should attend school, and many parishes scrambled to find suitable buildings, in Norbie the Gabrielsens were ready. They had their new school.

24th June 2000 – Norbie

Suddenly I look up and see it's 15.28. I've slept right through my meeting with Mary. I jump. Quick, boots on. Laced and downstairs to the kitchen, forgetting, till I pass his landing, the Bendigo book. I'm not really bothered anyway. It's Mary I need to see. She's there in the kitchen, apron on, standing by the stove.

'Mary, I'm sorry, I fell asleep,' I say.

'I know,' she says, smiling that kindly smile again. 'I called and when you didn't answer I peeped into your room. You were fast asleep, so I thought you probably needed the rest and just let you lie.'

'Did you have a look at the notebook?'

'Oh yes, though it's not very interesting as far as I can see.' She picks up a stainless steel pot from the draining board and sets it on the stove.

'Do you have time to tell me about it just now? I'll help you get the dinner ready, if you want.'

She shakes her head, the grey-black stripes of her hair waving. 'No, that's all right, I'm well ahead. Everything's ready in the pans just to cook. So yes, let's have a look at the wee book.'

She dries her hands on her apron and goes to the shelf by the table, from where she takes her glasses, the notebook and sheets of lined paper with scribbles on them.

'Now let me see,' she begins, settling herself down at the table. I sit next to her, and pull my chair around to be sitting so as I can see the papers from her angle. 'It doesn't make a lot of sense to me, but maybe you'll be able to figure some of it out.'

'Okay,' I say.

'Right then, here goes. It starts with this up here,' and she points a fingernail at a brief line of shorthand. It says 'I lived alone in the woods; a mile from any neighbour, in a house which I had built myself on the shore of Walden Pond in Concord, Massachusetts; and earned my living by the labour of my hands only.'

I say, 'Yes, I know what that is. I know what that's from. It's Thoreau. An American writer who went off into the woods to live for a while. Wrote this famous book about it.'

Mary seems impressed by my knowledge. She looks back at the notebook. 'Then there's just one line here, below. It reads: Solitude is the prerequisite for ecstatic experience.'

'Okay,' I say. 'No name or anything?'

CODE WILL SAVE

'No, just that. See here, it's on its own at the bottom of this page.' And she turns the pages of the notebook, to show me.

'Could be Thoreau again.' I'm disappointed. 'What's next?'

'Well, there's a long bit a couple of pages on.' She flips the pages over and shows me the shorthand, as meaningless as hieroglyphics.

'What does it say?' I ask, a bit impatiently.

CODE WILL SAVE

'It goes like this, roughly.'

And she reads this long passage which seems to be by a man exiled in some northern island, and I wonder if it is his writing till the details prove it isn't. I recognise it. It's MacDiarmid's, when he was marooned in the north in the thirties, complaining about having no intelligent company to speak to, of being surrounded by superstitious fishermen and their wives who can't do more than quote Churchill or *Old Moore's Almanac*. I let her read a while, then touch her arm to make her halt, mid-sentence.

'It's a quotation. I've read that before. One of my father's heroes, Hugh MacDiarmid.'

She stops, peers up at me over the rim of her glasses.

'Whoever he was, he was an arrogant bugger, that's for sure,' Mary laughs.

'What's next?' I ask.

She flips the page forward, starts reading again. I can't place it, but I know it's just another quotation, something to do with the idea of North, as the writer puts it.

'No?' She senses my disappointment. 'This isn't really helping much, is it?'

'Not so far,' I answer. 'But keep going.'

'All right.' So she does, she reads again, a page further on. This time it's about Karel Capek and how, as a boy, he dreamed of discovering a wonderful Arctic island, where mangoes would grow on the slopes of a volcano, even surrounded by ice.

It's a beautiful passage. So I let her read on, about how at last he made his journey, up through Norway and beyond the Arctic Circle to the end of Europe.

She closes the book. 'That's it,' she says. 'Apart from here, where it says Easter Sunday, Radio 3. I think maybe it's something he jotted down off the radio.'

I take the book from her. Flick the pages forward and back. So many marks, and so little meaning.

'Well thanks, anyway. It was stupid of me to think that ...'

That pitying look. 'What, my dear?'

'I don't know. I just thought that there might be something in there.'

'Well there is. Just not anything very interesting to us. Though he obviously thought it was, before he went to the trouble of copying it all down off the radio.'

But then something catches my eye. Below where it says Easter Sunday, in a different pen there are three numbers, 24, 6 and 3, and then something else in shorthand. 'Mary,' I ask, 'what does this say?'

'I told you,' she answers, 'Easter Sunday, Radio 3.'

'No, these numbers down here, below? 24 and 6 and 3?'

'I don't know. Maybe it's the frequency or something?'

'Is it not more like a date, the way it's written?' I think out loud. 'The 24th of June. That would be Monday coming, wouldn't it?'

'I suppose it would. Let me see that again.' And she takes the book from me, running her fingers over the text carefully.

'You're right,' she says. 'I did miss something … it's barely legible, but I think it says … I think it says "Salutation".'

'Salutation?' The Sallie, in Perth. 'Does it say hotel?'

CODE WILL SAVE!

Mary is still examining the page. After a while she says: 'No, but I think you're right, this is a date. Monday's date!'

'But what about the 3?'

'The time maybe?'

'Three o'clock? It would have to be afternoon, wouldn't it?'

'I suppose so.'

CODE WILL SAVE

I am running this possibility through my mind when the laird walks in, looking glum and grumpy, rather greyed by the mist, perhaps.

'Well well well,' he says. 'I was looking for you, to tell you the search has had to be abandoned because of the weather. I didn't think to find you in here.' And he notices the papers and the notebook on the table in front of me.

'What's this you've got here? Where did you get this?' he asks me.

'It was in the chalet.'

'You mean you took this?'

And then I realise that I've betrayed myself, that I've admitted to the very thing I'd promised him I would not do.

'And what may I ask have you discovered? Between you and Dr Watson here.' As if he thinks we aren't capable of having one intelligent thought between us.

'This.' I point it out to him. 'It's a date. Monday's date. And a time. Three in the afternoon. And a name. Salutation. It's in among all this stuff he's copied from the radio, we think. On Easter Sunday.'

'And?' He is boiling with fury at me. But I won't respond, just who is this man, this self-appointed master, to tell me what to do with my father's things?

'It's an appointment or something. So that could mean he was going away somewhere. Until at least tomorrow.'

Dr Hart snorts. First there is a preparatory cough, then a definite snort of scorn. 'Salutation? No, nothing of that name round here.'

'It's a hotel in Perth,' I add.

'Well, it's something,' Mary says. But there is no broom in her hand to shoo this man, no sign of her siding with me. Instead she seems small, nervous and only too willing to fit the jungle flower role.

'It's meaningless,' he says. 'He already had an appointment to see me and he missed that.'

But it is something, like Mary says. I know. And I know where.

'No,' he says, 'And I must say I'm deeply disappointed that you should have taken this from the chalet when I gave you express orders not to move anything. Police orders.'

'I'm sorry,' I say. 'It was just that I thought maybe there might be something …'

'Exactly. Police job. Not yours.' He glares at me, moustache trembling in silent fury. Then, noticing that Mary is watching, he calls out: 'Dinner under way, Mrs Mitchell?'

'Yes,' she answers meekly, smiles at him, stands up from the table and makes her excuse. She'll need to check the potatoes.

He turns to me again. 'And what else did you take?'

'From the chalet?'

He doesn't answer, just stands over me like an old-fashioned schoolmaster leaning on his desk, cane in hand. I sit there staring up at him, this man who has given me his hospitality, recalling the words of that tract I'd found at my father's: Having ignored my Sustainer, presumed on His resources, broken His laws, dishonoured His property …

'Nothing,' I say. 'Just this stuff. And that key I gave you yesterday.'

Dr Hart considers a while, then lifts the notebook up again. 'And what else does it say?'

'Mary thinks he might have copied it from a radio programme.'

He runs the pages through his hand. 'Perhaps it's just the time of another radio programme, the next instalment or something? Isn't there a radio programme called "Salutation"?'

'I don't know,' I answer. 'Maybe.'

'Well, we should give it to the police. I won't say how I came by it. Just that it was left here.' And he heads out with the notebook under his arm, confiscated.

Mary peeps round at me from the stove. Her expression is no longer friendly in the way it was. I make a face of apology, but she doesn't respond.

'Sorry, Mary,' I say.

Stirring a pot, she doesn't look at me. 'Now you've got me into trouble. He's a terrible ogre when he's in a bad mood.'

'I'm sorry,' I say again. 'I didn't mean to get you into ... I just didn't think.'

'That's exactly it,' she says. 'Folk don't think.'

'Can I help you with anything?'

'No.'

She's rattling the pots and pans, lifting lids and letting them drop. Opening the stove door and slamming it shut. Going over to the sink and clattering the crockery.

'Mary,' I say, 'You're angry with me.'

'Me? No.'

'You are. It's obvious.'

'No, I'm just busy, I've got the dinner to get ready. You'll be having cheese omelette. I hope that's all right.'

'You don't have to go to any bother. A salad's fine. And maybe some of that delicious homemade bread.' At that she stops rattling and crashing. 'You like my bread?'

'As good as any I've ever tasted.'

But then as if remembering she's angry, she turns back to the stove. 'Well it's nice to know not everybody thinks I'm just a skivvy.'

'A skivvy? Mary, you're wonderful.'

'Now now, no flattery.'

'I mean it. All that beautiful food and you have all these hidden skills as well.'

'What hidden skills?' she asks me, suspiciously, oven gloves in hand.

'Well, shorthand for one. And I bet you've a few more hidden away.'

She crosses to the table and lights a Silk Cut. And as she's doing so, I suddenly realise who it is she reminds me of.

'Are you insinuating something? Because if you are, you'd best be out of here now,' she says, not unkindly, even with a touch of good humour.

'Me? Not me,' I answer. 'Why, is there something worth insinuating?'

She laughs. 'I'll let you off then, seeing as you complimented my bread. But just remember, when Dr Hart is around you call me Mrs Mitchell, not Mary.'

She tells me this with utmost sincerity, like it was some unwritten law to be observed regardless. I don't mind, that's easy enough, now I know. Whatever the reason for the formality, whatever the touchy area being protected from insinuation, I can deal with that, accept it. That's not my business.

'Okay,' I say.

'Good. As long as you understand.'

Nobody's business but her own. She's still a good person, I have no reason to change my opinion.

'I'd better let you get on then,' I say.

She stubs out another half-smoked cigarette. 'Yes, you'd better.'

CODE WILL SAVE
    little learning
        salutations

I fetch my jacket from the attic room, stepping up and down as silently as I can. I slip out the back door. And then the fog strikes me, this total wall of cold grey nothing, like the clouds had fallen and are lying waiting on the wind to rise and lift them back to the skies where they belong. But it isn't going to happen in a hurry. Not even a breath of air in motion. Just this heavy quilted stillness, this ocean dampness everywhere.

I can barely see six feet ahead of me. But all the same I've mapped this place, I have the picture in my mind, which road to take and all that.

I've gone twenty strides and already I can't see the big house behind me. Twenty more and I'm through the gates, then twenty more and there's nothing, nothing but the rough tarmac road in front of me and my next three strides. I zip my jacket right up to the collar. Put on my hat. There's deep cold in this fog, chilling cold.

But I know where I'm going, there's that map in my mind, of this village and the few roads that exist. I can't go wrong. So I walk on, and still there's nothing but the road and the rich green summer verge, full of vetch and blooming cow parsley, then the deep ditch beyond that and a dry-stone wall. Lambs and ewes bleat somewhere in the greyness, but only occasionally, as if even they have been silenced by this oppressive weather. It should be daylight, broad daylight here at this time, at this time of year, but tonight, as evening falls, there's just thick white nothing.

Then I see two red lights and a shape looming, materialising. But it isn't the phone box, no, it's the green van again. The shepherd's van. And it's stopped right in the middle of the single-track road, with the doors wide open and the engine off. Warily, I approach. But I can see through the rear windows that there's nobody there. It's as if it was abandoned. But surely no one would block the road like that and then disappear? To get past, I have to leave the tarmac and walk on the verge. At the driver's door, I stop a second and peer inside.

Behind me a voice says, 'Aye, aye.' I jump two feet in the air and, spinning round, find that weathered old face smiling at me. The old man with pipe in mouth, his dog at his foot.

'Were you wanting something?' he asks, in that slow, easy drawl I remember.

'Me? No, no, I was just wondering why your van was standing here in the middle of the road. Wondering if you were all right.'

'Och, I was just here. Did you no see me?'

'Where?' I ask.

'Just right here. Where else would I be?'

That's a question to which I have no answer. But he just keeps on appearing out of nowhere, looking at me as if I was a stranger, but talking to me as if he knows me very well indeed.

'The mist's brawly thick,' he says.

'Yes,' I say. 'Sure is.'

'No much of a night for a walk,' he adds. And then he takes the pipe from his mouth, coughs and spits a jet into the ditch by the roadside.

'No,' I say. 'Not for a walk.'

'I could give you a lift,' he says. 'Where are you heading for?'

'The phone box. But it's all right, I like walking.'

'Weel weel, whatever you like.'

And then I should move on. I should turn and say cheerio, and walk off up the road. But I don't. Something holds me there, standing absolutely still, just as he is standing absolutely still, the pair of us, standing there, motionless in the motionless air. The dog is panting, there's a long plaintive bleat from somewhere far off in the fog, and a seagull's piercing squawk.

'You ken your road there, then?'

'My road?'

'Where the phone box is.'

'It's just up here a bit isn't it?' At this he laughs, as if I've said something very stupid indeed.

'No no no,' he says. 'That thing hasn't worked for years. The new one is ower the hill, doon in the Innertoon. Aye, in Innertoon, by the school. If it's a phone you want, you're a long way off course.'

'Innertoon?' I say, 'By the school?'

'Aye, just by the school.'

'Is it far?'

'Far? No.'

'What, a mile? Two?'

'Yes. Aboot that.'

'And where exactly is this Innertoon?'

'Oh, the Innertoon is in ower the hill. You would have to go up to the church, then bear right at the junction, go doon past the chalets, keep on going past the road into the bungalow, then the road swings round to your left and runs past the quarry. After the quarry there's a junction. There you would need to go to your left. Then carry straight on an you'll come in ower the hill to the Innertoon finally. You'll ken when you see it, there's a pier. And near the pier is the school. You'll see the phone box by it.'

All this he says as if each word had weight and meaning independent of each other, a slow melodious flowing of air through his mouth, rippling to my ear in the otherwise perfect stillness.

'I can gie you a lift noo,' he says. 'I'm goin that way mysel.'

I stop. I stand absolutely still, composing poise, neither taking of nor giving air.

'All right,' I say.

So I get into the van. The dog in the back has its tongue at my ear, panting slightly. The shepherd turns the key. The engine turns over, then picks up. He puts it into gear and lights his pipe, slowly sucking and sending blue smoke, a heavy aromatic reek, into the van space. But I don't cough, I'm thinking, why haven't I noticed this 'Innertoon' on my map? I pull the folded square from my pocket and open it out. But the light from the dash is too dim by far for me to see.

'We'll need tae go slow, in this mist.'

Slow is true. At ten miles an hour we edge forward through the retreating wall of whiteness lit by the beaming headlights of the green van. It stays just that distance away all the time, neither advancing nor retreating, not a void, but a fullness, a great and overwhelming fullness of moisture in the air. Like a body overcome with emotion.

'Will you be able to find you way back?'

'Back?' I say. 'Yes, I've got a map.'

'But in this mist?'

I've walked in mist before, I've climbed. I know when it's safe to move and time to sit it out. Here there's just a flat road to follow, and the key is on my map. Unless this Innertoon is Brigadoon and I'm on my way under the mountain for thirty timeless years.

I look at this spirit guide smoking his pipe, edging the van forward through the greyness, casting white beams of light though the fusion of air and water. And I trust him to take me where I need to go, to this Innertoon, or the hollow mountain. If that is my destiny I will not refuse it, to be taken by this troll.

'I hope so,' I say, looking out.

Staring out at the light beams, hypnotised by them, a sudden panic strikes me. My Maglite? I feel for the zip pocket on my arm. Yes, there it is. In case I need it to read the map coming back.

'You could always get a taxi,' he says.

That is a strange thought, away out here. A black hackney cab, to carry you home.

'There's a man, Johnnie Haa, has a taxi. He'll run you back.'

'Right,' I say. That could be useful. If the mist gets any worse, it's an option. 'How do I find him?'

'He'll be around the pier. Maybe in the Sail Loft.'

'The Sail Loft?'

'The pub.'

A pier, a school, a phone box, a taxi, a pub, this Innertoon is rapidly becoming a metropolis.

'What else is there at Innertoon?'

'Innertoon? Well, there's hooses,' he says, and laughs. 'A shop. An a kirk.'

'Another church?'

'Oh aye, there's nae want o kirks here. Though no that mony folk go tae them these days.'

Whether this is a good or a bad thing, he doesn't tell me. His face betrays just the outlines and inlines of a life of clenching a pipe between his teeth, screwing up his eyes to stop the crowding smoke from stinging too much. The van takes a sharp right turn and is heading down a slope now, hearse-slow. But true, somehow, too. The engine is happy, it's peaceful. I can feel every bump of the road through the suspension, but because we travel so slowly they are gentle rolling movements, not jerky or stressful.

The shepherd turns another corner and two lights appear in the fog, but stationary ones. A gravel track leads away, cutting through the verge to merge with the tarmac. It looks like the way to the chalets.

'You're fae Perth, aren't you?' he says, out of blue reek.

'Yes,' I answer, surprised.

'I used to go there once a year, when I was younger, to the agricultural show. I ken Perth weel. The Salutation Hotel.'

Maybe I should be amazed. But I'm not, because this is how life works, it throws up all these stray connections out of what we think is random chance and we just have to credit them. Follow them. Believe. There is a code and it will save.

'Oh aye, I've spent mony a day in Perth. There was a gang of us would go, when I was younger. We'd wander aroond, have a bit of a spree an that. I always looked forward tae Perth, every year. For the Show.'

'I used to go too. When I was wee,' I say. 'Every year.'

'Aye? Weel weel, the world is smaa, right enough.'

And then I see the signpost appearing out of the mist:

INNERTOON

And it's gone as quickly, as he turns in the direction of the arrow. The van begins a descent, down, down, down we go. I feel my body falling forward towards the light on the dash and the seat belt restrains me. He brakes and the braking halts my conversation. It is very steep at the end, and then behold, a streetlight or a floodlight of sorts, illuminating a flat tarmac turning place. Puddles of water everywhere reflect the hollow white glare of the fog-haloed light. It is hard for me to tell whether it is still daylight or not.

The van circles round the turning place slowly and comes to a halt under the light. He switches the engine off and turns to me.

'That way is the school.' And he points across my body through the passenger window. 'The phone box is just right there. Walk that way and you'll come to it. Here, this is the Sail Loft. There'll be a few fishermen in there, wi it being a Saturday, but if you want a bite to eat or a drink, the lady there will see to you. Maggie. Tell her it was me that sent you. And if Johnnie Haa isn't in there, he won't be far away. Maggie will ken where to find him.'

'Thanks,' I say, and I mean it. Really. I pat the dog's head. 'What's her name?'

'Her name? Well, she gets a few names,' he says and laughs. 'Depending on how she's behaving. But mostly she's just Gem.'

'Jem?'

'You ken, like a diamond. A gem.'

That's nice, I say, yes. Gem. And then I pause and stand peering in the door of the van a moment. The blue smoke is snaking out. I even kind of like it, like it's an incense of sorts.

I thank him, get out, cross to the phone box. The shepherd doesn't drive away, but stays there watching. The slot for the coins is blocked.

'No working?' he calls over. 'You'd better go in an see Maggie,' he says, like he's made the decision for you. 'She'll let you phone fae there.'

The van door clips shut, with a snap. Gem leaps forward into the passenger seat and sits looking out at me. Then she turns her head to look straight ahead, the engine starts, and off they go, intrepid, into the fullness of the mist. To rescue or to bury, whatever happens. Whenever, wherever, whatever.

All the buildings round the turning place are set with their gable ends outwards, except one where I can make out a well-kept garden and the rough facade. The entrance to the pub is signposted, another arrow, pointing me up a lane. A distance up the close I see a light, and signboard hanging. 'The Sail Loft', it says and there's a painting of a sailing ship in full rig.

The door opens on real warmth, a fiddle and some other instruments, the rumble and shriek of conversation. The pub is tiny, but full. There's a crack of pool balls from an adjacent chamber. Folk are busy talking.

Some turn to stare

at me

CHAPTER SEVEN

'THE SURGEON GENERAL COMES HAME'

> It little profits that an idle king,
> By this still hearth, among these barren crags,
> Matched with an aged wife, I mete and dole
> Unequal laws unto a savage race,
> That hoard, and sleep, and feed, and know not me.
>
> Alfred, Lord Tennyson, 'Ulysses'

The retiral of Dr Scot from the naval service and his subsequent return, accompanied by his young family, to Norbie in the summer of 1872 was the greatest event in the parish for over a generation.

Even the oldest of the parishioners could not recall a day more feted, more welcome, 'since John o' the *Doris* and his bonnie Margaret made their hamefarin'. The older denizens remembered, but had grown old with the great Hall closed for most of the year, open only occasionally, for the season.

The prospect of year-round occupation – and indeed the chance of employment for the fit and young – brightened the horizon a little further, in what were otherwise dark times in Zetland. The exodus then beginning would carry thousands from the 'Aald Rock', including the renowned voyage of the Thorwaldites, Rev. Thorwald Gabrielsen, a prodigy with unshakeable faith in his destiny.

Although the cod fishing on the Faroese banks was by then in decline, huge quantities of herring were being caught, greater even than in the days before the Great Herring Crash of 1842, when they had all but disappeared.

As James Gabrielsen explains, herring was at that time a great delicacy on the continent, and so the market was strong. For some divinely known reason, the size of the shoals around the shores of Scotland experienced around that time an uncanny swelling, so the industry grew suddenly. According to Gabrielsen, 'Where once herring fishing had been a seasonal activity, now hungry fishermen pursue the silver darlings round the coast, and because the herring is a fatty fish and has to be cured quickly in order to prevent rotting, in their wake comes a vast following of workers, men and women, employed ashore. Shoals move with or respond to the Gulf Stream, starting out on the Western Isles to arc around the north coast of Scotland into the North Sea, a great wave of Lord-given life that unfolds throughout the year. So a little army of barrelmakers, curers, merchants, labourers and "guttie lasses" make their way around the herring ports of Britain, touring the north coast of Scotland and here to Zetland during the summer months and, in the autumn, reaching as far south as East Anglia.'

At the height of this explosion of activity, Gabrielsen was not to know, there were as many as 30,000 vessels involved in herring fishing the East Coast, not to mention others in the Irish Sea.

Throughout the years of the herring boom, which was to last until the Great War, Zetland fishergirls were integral to the fishery in any port where herring was landed. From throughout the archipelago, they would walk to Larvik or one of the other smaller ports, often leaving behind crowded and hungry houses, to bring home valuable silver coins from the darlings of the sea. A girl might begin gutting and packing barrels as young as fifteen, and sail throughout the season from Stornoway to Larvik, to Peterhead, and down the east coast of Britain as far south as Great Yarmouth. The society of the 'guttie' lasses, with its matrons, was legendary.

The town of Larvik grew rapidly. A shantytown appeared on its northern fringes, a world of corrugated iron and jerry-rigged sheds where workers bunked, a mixed camp, though segregated, of women and men from all around the northern coasts of Scotland.

Respectable burghers and the town's finer society shunned them and their doings, yet made a great deal of money from the 'boom', by one means or another. New 'villas' began to appear, on the hillside above the old harbour, away from the steep dark lanes and old 'klosses' that encircled the shore. A new civic pride began to show, in plans for a new Town Hall, for public gardens and an opera house, to join the fine new school built after the Education Act, which Arthursen had financed.

The town was by this stage serviced by regular steamship connection to the port of Leith and the capital city. As trade links intensified, Leith itself developed a Zetlandic quarter, centred on Prince Regent Street, known locally as 'Zetlander's Avenue'.

Larvik, meanwhile, was becoming ever more Scotch, and ever more civilised. The old practice of drunken wharf-rats rolling their flaming barrels of tar through the main street on Antonsmas was banned, and those wild celebrations known locally as Op-Hell-Ya were transformed by the burghers into a pageant, as was fashionable during that period, involving various costumed troupes which would each perform a short sketch, or sing a topical song.

At the heart of this new civic pride was a sense of Zetlandicism, which drew on the archipelago's Nordic past and was expressed most obviously in the appointment of one man each year as the Faals Jarl, or 'false earl', who would then appoint from his friends a squad of men who, come the celebration, would each appear in a rather baroque mock version of what people of the Victorian era imagined Vikings may have worn.

A newspaper was begun, and a firm of publishers sprang up, dedicated to publishing the work of local bards and scholars. Among them was James Angus Stoot, fellow pupil of Lang of Quharv, and friend to James Gabrielsen. The unique dialect of Zetland thus found its way to print, and once it had found its way, there seemed no end of those willing to volunteer their own often eccentric rendition of the spoken tongue in the press, the mood of their work very often elegiac, focusing on emigration, loss and parting. At the end of the decade, the first major work of Zetlandic literature appeared, in the form of stories written by a Zetlander settled in Leith, where he and his brother had a store and an import-export business, George Stewart, author of *The Hermit of Trosswickness*.

Another key publication of the period was the long delayed appearance of the Reverend George Lowe's *Travels*, the account of a journey made in Zetland a century earlier. This extremely literate and observant churchman belatedly did Zetland a great favour, and his book spurred a new enthusiasm for history and antiquity, both of which the burghers of the swelling town were keen to promote.

So it was a changing Zetland that the laird returned to, one which appeared at last to be dragging itself into the nineteenth century. At that point in his own life, his two daughters were on the verge of womanhood, dressed always in the latest continental fashions through his wife's many Polish friends in Paris, and though neither had the sharply defined Slavic beauty of their mother, both Florence and Catherine (as she was known, though she had been christened Agnes like her mother) were certainly marriageable. They enjoyed the attentions of Zetlandic gentry, as the new girls on the circuit. Dr Scot's career was of such eminence that they carried an additional interest to would-be suitors.

The laird's son, Albert, or Bertie as he was known in the family, was a rather indulged nine-year-old when he first came to live in Norbie though, as a boarder at Cheltenham, his presence was infrequent. A curious child who could never sit still for long, but was always asking questions of people; always keen to know how things worked, he wandered the fields and buildings of Norbie as he chose, paying no heed to what might be growing, what kind of creature might be penned there, or any sense of the property of others. He became a familiar figure to the folk as they worked, always on his way to somewhere with some plan or 'ploy' in mind. He was, Gabrielsen tells us, 'once upbraided for walking through a field of corn by one of the old crofters, whereupon he threw this elder such a look of malice that the man feared not for his crops, but for his very tenure'.

Bertie habitually wore one of the then newly fashionable suits which his mother had fastened her eye upon when last in London, where all three parts are made of the same material. She had tried to persuade her husband to get one for himself, but he was firmly of the opinion that a suit consisted of three separate elements and always had done. His trousers would always be striped. His frock coat was far more serviceable than those short jackets, which were barely more than a second waistcoat. So she bought six for her son instead, and he was delighted, as they had so many pockets for him to fill with his gadgets.

Gabrielsen records that Bertie's brown tweed three-piece came to define him, and when he fell into an argument with one of the dairy maids working at the Home Farm, for poking a stick in the fresh milk, she made fun of him thus: 'Du's da felloo, de, gjaain aboot in dy peerie suit.' At which, Bertie, showing his comprehension not only of the dialect but the subtlety of the insult, replied, 'This is what people with some sense of fashion call a ditto suit, you dummy.' The girl, a few years his elder, and quick-witted, replied 'I doot da tree pairts a'de are da sam – aa tree made o da sam mischief.' The tale travelled through the Big House and the name stuck. He became 'Ditto' to all the servants, who tolerated his presence silently when he wasn't at school, and soon the soubriquet spread to the whole village.

The laird himself was also in the fields that summer, in the company of Gabrielsen, whose knowledge of surveying he employed in drawing up plans for the drainage and improvement of the meadow land of Norbie. Behind the beach, and the links, lay a small freshwater loch into which a number of small streams flowed, carrying all the great peathills' gathering of rainfall to the sea. Around this loch, on the flat land, the streams fragmented into an estuary of smaller streams, and submerged into a marshy siltland which had never been fully farmed. Behind this again lay an assembly of small fields, surrounded by rough stone walls, so covered with moss and ferns that they seemed part of the flora. These historically passed between the various crofters who had entitlement, on the old system of 'runrig'.

What the laird was up to was the subject of some debate in Norbie, it appears, as both he and Gabrielsen kept his scheme quiet until he was ready to present it as a fait accompli. Some said he was planning to build a new house by the loch, others that he had a whole new village in mind. What all but a few folk agreed upon was that the moss-covered stones which defined the boundaries of the fields had lain there since the first day, and that to move them would disturb 'da peerie fokk'. The old folk said that it was only with the blessing of the many creatures who lived among the stones that crops grew within their enclosure. If they were made angry, the land would be become 'as barren as da Sahara'. But none dared challenge the word of the Guid Doctor, for he had already made himself loved, when the day came to unveil the plans.

The laird wanted teams of young men. They were required to tear down the old walls, move the stones away and cover them with earth to make banks, and then dig a great channel to divert the two streams into, so that the land would dry out and become useful, ready for ploughing. For it was fertile ground, that they all knew by what grew there untended. This land would then be apportioned to the various crofts and fixed with them, so that whatever work they put in to improving it further would be to their own benefit, and not the next man whose turn it was to use it, as had been the custom with the old 'runrig' system.

The company did not object verbally, for they believed the laird was wise and loved him, though he could sense opposition. But when he threw in the promise of new houses, erected in time to match the new crofts, they were happy. This was, he said, as much about improving the people's conditions as the productivity of the estate. None could argue, for nothing like this had ever happened before, and they were all rather in shock, according to Gabrielsen, 'though predictions of doom followed right on through the years of work that lay ahead'.

Yet there was a greater shock ahead for all, for the master would not survive to see his plan executed. That winter, a messenger came from Vass to beg the laird, in his capacity as a surgeon, to aid a young fellow, one Malis Jarmsen, who had been 'messing around with an ancient carronade still sited overlooking the harbour since the Napoleonic wars. He and some friends had got their hands on some gunpowder from somewhere, and thought it would be fine fun to fire a shot from it and waken up the sleeping world. Things went agley and he had ended up blowing his arm off. So Dr Scot got on his pony and rode the eight miles over the moors, and managed to save the youth's life.' But on the way back, the benefactor faced such a blast of Arctic wind and rain that the poor man was chilled to the bone when he finally returned to Norbie Hall. He took to his bed and never recovered, pneumonia setting in and carrying him away within a week, despite the fact that he had been such robust soul.

Tributes poured in from all corners of the Empire. Lengthy obituaries appeared in all the main newspapers, most drawing on the portrait given by James Gabrielsen himself to *The Scotsman*, for whom he had become something of a Zetland correspondent, following his brief fame in the building of the school:

THE LATE DR SCOT OF NORBIE – In our obituary column notice has already appeared of the death of Dr Robert Scot of Norbie, Deputy-Lieutenant of the county of Zetland. His death was quite unexpected, for he had only been seriously ill for about three days, and his death has thrown a gloom over the Westside. Dr Scot was born on the 1st of January 1812, and in the following year he lost his father, Mr John Scot of Norbie, by the wreck of the Zetland trader *Doris*, on her return voyage to Zetland from Leith. Having been carefully prepared for College under the tuition of the Rev. A Webster, minister of Quharv he studied at Marischal College, Aberdeen; and having then attended the usual medical curriculum in the University of Edinburgh, obtained his LRCS at the early age of nineteen. Being passionately fond of the sea, he entered the navy as assistant-surgeon in 1833, and retired from the service as Deputy Inspector-General of Hospital and Fleets in 1870.

The principal scenes of his foreign service were the Pacific, China, the Baltic, and Mediterranean stations, in the second acting as senior medical officer. Amongst the honours conferred upon him were Sir G Blane's Gold Medal for a medical history of the Burmese War in 1852, while serving in HMS *Hastings*; the silver medal of HEIC for the same war; the Baltic Medal; the medal of the Royal Polytechnic Society of Cornwall, for Natural History; and his medical and surgical notes in the Royal Dockyard are printed in the Parliamentary Blue Book 1869. His letter to *The Lancet*, complaining of having been ordered to use the stomach pump as a punishment on board HMS *Vanguard*, shortly after entering the navy, led to an Admiralty Order for the immediate abolition of the practice, though at the time his friends expected that he would be tried by a court-martial and dismissed the service for what they considered an act of madness. On his retiring from the medical superintendence of Sheerness Dockyard, a splendid testimonial was presented to him by the workmen; and on his arrival in Zetland, a public dinner in honour of him was given at Vass.

In 1850 he succeeded his uncle John in the Norbie estates; but, till within the last few years, owing to his devotion to his profession, his tenants only received an occasional visit. For many years after his succession the rental was expended in building improved dwellings and making other improvements. He has left a valuable collection of curiosities and *objets d'art* gathered in his many wanderings, and presented by the many friends he had made in other lands. By his marriage with Agnes Catherine, he leaves two daughters and a son. This son, being a minor, the estates fall under the management of trustees.

The funeral took place in the churchyard of Vass on Tuesday, 12th, and notwithstanding the inclemency of the weather, was attended by about two hundred of his tenancy and friends from various parts of Zetland, with whom Dr Scot's name was a familiar and loved household word, and by whom his memory will be treasured as that of a just, generous and broad-minded man.

This turn of events threw darkness over the whole of the Westside, not just the Red Coast: 'in Norbie Hall itself, where there had been laughter, came tears, and where there was hope, abandonment and futility now reigned', Gabrielsen notes.

Letter from Peter A Scot,
to Rev. Archibald Nicol
March 3rd 2001

Miami

Dear Reverend Archibald

I am enclosing a brief essay I have authored on the subject of the Rev. Thorvald Gabrielsen & the Christian sect known as the 'Tirvalites', which I'm sure will be of interest to you as a man of the clergy. My own interest springs from the fact that my father, the eldest of the children of Albert and Robina Scot, was a member of this sect and, in fact, was precentor of one of their churches as a young man. Though he spoke little about this period of his life, which I think for him was overlaid by his experiences as an ANZAC at Gallipoli, I know that the foundation of his religious faith was laid as a boy in New Zetland, while listening to this amazing man preach. By then, the Reverend Gabrielsen was quite an old man, of course, but my father always kept a photograph of him which I came into possession of on his death. The portrait is of a white-bearded figure of stony visage but on close study I can detect the edges of a smile in his eyes, a mildness which I believe the old Zetlanders used to refer to as 'blydeness' or 'blitheness'.

I do not make any claims to authorship of a great work, you will understand. My aim was simply to share this story with my church here in Miami, by means of this brief sketch, recently published in our magazine, with the photograph I mention. I am pleased to have shared this with you.

Yrs in faith
Peter A Scot

THE STORY OF THE REV. THORVALD GABRIELSEN
& THE 'TIRVALITES'
BY PETER A SCOT

To the Memory of
the Reverend Thorvald Erasmus Gabrielsen
Born Norbie, Zetland 29th September 1856
Died Serrafir, New Zetland 14th March 1916
Leader – Minister – Teacher

'He led God's People over 12,000 miles of Ocean'

Born to James and Catherine Gabrielsen of Zetland, Thorvald (pronounced 'Tirval') was a prodigious and thoughtful child who read the Bible avidly. He reportedly spent his days roaming amongst the hills, lochs and peat bogs of remote Norbie while reciting great quantities of verse from the Good Book.

Thorvald became a pupil teacher in his father and mother's school in Zetland until, at the age of seventeen, he was at last able to fulfill his ambition by enrolling at the University of Aberdeen. On graduating in 1877, he was awarded the Gold Medal for Moral Philosophy. Then, to enable him to enter the ministry and be guaranteed a presbytery, he had to complete Theological studies in Edinburgh. In the summer before his departure he married Mary Georgeson, who had long been his sweetheart. During his studies he earned the respect and friendship of a number of influential men who would later support him in his attempt to establish a religious colony, a 'New Zetland' in the distant South Pacific.

On completion of his studies in Edinburgh, Thorvald and Mary returned to Zetland, where he had been appointed as a teacher at the SPCK school in Roovik. Teachers with the Society for the Propagation of Christian Knowledge also doubled as lay preachers, and he soon came into conflict with the established minister in nearby Skeld. Their differences were fundamental, so much so that when the Gabrielsens wanted their first-born son John Luther to be baptised, they took him to Vass, twenty miles to the west. As Thorvald refused even to attend services officiated by this minister, his living was at risk. His stipend was stopped and in 1878 he went to Larvik where he spent a year working in the herring fisheries.

It was on the quaint little main street of Larvik that he firstly began to preach the Word, 'pure and incorrupted, as God intended', to all who would listen. His fame spread quickly, for he was a inspirational orator, and he gathered around him a group of followers dubbed 'The Tirvalites' by the people of the town. Their Temperant attitudes were not in tune with the mood of times in the Zetlandic capital as it suffered the wild years of the 'Great Herring Boom', so Thorvald and his flock resolved to emigrate and establish his long-held dream of a religious colony.

Thorvald's father, the schoolmaster at Norbie and noted scholar James Gabrielsen, was at that time the agent for emigration to New Zealand, and coincidentally a friend of the then prominent New Zealand Zetlander Robert Stoot, who had been taught surveying by Gabrielsen's father-in-law.

Knowing of the troubles of the barbaric Zetlandic colony started by Captain Jake Kulliness, known to the natives as 'Kapiyaki' at Serrafir, Stoot and Gabrielsen applied to the New Zealand governor, Sir George Grey, for a land grant on the islands, with the primary aim of establishing a church in this notoriously heathen place. Governor Grey, whilst having no jurisdiction over the territory, told them to proceed if they thought they might make a profit from the endeavour, and bring this outlandish archipelago into the community of God.

So it was that in early November 1881, Thorvald and Mary with seven of their children, and 150 other 'Tirvalites' set sail aboard the *Isabella Browne*, a barque of 236 tons, and the smaller *Zetland Lass*. Having called at Cape Town en route, the *Isabella Browne* made Adelaide in April 1882. The *Zetland Lass*, carrying another 55 parishioners, arrived in October. Here they intended to winter and replenish the supplies required to establish their colony.

Adelaide was in the grip of gold fever, following a huge strike at Ballarat near Melbourne, and the accompanying greed and violence made the place a misery for the 'Tirvalites'. When typhus struck and carried off three of his six sons, Thorvald believed that the Old Testament prophecy of plague and pestilence as a punishment for the worship of a false god was coming true. So, having gathered the necessary provisions, including a flock of one hundred Zetland sheep from a farmer who had successfully transplanted the species to Australia, they set sail for the far distant islands which would become their home, and on 21st September 1883, they arrived at last in the harbour at Serrafir, where they planned to encamp until they had surveyed and divided the land.

In Tokumua, as 'New Zetland' is now known, following the death of 'Kapiyaki', it came as a great surprise when the *Isabella Browne* sailed into Serrafir Vo, bearing the first flocks, but the peace-loving congregation found ready friends among the similarly inclined Murikavi people.

By September 1884, a grand wooden Meeting House with seating for five hundred was overflowing every Sabbath with settlers and natives alike. Thorvald was surrounded by Zetlandic-speaking Presbyterian crofters and fishers, and their modest womenfolk, who with their God-fearing ways kept the Sabbath holy and packed his church. In 1889, they built a fine wooden school. The 'Tirvalites' had found their 'Happyland' and they were joined by further settlers during that decade.

Thorvald and his family lived happily in Serrafir until his sudden death of apoplexy on the 14th of March 1916. His flock continued in their Tirvalite ways, but as the years passed they intermarried with the natives. Many moved away and their Zetland roots dwindled. However, in Serrafir his memory is kept alive by a memorial statue, next to the fine timbered Presbyterian Church that survives to this day.

With thanks to John Inkstir,
'The House of Memories', Tokumua

Letter from Philippa Gabrielsen
to Rev. Archibald Nicol
May 12th 2001

Bon Hoga

Dear Archie

I am enclosing the transcript of the last short interview I did with Ms
Mimie Jeromsen, once again in the hope of getting your comments on
the language. John Inkstir says your comments have been very useful in
helping to decode this vital source, and he has asked me to pass on his
thanks.

She is a dear frail soul, almost as delicate as the lacework shawl she
wears, and I fear my visits tire her out, yet at the same time she is very
keen to meet and talk, as I think she has no one left in her life now who
knows anything of where she started her life, and what changes she has
seen. The nurses are very kind to her, and do indeed seem to treasure her,
but do so I feel without really understanding her, when she speaks in her
broad Zetland tongue. I have been studying this myself lately, and now
feel much more confident in our discussions, as I seem to be developing
an ear for this strange dialect. So much of it echoes words or expressions
I know from Alroki, it's quite amazing to see how much of that is
Zetlandic in origin.

I very much hope to see her again when she is well enough and in the
mood to tell me more.

Bestist,
Philippa

MISS MIMIE JEROMSEN: 2ND INTERVIEW

Mimie, I'd like today to ask you about the Cunninghame family who you used to work for. I believe they had been a landowning fanily and had quite a pedigree back in Scotland, in old Zetland?

Weel, ja, dey wir been lairds a'Noarbie fir lang, oh ja, ever sin syn da Scotch lairds first cam, awa back, gude kens foo far. An dey aaned aa da laand ati'da Wast, ja, Thula an Papa an Vaela an aa. Hit wis a graet koos a'laand, ane a'da biggest estates ati'da whole a'Breetain in laand alaen. Bit du kens, pooramis laand, da maest. An aa dem, dey wir aa caa'ed John, doon trow time till hit fell'at ane a'dem dee'd wi nae issue. An so hit cam'at da Surgeon General cam ta be laird, aboot da mid a'da hidmist centirrie.

The Surgeon General?

Ja ja, a graet man he wis, dey aye said. He wis da mester o aa da surgeons an da doctors an dat atill aald Queen Victoria's fleet, awa doon in Englan, doon aboot London sumwye. Greenwich mebbie. A most eminent man, ja ja, wis da Surgeon General, as he wis caa'd … (LAUGHS)

Was that what people called him in Norbie?

Weel at first, du sees, whan first he cam nort as laird and fetcht wi him his young leddy wife, da Polish lass, dat wis fu his first introduced himsel. He stude up afoar aa da fokk gaddirt an said 'I am the Surgeon General'. He hed a graet wad a paepir wi a mukkle lang oration aa set, but eftir he sed da first twartree wirds, aa da fokk startit to clap and dat wis dat. Because aa da fokk kent him oniewye, his tale hed been telt aboot da fires, an d'ir wis nae need fir him ta tell hit agen. Bit eftir a start, dey aa caa'd him da Guid Doctor.

And what was the Surgeon General like?

Weel du kens I never led een apo'im mesel, na, he wis lang ati'da grund afoar I wis boarn, tho we heard plenty o'im fae wir aald fokk an dat. He wis lang-loved. He wis a good laird at a time whan dey wir plenty a'da tiddir … whit's da wird … complexion. Fir da estate hed been saer neglectit fir a generation. Da last John Scot moved awa ta Edienburgh eftir da tragedy a'his heir's droonin aboard da *Doris*.

That was the sailing ship that sank in the early 1800s? I've heard something about that.
Du kens dy Zetlin history dan, I see. Hit wis a mostaffil tragedy, mostaffil. Ja ja, dat hit wis. Aa da young lairds, droon'd. Ja, Guid bliss dem. An Young John Scot da floo'er among dem aa, dey sed. Ja ja, hit brook his faidir's hert dey sed, could never face ta bide near wattir.

So old John Scot went off to live in the city?
Ja ja, an da estate wis run be dis factor, ja, he wis a bit o a rogue dey sed, a grippy man'at nevir tendit ta da hooses nor noght a'dat, but wrang eviry penny he myght oot a'da fokk. Danadays fokk wis little better as slaves, du kens.

So the Surgeon General changed things when he inherited the estate?
Weel, ja, as da story gjings, he set himsel ta improve things, an biggit fokk twartree spleet-new hoosis an rummilt dem as wis maest in need a'rummlin. An dan he hed a felloo come an lay oot new crofts, aa squared aff an dat, he did awa wi da aald runrig wye, an dey drained da moodoo an aa. An aa dis whan iddir lairds wir joost harryin da fokk ta dir end. So ja, da fokk hed raeson ta laek da Surgeon General. An dan if dey wir a bodie seek ir dan mebbie someen faain an brukkit demsels, he wid gjing, ja, he wid gjing oot ta dem. Dey sed he even rade aa da wy ta Vass eens. Sum laad hed been ployin'im wi some kind a'cannon ir dat an he'd blaan his haand aff. An so da Surgeon General, he got himsel apo his powny an he set aff, ja, eght mile trow da paethill du kens, nae med road nor dat, an he traetit da boy, ja, an saved his life dey sed. So dat wis wihit'na kind a'boadie he wis, da Surgeon General, ja. An aafil blyde man aboot da fokk.

So this period of improvement that he set about, this would have been around when?
Och weel hit widda been sumtime atween da mid-centrie an his daeth. Ja, ati'da saxties mebbie.

The 1860s?

Ja ja, fir I tink hit widda been aboot 1875 dat he de'ed. Ja, I tink I mind hearin dat. He wis still a young fit man, dat I do ken, bit da Loard took him maest sudden. He wis oot traetin sum poor bodie as wis his guidhertit wint, an cam hem ati'da sleet an da rogh gael, an took himsel a fivir an never raise maer. Da Polish wife wis nae maer as a ting a'lass'at he'd taen hem wi him ta Noarbie, weel, she wis joost distroght. An her wi tree peerie bairns.

Three little children?

Tree peerie bairns. He wis a aald man whan he marriet, du sees, a man a'fifty, an she wis joost a lass a'twinty-six. Ja. He wis dat'n muckle aalder dan her, ja. Twintie-fower year, ja, I mind hearin dat.

It was something that people commented on?

Na na, I mean I heard aa dis fae me leddy. Weel me mistress, fir she wisna a leddy dan, na. Nor wis she whan she startit, except in her naitur.

You mean she wasn't lady of the manor when she came out here?

She wis nevir da 'lady of the manor', na, no hir. For tho I myght ryghtly caa hir me leddy, she wis aye joost wir Robina, da sweetest naitirt craitir du myght waant ta meet, ja ja. She nevir axt wis ta caa hir onythin bit da … joost Robina. Fir she wis aye wan a'wis, du sees. She wisna boarn ta da big hoose, na. Tho du kens d'ir wis nevir aen boarn that wis maer in her naetril hem daer, fir aa da fokk loved hir an waantit ta please hir. Mesel da maest a'dem, ja.

So she was a good boss to work for?

Weel, I never kent nae iddir aen, an I nivir felt hir ta be muckle o a boss. She wis my freend an gaerdian in a unken wirld, yeah, feth, dat she wis!

So your mistress, Robina … the lady, she told you about the Scot family?

Oh ja ja, she wid news awa ta me aboot a lokk a'whit fell whan dey bed apo da Aald Rock, oh ja (LAUGHS) … du kens hit wis a mostaafil scandal, dat. At da time, dey sed. I wisna boarn mesel.

A scandal in the family?
Weel ja, dir wis dat aaright. Whan da young laird ran awa wi her.

With your mistress, Robina?
I doot A'm sed owir muckle aboot'it aaready. (AT THIS MIMIE BECAME QUITE UNSETTLED) Na, A'll better no tell de yon, na. Hit laekie widna be right apo dir memory, na. Tho du kens da fokk at spakk ill a'dem nevir kent da half a'whit gied on. (PAUSE)

There's no need to tell us anything that's … if that's going to make you uncomfortable, Mimie.
Du sees dir wis dat'n a steuch aboot hit aa. Tho hit wis lang owir whan I wis boarn, me middir kent aa aboot it, an she hed lang been tyght freends wi Bieni … as she aye caa'd her … no even Robina dan. Na, she wis joost Bieni ta me middir, whan dey wir growin up. An she aye took Robina's paert, me middir.

Can you tell us what actually happened?
(PAUSE) Lass, I dunna ken. A'll see. A'll tink apo'it, ja. Wheddir hit wid be ryght ir no, du sees. (PAUSE) Well, hit's a lang time ago I ken. D'ir mebbie nane as minds da fokk bit me disdays. An w'ir apo da tiddir side a'da glob, ja. So I suppose it laekie widna do a lokk a'herm.

As you know we're trying to gather as much of the history …
Dat dat, ja … I ken, lass, du's telt me. But du sees, fokk nevir spakk muckle aboot yon kinda thing eensadays. Na na. (PAUSE) I tink A'll awa an lay me doon a peerie start … (END OF THE 2ND INTERVIEW.)

~~Weeks have passed since I last added lines to this narrative, in which the illness has held sway with me, distracting my mind from all else. The pain was at times too overwhelming. I could do no more than barely survive, functioning at only the most basic level, while praying for deliverance. In the last few days I have returned to my study, at first to read – and now,~~

at last, to record again. I find the preceding pages to be rather a blotted copybook, with passages crossed out, intrusion and diversion dominant. It seems that I have repeatedly entered upon my scene as a player, then exited clumsily. I began with the intention of explaining the mystery of the pilgrim's 'wiedergeburt' and now I find I have added another layer to it.

I have been reading again Professor Gwatkin's volume on *Early Church History*, and note afresh how the first three hundred years of the Christian era were filled by passionate debate over the most fundamental of concerns. Concerns such as, was Jesus real or some kind of apparition, was he truly the Son of God? And what did it mean, then, to say that – or indeed, that he was born of the Flesh? How could there be such a thing as an Immaculate Conception? And so on. Before St Augustine and his influence, before the orthodoxies were defined. What strikes me now is how like the debates of the modern age these early speculations were, as if the definition of the earlier era and the decay of the latter were symmetrically related; and the latter was the unravelling of the construction.

And so I have come to consider afresh the wandering convert who sent me his story; and I see how he, in naïve response to divine revelation, required no reason for his belief. He had felt the power of the Lord and was without doubt. The Holy Spirit had touched him.

Once I too knew that joy of certainty, indeed ever since I was called to the ministry and all through the early years of marriage, I was remarkably untroubled by doubt. In my earlier days, what later generations dubbed 'the teenage years', I explored a little, read about other religions and tried to test the childhood beliefs I had inherited; but after I had settled on the ministry I never looked back again. I accepted my calling. Even up until Margaret's death I had, if not the ecstasy of recent conversion, then the lasting peace that comes with sure comfort. Now I can find no such easy solace. This suffering undermines my calm. I doubt Eternal Goodness; shun my fellow man; and bury my pain as best I can in

24th June 2000 – Innertoon

So I stand a moment at the door, overwhelmed by this little hive of life and laughter, a shock of congregation in the miserable fog. Then, making apologies, I weave my way to the bar between the tables, over stone flags. It isn't far, but circumnavigating the crowd is slow work, as tricky as the drive through the mist.

'Yes luv, what can I get you?' the dolled-up barmaid asks in a north of England voice – she smiles at me, as if she knows me.

'I'd like a beer, please. And is there a phone I can use?'

'Phone's round there by the bar. But you'll never hear, love. Listen, what I'll do is, I'll take you through the back and you can phone from there. I'm due a cup of tea. Phone box not working again?'

'No, the old man who gave me a lift, the shepherd with the green van, he said to ask in here.' And she nods her head.

'It's kids,' she says. 'Vandals. So he's out and about is he, even in this weather?'

'I'm glad he was,' I say. 'Or I'd never have made it.'

She hands me my pint, but won't take my money. 'It's all right, luv, on the house. I'm Maggie, by the way. Friend of your dad's. Give me five minutes to clear the glasses. See if anyone wants a drink.'

So I'm known here. I squeeze into a corner near the music and stand, leaning against the wall. There's a peat fire, like I've seen before in Donegal in what they call a kitchen bar. This is a Zetlandic one.

Two fiddlers play, a guitarist and someone with a bodhran, thrumming away. One fiddler is young, with shaven head, a piercing in her lower lip, extravagant earrings too. She uses every single millimetre of the bow, so that her arm travels in a far larger arc than the other fiddler, also a lassie, whose primmer manner involves more strokes of shorter length. It's fascinating to watch how they express their personalities through their playing, how they play off one against another, even as they play together. The guitarist I realise is not a guitarist, but a bouzouki player.

It's a fine noise they're making by the roaring fire, and folk's feet are tapping even though they're talking at tables.

Then Maggie beckons me to follow her, up the step onto the floor behind the bar, and through a little archway to the rear. She takes me up a flight of steps from a cellar, through a door at the top, where we emerge as if from an underworld into a hallway of complete domestic stillness.

'It's nice to get away from the noise for a while,' she says, 'And I'm due a cup of tea. I'll show you where the phone is and put the kettle on. I hope he's all right. Too tight with the big house for his own good.' she says.

I give her a what do you mean look.

'Oh, the estate might be a separate kingdom, but there is some traffic between them, I assure you.' And she laughs.

'Why do you say the estate's different?'

'Well, this isn't Dr Hart's land here. No, he owns the ness and all the land round Outertown, but this is a separate estate. It's a community cooperative. The quarry is the boundary. His quarry. And much fuss there is about that right now.'

I'm nodding as she's talking, leaning over the end of the bannister.

'But folk do come down here, as I say, and we get the latest news. It's been quite the talk lately. What with the fire and then your father. Then you turning up.'

I nod. 'What about that fire?'

'Strange business,' she says, but doesn't expand. 'And that weirdo couple.'

'In the other chalet?'

'You've met them?'

'I surely have.'

'Then you'll know,' she says, and laughs.

'So did my father come in here a lot?'

'He did, for a while. But then he got into an argument with somebody and he hadn't been around for while, before ... you know, disappearing.' Then she adds, 'I liked him, though.'

And she spins away and through the house, presumably to the kettle. I go to lift the receiver, but she's calling through to me: 'So why is it you can't phone from the laird's house?'

'Oh, I probably could, but ... I suppose I just didn't feel it was private.'

'What you mean is it's all too private, don't you? But not private for you.

From what I hear folk saying, there's been all sorts going on up there.'

'Oh?'

'All sorts. Of course how much of it is true is another question. But a big fuss. I'll let you get on with the phone call.'

But no, I say no, tell me, please, what's been said. I'm trying to piece together a picture of exactly what has been going on there.

'You sure you're okay, love? You know, I don't think you're well, are you?'

'I'm all right. I've been feeling a bit light headed. Dizzy. I had a fall, banged my head.'

'I heard,' she says. 'You met my son. When you fell. Let me see.' And Maggie lays her gentle barmaid's hands on my head, parts my hair at the lump.

'You do have a bump, don't you? You've been bleeding. You might be a bit concussed. Come through here then, chuck.'

After I'd made the phone call and spoken to Gran, sitting in the depths of her settee, Maggie introduces herself properly, and pours the tea.

'It's probably none of my business,' she says. 'But you know how it is, you see things going on and you wonder. Anyway, there's rumours being going around down here about Mary Mitchell and your father. And everybody knows that she and the laird have been together for a while, you know.'

And from the look she gives me, I can tell what she means.

'Mary may be a flirt, but ...' I say.

'No,' she says, 'It was more than flirting, what the person saw.'

For a while I just sit there. Something tells me that this woman, this sensible, reliable bar manager woman who likes my father, is telling me the truth.

'So I don't think that's something that Lord Snooty will be telling the police, if you get my drift.'

Yes, I do drift, drift into all sorts of scenarios.

'You okay, love?'

'I'm just thinking. You know, what difference that might make to the whole situation.'

'Well, don't think too hard. It's police business, not yours. I just thought you should hear what's been said.'

'Who said it?'

'Someone who knows. But they depend on the estate for their livelihood and wouldn't want to make enemies.'

But when she comes back with the tea tray, I have formed a question. 'You said my father had an argument. Who was that with?'

'One of the customers. A regular. It was stupid. Nothing at all. Want to use the phone now?'

I suddenly picture the horizon as I'd seen it from the ness that first day. The ships I saw. And it strikes me: 'Dr Hart says there's no other way off the island but the ferry and airport. Couldn't he have got aboard some other kind of boat? A fishing boat, maybe?'

'I suppose so. Is that likely?'

'It's just that there was this man who lived next door, he was a cook on a fishing boat and I wondered if maybe ...'

'I'll ask. Some of the lads from the boats are in. We'll see if they know anything.'

In the bar, the fiddlers have put down their bows. They're talking deeply, maybe swapping techniques. The one with the piercing and the shaven head looks up and smiles, as if maybe she recognises me as a comrade.

Maggie stops to serve whoever wants, and then she's going to take me to the poolroom, where the fishermen might be. The fiddler takes up her bow, and the bouzouki player strums a chord. Gently she sways out a melody, sad and somehow wrong for the mood of the pub, but slowly people hush and listen, as if they'd been waiting for just that tune, to help them set aside the business of the day and touch something deeper inside them. The other fiddler picks up, a contrastive harmony, and the man with the bodhran rumbles a soft but threatening percussion. And all in the pub sits transfixed as the tune is drawn out by the swaying arms and careful fingers, a glorious noise for a minute or so, that captures all like a common thought, bringing understanding and stillness.

But only for a moment, before the folk in the farthest away booth begin to talk, and the musicians are lost again in the fog of conversation. The peat fire burns fiercely. I'm too close for my liking, too warm, with my fleece and my jacket. Then Maggie is curving her tapered forefinger and hooking my attention with a follow me sign. And I do, brushing against strangers who hardly seem to notice or to care, through a small doorway into a back room. The pool room. It's cool in here, pleasant.

Inside five young guys are standing round the table.

'Any of you know Colin who comes in here sometimes,' Maggie asks. 'A cook on one of the boats.'

All look a little uncertain.

'That the auld bald guy?' says one.

'No, that's not him. Colin's the bloke fae sooth,' another says, digging him in the side with a pool cue.

'Oh ya, I ken him. He's on the *Sirius*. Or he wis, last I heard,' comes a third.

'Hey, Gansey, tak de shot!'

The speaker comes round the table to address the white ball. He's lining up a stripe for the far left-hand corner. He lets the cue go, the balls crack, and the target ball is thumping into the pocket. A couple of the fishermen cheer.

'Yeah,' he says. 'I'm sure it's the *Sirius* he's on.' And he gives his attention to the cue ball again. This time the shot is tight and requires a little spin to bring the white back into position for the next. He lines it up and fires it down.

'Do you know if any of the crew's around?' Maggie asks.

'No, she was going to be workin the Minch, last I heard.'

'When was that?'

'Week ago, maybe.'

'Can you radio them?'

'Maybe.'

'Okay, could you do that when you go back to the boat? Ask them if they've had a Rod Cunninghame aboard. It's important.'

'That the guy that's disappeared?'

'Aye, you ken him. He's in here sometimes. The one that spouts all the old poetry.'

'Oh, auld Wordsworth?' he laughs. 'Everybody kens Wordsworth. Why did you no say?'

The one who told us the boat's name rattles the black in and the game's over.

I ask when they'll hear from the *Sirius*.

'Dinna ken,' he answers. 'Whenever we do it.'

'When will that be?'

'When we go back to the boat. Could be any time.'

'Where is the boat?'

'In the harbour.'

'The harbour here?'

'Aye.'

Back in the inferno, the fiddlers are playing fast and loose with their bows, jazzing up the folk tune they're playing with. I lean against the dry-stone wall. It's like a burrow in here, a stone burrow. Like something medieval, unchanged since the dark ages. Except of course for the fruit machine, juke box, satellite TV and all the advertising packed in among the people.

Maggie sees me standing there and beckons me over. I weave through the crowd, brushing against bodies, and when I get to the bar, she hands me a wine glass with something rich and brown in it. 'My own tonic. Brandy, port, bitters. Get it down you.'

'Thanks,' I say, 'but I'd better get back.'

'Back to the big house tonight? In this weather?' she asks. 'Why not just stay over? You can have the spare room.'

I appreciate this. But I tell her that with all this going on I'd best get back. I've already missed dinner.

'You're sure now? You know, I think your father would have wanted you to stay.'

'Why?'

'Just my feeling.' Then she's gone, off to serve drinks, leaving me puzzled. But I don't care. It's just good to be among strangers, it's good to know that I have established that the clue is a clue. And I'll be there, yes, at three o'clock on Monday, I will be in that restaurant in Perth. At a table for three.

It strikes me as odd how kind she is. She seems to know all about me, even about my fall, which of course her son must have told her about.

What is it she's so interested in me for? Gossip from the big house? Maybe, maybe.

A round full moon face with florid cheeks and thinning grey hair is at my shoulder. 'Maggie says you're Rod's bairn. Any news?'

'No, still nothing.'

He nods his head slowly. 'Listen, why no come and sit down here with us?' And he points across the crowded floor to where four faces are all staring at me, smiling, invitingly, come over. Another man and two women. 'We kent him, you see. We were friends.'

All through this, the fiddler has been glancing towards me as she plays. It's as if she recognises me, or something. But I'm sure I don't know her. Not even from a very long time ago, somewhere completely different. But she keeps glancing at me as she sways around, swinging that bow. But then I realise they all know me now, the word has spread around the folk, of who I am.

'You're Rod's bairn, eh? I'm a friend. Roy. Convener of the community cooperative. But mind you, I make a point of never setting foot on that estate,' he says. 'Decadent fuckin feudal. Fuckin anachronism. But as long as people go along with it they keep the whole system going. The ones that'll turn up to every function in the big hoose minding their Ps and Qs like good fucking peasants.' I nod. 'Listen,' he says, 'I hope nothing's happened to your auld fella.'

And yes, I can see how my father would fit in and be a comrade here, why it was that Maggie'd been so kind. They liked him. 'Auld Rodie'. 'Wordsworth'. 'A Comrade'.

The fire's hot, but somebody throws another couple of peats on. The shaven-headed fiddler has stripped off her purple woollen jumper and she's throwing the bow like it was a javelin or a pool cue. People are roaring with laughter and I drink another, wedged in among them. The fiddler's belting it out, swinging the bow and the tune all round the room, she's possessed by the rhythm, contorting her face as if a demon's got her, a demon of a tune. I strip to my T-shirt, but still I'm too hot. Can't be bothered going anywhere, couldn't care less about murder

or dinner

just want to sway with the folk

Then Roy leans over, begs my ear: 'So you're the true heir, then?' He laughs, a wild look in his eye.

I don't understand.

'The true fuckin son and heir. Come back to claim your right.'

'I'm not much like my father,' I say. 'Not really.'

The fiddler's bow knocks down a pint glass and it smashes on the flag-stone floor, but nobody seems to care. She just goes on playing, winging ever higher, sloping ever lower. The fiddler's our leader, my feet are dancing, head is nodding, I'll follow her anywhere.

There are too many things to squeeze into my not-too-clever mind right now. Everything has a spin, nobody is without sin. It's a dark and deeply

depressing

world

CHAPTER EIGHT

'THE CROFTERS COMMISSION INVESTIGATES'

William Guthrie's 2nd Truck Commission Report of 1873 is a substantial document and demonstrates the thoroughness of the investigation, yet it had little actual effect. Commentators suggested that this was due to the fact that 'complaints of the men themselves were not loud or frequent' – that they were so cowed by the oppression of their masters that they were afraid to speak at liberty. It seemed the fundamental issue was land-tenure, and that this must needs be investigated. So the Crofters Commission of the following decade developed.

Reputable men were gathered under the presidence of Lord Napier and in the summer of 1883 the deputation took to the sea in a steam-yacht – the *Prometheus*, chartered from the Lighthouse Commission for Northern Waters. For the following close account, we must again thank James Gabrielsen, who was present on this voyage, and recorded the events for *The Scotsman*.

Sheriff Elfinston was chair, Lords Cameron and Frazer-Mackintosh his primary investigators. Their intention was to call at a number of the more isolated places in addition to the main ports, and there hear directly the grievances of the people regarding their landlords.

By July, they had completed their exertions in the south of Zetland, and the Commissioners' yacht sailed from Skallvaa to Thulay, the fabled isle to the west of the Westness.

Looking at their records the Commissioners saw that the two hundred and seventy inhabitants paid a yearly rental amongst them of £140 to the estate owned by Mr Albert Scot of Norbie, which was administered by the firm of Berrick & Co, factors, the laird being in his minority. Of thirty-eight families living there, all were headed by crofter-fishermen, catching cod and ling from six-oared boats. In addition, the islanders supplied crew for two herring boats fishing out of Berrick's station at Vass.

As the yacht approached the island, the sheer magnitude of Thulay's cliffs astounded the Commissioners, appearing to rise from nowhere out of the Western Ocean and growing steadily, from a distant three-stepped outline into a vast mountainous steeps, towering over the vessel, as if it were a 'gigantic green iceberg, floating northwards, having broken away from the west of Europe', Cameron observed.

'All manner of sea-fowl are studded into the rock-face, like jewel seams in a mine,' Sheriff Elfinston added.

The harbour was barely more than a cleft in the rock face, with a tiny jetty across its mouth, and so landing on Thulay was never easy if the sea was against it. Ships had been known to turn back many a time, with frustrated passengers and cargo undelivered after an eventless crossing. But the Commissioners were blessed in this respect and they came ashore to a great welcome. It seemed the whole population of the island, including babes in arms, had congregated at the tiny harbour to greet them.

They proceeded to the schoolhouse in a great mass, led by the Thulay 'parliemen', while the rest of the population followed on as best as legs and curiosity could carry them. The Commissioners were glad to be ashore, and ever more amazed by the isolation of the rock.

It was remarked by one of the welcoming party, a Mr Gaer, that no person not born there could ever shake the sense of being at the absolute outer limit of the world that Thulay engendered – and that no Thulay person ever felt themselves to be anything other than at the centre of civilisation there, while life on the Zetland mainland was at least one step removed from the heart of their solar system, and London as distant as Uranus.

'No matter how dreadful or marvellous their deeds elsewhere in the globe, those are as nothing next to their conduct under the Thulay fells,' he added.

The Commissioners had intended to hold their meeting in the school, but the day was so inviting that it was resolved to do so in the open air and a table was brought out to act as the bench. With the Commissioners seated, proceedings began.

The folk of Thulay, in readiness for their arrival, had assembled their 'parliemen', or 'Da Ting' as it was called in the local tongue, and had elected this Robert Gaer, Church of Scotland catechist and crofter, and Mr

Andrew Robertson, crofter, to represent their views, as 'the best speakers on Thulay'.

Robertson read the minutes of a meeting held on the 11th June at the Congregational Manse, presided over by Mr George Morrison, the minister, which bore that the Thulay folk had raised a subscription to send delegates to see the Commission at Larvik, should they fail to call at Thulay while on their tour. This memorial was to have been presented to the Commissioners, as a faithful expression of their wishes, in such an event.

Now that they had in fact arrived, Gaer said the paper in question set forth that they respectfully submitted that rents were excessive, and out of all proportion either to the value of what the soil could produce, or to the value of rich farming land in other parts of Scotland. They were 'unable to state the exact sum paid by each tenant, as the public burdens were collected along with them and they got no receipts; but as nearly as they could calculate, the best portion of the isle was rented all over at 23 shillings per acre for arable land, including the right to hill pasturage.'

'The soil is very poor and exhausted, and owing to the parlous position of the isle a large part of the crop is often either blasted by sea, or shaken and destroyed by violent gales,' said Robertson. 'We have calculated that on an average our crops do not provide us with bread for more than four or five months a year. All the rest we must buy.'

'In recent years the rents have fallen in certain parts of Scotland, but here no man has ever heard of rent decreases; it has been rising, rising, rising, for generations,' Gaer said, and added that 'Whenever church or manse repairs are executed in Vass, there is an increase of rent all over the Norbie estate to cover the cost, and that remains till the next repairs are called for, where increase number two is made in addition to increase number one.' Gaer went on: 'The manse of Vass was built about 1867. Most of us have paid 10 shillings a year since towards its cost, and there is no indication of the charge ceasing. The people get no advantage from the parish of Vass. The minister is supposed to come to preach twice a year, but is afraid of the sea.'

Commissioner Cameron then observed that 'even if he did come, he would no doubt omit to bring the new manse with him,' and laughter broke out among the folk.

Gaer went on with his report. 'There is no work to be had in the island. We must depend on the sea for our often precarious enough means of existence, and respectfully submit that it is entirely unjust for us to be charged rents that our crofts cannot produce, but which must be fished out of the sea. Even if rents were more equitable, we would still be at a disadvantage, our situation compelling us to sell in the cheapest and buy in the dearest market.'

Robertson, a more placatory individual, intervened, as if fearing Gaer had spoken too forcefully: 'For a long time the landlord has been of a good type, and the factor as sympathetic and forbearing as possible: but we cannot tell how soon changes might come, and we respectfully submit that tenancy should be secured by something more than the good disposition of a factor, who might soon be removed.'

Robertson's assessment had some support amongst the people, but there arose from a certain quarter a strange, dissenting hiss. He glanced briefly in the direction it appeared from, frowned, and carried on thus: 'As tenants we have nothing but praise to give the current factor. He has ever been considerate and merciful; and as islanders we owe much to the merchants for whom we fish, Messrs Berrick & Co of Roovik. Whether we are in debt or not they always supply the necessaries of life, and they have done so in cases where there was little probability they would ever be paid.'

Though they clearly represented different parties within the population, Gaer and Robertson both regretted that so many of the Thulay folk were falling deep in debt, and were barely able to pay their way. They respectfully gave the following practical suggestions, the considered verdict of the Thulay Ting. Some of the proposals would be mainly for the benefit of Thulay itself, while others would be to the public advantage in the world outside.

1) That a substantial reduction be made on existing rents; *and*
2) that the power of eviction be curtailed by leases and otherwise; *and*
3) that compensation be given for tenants' improvements; *and*
4) that the attention of the government be called to the very

unsatisfactory mail service, *and*

5) that the necessity of obtaining a more suitable vessel be emphasised; *and*

6) that the port of departure instead of Gaerdirhuis be Vass, as that is much nearer to Thulay; *and*

7) that in the interests not only of the island, but of the national fisheries, so advantageously situated a fishing station as Thulay should be turned to account by the construction of a proper harbour; *and*

8) that in the interest of the fishing, and for the safety of the mercantile marine, a lighthouse should be erected here.

In addition to this, Gaer then read out the following list of grievances:

1) The whole trade of the island is a monopoly in the hands of Messrs Berrick & Co and the inhabitants do not therefore enjoy the benefits of competition, and, although most industrious, are kept in a state of hopeless poverty.

2) The want of fixity of tenure perpetuates this system by deterring competition.

3) The want of a proper mail service retards the development of the island's resources. A small packet of about fourteen tons burden at present carries the mail from Roovik. She ought to call at Thulay once a fortnight but it frequently happens that due to the lack of a proper harbour there is often no communication between Thulay and the outside world for perhaps two months at a time, which is clearly to the disadvantage of both the island and the world.

4) The continued charge for building a manse at Vass, of which parish Thulay is a part, and the cost of which we believe should have been defrayed long ago from the revenue derivable from Church lands.

Mr Gaer went on to say that he hoped the Commissioners would heed the words of the Thulay Ting, for they had thought hard of the best solutions. He also trusted that the Commissioners would use their influence in protecting him from any annoyance which those in power might feel inclined to inflict, in consequence of his having given a true description of the condition and wishes of the inhabitants of Thulay from personal experience.

The Commissioners then began to question him. When they asked about leases, the whole company laughed.

Gaer said, 'There was never such a thing as a lease. Folk are tenants at will. There is none individual proprietor of his place.'

A voice from the crowd shouted, 'It is simply a republic,' and this drew further laughter, to which Frazer-Mackintosh rejoindered, 'A republic without liberty?'

Sheriff Elfinston wanted to know of Gaer, 'Did not Messrs Berrick offer to give up their business about ten or twelve years ago and did the people of Thulay not to a man sign a paper that the monopoly should not be given up?'

Gaer answered, 'Yes, I believe they signed Mr Berrick's paper to fish for him.'

'Why did they do that if they wanted the monopoly broken up?'

'Because folk have been so long in slavery, not only here but all over Zetland, and are afraid of the evil that might result if they oppose the factors.'

At this bold statement, expressed with a burst of visible anger, a gasp passed through the crowd, and a dog began to bark, which was rapidly silenced with a guttural roar. Another strange hiss of dissent arose. From the rear came a voice: 'If it hadna been for Mr Berrick some of us would not be alive the day. He has done like a gentleman for us, an we ought tae be thankful tae him for it.' At which several others murmured their support.

Another stepped forward, as if to speak for these dissenters. The Commissioners asked him to identify himself for the record. He said that he was George Morrison, missionary, not an ordained minister, but connected to the Congregational Union. He had been in Thulay for two years and had attended the meetings of Da Ting in order to help translate their wishes into language that the Commissioners would comprehend.

'I have heard all the discussions and it is clear to me now that Mr Gaer has gone far beyond his role, in handing this supplement to your Lordships. His is not the opinion of the majority of people by any means.'

More of the curious hissing followed, this time from the other party, and Sheriff Elfinston called order, before instructing Morrison to continue.

Personally, Morrison thought that another shop on the island would not improve things at all, for 'there is so little profit in the trade with the island, both businesses might give up, were it to be halved'.

Mr Frazer-Mackintosh asked if he considered that it was for the benefit of Messrs Berrick that they maintained a shop there, to which no reply came. Then he added, 'Is it not a fact that the proprietor forbids any contact with other traders?'

Morrison conceded that he could not answer.

Sheriff Elfinston wished to know about the religious habits of the people. 'Are many of you Congregational?'

Morrison replied, 'Most of us. Indeed, few have connection with the Church of Scotland here, unlike the mainland part of the parish.'

'Which perhaps accounts for the strong objection to the rent increase for the Vass manse,' Frazer-Mackintosh noted, smiling.

The sun was blessing the meeting and tempers improved. Sheriff Elfinston inquired as to the level of attendance, to which Morrison answered that 'all attend regularly, though they are not as strict Sabbatarians as in the West Highlands and the Hebrides'.

'Do they consider it a sin to wander about admiring the beauties of nature on a Sunday?' asked Lord Cameron.

'No, they do not. They are not so straight-laced as that.'

'Are they against such vain things as the singing of songs?' Frazer-Mackintosh inquired.

'No, the inhabitants are very musical, very fond of sacred music. And their fiddles, of course.'

The mention of the fiddle brought whistles and cheers from the crowd. And so towards the close of the meeting, proceedings took on a more conversational shape, with various voices speaking as they felt the spirit move them.

The Commissioners inquired as to stock, and were told that they averaged three cows and six sheep. None of them kept ponies, as only the proprietor was allowed that, which all complained of as the ponies would be very useful for transporting fuel from the hill where the turf was cut. At present the womenfolk had to carry it their wicker 'kyshies' about a mile on their backs, knitting all the while as they walked. They also said that they still had the fire in the middle of the roof, though none of them now kept cows in the family home as their forebears had done.

The soil, the Commissioners learned, was 'mostly peat and clay'. Elfinston asked what crop grew best, to which a wag at the back shouted 'None of them.'

When asked about emigration, they answered that a good many of the young men had gone for sailors, and about twenty years ago a number of families went to New Zetland, aboard a ship chartered by Berrick on behalf of the laird, an expedition led by the son of the schoolmaster at Norbie.

'Nane o those wha left hae ever come back hame tae Thulay,' said one matron, perhaps thinking of a child of her own.

The young women, when asked, said they would never leave Thulay. One explained, shyly, that the world away from there 'could never be hame tae them'.

'And we could not raise our children in an unhomely place, for they would not then be Thulay folk,' a second said.

Another added: 'And how could a mother not belong to the same place as her child?'

The young men, when asked if they would leave, said that if they had a powerful steamboat here, like the one the Commissioners came in, to carry away the fish they caught to market fresh, they 'would make a lot more money and grow rich, and live well here', at which the girls all giggled happily.

The matrons and the older men complained of the high price of certain luxuries. Sugar was 6d. per pound, while tobacco the men considered very dear at 6s. per pound. In contrast, the price paid to them by Berrick's for their eggs was a pittance.

As to the matter of diet, fish was common. In winter they had bread and milk for breakfast when they could get it, but there was a great scarcity of the latter for want of cattle; sometimes just a little black bread and black tea was all they managed. They had fish and potatoes for dinner, but the potatoes were so very wet, you could wring the water from them. They rarely killed a cow, but ate their old sheep. They had no doctor on the island, the nearest being in Vass, but most of them had good health.

'Perhaps none the worse for not having a doctor?' observed Commissioner Cameron.

'Ah well, maybe,' came the general answer.

'Potatoes and fish seem to make you as big and strong as we have seen anywhere,' said Sheriff Elfinston, and they laughed.

'Or indeed as pretty,' Cameron added, 'as any of the lasses.' At which all, even the ugliest, of the Thulay girls felt a little shiver of pleasure, and stared hard at the particular young man she had her eye on.

This was a perfect note on which to conclude the meeting, as the Commissioners at last fell silent, their questions done, and the people seemed indulged by this closing kindness.

But then, just as they were preparing to leave the makeshift bench, there stepped forward a very old man, a tiny wizened figure with a staff, who immediately appeared to command the respect of the assembly as some kind of tribal elder. His white beard hung below his waistband, yet his eyes seemed to gleam with youth. He said, in a heavy Norse accent, that he spoke English poorly, being the last Norn speaker on the island, but begged leave to have his say. Morrison agreed to translate if required.

Commissioner Cameron asked who he was, and he replied that his Lordships might address him as 'Daldmana Thulay', which he spelled out. The folk all laughed, but it took a minute for the Commissioners to see the joke. Despite his disclaimer, he continued perfectly clearly in heavily accented English, speaking very slowly, as if translating every phrase carefully in his mind beforehand.

'Most of us reckon James Berrick ... a merciful man ... though we are less sure about his older brother. Whatever name you may give ... to the system ... whether monopoly as you have termed it or godsend ... he is our current means of ... winning our living ... and none of us would harm that. But,' he said, 'the Thulay folk have forgotten the courage of their fathers ... and no longer do they take wildfowl from the cliffs. In my bairndom ... it was the fowling ... kept us alive ... when other foods were scarce … and now so few of the young men know the cliffs … they have lost the taste for all seabirds except pirisolan.'

The Commissioners asked of him what 'pirisolan' was and were told it was the greatest of delicacies, young gannets specially prepared, and that they would have the chance to sample some after the meeting.

'It is a terrible waste,' the old man said, 'of the island's resources to be letting so many fowl escape.' He spat a dark tobacco jet on the ground and cast his gaze across the men assembled and they averted their eyes, as if they knew that he was right.

'If I was three score years younger … I would show them all … how to scale the steeps.'

They brightened at this, and Gaer muttered to the Commissioners that if only he could show them, they would gladly go with him, for it was the pox that had wiped out the knowledge, there being only six fit men left alive when it was done with them, and none of them cliffmasters.

But the old man ignored them. 'I do not think,' he said, 'that these times are any worse … than the past. Life has always been hard and … it is true that the people … have been enlightened … as to the ways of the world. But … I doubt they will require a great deal more light … before they make anything of it.' He went on, 'Things being as they are, we must do what we can … the crofter has had a hard and bitter time … we work a good deal harder than many a rich man's horse and we have had to do it to keep alive our families. The crofters are the true strength of the nation … they ought to get a little more fair play in time to come … than they have had at the hands of the landlords in the past … but I do not blame them as much as the land laws … that allow them … to behave as they do.'

The company as one agreed, bending their heads to nodding and murmuring, as he spat again. 'Every man is selfish,' he said, 'so why not the landowners too, just the same as others. Yet something should be done for the crofters and not only of Thulay … I do not wish it for myself, but for the rising generation … it is not right that any part of the British Dominions … should live as if they were in slavery.'

At this he fell silent and the Commissioners could do little but nod in agreement at the words of the old man. Then proceedings were terminated by the chairman thanking all the islanders for coming out to speak with them. The Thulay folk thanked the Commissioners for coming, and hoped that they would not forget their visit. The Commissioners promised to give their memorial their best attentions.

The majority of the company arose and retreated a little, but a large number remained at a discreet distance, watching as the women brought a selection of platters and the Commissioners were honoured by a repast of Thulay delicacies, which they found interesting – the delicacy that was the pirisolan lay rather uncomfortably in the Commissioners' stomachs afterwards.

Led by Mr Gaer, they then proceeded to the top of the high cliffs, and enjoyed a splendid lookout on all sides. They were shown a number of curiosities, and heard about 'Hell's Lum', a hole which descended from the heights into the earth and was reckoned to be 'bottomless, for none that had gone down there had ever come back, and must be climbing down still,' as one wag said. But the exact whereabouts of this amazing feature had been forgotten, it was said, like much of the old lore, with the plague and the death of the old Norse language – though curiously they retained the Norse fiddle of their ancestors.

On descending again to the shore, they were met once more by the whole population, who said their farewells in such fond measure that it seemed to the Commissioners they were parting from old friends.

The steamship sailed round to the face of the great cliffs and again they all marvelled at the sheer scale of them, saying that they had never seen such steeps anywhere. The mass of seabirds nesting there gave off such a stench of guano that their stomachs were rather tested.

A great number of the Thulay folk had scaled the fell at the lowest point and were waving. Over the surface of the swelling waves, as if bouncing off it, there seemed to sound the echo of some song of parting, though 'Auld Lang Syne' it was not. A few, no doubt the youngest and the fittest, had even climbed as far as the shoulder of the Great Kame itself.

As the sun began to move through the western sky, the helmsman turned the bow away from it, and steamed towards Skallvaa. The Commissioners conferred and agreed that, strange and ignorant of the world outside though they be, and entirely mistaken as to the value and standing of their quaint place within it, yet the Thulay folk had made a great deal of sense. There was, in their geographical extremity and their methods of arranging their mental map to ignore it, something of the condition of all people.

'For is not every one of us naïve in assumption of our own centrality, of our own importance?' said Lord Frazer-Mackintosh, obviously quite moved. 'Yet without such solipsism, how could one motivate oneself to live to the fullest harvest of our God-given potential?'

This had been the most memorable of the hearings thus far and their pirisolan, particularly, was unforgettable. 'Some deep understanding of the condition of man seemed to be stirred by this outpost,' Gabrielsen tells us, 'and all were affected by it.'

As the distinctive three-stepped outline of the mysterious isle slipped into the distance, the sun from the west shadowing it into darkest relief, they were struck again by its remoteness, and were glad to see the tiny lighthouse ahead signal the comparative civilisation of the ramshackle little old capital, skirting the old Stewart castle of the former tyrant, 'Black Patie'.

This dominating fortress of Skallvaa seemed to spark a thought in Sheriff Elfinston. 'Thulay is a variety of stronghold,' he said to Cameron, almost idly, as the *Prometheus* dropped the hook and they prepared to descend into the 'flit-boat' which would take them ashore.

'But I rather feel that through us the Thulay folk have opened their portcullis and wish to share their riches with world,' said Frazer-Mackintosh, with a smirk.

'And is the world able to evaluate them?' Cameron asked of him.

'We shall see,' Elfinston answered as he stepped tentatively into the rowing boat. 'We shall see what becomes of them, and Mr Robert Gaer.'

'I wish them well,' said Cameron, as he followed, 'Those strange creatures who live permanently in the sublime.'

The Thulay folk had spoken to the world and the world, wisely, had seemed to listen.

25th June 2000 – Innertoon

Breathe a warm rush of clean linen, those fake natural fabric conditioners, turn over and snuggle in the chemical summer meadow of the quilt I'm wrapped in, dreaming of

home

The room is so pink, it makes me feel a little sick. I rise and stagger towards the smell of cooking, and Maggie is in there, for of course it is Maggie's pink I've slept in.

'Morning,' she says. 'You look as if you could do with a coffee.'

'I have to get back to the big house,' I say, calling it as the folk here do. Maggie's surprised. She stops her buttering of toast. Stands there, knife in hand glinting in the sunshine coming through the window.

'There's no hurry, is there? You could stay a while. Till you feel better. I'll make us brunch. The bar doesn't open till late today. I usually eat just before.'

'But really, no, I should get back. I've got to get moving. Thanks,' I say, 'for putting me up and everything. That was kind.'

'Luv, you passed out, there was no choice in the matter,' she answers.

'I'm sorry if I did anything silly last night. I never usually drink much.'

'You're excused. And you're welcome to stay here as long as you like, as I said. Your father and me, we got on, you know. Me and Rod.'

Is this another confession? Is this why she cast suspicion on Mary? Anything seems possible, but I liked this place better last night when the world was full of fiddles.

'The shepherd said there's someone here who has a taxi?'

Maggie looks disappointed. 'Yes. But you don't have to go right away or anything. You and me, we could have a nice chat if you wanted, I could get somebody to cover the bar for me and we could go out a walk or something. It's a nice day. The fog's cleared completely.'

'Maggie, I'd like to hear what you have to tell me, but I've got to go. I have to catch the ferry. And I went off last night to phone, and was going to go back for dinner. They were expecting me. They'll be worried.'

'Oh, no, don't worry about that. The big house know you're safe here.' And she smiles a perfect-toothed smile.

'How come?'

'The shepherd told them.'

'No,' I say. 'I'm going to walk back. I need the air.'

And so it comes to pass that on this Sunday morning I am walking up the hill from Innertoon with a heavy head and a heavier soul, repentant for my intemperance, with Maggie's boy guiding me along the shortest route back to the Norbie Haa at Outertown, along an ancient path. The route leads straight up, over the top of the hill, rather than all the way around its base as the road goes.

I scan over the little harbour and the huddling of houses. A dozen maybe fifteen. It seems organic, somehow, like a little colony of mussels clutching to a rock, as much a part of the natural environment as the grass or the sand, the sea or the rocks.

The pathway is narrow. At its centre is a thin line of worn-down earth with some large flat stones buried deep. It's an old route, for sure. I'm sweating quite heavily. The wind has risen from the south and blown the fog away through the night, and the sun is out. It's hot, even. On the one side, my right, there's a ruined dyke with a fence built slightly inside it. To the left, a steeper bank and a more complete wall, with no fence. The bank is lined with vetch and dockens. Sorrel and daisy. Meadowsweet. I notice how the green growth is eaten sharply back as far as a sheep's head can reach through the fence. The fields are all full of that white woolly life, bleating desperately, charging about playing chase, just like bairns at nursery. It's a playground for sheep-kids, this hillside.

The path begins to level out and the boy's feet in front of me don't seem to be stepping ahead as quickly. We're a few hundred metres high now. About another fifty and we're onto a rounded hilltop, a shoulder to a higher hill to the north. There's a little lochan ahead of us, shining brilliant azure blue, the sky reflected, a totally other land from the tight-bound village below. Here it's a heather desert, open and bare like a moonscape. Except when I look closely, I see that the heather's like a coat of wool, tightly woven and curled, gnarled to the land's skin. The blue loch is bonnie, lying there with the ripples of wind speeding across it. No artist could make it better. I realise that I love this strange place already, as if it was an old friend.

'Mind if we stop?' I shout. The wind's quite strong up here, but southerly and warm.

'Okay.'

We both sit down on the bank, at the side of the path. I take out a bottle of water I got from the bar before I left.

'This is an old route, this,' I say.

'They call it the Coffin Road,' the boy says, and looks away.

'Coffin Road?'

'The path they used to carry the coffins to the churchyard.'

Of course. It makes sense. The people of the village would bring their dead bodies to the priests for their blessing and the reassurance that they would rest in peace. The fathers would see to that. That was their task. To receive the dead. To set folk's minds at ease about death too. Safe in the arms of the Lord.

'From Innertoon straight up the hill here and then down to the old church by the beach, on Dr Hart's land.'

'To St Mary's? The old arch by the beach?' He nods. 'Innertoon's probably the oldest bit of the village, then?'

He nods again, flicks that blond fringe out of the way. Again I glimpse Martin briefly.

'You should see some of the buildings down by the water. Look like they've been there since the dinosaurs,' he says.

Long before the first laird came and built his Big House. Long before the church fathers decided they needed a barn for the congregation, there would have been a few houses here, maybe even supporting more folk than the place does now, as folk needed less. And a path from there to the church. But they wouldn't just have carried coffins along it. They'd have carried squawking bairns, for a blessing. And wedding bouquets too, maybe. And they would have brought gifts and presents for the fathers. Up past this loch here. Carrying their gear. It would have been shorter to walk than to sail, because of the long ness, that finger of land they'd have had to round if they were going to St Mary's by boat. Yes, I'm mapping it now, the ancient history of this place, the first layers of civilisation. The Irish monks in their chapel. And who knows what the natives are? Picts maybe? Norsemen? Or the descendants of the broch-builders, beaker people? Probably all of them, different waves of emigrants and stray shipwrecked sailors. All mixing their drinks in the pub down at Innertoon.

'Listen,' the boy says, 'I ken Mum said to walk you all the way, but you can't go wrong. You just follow this path. Thing is, I want to go up there.' He points up the hill. 'That's where my cave is.'

'Your cave?'

'Aye. Don't tell, mind.'

'No. I won't tell.'

'See, just up there on the side of the hill, that ridge?'

I screw my eyes up, realising again that my binoculars are in my closet. But I can see there's a line of bracken, a stony ridge and then a further heathery rise. 'Away up there?'

'Aye.' He sniffs, starts poking around among the plants, plucking long threaded roots of vetch and squeezing them into tight balls of green, till the sap oozes out and his palms are stained. 'I'm gonna make it better, like. Get a bed there. Maybe live there in the summer holidays.' He pulls another clump of foliage. 'Maybe a chair.'

'Could you not use bracken for a bed?' I say.

'Bracken?'

'Dried ferns. You know, like they used to do. See, there's a strip of it over there.' I point towards the hillside.

'Did they?'

I nod. 'Yes. They'd use dried ferns for bedding.'

'Gen?'

'Gen.'

I can see his brain working out the task: the gathering, the drying in the sun, the piling up, the use of stones, maybe, to build some kind of shape. 'So do you ken aboot caves?'

'Caves?'

'Likes ae stone age an that?'

'No. Not really. I mean who does, really, these days, what it was like to live then?'

He looks concerned. 'But there's scientists, ken, archaeologists, eh no?'

'Yes, there's a lot of folk that study it, all the same.'

'That's what I'm gonna do,' he says. And from the grim look of determination on his face I might as well believe him. I lie back on the bank of green. There's a bee buzzing around the purple vetch blossom, a warm and peaceful hum in the middle of the staccato bleating and squawking.

'GET!' the boy shouts, and leaps up. Then, to me, 'Hate they things,' he says.

I laugh. 'Och, they're only gathering nectar, they're not interested in you. Besides, stone age folk knew that honey was good for them, didn't they?'

'Did they?'

'Folk and bees go together, like people and dogs. Honey's one of the best things you can eat. For health. It's like the bears. Bears go mad for honey.'

He's on his feet now, dancing around nervously. 'You're gonna leave tonight, eh?' he says.

'Yes. Got to really. Got to get to Perth.'

'Will you be back?'

'Dunno. Depends on what happens, you know, with my dad.'

The boy's twisting up stalks of grass, tying knots in them with speedy fingers. His forehead's lined with frowns. 'I never minded him coming round.'

He peeks at me from under that blond fringe. It's the first time that morning I've seen the blue eyes looking at me full on. 'I'm gonna go now. Okay with the path?'

'Aye. Thanks. Take care.'

He turns and walks away, skips over the fence, away through the flock of sheep, herding the lambs before him, up towards the higher hill and the cave. And then I think of something. In the pocket of my coat. Yes, it's still there. I shout his name as loud as I can. The sheep begin to bleat and stare. I shout again. He turns on my third call.

I shout, and he comes running speedily over the grass towards me. I hand him the Maglite from my pocket.

'For the cave,' I say. And I show him how it works, how to open it and switch it on, the different beams it can cast. It's a good torch.

'Thanks,' he says, and off he goes again, turning the thing over and over in his hands, but this time walking faster, more spring in his stride. After a hundred yards or so, he turns and looks back and I wave.

I lie there a bit, letting last night go. Letting the fiddle be replaced by the skylark. The fresh sea air washes the peat and the cigarette smoke smell from my clothes and skin. The sunlight bathes my puffy hungover skin, soothing it, salving. What did he mean, that Roy, that I am the true son and heir? To being lost, alone

    cut

       hung?

25th June 2000 – Norbie

And now I go back to my life, cut and bruised,

    dizzily

along the Coffin Road towards the blue lochan. Slowly the landscape of Outertown begins to emerge on the far side of the hilltop. Norbie Haa, the curve of the beach though I can't see the sand from here, the ness and the old church. Wish I'd brought my binoculars because I can see that there's activity down by the pier. And it's then that I hear the sound of the chopper, very far away. Just the heavy chug, the chop of rotors through the air.

It's happening. The search.

Up here in the hills with the sun belting down and a skylark singing so high up I can't even see it, even the sealman they think to pull ashore seems bearable. On I walk, until the path begins to descend the other side of the hill. I look back towards the crags where the boy has gone one last time before they dip out sight. But there's no sign of him.

Now the path turns steeply down. Ahead lies the manse of Reverend Pirie, the church. There are cars parked round about and a few folk are hesitating in the sunshine, before committing themselves to the gloom inside. It's Sunday meeting time.

The laird's Land Rover is there. Mary's Fiesta and the shepherd's green van too. The service is set for eleven o'clock, which means they'll all be inside in a few minutes.

So I wait. I sit down on the heathery brow of the hill, making sure I'm out of sight. I watch the congregation sidling up to the door and filing inside, the dark-besuited men, the ladies in their frocks. I see them all in and then continue down the hill. I have no reason to join them.

What it is, then, that makes me stop and stand outside the church listening to the sound of the first hymn being sung? Why is it that I'm so keen to identify it? Somewhere deep inside are ready responses to all catechisms, bursting to emerge, buried for the whole of my adult life. But they aren't forgotten, no. I remember this ritual very well. The church in Perth. Far bigger, far more ornate than this stone barn.

And this overwhelming urge to see inside strikes me, to go in and join the worshippers, to confirm allegiance, however residual. To give my responses. Despite everything I have learned about the world and its ways, nothing has come close to filling this church-sized space inside.

So I do. I push open the outside door, and go into the little porch. The scent is immediately familiar. The organ is playing, squeaking out a few notes. I hear 'Amen' being sung at the end of a hymn and the shuffle, rumble and cough as the faithful sit down. Inside the first door, there's a porch and various leaflets about this event or that charity.

The voice of Reverend Pirie sounds from the main chamber, a sonorous tone, as he might say. And there's the stairs leading to the gallery. I could just slip upstairs, couldn't I? So I do. The voice comes loud and clear.

'Our text for this morning is taken from Deuteronomy, Chapter 11, verses 26 to 28. "Behold, I set before you a blessing and a curse. A blessing, if ye obey the commandments of the Lord your God, which I command you this day: And a curse, if ye will not obey the commandments of the Lord your God, but turn aside out of the way which I command you this day, to go after other Gods, which ye have not known."'

Then a shuffling, and he speaks again: 'Blessed be the word of the Lord, our God.' A little coughing breaks out, then the organ begins to sound and I push the door open into the gallery, while the sounds provide cover. The air inside the church is cool, though the sun streams in through south-facing windows. Motes of dust dance in the light shafts. Below the congregation stand, ready for the next hymn. I move closer, till I can see the spread of the interior. In the roof, hanging from a cord, the model of a sailing is ship rotating very slowly.

The gallery is empty, as I thought it would be. All the faithful souls are gathered in the lower space. I can see the tops of their heads as the singing begins. There's the laird's bald pate, sticking up in a particularly impressive pew to the side of the church – the Laird's Pew, no doubt, built for his predecessors and their families.

The minister stands in the pulpit staring down at the assembly, the symbol of his creed near at hand – the dying man hanging from a dead tree, like Odin awaiting enlightenment.

The second hymn begins. I know it well. It's one of Gran's favourites: 'Rock of Ages, cleft for me. Let me hide myself in Thee.' A beautiful song. Yes, whatever else I might say about it, the sentiment is comforting. However atheistic or agnostic I may have become, I can't deny the solace that this offers for the lost soul. The suffering. And aren't we all suffering, in one way or another, the trials of this earth? For whatever reason, whoever's plan – God's or the aliens' – whoever thought up this strange turmoil we live in.

The singing is over and my inner voice is almost released from agnosticism. The announcements are read and the collection is taken. Another hymn. And then the Reverend Pirie settles to his sermon.

'In the old calendar, the 24th of June was the festival of midsummer, or St John's Day, which commemorates the life and the culmination of the mission of John the Baptist. All old traditions of this festival lay stress upon the fire of midsummer. Fire is a purifying and refining element. If spiritual fire enters into the thoughts of men, it enables them to distinguish not only the creative, but also the destructive forces in the world. If we put this fact together with the Whitsuntide picture of the "tongues of fire" and the disciples' realisation of the eternal spiritual truth of Christianity, it seems as though these two summer festivals have, in their different ways, to reveal the same things. They have to reveal the Trinity that rules everywhere in the world; and they have to reveal also the moral responsibility that rests with each human individual for the events of history.'

He pauses, looks up in my direction, sees me in the gallery and looks surprised, then pleased. His voice lifts a fraction, as if now he must project to even the most distant corner of the church, to even the most distant of souls. Mine.

'Whitsuntide, with its outpouring of the sense of individual spirituality, and St John's Day with its reminder of the great uniform spirit of the world, form a connected whole which brings to light something else. When a great moral impulse arises, it is received by different individuals in different ways, and is furthered by them from the standpoint of their own special relation to it. The case of the greatest of all moral impulses – the Christ-impulse – is no exception to this rule. Only it was given and received in freedom: and this ensures its continuity. The Gospels are not something which are created once and for all, but when received by the free spirit of individuals, can continue as an impulse that is freshly renewable in every epoch of history to the end of the world.'

He looks again, right at me, his dark black eyes sparkling. Dancing. Then he holds up three fingers. 'Three sayings occur in the Gospels which point to this clearly. One is: "When the Spirit enters into the human spirit, when the Comforter is come, Ye shall know the Truth, and the Truth shall make you free". The Truth may ever and again find new words with which to express itself. Another is: "I am with you always, even unto the end of the world". No matter what external changes history and evolution may bring forth, the Christ-force remains. And the third saying is St John's: "He must increase".'

He lifts his head to face heaven and speaks the phrase again, as if he's trying to launch it towards the world: 'He must increase!' And again: 'He must increase!'

Then a long pause. A long breath, a gathering pause.

'At the Easter Festival we spoke of reincarnation. It was pointed out that reincarnation alone, without the Death and Resurrection of Christ, would not be sufficient to atone for human errors. Why not? Because man, by himself, cannot do more than try to make good, in repeated earthly lives, the mistakes that shadow his relation with other human beings. What happens to the Earth as a result of man's sins, must be healed by a Divine Being. These are the "sins of the world". Those errors which affect the actual destiny of the planet. And such there certainly are. It is not possible for any human being clearly to foresee how far his personal sins do really affect the Earth, but the fact that man has this power of inflicting suffering upon it is irrefutable.'

And now, by the rise in the pitch of his voice, I know that his climax is near. 'Could we but trace every consequence, large or small, of a great sin, it would be impossible to endure the pain of it. And so it is taken away from us. To recognise this is to know Conscience, in such a way that its warning voice is heard not only in the personal life, but in the history of mankind. That is why in the light and fire of summer, it is not only the beauty of the world and the heights of ecstasy that gleam into the human soul as it receives its midsummer message of fertilisation, but the shadows of the depths are also roused, and the "historical Conscience" is awakened. When we let ourselves take part in the summer ecstasy, it is because other beings desire to come to meet us. It is not our affair alone, for the Cosmos wants something from us. Uriel, the archangel associated with the season of summer, through whom the wisdom of the world reveals itself in Light and Fire, is described as the teacher of Esdras. There he teaches the prophet by telling him of the vastness of the divine wisdom; he presents to him the most wonderful pictures from the mysteries of Nature, and by means of them awakens the conscience of Esdras and his understanding of the history of his people. Uriel discloses himself to Esdras, in a certain sense, as the Creator of the world, and this indication occurs elsewhere as well. There is too a legend which is the subject of a poem by Ralph Waldo Emerson; Uriel is described as one among the beings of Heaven who rejected the principle that line, a continuous sequence of things ruled in the Universe, and who instead insisted that the circle, the going forth and returning of cause and effect, was the truth. The legend thereby hints at the truth of repeated lives on Earth – reincarnation, with the final salvation that is redemption.'

The folk below me shuffle and while the pan-drop packets rustle, and before the benedictions and the next hymn and the announcements and whatever else he has to do, the special prayer for my father, the finalities of the service, I slip quietly down the steps, unseen, and out into warm sun and sea breeze once more. My heart is thumping, thumping.

So I walk on down the old Coffin Road, and in my head the voice of the sonorous Reverend Pirie sounds and resounds.

Time is no more required to flow than space.

So I flow. What else can I do, but flow? If time doesn't move and space doesn't move, than surely it must be down to me, to move through it, the current of this river that is always going nowhere? It is a simple case of putting one foot in front of the other. No alternative, but alternation. Left. Right, left, right. I am on the Coffin Road and it is taking me to St Mary's. That's all I need to know. I can see the dotted line on the map that denotes this track, how it bisects the main road, if such it might be called.

And there, at this crossroads of single-track tarmac with the barely visible line in the green fields that is the Coffin Road, stand John and Lena, dressed for Sunday, their banner rolled up. He's carrying a stickered guitar case and she has a big multi-coloured patchwork bag slung over her shoulder. It bulges out here and there. There's something distinctly tambourine-like about one lumpy bit.

'Hello,' she says. 'Is church out, then?'

'Nearly. I thought you'd be there,' I answer. 'With your banner.'

'No,' he says. 'That's not our church. We went there at first, but now we go into town. Pentecostal. We like to get out where people can see us. Spread the gospel.'

I nod.

'No news of your father?' she asks.

'No.'

'The helicopter's out. I guess that means they're searching.'

'Listen,' says Lena, 'you could come with us if you wanted, there's plenty of room in the minibus. You may find it a comfort. We ...'

'No,' I say, sharply. 'I'm leaving tonight. I have to go back. Thanks, but ... it's kind, but ... no thanks.'

'Well, let's hope they're wrong and they don't find him,' she says, 'God bless you.' She gives me a sweet little kiss on my cheek. And as she's doing so she whispers in my ear, 'Thanks, you know ...'

I catch her gaze straight on for a second. John holds out his hand, shakes mine. He squeezes it and won't let it go.

'Thank you,' he grunts.

'Yes,' she says. 'Thanks.'

'Some people think I haven't changed.'

'Yes,' she says, 'Some people. Give a dog a bad name.'

'Sticks,' he adds.

Then there's a rumbling engine approaching and a toot. A Volkswagen van with seats in the back pulls up. There's a couple of folk in there already. They wave and smile. Three small children are seat-belted together like a job-lot at an auction. Hairy wild creatures, faces smeared with peanut butter or something. They're shaking their heads in some kind of ecstatic frenzy. One of them sees me, says something to the others and points, and then they go all shy, like sea anemones disappearing inside themselves.

'This is our lift,' the Holy Ghost says.

But now he's just John. Strange, brown-suited, lopsided John with his Bible in his pocket. Code will save him.

'Well goodbye. It was nice meeting you,' says Lena. 'God bless.' She takes the patchwork bag from her shoulder as if remembering something and pulls the cord open. From inside she takes a book and hands it to me. It's gold in colour, rather flimsy, and printed in red on the gold cover in big capitals is JESUS CHRIST. And under that, there's a stylised representation of a flame in the same red outline, with '21st' written into the design. And below that again, the words:

A MILLENNIUM KEEPSAKE

'Thanks,' I say, and she smiles, and kisses me on the cheek again.

I stand out of the way as the driver does a three-point turn. The van comes very close to me. A windscreen sticker comes right up to my chin. It's rainbow-coloured:

†HERE IS HOPE

Sincerely I hope that it is true, that hope is there. For the bairn's sake. John and Lena get in the sliding side door, wayfarers heading for the H-A-P-P-Y land.

The rolling rhythm of the vw engine slips away among the bleating and the cries of the gulls from the

shore

Letter from Philippa Gabrielsen
to Rev. Archibald Nicol,
May 20th 2001

Bon Hoga
Tokamua

Dear Archie

These following anecdotes were written by Doctor Robert Scot of
Norbie, Zetland, father to the immigrant, Albert, who was born in 1812.
His mother, Mary Scott of Skallvaa b.1788, father John Scot, b.1788,
d.1813. Paternal grandparents were John Scot of Norbie 1760–1850
and Elizabeth Scott of Skallvaa 1761–c.1837. Maternal grandparents
were John Scott of Skallvaa 1756–1833 and Clementina Scot of Norbie
c.1759–1826.

These are copies I send to you, obtained from Miss Mimie Jeromsen,
who has the original notebook. I don't know any more than that he
started when in Plymouth in 1833, continued when he returned to
Plymouth in 1860 and finished in 1864. It was only when I read through
them that I was able to find him and his family on the 1861 census as he
gave his address as 6 Portland Villas.

That was the third time I had looked. I was very surprised to find his
mother with the family as I had not been able to find her on the 1851
census in Zetland and thought she had died. I feel that the anecdotes
were stories that his mother and grandfathers had told him.

I would love to know which grandfather he is referring to here.
Have you found any other stories that have references to any of the
happenings which have been recorded here about Zetland families? How
much truth is there to them, do you think?

Best wishes

Philippa

Dr Scot's Jottings

1833 November 16th – Plymouth
'Well, John,' said my Great Grandfather of Skallvaa to Grandpapa when he was young, speaking of a protégé of the latter for whom he wished to procure the berth of Village Schoolmaster:

'I cut a pretty figure in Edinburgh with Jerome Smith at my tail: your candidate could not pass the accessary examination and thus summed up the account of his failure – "I just arred ae wird an' they sould hae glaapit me!"'

Poor old J. I remember him well in my younger days, but he, like his venerated Patron, is long since gathered to his fathers.

I cannot afford to lose an anecdote of a lovely young Cyprian that Grandpapa was fond of telling of an evening, after supper as he sat with his feet upon the fender, his glass of Brandy Toddy on the side of the grate, the left hand supporting the right elbow as he held up his Pocket Handkerchief for a fire screen. It is impossible to forget it so it need not be written.

Mem. His story of the Privateer off Peterhead – His own watch and Walter Scott's ring –

16th November 1860. 6 Portland Villas, Plymouth.
Twenty-seven years have passed away since the above was written, and now with my beloved mother seated by my side, a darling wife and baby – our first born – to cheer me, and my cherished niece Jeanie Gifford and sister Clementina to lend light to our household, while I hold the position of Staff Surgeon of HMS *Impregnable*, flagship at this port, when I commenced my naval career, I resume at this distant period, the chronicle of events, the recital of which in earlier days have proved so powerfully interesting to me –

In the Privateer affair, one of the marauders asked my Grandfather to favour him with his watch, and on his suggesting the possibility of his having none, the pirate replied 'You're a d—d liar for I saw the chain'!!!

Mr Scott, the sheriff, on being pressed to surrender his ring and [demeaning threats sic], the Privateer said 'You had better give it to me as I will return it to you but any of the rest would keep it.'

It was accordingly given up and as the robber was leaving the vessel, the Sheriff said 'But you forgot to return my ring!'

'So I did,' said the honest rogue and immediately replaced it on his finger! It contained Mrs Scot's hair. The Privateer was captured by a King's Cutter the very same day, and the plundered passengers recovered all their property.

Story of Burris (Borcas) Lyons and the whaler. This heroic Zetlander when in command of a whaler on her homeward passage from Greenland, was captured by a French Privateer. They removed all his own men except himself and a boy, replacing them with a prize crew of Frenchmen.

At an opportune moment when all the Frenchmen happened to be below, he suddenly closed the hatches, effectually securing them, and shaped his course for Larvik, which he actually reached in three days, assisted only by the cabin boy, but latterly almost overpowered by sleep. It is said that in order to support himself, he was obliged to get into a barrel at times, while his boy steered.

His only weapon of defence was a large knife which my mother saw in Burrell's Museum when at school at Edinburgh in 1800, exhibited as a great curiosity, its history being detailed by the exhibitor on my grandfather asking 'what interest attached to that old rusty knife'? She adds that 'it was just like a splitting knife with a wooden handle.'

Burris Lyons had two brothers, James and Matthew, and one sister, Mary, a twin with James. The latter was famous – or infamous – by having forged a cheque on the Bank for Ten Thousand Pounds, which was cashed by his sister Mary – dressed in men's clothes, he being little and she very tall – and escaping safely with the approved money to France was never again heard of. Yet her identity was suspected by one of the Bank Clerks, for while waiting for the money in a private room, some refreshment was offered according to the custom of the times, and the acute scribe remarked that he was certain 'she was not a gentleman but a lady, as she sipped her wine'!

Shortly after her departure, further suspicion was excited; the 'hue and cry' was raised. She was pursued, arrested and tried, but no complicity could be proved and she was fully acquitted.

Sandy Chalmers: A son of Auntie Chalmers of Wastshore.
Memory: A man of considerable genius, the painter of the miniatures of my Uncle John of Skallvaa and William of Norbie, was distinguished by his filial affection having taken his mother to Aberdeen to live with him. She did not however, appreciate his attention, but soon returned and on being questioned by my mother as to her reasons for her speedy return, replied that 'she had been nearly poisoned with dirt'!!!

The Night of Eddy White
Eddy White was sent to Skallvaa in charge of a party of Soldiers for the purpose of warding off from Nelly Mansen, a fair, though frail protégée of the sheriff, Walter Scott, (and mother of Andro Scot still living in Quharv: she subsequently married James Lang and was the mother also of Betty Laing, married James Jamesen of Vass, still alive), the unappreciated attentions of the officers of three Greenland ships – Capts: Clay, Kay and Hansen. (Clay's ship was the *Vigilant*.)

Nelly Mansen lived at Blacksness, and the officers and men kept refreshing themselves at John Mulin's (Mary Mulin's father) little Public House until they became unduly excited and called Eddy White's defensive function into play. He used his cutlass freely, and inflicted severe wounds on several men, including Charlie Pottingir, father of Ertie of Gupigirt, William Davisen, husband of Inga [?] Tho Blymen and others. She made a poem on the marriage of young James Ollasen, (brother of Lieut. James, and father of Mary). It had reference to 'the Cart Horse Riding wi' the Deil', the carthorse being my Grandfather's old favourite which 'the Deil' (old James Ollasen) was suspected of having driven over the banks. One stanza was thus:

> *Diabolus Coquestus*
> *Now as for the Clergy, it truly is a fun*
> *To see them so respectful to my favorite son*

Eddy took his stand behind the stack in the court, from whence he issued forth to the attack, and Uncle Charles dressed the wounded men in the kitchen. No public inquiry took place, as the vessel sailed. This occurred in 1798: it was fully narrated in the papers of the day.

Old John Hendersen of Glup, married to a sister of Robert Robertsen of Gopaburg, was father of Willie a'Glup, who was a captain in the 27th Enniskillans at Waterloo, and once said to my Grandfather of Norbie 'I'll tell you an aneckdote of my William' as he called it! This same 'Willie' after his return was spinning awfully long and improbable yarns about his service at Waterloo when at Skallvaa, when my Grandfather cut him short by asking if he had heard what Napoleon said to his guards when observing his deeds of valour. 'No,' replied Willie, who stood 6 feet 3 inches in his stockings, modestly. My Grandfather replied as follows: "Here, boys, here, cried Napoleon. There's Lang Willie a'Glup: shoot him, boys, shoot him!"'

Willie did not say much more that night! It was he who wrote from Happyhansel, 'Dear Mother you know it is but little that I eat, but that little I can't get!' His letter was intercepted, and brought down on him condign and speedy punishment!

It was Robbie Dul who asked there if he should read one of Hudge (Hugh) Blair's Sermons!
The same classical locality was the scene of my Uncle William's' reply to Robert Robertsen's question 'if he had seen his father?'

'Yes' said William, 'I met him going along the beach with a tangle in his mouth.'

Good old Henry Robertsen was small of stature and very dark, enjoying the soubriquet of 'The Crow', and as it was the building season, when the crows employ tangles largely for their nests, the witticism was very annoying and led to an immediate and severe personal conflict.

He was the son of the same Father Scot who died at the hill carting Peat for the poor people. Father Scot was a brother of John Scot of Norbie and Gibbiestaen, uncle of my Grandfather of Skallvaa. He dropped the title of Gibbiestaen because its land was confiscated to the crown on account of the burning of the three witches on the Galloo Hill at Wastshore, or rather of another burning of the weird sisterhood in the South by some enlightened ancestors of ours whose name is lost in antiquity!

Jonathan's pranks (for he was half-witted owing to a fall from aloft in one of her Majesty's ships about the middle of the last century) was nervous and eccentric. He once laid Eppie Ollasen on the gridiron and her clothes were on fire when old Uncle Charles arrived and found him holding her down with a piece of wood. Uncle remarked, 'You wretch, you might have burnt the woman' 'D—d scoundrel! She angered John!' (my Grandfather) was the brief but pithy rejoinder! He used to carry off a whole roast joint from the table, eating as he ran along, 'having' as Mam says 'a fearful appetite'! He used to wash down the ravenous meal with a dish of melted butter, which he also employed while eating fat mutton.

'Come now Minnie Mary,' he would say to Mam, 'play the Diana to Donna and Donna will dance'!

Jonathan had a sister Mary, a very sensible, nice, lady – their father's name was James – brother of John Scot of Gibbiestaen as before noted.

'It's a light from aboove'! This classical expression had its origin at a Religious Meeting at Skallvaa in the last century.

On one occasion at Busta, where the ladies always had a pet child, about the early part of this century, and the then cherished one entered the drawing room, robed in a flannel garment made by her patroness, of which she was very proud. She went up to Grace Gray who was on a visit, looking out for admiration, and said: 'Sees du my panny Jaekie?' (my flannel Jacket). 'And who,' said the caustic spinster, as she was destined to be (still alive, 14th March, 1862), 'cares for de an dy filthie Jaekit'!!!. The unfortunate child, quite abashed and still defiant, replied with reference to Miss Gray's terrific squint, 'Du needsna set dir ears ups, Ma!' She is now nearly blind, having been operated on for cataract!

March 12th 1861 Plymouth
Old Laurence Arthursen (owner of the *Quiz*) married Katie Crowan,

whom my Great Grandmother of Skallvaa brought from Aberdeen with her. Katie was a sister of James Crowan a schoolmaster and a servant in Mr Forbes' house where Grandpapa lived. She described my Great Grandmother as a very beautiful woman, dressed in a scarlet riding habit, trimmed with gold lace. Owing to her kindness to my Grandfather, his mother went to Aberdeen on purpose to bring Katie Crowan home. After her death Laurence married Katie Jamesen, still (1861) alive! Laurence was however Katie Crowan's second husband, as she was first married to John Martin, Mary Martin's father, and at her dying request he married Katie Jamesen, who repaid his courtesy by frequently beating him! I remember my Grandmother once blowing him up 'sky high' (a.c.s) for some maltreatment of me after I had provoked him beyond endurance.

The following was a Latin witticism of good old Mr Sands: '*Hic Jacit Jacobus juventa*' – '*Templum Bellum Spelumea*' – Translation, 'Here lies James Bullock, church warden.'

Another of Mr Sands: A fellow suspected of having stolen a mare suddenly absconded, and ten years subsequently appeared in the neighbourhood as a preacher, but his identity being discerned by the precentor on his giving out the line for the hymn beginning 'within the congregation great' – 'and Lilytodel he was there, who stole Josiah Tucker's mare!' was substituted by the acute and humorous harmonist for the proper words. At which the felonious minister descended from the pulpit without waiting for the conclusion of the verse and was never more seen! 15th March, Mr Sands died at the age of only 63, while smoking his pipe and joking with the servants, of apoplexy.

On the occasion of Mr Bolt informing Mrs Gray, Grace Gray's mother, that he had brought his correspondence with the Countess of Sutherland to a successful close, regarding permission for her to retain her cottage in the Highlands rent-free, she having nine daughters and one son wholly unprovided for, her grateful reply was that 'she did not know what he was making such a work about, as pecuniary considerations had never given her a thought in her life!' On narrating the anecdote to Mam he mildly called her 'a dammed Trooker', rapping on his snuffbox rather impatiently.

4th April 1862: Old Sinclair of Brue on one occasion, and one only, attended the church of Dunrossness with his wife and sixteen children of whom Miss Craigie Sinclair, whom I well knew and loved, a perfect specimen of a lady of the old school, and who died at Papay upwards of ninety, and Gideon Hendersen's mother were members; old Mrs Sinclair of Brue, a Miss Tanele of London who was very kind to me in my boyhood, and who died also upwards of ninety, was the widow of Arthur Sinclair one of the brothers. She was a relation of Gibby Tanele, and originally belonged to the Niep.

2nd February 1863: Robert Sinclair of Houss having accidentally strayed into Sir John Dalmahoy's Gardens, near Edinburgh, espied two ladies attempting to climb a tree, and having assisted one of them, named Philadelphia, to descend, was introduced by her to her father, and forgiven for his intrusion.

It was just as well, for he immediately afterwards married the lady, and when he went to Zetland, they took the younger sister Alicia with them; the latter married Mr Bruce of Zumburg, and was the Great Grandmother of the present proprietor.

My Great Grandmother of Skallvaa, Katherine Sinclair, was a daughter of Philadelphia Dalmahoy, to whom belonged the small silver rule and crimping knife with silver handles now in my dear mother's possession. They descended to my Grand Aunt, Philadelphia Scot, who gave them to her grandson James Scott of Skallvaa, who left them to his brother Charles, who in order to raise money to buy a top, sold them to my mother for Fivepence Sterling.

John Scot of Norbie, my Great Great-Grandfather, while pursuing his travels on the Continent in the early part of the last century, with John Gray as his servant, was attacked and nearly murdered, his life having been saved by the gallantry and devotion of John Gray, who threw himself in front of the assassins, and received a stab intended for his master which proved all but fatal.

In grateful recognition of his self-sacrificing bravery and fidelity, he had a living cow led to his door every year during the remaining portion of his existence which was prolonged till the year 1793.

He was the father of Kirstin Gray, whom I well remember, and grandfather of Andro and Meggie Williamsen of Skallvaa. In John Gray's absence Kirstin Gray was sent to the dancing school with the ladies as Miss Christin Gray. She eventually became a celebrated *accoucheuse*, attending my Grandmother of Norbie on the occasion of the births of several of her children, among the rest, that of my father in 1782, and Jessie Henry, and also that of my dear mother in 1788 who was the first, (but not the last) of the Skallvaa family she ushered into the world.

William Hendersen of East Frampton, Quebec, is a son of Saunders Hendersen and Mary Umphray – sister of Clemie Umphray, and Lillie Umphray of Skallvaa. His father and the father of Gideon Hendersen of Papa were brothers. Old Auntie Chalmers was a sister of my Grandmother of Skallvaa and Auntie Mary, and consequently a daughter of Old Norbie.

14th March 1864, Dr R Scot

25th June 2000 – Norbie

I step on, down the steep bank to the lower side of the path. Here it converges with a burn and runs along its side towards the sea.

There's a building ahead. As I approach I can make out the easy sloping roof and the square-ground plan of a bungalow. I'm approaching from behind. It's quite a long way off the path, but there's a track a couple of hundred yards away running almost parallel to mine, slowly converging. A new, gravel road

below

Around the bungalow is a concrete garden wall, high enough to keep the sheep out. It's grown over with yellow lichen. On the side of the house that faces the sea, there is a gate, leading out. Its position is determined by the symmetry of the design, not the logic of exit and entry. But the thing is, the road comes to the house from the rear, and this front gate goes nowhere. There's just a lot of sheep and lambs on the other side, basking, sporting. The ground is beaten down to mud by their sharp little hooves and there's sheep shit everywhere. But inside the wall there's a great growth, of green, half a summer's growth uncut. I wonder if this is why they come, the sheep, so they can at least smell those sweet herbaceous plants, that great rush of growth so full of the goodness denied them by these barren, over-grazed fields. I'd like to let them in to have a real good feast. Those scrawny lambs, those ewes sucked dry of milk and desperate for sweet meadow grass to make more.

Yes, I should let them in. What's the point of letting it all just grow like that, unused, untended. This little oasis of green, with even some long ornamental grasses out in front of the veranda in the middle and a wall of willows and elders round about. Some great big red-hot pokers like at Gran's house. Lupins too, inside the walls. And fruit-bushes. Gooseberries. Currants. It's all been left unattended and only the tallest of plants have survived the onslaught of the grass. Something draws me in. I could just disappear between the bushes, and though this position is right in the middle of Outertown and visible from all round about, I do just that, I swing inside over the garden gate. The windows are boarded. Tightly secure. I can see that the frames have at one time been painted dark red. I walk all the way round the house. Everywhere the lichen, like an extension of nature to reclaim its own. Swallowing the stuff that somebody's straining ego managed to throw up above the soil, for a while, back underneath again.

It's not a design that seems to be at home here, like a flying carpet, waiting for the ocean wind to lift it off. But the house is clearly not new and still the roof is there. Round the back in the overgrown, dank-shadowed area between the house and the earth bank behind, there's a shed with an open door. I push my head inside, as if I was pushing away

the years

TIME IS NO MORE REQUIRED TO FLOW THAN SPACE

Was that what he'd said? The minister? In which case right here and now are all the moments that ever there *were* here, all happening together. Stand where hundreds of other people are standing, in their moment, wherever it is in time. Before this house was built. And since. They're all here with me. But not Martin.

Some spirits are ignoring me.

There is a door open at the back. It leads into a kind of lean-to, the back porch, two Belfast sinks, great deep things for washing. Bolted to the wooden draining boards of both is a huge mangle. I push the door open slightly further. Further in there's a trail of rotten timber and I see that a part of the roof has fallen in.

Tentatively, in through the main house I go, into what I know must have been the kitchen by the rusty black range, then a small dining room. In there's a dresser with some fine crockery. The dresser is oak, but the base of it is rotten too. The house is in much worse condition inside than it appears from outside. The floor feels distinctly rubbery underfoot, as if the beams are rotten and weak. I wouldn't really like another fall. Carefully feeling for where the floor is strongest with my left foot, I progress through the bungalow. The rooms are generous, but somehow the walls seem very thin after the laird's, and the stone burrows of the old village at Innertoon.

Very little seems to have been moved since the house was shut down, by whoever, whenever. There are ornaments on shelves, the skeleton stems of dried plants still in pots on the dusty paint-flaking window ledges. Pictures still on the walls. And in the lounge, a huge leather settee, one that would fetch hundreds of pounds at auction even in the state it was in, assuming no rot, no worm.

In an alcove there are some photographs in frames, set on shelves. Of happy, smiling young people. In long shorts and cool tropical dresses, in sandals, with sun-streaked hair, smiling, and all of them smoking, in almost every picture. Could it be that this handsome young buck with his fine blond hair swept back in a Brylcreem curve, wearing a flying jacket with a sheepskin collar, and crisp-creased flannels, could it be that this is the doctor, the laird? It could. And the woman standing with her arm under the open jacket, around his waist and holding on so tight with both arms it looks as if she's madly in love with him, is she not the beauty with the jungle blossom from the painting in the big house? Yes, it could be her. I feel guilty now, like an intruder. A trespasser. As if this is a mausoleum to a former life, and sacred, so that I have defiled a holy place.

But then the sound of a helicopter enters my head. The whum-whum-whumping of the blades. Out through the front of the bungalow, a shadow suddenly appears as the sun brightens and it swoops at high speed along the finger of land, heading towards the shore. It's coming towards me. Getting louder!

I sit down on the old leather settee, numbed, frozen by this grandstand view of the beachhead, as the shadow gets larger and larger, and the noise louder and louder, and the copter lands on the flat machair. The men are just too far away for me to see them clearly, but there is activity, a busying of black flea-size creatures, as the whumping ceases. I don't want to look. No doubt this is why I had to forget my binoculars.

But I'll go there now. I'll leave this coffin-house to see for myself. I'm ready for the sealman, if this be he. I go quickly from the house of spirits, pulling the door shut, down the garden and over the wall, down the bank to the burn-course and onto the old path. I understand now why the sheep can't have the garden grass. They'd be in the house and in no time the place would be covered in shit and the delicate web of decaying past destroyed. Though maybe the sheep would be happier.

Very marshy next to the water, churned up by their hooves, but further down where it's fenced off is this incredible rush of marigolds, of yellow and green, growing through the water, and slim willows sprouting above. When I emerge from the burn's curves onto the machair at the beachhead, the helicopter is still. No one there. The black fleas are bigger now, they're bluebottles, and they're over by the cars. Along the narrow road from the church the laird's Land Rover approaches.

I decide to hang back a little. To wait and see what happens. I'll be able to tell what the outcome is. The sealman. Or not.

The laird gets out and goes over to the policemen. I see them talking. The policeman who came to use the laird's toilet is holding his hands up, like a surrender. Or resignation. But does that mean the search is over because they've found him, or because they've finished searching? No, surely even if they hadn't found him but had searched everywhere, they'd go back and look again, and again. It must take longer than this

    Surely

TIME DOES NOT FLOW

The past is alive in the present, the future too. Not the line
     but the
         circle

My heads spins like the rotors. If I simply stand here, am I not travelling anyway, waiting for the inevitable to come to me?

Then there is the old archway. It comes into my consciousness at a tangent to the helicopter, which I anticipate will rise from the beachhead and swoop away again, when whatever brought them to ground is done. Why should they land? And if they'd found a body, would they bring it here, or take it straight to wherever the mortuary is? Then a group of them return to the helicopter and it does take off. Joining them on board this time is the burly figure of the laird.

And this is when the archway of St Mary's comes into my sight fully. I realise that it has been my destination since I left home in Edinburgh, and especially since I crossed the hill with the boy. This is where the old Coffin Road leads. And I know I am here because I need peace. Stillness is crucial. If I'm active in my time-space, how can I slip into another? Breathing must slow until I am part of the ocean, rushing and dragging.

Then maybe I can be the ancient monk, the father, the papa, here by this beach in the beautiful place, receiving the coffins from all the Innertoons within their spiritual reach. Accepting the offerings of the folk. Blessing bairns and teaching the folk how to pray

TIME IS NOT REQUIRED TO

There's a family group of ducks making its way down the burn past the archway where I sit. What was that charm? That poem I learned, that blessing from the *Carmina Gadelica*, the one I spoke over my own son in Roslin Glen when he was just a baby after my mother died, when I went there, seeking peace and tranquillity? Such a sweet word that, and an even sweeter thing, the times I've felt it. Not many, no, but times, yes, usually out here among nature, then sometimes I have felt a sense of tranquillity

If it may be a lengthening of thy tranquillity

I let the sea wind blow through my hair. Relax. Meditate on Mary of the Peace and why she won't come to me here, in her chapel, her place, sitting as I am under the bright light of heaven, dedicating myself to her.

What is it that keeps her from me?

Martin? Maybe if I pray.

The time thou shalt have closed thine eye, thou shalt not bend thy knee nor move, thou shalt not wound the duck that is swimming, never shalt thou harry her of her young. The white swan of the sweet gurgle, the speckled dun of the brown tuft, thou shalt not cut a feather from their backs, till the doom-day, on the crest of the wave. On the wing be they always ere thou place missile to thine ear, and the fair Mary will give thee of her love, and the lovely Bride will give thee of her kine. Thou shalt not eat fallen fish nor fallen flesh, nor one bird that thy hand shall not bring down, be thou thankful for the one, though nine should be swimming. The fairy swan of Bride of flocks, the fairy duck of Mary of peace.

Yes, this is Mary's place. I sense it. A place of Marianism long before the Reformation, where the icon of birth, the mother and her child, was worshipped. Such extremes, these Christian symbols. That young man sacrificed, nailed to a crosstree, the end of life. And a young mother untainted by the world, immaculate, the beginning of life. Opposites.

And then I'm ready to leave this sanctuary. I'm ready to say goodbyes. Now it is a question of faith. From here until the Sallie, I will walk a line of faith towards the fact that my father liveth. Unless the sealman comes before I escape.

So the gravel is crunching under my boots, I've shut out the stupid questions and have set myself the simple project of getting my rucksack, of travelling twelve miles before six o'clock, and being aboard that ferry when it heads south. I'll even face the sickness.

Though the sea is sparkling today, glinting in the sun, as if it would do me

no harm

CHAPTER 8 (CONT.)

On the day following their memorable voyage to the rocky fortress of Thulay, the Commissioners proceeded to Larvik by gig, where a special hearing had been convened. Again, Gabrielsen was present and recorded the following detail.

The names of twenty-four delegates from all the various parishes had been offered, and all had made their way to the new capital, and were hanging around the Toll House to be heard. But when confronted with such a crowd, the Commissioners decided this was far too many, and asked that the number be reduced to representatives from all classes, and as broad as a range of parishes as possible. So the list was rapidly cut to ten, and those selected were summoned, leaving the other delegates to kick their heels.

Among those who gave evidence was James Berrick, younger partner in the firm of factors managing the Norbie estates. In his opening description, he said that when the late Dr Scot inherited the estate, he found the houses fallen into a state of dilapidation, and the crofts all cultivated on the old run-rig system. On his instruction, the factors had overseen the building of a number of new houses, some of which cost as much as £30, and Dr Scot had also gone to the expense of dividing and draining the meadowland where necessary. This venture had been successfully completed in Norbie itself, and at the moment of his untimely death, he had just engaged a land surveyor to measure all the other crofts on his estates.

Berrick then said that there were two hundred and forty tenants and not one of them was treated unkindly by Dr Scot, but that they loved him as a good laird, as demonstrated by the great number who came to his funeral. The current proprietor, his son Mr Albert Scot, lived at Norbie but was under age, so the management was carried out almost entirely by his company.

Frazer-Mackintosh asked Berrick about Thulay in particular, as the previous day's voyage was still much to the fore of their minds.

'Would you continue to supply the people of Thulay, if you did not have the bulk of their dealings?' he inquired.

Berrick shook his head, and looked around the company gathered. 'No,' he said, turning his gaze back to the Commissioner, 'we would not keep a shop if we did not have the bulk of their trade. It would not be worthwhile. I may explain that, a few years ago, some of the young men wished to cure their own fish, and go out with them to the Mainland to sell. There was a little discussion amongst them about it, and we put it to them whether they wished to have that liberty or not.'

'And what response did you receive?' Cameron asked.

'We sent a paper to the schoolmaster, and asked him to circulate it among the men. This is the content,' Berrick said, and began to read from a document he took from his pocket. 'Berrick & Co, who have for the last fourteen years kept a curing establishment on the island of Thulay, and found the undivided produce enough to pay for the trouble and risk of it, while furnishing the necessaries of life, fishing material, etc, at ordinary rates, would, now that some parties have shown an inclination and even begun to cure their own fish, wish to ascertain the views of the people as to whether they desire Berrick & Co to continue their establishment as before; or would they prefer each to cure as it suits him, and provide his necessaries as he can? Whilst there is always the most perfect freedom to all to fish, labour and sell their produce in what appears to them the best market, the isolated position of the island appears to require that one system be followed by all. The heads of families and other fishermen will therefore please indicate their views by subscribing below, adding yes if the former system be preferred; or no, if otherwise.'

After reading this, Berrick paused. He raised his eyes slowly and met the gaze of the Commissioners with easy assurance. 'I have the signatures of fifty-six men at the bottom of the paper, all in favour of our continuance.'

'Were there any negatives to the paper?'

Berrick shook his head. 'It created great alarm amongst the people, because they were afraid they would be left to their own resources.'

'In consequence of that, you continued to supply the islanders?'

'Yes, we went on as before.'

'Since you sent them that paper, has any attempt been made by the inhabitants of Thulay to cure their fish themselves?'

'No, it was needless to have sent that paper, because they had given it up themselves, as it had not been paying them.'

'But that paper had the effect of making it quite clear to the inhabitants of Thulay that they must either give their fish to you green, or you would remove your shop?'

Berrick's response was thus: 'We would either have their whole trade or none of it. It is a great risk to send vessels and boats there, and a small part of their trade would not pay.'

The Commissioners quizzed him on the matter of the expense of the manse at Vass, which the Thulay folk took such exception to. Berrick said that the call had come from the minister himself, and the landlords were obliged to expend something like £2,200 in less than eighteen months. There was a slight increase made in the rents, to defray this cost.

Then he was asked by Sheriff Elfinston if it was true that Berrick's paid for the Thulay fish and eggs at a lower rate than elsewhere, and that commodities were made more expensive to the Thulay folk than was justified by cost, for the company's profit.

'We supply goods there at the same price as we do at our shop at Roovik,' he said, then added 'although it is true that the price paid for eggs at Thulay is one penny per dozen less, but this is because the shells are very thin and apt to break. Anyway,' he said, 'I doubt that the Thulaymen have any idea of the cost of anything outside their island. The prices Berrick's charge are the same as at Larvik, with the exception of flour which is due to the freight,' he added.

Cameron then asked him if he did not think the rents too high, and a cheer went up among the members of the audience.

'No,' said Berrick, 'the people might complain but I do not think that there's much wrong with the current arrangements. If they are ardent in their work, and have good fortune with the catch, then folk live well enough. Nobody had ever been put off their croft in my time.'

Sheriff Elfinston asked, 'Are many among the tenants endebted to your firm?'

Berrick answered, 'As the accounts are only settled once a year, at this time all the tenants are in debt, but I expect all will clear their outstanding balance come settling time. I cannot be certain that all will, but that is my hope.'

Napier enquired whether this was the normal annual outcome. Berrick admitted that it was not, as there were a number who carried over debt. When asked to put a figure on the proportion, he declined to do so, 'as it is variable, year to year'.

Asked by Cameron what initiative he thought might make a difference to the tenants, he said that he thought Norbie was now at a great disadvantage over certain other places which had been, in the last thirty years, connected to rest of the mainland by road.

Napier wondered if the enlightened late proprietor had ever considered building a road at which a shout came from the hall: 'Considered, maybe, but they haena ever done a thing worthy o the name o road-makkin.'

Cameron asked whether they had ever done anything unworthy of the name, and the assembly laughed at that witticism from the bench.

Berrick said 'Yes, the late Dr Scot desired it, and subsequent to his death, myself and the factors of neighbouring estates had indeed considered it. We surveyed the terrain, which amounts to seven miles of peat moor to the next nearest habitation.'

He added that much debate had arisen over the route, 'which if it came in one way would favour one set of tenants, and if it came another would favour others. So it was impossible to get folk to agree. Factions grew behind the possible routes concerned and the tenants were split, almost to the point of violence. I don't think they would all help the proprietor now unless they are paid, even if it would be to all their advantage in the long term.'

When asked if he had anything else he wanted to say, James Berrick replied that he thought 'the people have nothing much to say against the landlord or factor in Norbie. While other lairds had been clearing people off the land to make way for sheep, they had had a benefactor for a laird, who only wanted their betterment. There has been none like him in memory. If they have complaint, it is not against him but against the law, for they want leases of at least twenty years.'

Lord Napier observed, 'You make Norbie sound a model estate, yet have you not immediately before remarked on the conflict over the possibility of a road? And is it not the case that some two hundred people have left the area in the last twenty years?'

Berrick said this was so, but that they were encouraged to go to New Zealand by the system of free emigration offered by the government there. 'A local man, a minister, had with the help and encouragement of his father, who is the agent for New Zealand and a friend to the Prime Minister, Robert Stoot, arranged for two ships to carry them to a colony there.'

Asked if this did not suggest a rather unhappier land than Berrick himself portrayed, he answered thus: 'The population was so great at that time that the land was hard pressed to support them all, and many saw a better opportunity there.' He recalled the day they left, 'walking overland to Vass to begin their voyage, across the seven miles of peathill, the young women carrying their babes, the men porting their sea-chests, with the few mementos they would take with them to the other side of the world'. He wished them all well there, but doubted how much better their fortunes might be. 'It isn't everybody who finds gold like the men of Bendigo, or becomes a Prime Minister like Robert Stoot had done in New Zealand.'

James Berrick, factor of Norbie, Valay and Thulay had then said his piece. It seemed he truly believed he could hold his head up and speak of the laird's good deeds – and his part in carrying them out – with pride. The Commissioners thanked him for his frankness and dismissed him.

Others too gave their testimony at the Larvik hearing, the ten selected as representative, but they add nothing to the story of our parish.

The complaints and the defences were as you have already seen them from the Thulay folk and the Berricks. There was a couple of 'Robert Gaers' among the representatives, brave spokesmen who told their own extreme view of the truth, who took a chance with fortune by doing so.

The meeting ran its course and the following day the Commissioners' steam-yacht sailed for the Orcades. But that is not the end of the story – repercussions followed soon enough, first of all when the original Robert Gaer, crofter and catechiser of Thulay, features again later that same year.

It seems Gaer was justified in his fear of 'annoyance which those in power might feel inclined to inflict in consequence of my having thus given a true description of the condition and wishes of the inhabitants of Thulay from personal experience.'

Lewis Berrick, whom Gabrielsen says was 'infuriated' by the events of the Commissioners' voyage to Thulay when they were reported to him by George Morrison, took control of his younger brother's charge of Norbie estate, and obtained a decree of eviction at the Zetland Sheriff Court against Gaer a few weeks later – for good measure, he added another for a sum of £40 he claimed Gaer owed them, demanding immediate settlement.

'We hear the island of Thulay is in a great excitement,' Gabrielsen records, 'For the decree has been charged upon, and as Gaer has so little about him, besides farm stock and his few sticks of furniture, an officer is expected from Larvik to conduct a poinding and rouping of his effects.'

There is no lengthy account of the scene, unfortunately, for it would have been a spectacle indeed to see the officer come ashore at the island fortress and march with his constables to the door of the catechist, with the gathering crowd of Thulay folk around their heels. Did the brave catechist stride out to meet them, or did he bar the door? Were the children hiding, terrified, in the boxbeds? This we can but conjecture.

But the outcome is on record, because the officer was 'deforced; nearly the whole of the people taking part with Gaer; and although no violence was offered to the officer, the people refused to bid for a single item offered at the auction.'

The Thulay folk exerted their non-violent will – and the officer and his constables left the island, disappointed, but threatening 'further steps'.

25th June 2000 – Norbie

The front door of Norbie Hall is locked, of course, so I have to go round to the rear. Through the window I see Mrs Mitchell, as she looks up – and what kind of a look was that?

'Well well well, see what the cat's dragged in,' she says, flatly, so it's hard to know the mood behind it.

'Morning,' I say. 'I'm sorry for not coming back last night.'

'Well, we were worried for a while, till the shepherd looked in and told us where you were. We expected a phone call at least, to say you were staying.'

'I didn't really mean to stay. I just fell asleep …'

And she comes over to the table, settles down with her cigarettes and her lighter, beckoning me to sit. She gives me that look of compliant defiance, takes a cigarette from the packet, but doesn't light it right away.

'I was thinking. I want to tell you about something that happened. It was a few weeks ago,' she says. 'Just a mad thing, one of those summer nights. I'd been here working till late. There was a party of guests due. Your father came in here, quite late on. He was drunk. I'd had a couple just to keep me interested in what I had to do. The oven was on and it was unbearable hot, the heat in there. So we walked down to the beach. It was a beautiful evening. And we were talking, laughing like we always did, we always laughed. And then I kissed him …'

'And what's that got to do with Maggie?'

Mary, Mrs Mitchell, flicks the lid of her lighter and sucks the smoke: 'Well, it was the day after that him and her fell out. I don't know what happened exactly, but he swore he'd never go back there. I think he told her what happened between us.' Then she winks. 'Sunday lunch will be a bit late,' she says, in a Mrs Mitchell way. 'The laird's got himself a trip in the helicopter,' she smiles, starting to rattle her pot-lids.

'What's the story between him and Maggie, down at the pub?'

'Your father?' She snorts two jet streams of smoke from her nostrils. 'Ach, she looked after him. Did his washing. Fed him. And whatever else. He spent a lot of time down there last year. Or so I believe. He wasn't coming up here so much then, so I don't really know. I don't think your father was too involved, all the same. He could be quite heartless talking about her, sometimes.' She stubs out her cigarette, only half-smoked. 'He was always hankering after the things he couldn't have, it seems to me.'

Her accuracy shocks me. 'That's the truth. That is my father you've just described,' I say.

She picks up her cigarettes and lighter as if she's about to get up. But then she hesitates, as if she's had a thought. She smiles: 'I wonder sometimes what it is that makes everybody so different. It's kinda marvellous in a way, don't you think, how what happens to us when we're bairns seems to shape us? I mean there's your father growing up in Australia, dreaming about the old country, wanting to go back there. Always looking at the horizon and wondering what lay beyond. Thinking what was out there is better than what's here. Wherever "here" is. I suppose wherever your head is. At that time.'

She gives me a sideways glance: 'Do you really believe he's going to be at that Salutation Hotel tomorrow?' What can I do but nod? 'You don't need to explain. We understand what you're going through. The not knowing.'

'One way or another would be easier. Sometimes I think anything could have happened ...'

A beat.

'Not short of murder?' she asks.

I look her over closely at that. 'Maybe,' I say. 'I don't know anything any more. Until I see for myself that he isn't there tomorrow, I'm going to keep on believing. I have to go back.'

'I can understand that.'

And then a silence falls. It's easy to be silent with Mary, somehow. It would be easy, yes, easy, to fall in love with her ordered peacefulness as she ghosts confidently around this well-appointed kitchen, keeping down on the dust and madness with her sane sense of proportion. If it wasn't for the thought of murder.

'It's a shock for me,' I say, 'being back in his life like this. It's been a long time. I've changed. But maybe what's hardest to appreciate is just how he's changed from the man I thought he always had been and always would be.'

Mary puts her head on one side, thinking: 'When I came back from Glasgow to look after my mother, that was a shock too.' She sighs, heaving her chest, her whole body, outwards as it fills with the kitchen smells, then falling. A sad sigh of resignation. 'I realised then how much we'd both changed.' And then she brightens: 'But it wasn't a bad thing entirely, I think we both knew that in fact we could get along all right now, even though we couldn't be really close, as we'd been long ago, when I was just a bairn.'

And then there's silence again, a long warm silence in which I can rest the idea of murder. A tiredness comes over me; the first time today that the stresses of the night have really gripped me. It's easy just to snuggle in Mary's warm and silent kitchen, to smell the smells of good food rising from her clatter orchestra of pans and pots and spoons and ladles. Here I could just drift

TIME DOES NOT

But no. I can't allow it.

Up the winding stairs I go for the last time. I look again out of the window the fog had pressed against, the window where I stood and saw the midsummer light. Sad, yes, a little, to be packing up my things, so soon departing. Backwards, yes,

backwards go I

again

It seems like days since I was here last, as if I've reached some kind of turning place on my journey since then. At Innertoon, was it? Or at St Mary's. My fall?

Back to Perth

you go

The sound of the chopper from the beach begins to grow louder and I know that the hour of reckoning is approaching.

'You're going to have something to eat before you leave,' Mary says. 'I'm not allowing you to go away off on that ferry without a good meal inside you.'

And before I can protest the door bursts open and the laird comes in, looking more like an excited seven-year-old than seventy.

'Hello, hello,' he says, all jolly again. 'Remarkable things, helicopters,' he says. 'I've just seen round the whole estate in about five minutes.' And then, remembering: 'No sign of your father, yet.'

'He's leaving,' Mary says to him.

'Leaving?'

'Aren't you, dear?'

'Yes,' I say.

Dr Hart is brought up short. Yes, short of breath he is, so he sits, the exhilarated seven-year-old becalmed again,

gasping for wind

I've said my farewell to Mary, with a kiss and 'all the very best, take care'. And she has extracted from me a promise to come back, to bring my boy. Then I'm climbing into the passenger seat, engine starting. My rucksack's in the back, with the Millennium Bible, the stone that I took from St Mary's and the sea curiosity, that egg-sac thing, and the black-tipped feather. And my father's papers. There's no pain in my side any more, my hangover's gone. The day is bright, I'm hopeful. There is hope in believing. And I will not listen to the chopping of the rotors.

The Land Rover turns and sets off, pointing down the gravel pathway, away from the house, heading towards the gates with the two round stones on the gateposts. Looking back up the drive, I see the figure of Mary, her kiss still wet on my cheek, standing in front of the big house, waving. Lady Mary for the day. While the laird's away.

At the bottom of the drive, there's a gathering of policemen just beyond the gateposts. They turn to look and I can tell from their body language that the search is still fruitless. A brief sense of triumph surges through me, as if now I am a step closer to my quest. The laird stops and screws down his window.

'Anything?'

'Nothing.'

'Carrying on?'

'Till darkness if need be.'

And the laird nods, puts his window up again and drives on. Up the road he goes towards the top of the hill.

I look back over my shoulder and see the finger of land stretching towards the south, pointing me back home. St Mary's at the beach-head. The bungalow in the centre of the village. The two and a bit chalets cut into the side of the hill. And the road that I know now goes to Innertoon and the past. On he drives, up to the junction, closing in on the church, and the little green stripe going up the hill beyond it I now know to be the road to the caves. The crossroads of the old and the new. But instead of turning towards the past, he goes left.

It is like emerging from a dream. This surge of energy. This sense of freedom, escaping the village. And I'm not looking back as the laird crests the hill and away we go, accelerating along a straight, out of sight of Outertown, out of sight of Innertoon, out of my father's life.

'Thanks,' I say, 'for everything. It's been difficult, but …'

'You're welcome,' he interrupts. 'More than welcome.'

Then an awkward silence ensues, as if it's difficult to talk with him out of the environment we've shared, away from the scene of the mystery that has bound us these last few days. But I want to tell him I'm grateful.

He just snatches at the gear stick and revs the engine. So to put him at his ease I ask him what it was that brought him here in the first place.

'You were telling me about it all the first day I was here, but I felt so tired I didn't really take it in.'

'Ah well, that is a very convoluted story,' he smiles. And the tale starts to unfold. Telling it relaxes him, and so I relax, listening to talk of a rubber plantation in Selangor and an old river boat captain he got to know.

'Came from here, he did, went to sea as a boy, never came back. Ended up working his whole life going up and down the Mekong River, till they finally retired him because of his eyes and he ended up out our way.'

And the story goes on, of how Dr and Mrs Hart had been yachting in the isles with friends, had seen the house from the sea, then out of curiosity visited the island, saw the Outertown estate for sale and fell in love with it. When it was time to think about coming home again from the East …

I'm listening, watching out the window, noticing how red the cliffs are here. Old Red Sandstone

crumbling

Dr Hart coughs, sniffs. 'The big house was in an awful state when we bought it. We lived in the bungalow overlooking the beach for the first three years, while renovations went on. Sadly, the old gal never saw the big house complete.' And the quivering of his voice and the twitching of his moustache tells me that he's letting me see inside a very tender place. 'That was something your father and I had in common. We both lost our wives.'

Yes, I can appreciate that now. I'm leaving with a changed perspective on my father. When I only saw the chunk of his life that was Perth, I saw him in a certain way, at a certain angle, and when his Australian past emerged, I couldn't handle that. Now, having this part of his life mapped out seems to help.

'Yes, I saw the bungalow,' I say, and again I've spoken without thinking. 'Yesterday. I walked the old Coffin Road to St Mary's from Innertoon.'

'Did you indeed?' he says, and nods thoughtfully.

'It looked sad,' I say. 'The bungalow.'

This makes him smile. 'Sad, yes, but it was pretty. Pretty impractical, really, trying to replant to somewhere like this. If I'd thought about it, you know, really thought about it. But the land was cheap here. And we saw it at midsummer, this time of year, when the light is so marvellous. But she hated the winter darkness. Went mad with it, really. Poor girl.'

We come to the old Victorian mansion where I'd first seen the shepherd. But there's no one out today. Backwards go I.

Dr Hart laughs to himself. 'Grew up with servants. In Lahore.' And then a heavy gloomy old man sadness falls. 'By then we were too old to think again. We'd started this enterprise with such high hopes. And … here I am, now, alone.'

'But you're not alone, are you?'

'What do you mean?'

'Well,' I say, 'there's people around you who respect you, who need you in some way. Mrs Mitchell, for instance.'

'Need me?' He smiles ruefully. 'Is it me they need or just someone with enough wealth to keep the wheels turning?' And then he looks at me, partly amused, partly confused. His moustache twitches. 'Why am I telling you all this?'

I shrug. 'Maybe because I didn't understand it the first time. Or because you know you can safely. Because I'm the outsider, I'm leaving. You know whatever you say to me won't come back around to haunt you.'

'Perhaps so.' He nods, turns to me and smiles. 'Your resilience impresses me.'

For some reason that brings a tear to the corner of my eye, but I laugh. 'Resilience?'

'I mean your refusal to bow down in front of fate.'

'I suppose I haven't stopped believing yet despite everything. Here I am going back to Perth, thinking he'll be there. Am I crazy, heading off like this, do you think, Dr Hart? Honestly?'

Now it's me who's rueful. He smiles. 'You may be a little mad. Temporary insanity would be understandable at this time.'

The road towards the port is wider and smoother than the narrow single-track with passing places that culminates at the pier in Innertoon. Now the Land Rover starts to power, a different vehicle from the one that had dodged the potholes on the way to the chalet the first morning. Though the smell of wet dogs and alcohol is no less strong.

The laird coughs. 'You know, Mrs Mitchell gave me some good advice where you were concerned. Last night it was, while you were out. She said that you were dealing with this thing in your own way and that it was important not to interfere. I rather think she meant that you would work things out yourself, somehow.'

'She's wise as well, Mary.' He doesn't object to her Christian name this time.

'My own thought was to prescribe something,' he says. 'But you've dealt with it in your own way, as she said you would.'

He stares at me not best pleased, his head shaking slightly, then turns his attention to the road. The car is heading up a steep hill and he's hanging on to the steering wheel as if

for guidance

Letter from Philippa Gabrielsen
to Rev. Archibald Nicol,
June 25th 2001

Bon Hoga
Serrafir

Dear Archie

How are you, my dear friend? I haven't heard much from you lately. I do hope your health is keeping up. I wanted to share with you another short interview with Miss Mimie Jeromsen. In the time between this and my first visit, while she was ill, I learned more about those early settlers and what they were met with when they first landed here, back in the 1870s, through the letters, papers and the mementos which we have been gathering as part of our local history project. It is so exciting!

Reading them, I have felt as if we – I – was one of only a few persons in the world who knew these wonderful things, about the old folks and who they really were, when they arrived here, before the colony changed them, and their children, and their children's children. The evidence is there, in the knitting patterns, the stonework, the tools they fashioned, even if the weather they warded off was different, the stone itself, the soil they tilled, the fish they caught and the fruits they ate. And it was there too in the faces they had brought with them, in the early photos; they had a different cast about them, a sort of a 'weatherwornness' different from the kind we wear today. Something that came from 'The Northern', as we sometimes refer to old Zetland.

A key figure in it all was Thorvald Gabrielsen: 'The Minister', as we refer to him. He seems to have been a very charismatic person, and held a kind of power over his congregation. As a man of the church yourself, you will probably understand this much better than I do, but it seems to me that when people invest their faith in another person, who is anointed with the task of guiding them spiritually, then they sometimes also confer a kind of secular authority on them too. So they were willing to follow him, on his mission, to settle here and build a religious colony in the South Pacific where the old ways would be preserved, yet paradoxically a 'New Zetland' would be made. The Minister led, with the blessing of his own father in Norbie, the bravest of the surplus population to establish an outpost of Zetlandic civilisation where the old ways would survive.

We have searched, so far without success, for the manuscripts of his sermons, which were kept in the family here in New Zetland until the grandchildren fell out over the property. By then most had left the colony, settling in New Zealand or Australia. I haven't yet been able to make contact with them all, but I am working on it. There was a schism in the church, between two sons of The Minister, after he died, and although the two lived together in harmonic enmity, if I can call it that, for some time, the bad blood flowed in time, away from Serrafir. Somewhere along the line, The Minister's own papers, which he kept so meticulously, were lost or destroyed. There was talk about a box, kept latterly by a grand-niece of his, who had moved back to the North as an old woman, but this too seems to have disappeared.

Aa da bestist,
Philippa

MISS MIMIE JEROMSEN: 3RD INTERVIEW

Miss Mimie, I'm glad to see you've recovered your strength and feel well enough to do another session. We're very grateful at the Heritage Society.
A'm been tinkin.

Yes?
I wid laek ta tell Robina's tale, dat is, her an Albert's story. Ja, du sees whan du axt me da hidmist time we spakk, I wisna joost sure, du kens. Bit noo A'm toght an toght aboot'it an I wid laek ta.

You're talking about your former mistress Robina Cunninghame or Scot, and her husband Albert?

Dat's dem, ja. Bit dey wirna aye Cunninghame ta nem, na, dat wis joost whan dey cam oot here.

The family changed its name, didn't it?
Ja, da young laird, hit wis'at did it, Mestir Albert Scot, only son ta da Surgeon General, tho he hed twa aalder sisters. Wir Bertie Cunninghame. Dey wir aa boarn doon aboot London somewye, an dan moved ta Noarbie whan da faidir retired fae da Navy. Du minds, I telt de dat, fu he wis an aafil lokk aalder as his wife, an merriet laet?

Sure, yes.
Bit whan Albert took up wi Robina dat wis da end a'aa dat.

So we're talking here about the man we knew here as Albert Cunninghame, elder of the council of New Zetland, the first garage owner on Tokumua? I have his dates here somewhere: born Norbie, Zetland in 1864, died at Snarrniss, New Zetland in 1937.
Ja, dat wis right, I mind dat weel. A sad day whan Albert de'ed for Robina an aa a'wis, da peerie lasses an aa. Ja ja ... (PAUSE)

Yes, Mimie, I'm sure it must have been. But why did the family change its name?
Ah weel, dat is da story, ja. A lang aald story I sall tell ta de if du'll hear me. I dunna ken da hail o'im, na, bit whit I ken I sall tell. Ja ... du sees, Albert lost da estate ati'da 1890s. Ja, hit aa fell ati'brukk. Da Scots wir lairds a'Norbie nae maer. An hit brook his hert, I tink. Whan he left Zetlan he tried ta cut aff aa connection wi da faemily, fir he wis faan oot maest terrible wi his middir an twa sisters, ower Robina first an dan da will. An so whan he wan here, he took da Cunninghame name, hoopin I doot at dey wid nevir fin'im maer, fir he waantit nae maer ta do wi ony o'dim. He cut himsel aff aatagiddir, joost da wye'at his middir hed cut him aff.

That was in 1893 if the details I have are correct. And can you tell us what happened to the family estate back home in Zetland?
Weel du minds I telt de fu da Surgeon General wis a good laird an kinda

cukkirt aboot da fokk, an widna harry dem fir dir rent an dat? Du sees dat wis his doonfaa, fir da hail estate wis riddled wi unpaid debts. Dat wis common knowledge, ja, I mind me faider tellin me dat, ja. Whan dey cam ta look at da books, dir wis a gret lokk a'rent money at fokk wir due so hit kinda lookit aaright an dat, bit dan dey wid nevir pay an nevir pay, an he'd led oot dis an dat wi his 'improvements'.

So the Surgeon General's good intentions were undone because people couldn't pay their rents?
Da fokk hed naethin ta pey wi, lass. Naethin ava! Dey hed naethin firbye da fysh dey wir catcht, an da bits a'haps an ganseys dey might sell ta da shop, an aa dat wis coontit agenst whit bit a'vittals dey wid get, an so dey wir nevir seen money, hit wis aa joost barter. So whit wye wir dey gjaain ever ta hae da gaer ta settle up wi da laird?

No, I suppose it was difficult under the Truck system.
Truck? Hit wis joost laek slavery, lass, slavery. Fir da lairds dey wir joost laek royalty, du kens, no fokk laek wirsels. An dat wis whit da graet vexation wis whan da young laird, Albert, staartit coortin wir Bieni. Fir hit wis joost unheard o, ja. No for a young laird ta mak siccar a young lass's life wi a unwaantit bairn or dat, na dat wisna unken ava, bit fir him ta waant ta merry her, weel noo, dat du kens wisna don ava. Na na.

So Albert went against convention, did he ... (MIMIE IS PUZZLED) *... he was breaking the rules?*
Oh ja, da baeth a'dem did dat, nae doot. Ati'da times dey lived, whan dey wir young, ja. Bit a maer respeckable couple you wid never a'met, whan dey wir aaldir. Bit du kens, hit wis joost pure love atween dem, ja. Dat wis aa.

A great love affair?
Weel I doot hit most a'been, ja, fir dey wir tagiddir aa dir days. Ja, an a gret skreed a'baerns dey hed dim as weel.

Now there were nine children? In the Cunninghame family, I mean.
Nine boarn, ja, twa dee'd as infants. Fower boys and tree lasses, da lasses

were da last boarn. Dey wir da anes'at I took care o. Da boys I never kent as weel, dey wir grown men be da time I wis come oot here, an twa o dem wir gien back ta Breetain, somewy aboot London. An dir wis ane gied to bide in Australia, ta da gold at Bendigo or somethien laek dat, I mind hearin. Wid dat a'been hit? Bendigo?

Yes, one went to Bendigo. The three sons were older, but the three girls, they were born here in New Zetland, weren't they? And so it was the three daughters who you helped to bring up – Miss Agnes, Miss Catherine and Miss …
Eleanor, ja, da peerie ane wis Eleanor, Guid bliss her. An aafil blyde peerie sowl. Guid bliss dem aa. Ta tink I sood a'lived ta see dem aa buriet. Less a'less, whit did I do ta deserve ta liv sae lang, tinks du?

Is it not such a good thing then, to be a centenarian?
Ah weel A'm been blisst, truly, wi a lang life bit fir aa dat whan du comes ta be as aald as me, dey irna muckle left'at isna unken. But da Loard haes preservit me fir some raeson an weel, I wis tinkin, hit wis mebbie fir joost dis, so as I wis able to tell de da story …

Of Robina and Albert?
Mebbie dat, ja … du kens hit wis a scandal, ja.

Because the landlord wanted to wed some girl who was beneath him?
Ja weel, she wis dat, du sees, her family wis aboot da maest pooramis ati'da hail parish. Fir he could a'hed a choice a'weel-boarn lasses, dir wisna joost da ae laird, na, du widda fun a lokk a'peerie lairds danadays, wi a pocky a'laand, fir aa da Scots wir da main anes. Dey widda been nae waant a'matches fir him, lasses maer his ane kind, or he might a'gien an soght a wife awa sooth himsel. But whan he set een apo Robina, dat wis him. Bit dat wisna da warst o'it, na. Du sees hit wisna joost'at she wis dat'n low-boarn, na, she wis a lokk aalder as'im as weel. She wis near seevin year aalder, ja. An he wisna maer as a laad a'nineteen whan dey began koortin. So du sees da Aald Leddy, she toght he wis been bewitcht, laek sum vaam hed come apo'im. Ja, dat wis whit sum a'da fokk sed, at

335

wir boannie Bieni wis taen him straight fae his cradle wi some charm or aniddir.

They thought she was a witch? Surely not?
Weel, mebbie no choost a witch, bit hit wis dat'n uncanny, du sees, fir onythin laek dat ta happen. Fir ane a'da mestirs ta be taen dat'n aabir eftir ane a'da lasses, laek as ta staand up dat wy an say'at he wid mairry her. Ja, hit wis laek some kind o a magic spell, some toght, fir hit wis dat'n quaint a thing ta happen. Fir da laird ta waant ta merry a poor ting a'lass fae a blackhoose.

I guess it must have been, yes.
Me middir aye spakk aboot day he gied waakin across da links, his kist apo his back, ja, fae da muckle Haa ta da peerie aald hoos at Snooskie, whar Bieni's fokk bed, da fokk atid'a rigs aa waatchin him gjing. Hit wis a terrible scandal, bit du kens hit wis choost love, ja. Nae vaam ava. Na.

So how was it that they came to fall in love. Was she a maid or a servant at the Hall?
Ah weel noo, da wye'at Bieni telt hit, shu furst led een apo'im, an him her, ae day whan shu wis broght some o her makkin ta da shop ta sell fir tea, an he wis hingin aboot, choost a laad a'nineteen, du kens. He hed a peerie lean-to'at he wis gotten biggit ta himsel whar he wid elt aboot wi engines an dat, he wis a bit o an inventor, wis Albert, an he'd wired up da big hoose fir electricity, hed pittin in twartree lights an dan a lokk a'electric bells so his middir could ring fir her servants an dat. Hit aa ran fae a peerie windmill, du kens. Ja, he wis joost fairlie taen up wi aa things mechanical, wis Albert, right fae he wis a peerie ting, Robina sed. Dis wis awa afore dey wir cars, du understaands. Bit onywye, dis day, Bieni as she wis dan, fetches up at da shop wi her makkin, an du kens she's a bonnie lass an twartree a'da boys hingin roond da pierhead are kinda takkin a interest in her, whan dir's dis mostaafil explosion an Albert cam staggin oot fae his shed joost black wi da sute an dat wis da first sight she hed o'im. An didn she get dat'n a gluff she drappit da parcel wi her makkin an oot da hap burst apo da aert.

Makkin? By makkin, you mean knitting?
Ja, knittin, makkin as we aye caa'ed it. Du sees noo, Bieni wis da most special haand'at makkin lacewark haps an dat ...

Haps, those are shawls, aren't they?
Ja, ja, shaals as du says ... hit wis a graet makkin, dat, eensadays in Zetlan, fir du sees dey wir dis man, an Engliesh gentleman, cam nort an saa whit da wiemin wir makkin an whan he left he took wi'im twartree samples an gied ta da aald Queen Victoria an med a present ta her a'ane o da lacewark haps, an hit wis ati'aa da paepirs an dat, du kens. Feth ja, hit wis a wark.

And this set a fashion then, for the Zetland lacework shawls, didn't it, this presentation to Queen Victoria?
Oh ja, fir a peerie start da wiemin joost wis makkin makkin ... dey wir herdly able ta keep up wi da demaand. Aa da leddies ati'da sooth aa hed ta hae dir Zetlan hap, sam as da royalty du sees. An dan d'ir yun Duchess, da Duchess a'Bedford, she wis a aviator, du kens, laek yun Amelia Erhardt wife, she took an aafil gjaain t'da Fair Isle, she wis a orneitholigist, du sees. She med a graet wark owir da Fair Isle, an da fokk wir med hir an da Duke a present o a Fair Isle rig oot. Ja, a suit an a goon an dat ...

And this tradition of makkin, or knitting, it was kept alive in New Zetland, wasn't it, when the first settlers came out here?
Ja, fir mony a year dat wis true. Bit I never ken if da young anes still makk da day. Does du ken, lass?

Well, you know, Mimie, there isn't so much of the old tradition today. Which is a great shame. But there are still a few ladies who know. And that's one of the reasons why the Heritage Society wants to gather people's memories of the old ways. From folk like yourself who remember. Not that there's any who are really like Miss Mimie Jeromsen, now is there?
Weel dey ir nane as aald as me an dat's a fack, me lass. Na na ... I im heard dim spaekin aboot dis Hoos a'Myndin'at you hae, an I wis tinkin t'try an tak me alang daer some day. Tinks du wid I win? If I wis able?

I'm sure we can arrange that. But you seem tired now, Mimie. Shall we
abandon this for today?

Na, lass, A'm ower weel. I wis set ta tell de aa aboot Robina an Albert, bit
boy noo A'm forgotten whit it wis I wis gjaain ta say … will we hae a cup
a'tae an A'll see if I canna mind?

(TAPE OFF – DURING OUR BREAK, MIMIE SEEMED A LITTLE FRAIL AND SO
WE AGREED TO CURTAIL OUR SESSION.)

Carbon Copy retained of a
Letter from Rev. Archibald Nicol
to Peter A Scot,
July 13th 2001

Perth

Dear Peter

Thank you for your letter. I have been ill, hence the delay in replying.
What you have to tell me about Albert and Robina is interesting, and I
very much enjoyed your story of the Tirvalites. I knew something about
this venture already, but was glad to hear the full story.

Despite ill health, I have reached the end of typing out and editing
Gabrielsen's history, except of course the non-existent chapter nine,
along with some additional detective work done by myself when the good
Lord has allowed me the health to visit the library.

It has been a long process as I find my concentration wanders and I
end up far from the topic, but it is good for me to have something to do,
since Margaret died.

Yours faithfully
Archibald Nicol (Reverend)

Letter from Peter A Scot
to Rev. Archibald Nicol,
July 23rd 2001

Miami

Dear Reverend Archibald

It was good to get your letter and I am very sorry to hear you have not
been well. You have shown remarkable determination if you have typed
out all of Gabrielsen's manuscript, incomplete or not.

Regarding Albert and Robina, I can do better than tell you the story.
I will allow them to tell it themselves, by sending you these extracts from
some of their letters. It is a romantic story and very touching to think
that they were so in love as to go completely against social convention.

I'm not sure that any part of these should be included in your version
of the history, as they are not for publication, should you have this in
mind.

I send them merely in answer to your question as to what happened
next.

Do keep well, my Scotch friend,

Yours faithfully,
Peter A Scot

A History of Zetland with particular attention
to the Parish of Norbie, Valay and Thulay:

CHAPTER NINE

'THE LAST OF THE LAIRDS'

*(The text for this chapter in James Gabrielsen's history is limited, and
although there are a number of notes, they are not integrated into narrative.
We may assume that he was, as testimony suggests, working on this at the
time of his death in 1899. However, I have been able to piece together the
main events and personalities involved in the fall of the Scots of Norbie
from the letters of Albert and Robina Scot, later Cunninghame – AN)*

The visit of the Commissioners in 1883 coincided with the return to
Norbie Hall of Bertie 'Ditto', following completion of his schooling at
Cheltenham Boys School in far distant England, and a year spent in Paris
and in Warsaw with his maternal relatives. He now returned a fully grown
eighteen-year-old, with the prospect ahead of a university education in
Edinburgh.

The curious nine-year-old, always poking his fingers into things, had
matured into a young scientist of some gifts and considerable passion.
He was fascinated, in particular, by engines of all sorts – steam-driven,
obviously, but particularly a new invention currently being developed on
the Continent, the internal combustion engine, which promised a much
less cumbersome system of power, a machine capable of driving itself from
within. The dream prospect of horseless carriages seemed almost real.

While not a particularly commanding figure, as his father had been,
Bertie had about him a quick and bold intelligence that made him noticed,
and a boundless energy for activity. He set himself to build a workshop,
fetched the local carpenter and builder and sat over them till the job was
done in record time. In this shed, no more than a lean-to against the wall
of the old Haa and shop, he began to gather the wherewithal he required.
Each ship from Larvik brought more wooden crates, filled with more

mysterious materials and tools, for what purpose no one knew but Ditto.

Long summer days passed, with candles burning in the shed in the dim of night, till at last one evening, when the butler looked out, he feared the building was on fire, so bright was the glare shining from within. But when they rushed down to rescue him and threw open the door they found young Bertie laughing like a madman, bathed in blazing light, and saw that he was sitting in front of a great bank of strange glass orbs that glowed brightly.

No time at all passed, it seemed, before these magical lights had been transferred to the big house, and a large windmill – for that was the planned source of his brilliance and the reason for all the crates – stood on the brow of the hill behind, a whirring Goliath seeming to come striding at them when the wind blew. People said the stays wouldn't hold it when the winter gales came, but nonetheless it was an impressive structure. And the word 'dynamo' was added to the Norbie vocabulary.

Indeed, by this single act, Bertie changed from being a figure of fun to the local folk to a man whose knowledge was respected, even if he was very strange in many ways. He took little interest in the running of the estate, this having been administered since the death of his father by the younger of the Berrick brothers, James.

This fellow had in fact established something of fiefdom in Norbie, and was favoured by Bertie's mother, who had come to rely upon him since she was widowed. For her part, Agnes worried about her son, with his wild enthusiasms and impractical ideas, and her girls agreed. He wasn't quite comfortable in the role of patron, and showed little sign of growing into it. Much as Mama liked him to be acquainted with the latest ideas and inventions – and she really did like the electricity, even if she had nightmares about the windmill's collapse – she wished he were less self-involved and better able to manage a number of things simultaneously, rather than ignore all in order to follow the latest scheme with total abandon, or without proper foresight. She understood him all too well, had gladly encouraged his intelligent precocity as a boy, but nothing could have prepared Agnes, nor her daughters, for the next enthusiasm which was about to strike Bertie.

Though there was only one laird's house, and all the folk were common beneath it, there was nonetheless in the parish at this time a range of character and situation, from those who owned a little land independent of Norbie, who were in their less obvious way 'well-to-do', to those who subsisted in the meanest of dwellings and were barely sure of those.

Some families were original Norbie dwellers, had been resident there since before records began, and had surnames which denoted this, being the relic of the old Scandinavian fashion of patronymics which prevailed there till the mid eighteenth century – all ended in the same suffix: 'sen'. Others had Scotch names, though most of those had habituated over generations and so contained much Zetland blood, hidden behind the Caledonian.

Those who had risen had largely done so by means of making a living elsewhere. There were many merchant seamen among the breadwinners in this class, and five sea captains among those.

One, a Captain Wylimsen, had even obtained a large area of land from Berrick, beyond the hill dykes that marked the boundary between arable and rough pasture, and there had built a house for himself which he called 'Rangoon', in honour of the time when, as a young seaman, he had found himself stuck in that teeming city without possessions or purpose when his vessel foundered in the river there, and he was rescued by a Norbie man, a sea captain himself of that period, who happened to recognise the young sailor sitting by the roadside in the eastern metropolis, ordered the driver to stop, and shouted the immortal words: 'Is du no Jiemie Wylimsen's boy fae Norbie?'

Among the 'pooramis' people who had been forced to live partly by the charity of others was a widow resident at the ancient hovel of Snooskie, a rough shackle of mossy stones in the midst of a few overworked fields to the west of the westmost track, where none ventured by accident. This woman had lost her seaman husband when her children were very young, and had struggled to bring them up herself, with some help from the parish, her only source of credit what she might gain from knitwear. She was, humble soul, as fine an exponent of the art of lacework as any, and she brought her daughters up to do as she and others did, to knit constantly unless hands were busy doing other necessary work.

Consequently, the widow of Snooskie's two girls grew up expert as their mother, and from a very early age, were able to contribute to the household by the bartering of their wares to the factor's shop.

The oldest of the two, christened Robina, but known as 'Bieni', was particularly gifted at the lacework patterns then becoming so popular. In fact, Bieni had many gifts and she, with her sister Eliza's help, had made of the smoke-filled old blackhouse a warm and attractive interior, which surprised the few souls who ever ventured there, with its sense of wellbeing, of a healthy life and gentle ease, the order of the well-kept yard with its neat corn-stook and peat stack. There was little sign that the croft had no man about.

Bieni and Eliza had many admirers in the parish, and were always surrounded by young men on the long walk to church and back. Eliza married, and soon became a mother, as she left the Snooskie darkness for a bright new nineteenth-century home in Vass, the wife of an able seaman who, folk said, was sure to 'pass his ticket as a master'.

Bieni stayed on with her mother, managing everything, industrious and virtuous as any parent could wish. She seemed cold to the advances that came her way, though she was always polite with the lads who approached her, so much so that her mother began to fear she might end up a spinster. But Bieni had a secret that she had kept faithfully since her twelfth year, and which had caused her much sorrow since her fifteenth, when her lover Rasmi left Norbie aboard the *Isabella Browne*, in the company of the schoolmaster's son, Tirval, leader of that determined sect, the Tirvalites. He and she had been first sweethearts at the school together, and she was promised to him from the day of his departure when they'd walked the sweet heather hill behind Snooskie, and proved their love there, the air heavy with honey perfume.

Years had passed since then without word from him, but she knew how far away it was quite well enough, how ill-served it was by the mail, and that people rarely made the return trip. Yet she continued to hope that one of the seamen, home on leave, might have voyaged there, and might have carried home even a single letter. But then Rasmi had never been a scholar, and wrote with difficulty. His virtues were composed of action and enterprise.

So Bieni waited. One day, she believed, he would reappear, coming ashore down at the pier in the flit-boat from the steamer that now called twice a week from Skallvaa. She wouldn't know, she would be here, working, waiting. He would come straight here, even before he went to see his old mother, might even borrow a pony and come riding up the path as fast as that horse could gallop.

And then it would all be worthwhile. They would wed as quickly as possible. She and her mother would go with him, back to the fine home he had been buiding in New Zetland for her. She would close the door on the smoky fire and the black pots of Snooskie, she would shove down the wooden latch, she would secure the boards over the well for the last time, and leave her plants to grow as they could, or die, without her, inside the old mossy walls of the kailyard, the stones that she knew like a part of her body.

And together they would go, by steamer to Skallvaa, maybe over the hill to Larvik with their gear in a gig, and from there to Leith, where her mother would see her sister for the first time in fifteen years. They would stay a while there, and she would see the castle that she'd read about. And then, maybe to Glasgow, to the Clyde for the long voyage out.

There was nothing too much she wanted to carry with her. A single kist would do, near enough. She had gathered those few things together long ago, and kept them polished, ready. In New Zetland, she would begin over, and start a family. So she had no intention of being a spinster, as her mother feared.

Another two years passed, and still no word came. Bieni still hoped – still believed – but a little less than before. So when the factor, James Berrick, began to show an interest in her, she didn't put him off entirely, though she held him at arm's length as best she could. But if he were to offer marriage, well, she would be a fool not to consider it, he being successful in business and likely to provide her with a fine home.

But no matter how often Berrick called along, no matter how many times she laughed at his stories of what the Norbie folk were up to, whatever news he had to share from Skallvaa or Roovik or wherever, she did not find him handsome, did not feel that tug at the heart, that strange sickness in the stomach. He was too clumsy, too insensitive, too manly, by comparison with the quickness and intelligence of Rasmi, her lost boy, whom she hadn't seen in so very long.

Bieni had reached the age of twenty-five and was still without a husband in 1883 when the young laird returned. She was, therefore, some six or seven years older than him, but from their first encounter, she writes, there was a 'magnetic attraction' between them, even though she resisted him at first, and would 'not simply fall down in front of him willingly', as was the tradition between master and tenant.

She describes how she was on her way to the factor's shop with a parcel of lacework, some scarves and a hap, for which she would get the necessary household goods – usually much tea – in exchange. Outside the shop a gang of boys were gathered, and they began to whistle and make cheeky comments as she passed, about her 'needin a man'.

Distracted, she stumbled, just as a great bang came from inside a shed to her left, and out from within came a black-faced fellow, coughing and spluttering. He raced right into her, blind from the smoke, and she completed her stumble by falling. Her parcel, loosely wrapped in an old piece of linen, but not tied, sprang open and the wares inside which she had cleaned and dried so carefully before wrapping them, landed in a 'stank'. She had no idea who this lout was, and lowsed her tongue on him. It was only when she noticed that the wharf-rats had all stopped laughing that she hesitated.

It was not an auspicious beginning, but he was so apologetic and well-mannered about the incident that she felt quite sorry afterwards to have been so forthright in venting her vexation. After that, she noticed him in the church, in the Laird's Pew of course, sitting with his mother in black lace veil and the remaining unmarried sister, similarly in dressed in grief though her eyes danced rather too much – the oldest was married and living in Larvik by then, and it was said that Florence was keen to follow her out of the darkness that still rested on Norbie Hall, even eight years after the death of the good doctor.

As Bertie noticed her, she noticed him. So the next time she was down from Snooskie at the shop, she went to the door of the mysterious shed, as she had decided to do, on reflection, and knocked upon it. There was no answer from within, and she was disappointed by that, for she had rehearsed her apology carefully and was ready to make it – she, on consideration, thought it wise not to offend one's better.

The next Sunday he was not there at church either, and she wondered why. James Berrick was, however, so she consoled herself with him afterwards, walking the long path home round the shore. But she was even less taken with his lumbering ways, after the explosion of young 'Bertie Ditto' in her life. 'Such a silly name,' she wrote, 'and unkind of the folk to call you it.'

Another Sunday came and went, and another trip to the shop. Bieni was surprised to find herself even thinking about it, as if it mattered to her. And who cared, anyway? Any day now, Rasmi would return, carry her away as he had promised that day among the heather. She had his word.

Then on the fourth Sunday he was there, and he not only smiled at her, but afterwards came over and apologised again, and jokingly asked if she recognised him with a clean face. She laughed at that, and for just the merest fraction of a second she and he looked at one another without speaking, a moment that seemed 'to last at least a hundred years'.

On Monday she needed to go to the shop, for they were running low on flour at Snooskie, and she would bake if she had some. But the weather had turned so bad that she had to wait. And if she was to knock on the door of the shed again, then maybe it was best to wait a day or two, and not seem to rush after him just because he had looked at her so? It may mean nothing at all. But those blue eyes that had first peeped out from his sooty face, they were printed now on her mind's eye. It made no sense, but she felt that this man would become important in her life.

'For the first time in ten years,' she confessed to him later in a letter, 'I forgot my promise.'

On the Thursday the gale was over, and they desperately needed flour. The sugar too was running low, and so she took her thickest hap and, changing out of her 'rivliens' or hide slippers, put on her Sunday boots.

It was a storm-tossed village she passed through. The crops had taken a fair battering and a lot of folk were out tidying up the debris. More than one commented critically on her boots as she strode past, but the strange thing was that she didn't care one bit, for she felt her boots were carrying her where she needed to go. 'And so they did,' she recalls.

On this day she found the young laird was in, and he was glad to see her, for he had something to show that he was proud of – glass lamps that lit up brighter than any oil-lamp would, powered by the wind. His eyes danced wildly when he spoke of the windmill he was going to build, and how he would lay wires in Norbie Hall so there could be lamps in all the rooms.

Bieni liked the excitement, the novelty that seemed to mantle him like a cloak. He told her about the engine he was going to make, which would drive a horseless carriage, and said that a day was coming soon when all kinds of things like that would be possible, because men of science were at last cracking the secret codes of nature and casting off superstition. She wasn't knowledgeble about any of it, but found the way he explained it made sense to her in some manner, even if she had to ask him questions along the way. She understood, at last, that he didn't go to the church much because he was 'a man of science'.

And as they pored over some object or another that lay on his bench, she stood so close to him she felt a strange warmth radiate, some kind of heat that made her tingle. Once and once only had she felt that before.

An hour or more had passed by the time he opened the door for her, and she stepped out into the light. Her head was abuzz with a whole new vocabulary, as she stopped a moment on the threshold.

Suddenly he kissed her. Bertie seemed as shocked as she at first, but when she looked at him closely, she saw that he had changed, from 'the friendly scholar sharing his enthusiasm to a man eager to have her in his arms'.

For a moment, she almost went with him, back into the glow of the strange light within, but then she came to herself, pulled away and went as she had intended to the shop.

Back at Snooskie she did her best to forget about it and busied herself around the croft, but all the while she worked she had the image of his eyes inside her mind, 'dancing'. It was impossible that it might be anything more than just another affair between master and servant, though, and so she dismissed it.

What Bieni didn't know was that when Bertie had fixed on a thing, there was no putting him off, as his own mother might have warned her. His methods of courting were as intense as his devotion to invention. As the summer passed on into harvest, there came a spell of perfect weather such as not even the old folk could recall, and in the long warm evenings he would come to call on her, walking unseen along the shore from Norbie Hall to the west, until he came to the foot of the Snooskie rigs, then heading up across the burn. He would appear at the tiny window late at night, press his face against the glass, and knock, as late as midnight sometimes, after her mother was asleep, and beg her to come to him. And the more she put him off, the more determined Bertie became. He would bring her gifts, which she had no need of and no place for, but often after he had gone, when she looked again at this or that thing he had pressed into her palm, she was glad of them.

'The bracelet is beautiful. The writing paper and the pencils, too. And of course, the books,' she wrote.

Bertie was adamant. He loved her, he said, and wanted to marry her. Bieni scoffed at first, for such a thing was completely unheard of, had never happened and never would. He was hardly more than a boy anyway, and 'has probably never been in love before', as she had. But in spite of herself, despite the difference in status and the years between them, besieged as she was by his ardour and her loss, what hope did she have of resisting forever, when in her heart she believed their 'fates to be twinned?'

The letters between Robina and Albert cover only a short period, from October of 1883 until June of 1884. Their story is therefore far from completed by this correspondence, and it is to official records and the remaining notes of Gabrielsen's history we must turn, in order to discover what that twinned fate was to entail.

We know that a fine new house is built across the bay, named Robinaville, during the next year, and that on the 13th of December a son is born to Robina, and the father is named as Albert Scot.

We know that on the 16th of July 1885, Albert achieves majority, and that he marries Robina on her birthday, two weeks later, in Norbie Hall – and we know that a second child is stillborn the following year.

In addition, we know that during these years, while the Commissioners wrote their report, rumours began to circulate about the outcome. News travelled rapidly from Edinburgh, via Leith, to Larvik and Skallvaa, and finally to Norbie and the Red Coast beyond, aboard the *Jarl of Zetland* steamer. It was said that the recommendation was that rents be cut by a half, and that all the tenants' debts be erased.

In Norbie Hall, Gabrielsen reports, this was met with a sense of deep shock. James Berrick went to see Agnes with the news, and was forced to explain to her the perilous state of affairs which would arise, should such a scything cut and supposed strong remedy be applied. Many of the improvements Dr Scot had instituted remained to be paid for, and although the bank had been willing to advance on the basis of what was owed in the rentbook, if that was now to be wiped out, and future income from the rental so curtailed, then the estate was far from healthy.

We can only guess at the tensions which must have riven the rooms of Norbie Hall during these years of turbulence within the Scot family, with the social core of their cloistered lives shaken through the marriage of the laird to a peasant, as the very system they lived atop also shook with the political tremors underfoot.

Lewis Berrick was not so downhearted with the news as his younger brother, who had come to feel part of the Scot family, and quietly loved the widow he served. For Lewis, it seems, this was a great opportunity. He acted swiftly, demanding full settlement by Albert Scot of various great expenses which Berrick's had incurred on the estate's behalf, and when the young laird did nothing, despite his mother's appeals, Berrick had him sequestered. Then some of the other creditors heard this, and they immediately acted by appealing the sequestration, for fear that they could lose out. No solution was possible, until the outcome of the Commission's report was known.

In 1889, the long-awaited news was published. Estate rents would be cut by up to a third and all debts cancelled. James Berrick, by and large a kindly man whose own finances were perilously linked to those of the estate, was bankrupted by it. Lewis, rather than have the firm tainted, allowed his brother to sink alone, but brought an action against the Norbie estate for the settlement of the sum he said was owed.

In the hope of finding a way out, Albert and his mother agreed to sell the island of Valay, where the first John Scot had built his tower centuries before, and this sale we know to have gone ahead in 1893, the new owner being a nouveau riche mill-owner from Yorkshire.

This is all we have from Gabrielsen's history. But the advert in *The Scotsman* newspaper, with which I began this historical account dates from the next year, 1894, so we can assume that this land sacrifice was not enough.

And so I have reached the conclusion of James Gabrielsen's unfinished history, yet there is one further digression into the year 1894, which is certainly worthy of note, in that it involves the author himself.

This is the arrival in Norbie of Dr Jakup Jakupsen, a key figure in Zetland's culture, as well as his native Faroe. Jakupsen's work in the field of Faroese folklore and oral poetry played an important role in the rise of modern Faroese written literature, with his collection of Faroese legends and folktales. He looked upon folk tales as a kind of fictional literature, while the legends to him were a kind of source about early Faroese history. He also collected oral poetry, studied Faroese place-names, and was the first to point out that many of them were Celtic in origin. Jakupsen created a new Faroese orthography based on the new science of Phonetics, its principle being that there must be a one-to-one correspondence between phoneme and letter, and that the written language should be easy to learn by children, but his 'outlandish' scheme was not adopted.

Jakupsen had long been interested in the old language of Zetland, which he understood to be very similar to the contemporary Faroese he was studying, and he decided to make a field-trip to establish whether this relationship might make a suitable doctoral thesis.

When Jakupsen left Faroe for Leith, his only knowledge of the language of Zetland was drawn from Thomas Edmondston's glossary and those parts of George Stewart's *Zetland Fireside Tales* that are written in dialect. In Edinburgh he met Gilbert Goudie, and there he read 'a valuable manuscript supplement' to Edmondston's work written by a Zetland-born minister, Thomas Barclay.

During his fieldwork in the isles, he interviewed a large number of Zetlandic speakers and scholars, including Haldane Burgess, James Stout Angus, John Irvine, James Inkster, John Nicolson, and Laurence Williamson. And when he came to Norbie, he sought out James Gabrielsen, himself a well-known Scandinavian scholar of many years' standing. So useful a source was Gabrielsen that Jakupsen returned by Norbie from Thulay, in order to spend more time at the fine schoolhouse and library that the teacher and his wife had built.

Indeed, Jakupsen paints us a brief sketch: 'There, by a glowing peat fire, the old-fashioned oil lamps aflame, the two of us sat, far into the Zetland summer night, a young man and an old man equally eager to know what the other knew, to share their thoughts and stories, united in their shared fascination, smoking pipes and comparing Faroese and Zetlandic, teasing out the subtleties of pronounciation or meaning for one another – while I made copious notes on when and how this word or that might be used.'

Between this consultation and the many others he held, Jakup Jakupsen recorded as many as 10,000 words of old Norn, still extant even then, in the great age of the British Empire, with centuries of Scotticisation having elapsed since the archipelago changed hands.

As the scholar John J Graham writes in his preface to the second edition, Jakupsen's *Dictionary of the Norn Language in Zetland* is the unrivalled source-book of information on the origins and usage of the Zetlandic tongue.

So with this footnote, I complete the incomplete history of the parish of Norbie, Valay and Thulay, as I have found it. In finishing, I realise I have little else to say, except that it has occupied me, and I have learned something of my own country, and that it is unfinished.

My key source, James Gabrielsen, died suddenly in 1899, at home in the schoolhouse he and his dear companion wife had struggled to build so many years before, and which had seen, by popular testimony, scholars of note including professors, politicians and churchmen as well as honest fishermen and fisherwives pass through its humble portals. As a man of learning and religious conscience, as a force for good within his own community, and father to a remarkable missionary, it seems he stands on a level with any to emerge from that distant parish, low born or high.

After our cup of tea with traditional Zetland 'banniks' and jam, when I told her more about the work we are doing at 'Da Hus a'Myndins', Miss Jeromsen began her tale again:

Weel, du sees noo, his middir, da Polish wife, she wisna best-plaesed wi da news'at her peerie jewel wis gjaain aboot wi a pooramis bit a'lass wi naethin aboot hir ava. Na, far fae hit. Dir wis da mostaafil onkerrie, da fokk aa sed, choost laek a waar atwien middir an son, wi da sister'at wis still hem kaatcht in atwien dim, du sies.

A war between Mrs Agnes Scot and her son Albert?

Ja ja, dat dir wis. Bit da warst o hit wis, dey waantit ta maerrie. An Bieni, she wis sievin year aaldir as him. Ja, hit wis a wark, a aafil onkerrie. Feth, ja.

And this would have been when, exactly?

Weel, I kan tell de, fir hit wis choos aboot da time a'da Crofters Commission – du's heard a'dat?

Yes, in the 1880s, when the crofters in Zetland finally got rights to their traditional lands back.

Ja, weel, hit wis aboot dan. An da aaldist baern, he widda bien boarn ati'da hert a'aa dat. An Albert insistit apo'pittin his nem ati'da regiestir as da faidir, du sees. Ja ...

The official registry of the birth?

Ja, da parish register. Bit he did dat, ja. He acknowledged his baern. An he widda maeried hir der an dan, hed he no been a legal minor. Da middir widna lat'im. Bit dan, as shune as he wis turned twenty-one, dey maeried ati'da Haa, an da middir kynda cam around wi time, du sees, fir dir wisna a boadie at didna laek Bieni whan dey wir kent her a start.

And did they go to live in Norbie Hall after that?

Na, Berti wis biggit dim a hoose du sees, a new hoose. A proper moadrin hoose, wi a generator ta run lights an dat, ja, he designed hit aa himsel. He biggit an biggit, an spent maer an maer, an dan dey sued him, ja. Da factors. Berrick. An dan didn' Bieni loss hir second baern, stillboarn, poor ting.

That must have been terrible for them. Nothing so sad, so awful.
Ja most terribil aafil, hi mann a'been. Bit he wis a grippie laad wis Lewis Berrick. Cam ta be a weltie man, aaned half a'Skallva, an a graet curin business doon aboot Arbroath. An dan du sees da Crofters Commission choost led da laast straa apo dim, whan dey wypit oot aa dey wir owed.

The Crofters Commission brought about an Act of Parliament, didn't it, and slashed the landlords' income as well as what the estate was owed?
Ja, choost as I tell de. So dat wis dan hael thing ati'brukk, choost in nae time ava. Da hoos a'da Scots lairds, nine or ten a'dim dey wir, I doot, aa faan in twartree year, ja. Bit du kens, lass, hit wis a evil wye, back ati'da aald days, ja Feth! Da fokk choost coodna prosper, an hit hed ta aaltir, ja. Hit wis hed its day, hit wisna Berti's faat. Hit hed choost come dune, laek mesel disdays.

Miss Mimie, you are far from done!
Weel, mebbie … bit ja, dey selt da estate, nae iddir choice. An Bieni, weel, she'd aye toght ta emigrate, du kens, syn she wis a lass, an saa dat Tirvalites aa sail awa fae Norbie. She aye spakk abooot dat.

And so they came out here?
Ja, but no choos straight awa, du kens. Na, dey wir a start ati'da toon a'Larvik, first. Albert got himsel his car an he wid run folk aboot, kynda laek a holiday trip, fir dey wir nae cars ava dan, an fokk wid pey to gjing a peerie hurl. Whan dey cam oot here, he set himsel up wi da money dey hed fae sellin da estate, an he opened him a garage. Ja, he hed men makk rodds, an aa … dat wis him, happy, wirkin wi his engines. An Bieni, weel, she wis among fokk she kent. But no as well as ta be a vexation ta her. She cood kynda leave da past ahint her.

And what happened to the family, to take them away from New Zetland?

Weel, I never did hear it aa, bit dey wir buddir atwien Berti an dir aaldist boy. He wis kynda o a religious felloo, an wan o da precentors. Bit his faidir an him nevir saa ee ta ee, Bieni sed. He set aff fir Australia, an I doot he wis nevir back here. Ja, hit grieved his middir, I ken, no ta hear. An dan da iddir twa boys, dey gied back ta Breetain whan dey wir grown. So hit wis choost me an da tree peerie lasses, whan I cam oot.

And did any of the three sons have children themselves?
Ja, dey wir baerns. In da United States, an Breetain, an Australia as weel. I hae pictures a'some o dim, I sall try an fin ta de, if du wants?

That would be wonderful. Mimie. I wonder if the name Rod Cunninghame means anything to you?
Rod? Ja, dat wis da son a'da aaldist baern. Da ane at wis boarn oot a wedlock, in Norbie. Bieni an Bertie's grandson.

Wonderful. I've had contact with a man in Scotland, a minister actually, who has been trying to find the Cunninghames there. I'll tell him. And do you know whether any of their children ever made it back to Norbie?
Na, dat I widna ken. Norbie is a lang lang wye awa.

(TAPE OFF. AT THIS, MIMIE SEEMED TIRED, SO WE ENDED OUR INTERVIEW.)

25th June 2000 – Ferry

Up on deck, the rail is lined with passengers waving to folk on the pier. The ferry is too far out, but there's still one or two aboard ship, shouting goodbyes to those ashore as if they could be heard. There's a family, mother, father and two kids, hugging each other tightly, as if the danger of the journey might separate them. A few young lads capering around, showing off. Two old women with headscarves and coats. A couple of German backpackers.

The ship glides slowly out from the pier through the summer light.

The surface of the water is glassy and the peaked shape of the hill across the harbour reflects there, slightly warped. On the other side, where the town is straggled along the waterfront, there's some kind of a gathering going on. I can see a small crowd and some bright colours.

I take my binoculars out. There's a small crowd of folk standing next to what could be a war memorial. They seem to be singing. Some have instruments. I shift the gaze of the lens along the crowd slowly, and then catch sight of something waving above their heads. Something white, waving. It looks like a banner.

Then for a second the waving stops, and I see the words

LOVE HIM

That's all it says. But it's enough. I know where the rest is, and why the white sheet is moving. It's so that folk can see both sides. It's a parting gift from this island, this last message: 'Love him'. Dead or alive, whether I like him or not, I know I have to love him.

I scan the crowd. There's no sign of John or Lena, but if the banner's vitality is anything to go by, they're having a good time. And as the white lighthouse seems to drift towards the ship, I think why not? Why not praise the Lord?

So I go back to my cabin, my bunk and just let it all drift away

this time, I drift
    away from

Zetland

Feelings swell up and surprise me, like the motion of this ship. Six hours out from port, there's no land on the horizon. The world is floating through a summer midnight, streaks of dawn and evening indistinguishable. But I want to shut myself away from that world, in the depths of cabin hell, in the belly of this metal whale that swoops and swoons through a heavy sea, spraying the foam, chucking me up, sucking me down. Sickening me in the engine of the night, the hellish stifling heat, heart-sick in a half-sleep that flows through me and won't stay still, till I sit up and reach for the sick bag.

And the night is far longer than any I've endured. The ocean is endless. It's frothed up the oil I've poured on my troubles, and sprayed it all over my white-starched sheet. And I can't sleep. The boat is rocking too much, there's this creaking everywhere. So I switch on the light above my bunk and glance at my watch. It's nearly three o'clock in the morning. Still five hours to go. And I can't sleep. I just lie there staring at nothing, panting with the heat. And after a while, look down and fix on the book. The blue cover, gold writing, lying there. Holy Bible. Placed by the Gideons. A few feet away, it looks so small. How these scriptures haunted the first dozen years of my life and now I'm a stranger to them. And I think of those coloured stickers I used to get at Sunday School, how I stuck them in that album faithfully, memorised the verse they illustrated.

I reach down from my bunk and lift the Bible up. I flick through the pages. Matthew, Mark, Luke and John. Never forgotten, four names imprinted forever, like John, Paul, George and Ringo. Harpo, Groucho, Chico and Zeppo.

I try to find the Lord's Prayer. And there it is, marked in pencil. Somebody's marked the passage, some poor soul caught in a force ten gale thinking the end was nigh, maybe.

'Our Father which art ...'

It's all there, just as I remember it. And then my eye goes back, midnight curious, back to which bit the words are from. Of course, the Sermon on the Mount.

But this ship's not bound for Zion. It's not bound for anywhere I'm sure of. A red light pulses on my eye, morsing out a message. The message is that I am still a child, moving towards the unknown absence, caught in the cold sea and the north wind, the empty lands and the big skies.

Lost.

You're walking on a smooth sheen of water. Yes. And then a car slows, pulls in and stops beside you. Is it a Range or a Land Rover? You glide slowly towards it. Inside are four men in suits and as you come up to the car, the one in the front passenger seat winds down the window. You recognise him right away. It's Paul McCartney. Can we give you a lift? he asks. They're going your way but not all the way. You take your rucksack and try to fit it into the back behind the rear seat. There's cardboard boxes piled up in there and it's a tight manouevre. Accidentally you spring the lid on one. Bibles! Dozens of Bibles! You hesitate a second but they look friendly enough and anyway you feel you know Paul. The driver turns round to you. Hi I'm Brother Groucho, he says, This is Brother Harpo, Brother Paul and Brother Ringo. We're on a mission, says Paul. Out of the speakers snakes the jangle of 'A time to love, a time to die'. A Christian rendition with organ and Beatle harmonies. And then the driver peeks round at you and says, So tell me, do you know Jesus? You stammer non-committally, something about being agnostic-socialist-antiracist. A social anarchist. Brother Paul looks shocked. Brother Groucho frowns in the rear-view mirror. This is no time for vacillation, he says, Jesus is present through the power of the Holy Spirit, right here in this car right now. And he wants to meet every need. The Lord God is going to claim his own and only those who know Christ will be saved. Brother Ringo turns, stares at you, his fingers dripping gold rings with keys dangling from them. Have you ever thought about eternal life? Shocked, you answer I do have a life insurance policy if that's what you mean. He grins and his teeth are so white that they shine to the point of blinding you. When you're with the Lord you need no assurance, none whatsoever! He is our assurance! The others let out a Hallelujah in Beatle harmony. Paul: When you have given yourself to the Lord God Almighty you need worry over nothing. You see these people who peddle life assurance, now some of them are good people but there are many that are in the pay of Satan! Groucho: They don't know Jesus. Ringo: They do not! Paul: And they prey on the fears of poor people! Groucho: Promising them and their children security. Ringo: The only true security we have is in the Lord! And behold HARPO SPEAKS! His mouth opens and out of it emerges the sweetest child's voice you've ever heard in your life. Hallelujah! he says. The road narrows. Now it's a twisty single track with passing places and the car is bouncing over the bumps. You feel like you're on a ferry as it rolls and sways over the bumps. There's sheep wandering along the side of the road. Lots of them and lots of green shepherds, and black and white dogs staring into the car as it passes, bold as can be and the brothers seem to be distracted. It goes quiet. You feel the shape of the road through the wheels but not the land's curves. And then you see a signpost. INNERTOON, it says. It's my turning! Stop please! you shout. But the car carries on past! And for one terrible moment you think they've kidnapped you. Like you have been disappeared. But the line of green shepherds closes in and surrounds the car so it comes slowly to a halt. You open the door. Brother Harpo leans over smiling. You have many miles to go, he says, but let the Lord guide you and you will find your way. And you go to grab your rucksack from the back but Brother Ringo's in there first. He's got hold of a Bible, the tracts all fluttering in the wind. Sinners would rather go their own way, he says, than follow the Lord's. They favour the broad path to Hell, not the narrow one that leads to Heaven, says Brother Harpo. Brother Ringo hands you the tract. But we have a mission and that mission includes you. We want you to take these shoes with you and wear them on your travels. And he stuffs into my hands a pair of worn out sandals. All of God's chillun got to have their shoes, says Groucho. You say nothing just take them. Just thanks. You will see the light one day, have faith in that, says Groucho. You take the Bible. Thanks again, you say, and cheerio. The four brothers bid you farewell driving away on their Christian mission. You're left standing there on the roadside with your rucksack over your shoulder, a Bible in your hands and a folded paper with the words

Then the curly-haired bright-eyed figure of the minister appears among the flock of little green shepherds.

    'Split the stick,' he says.

        'Split the stick and there's

                Jesus

And the stick is a shepherd's crook, the staff of love that
    cleeks the
        lost

Perth

Dear Mr Scot

As I have not heard from you again, I thought I might write to remind you that I am still searching for the mysterious David Cunninghame or Scot.

I appreciate that you may have many other concerns more pressing, or that some misfortune may have befallen you to put an end to our correspondence (what terrible times we have all witnessed so recently in New York – I trust you have not been affected personally?) but I have been rather ill and my eyesight is now failing badly. I write, as you will see from this shaky script, with difficulty now, so I am conscious of time's measure running out if I am to tend to my lost sheep.

I would like to help him find his pathway to righteousness in the Lord and bring him home to the happy land. I have prayed for his salvation.

Yours sincerely

Archibald

6th July 2000 – Perth

It was on the train that I came to myself again. For the first time since I'd left, really. Those midsummer days on the island were a kind of dream, a swathe of ideas, voices and images all woven into one.

It was the realisation that I was finally going back to Perth that woke me. I'd studiously avoided it, since the second funeral. But on the train south, I warmed to the idea that I'd be walking those streets again. I began to feel the pull of the river energy flowing ceaselessly to the estuary. And I realised too that you can't go through life keeping a door closed between you and your past, no matter how terrible, how tragic, how humiliating. Otherwise you leave something of yourself behind you. And so you can't be whole.

Did I really expect him to be there at the restaurant? I don't think so. But it was an act of faith. I believed that CODE WILL SAVE. It was a sign.

The stations were a kind of countdown to home. As the rocky ridge rose above the green plain of the Carse, Kinnoull Hill grew closer, the folly and the sheer stone face with the mad earl's stone dining table at the top. Like a sacrificial slab. Could I go up there again?

The judder of the train over the railway bridge across the River Tay signalled arrival. I took my rucksack and stepped onto that platform. The air was familiar. I never think of the crispness of the air in Perth, its freshness, without thinking of all the corrie lochans and the mountain springs that flow together to make the Tay. The wind that blows through the strath seems to carry all the scents of the Highlands.

I couldn't decide which way to go. I just stood there in the station, the great Victorian station where Queen Victoria and Prince Albert used to stop off on their way to Balmoral, now with half its lines redundant. So I let my feet decide, started walking and before I knew it I was at the cemetery at Jeanfield.

I sat for a while on a bench, staring at my mother's gravestone. I had no choice, then, but to acknowledge my guilt. That it was me who told her about Tanya, that is was me who gave her the news that broke her heart.

And then I took the stone I'd brought from the old church on the island out of my rucksack. It was an Old Red Sandstone pebble. Small and plain, it looked like nothing but what it was. I bent down and pressed it into the turf on the grave, till it was completely hidden, thinking how its plainness suited her. She didn't like glitter. And in my confused state, I felt as if I was giving her the peace of Mary.

And then I stared at Martin's gravestone for a while. I hated him, then, for being so brilliant he could have soared, and for being so stupid as to waste the miracle of life. I took the black-tipped feather I'd brought from the island and stuck it into the turf, so that only the feathered part was showing. To symbolise flight, angels and all that. But I knew I could never climb Kinnoull Hill again, without wanting to leap over that edge, to try to bring him back. I was a coward, Martin.

Time to go to the Salutation Hotel. I slung my rucksack over my shoulder, and back I went, over the railway, past the new library, into the centre of town. And into the old hotel, the low ceilings, the ghosts of Bonnie Prince Charlie and his military that still seem to infuse the air of the place.

There was nobody in the restaurant when I arrived. I was ten minutes early. A waiter showed me to the table reserved for Cunninghame. I concentrated my mind on the forks and knives, the salt and pepper, the napkins and the place mats. The door hadn't opened. So I looked again at the napkins, the emblem sewn into them. The sway of the ferry swept over me again, as if I was still at sea, full to overflowing, sick. Something had to happen.

And then it did. The door did open and a man came in. He spoke to the waiter and he pointed over to where I was waiting. The Cunninghame reservation. He was surprised to see me. Asked if he had the right table. So I introduced myself and asked him who he was. He said he was a book-dealer, that he was meant to be meeting my father to negotiate the purchase of a quantity of my father's books which had gone to my Gran's in Blair when the house in Perth was sold.

I crumbled then. Some part of me had been expecting something significant to happen, that some new part of my family's story would unfold. Even that Tanya would appear. Instead there was a stranger, oblivious to all that had happened and was happening.

And then the police arrived. Mary had told the laird where I was going, and the laird told the police. And that was when the mystery of my father's disappearance was solved. It was the boy who found him, in the little blue lochan we'd visited together the day before, next to the old Coffin Road. He must have been there, dead in the water all the time we lay in the sun and talked, with the skylark singing high above us. The corgi was dead too, drowned. Caught in an old piece of net. Hard to say what exactly had happened. Afterwards I tried to work out a scenario where the dog might have chased an otter into the water, and been snared in an unintentional trap. My father might have gone in to try to rescue it, but I don't know. It's all guesswork. And at the time, there in the restaurant, the detail didn't matter. Then Gran died suddenly, the following Friday. It didn't surprise me. She'd looked dead in the church. I felt as if there was nothing left. Or rather nobody. Of the happy family in that photograph taken in Princes Street Gardens in 1969, only I'm left. And now there are four graves to visit

in Jeanfield cemetery

On the gravestones is carved a code that
　　　　saves

———————————————————

Letter from Peter A Scot
to Rev. Archibald Nicol,
October 1st 2001

Miami

Dear Reverend Archibald

I have tried, via my son-in-law, unsuccessfully to contact David Cunninghame or Scot via the internet thus far.

The contents of the notebooks are puzzling. At the beginning the voice seems quite rational but by the end I have difficulty following the scribbled insertions and/or marginal notes, whatever they are. Were they written at the time? Is this a record of actual events, the words people really spoke to one another? And am I meant to understand you read this document as the product of some kind of religious ecstasy?

I'd feel happier with a psychological explanation, personally – the idea that the writer has been traumatised by a sequence of major life-events and this is his way of coming to terms with that. Even so it doesn't make sense. Perhaps because of the fact that he is a distant cousin, I find this strangely intriguing – but frankly, there are blasphemies here which I find surprising a man of God should circulate. Thank you for sending it to me all the same. I wish you God's guidance in all.

Yours in faith
Peter A Scot

Letter from Rev. Archibald Nicol
to Peter A Scot,
October 3rd 2001

Perth

Dear Peter

What profoundly terrible times we live in! My prayers have been with you and your countrymen these last few days. This is truly a test of faith.

The notebooks may be a testimony of a conversion – what the Pietists referred to as a Wiedergeburt. The story of a rebirth, a person's life being touched by God, called to account by a time of great stress, as indeed are we all, at this time.

I hope you will be able to help me find your cousin. I have prayed for him constantly, that he should find his way to the Lord. The child

I baptised, the lost. I recalled these words from Bunyan this morning: 'And by and by the day broke; then said Christian, "He hath turned the shadow of death into morning."'

Yours sincerely

Archibald

PS – apologies for the scrawl. I only write by hand poorly now, and I can't type any more, but I have now finished typing all the documents David left here, should he ever come back.

7th July 2000 – Perth

When I think of that midsummer weekend, terrible suspicions well up. Even though accidental death is what it says on the certificate, I can't help but wonder what really went on between them all. I become infected with it, with suspicion – and the bad smell of a rotting carcass, the same putrid stink that I found when I opened the door of his chalet, lingers.

Somehow I know I'll never know the truth. It's too late for that. And I don't care now. I can't afford to. I went deep into depression, as if a dark gloom descended, after the two funerals.

I found some solace in the idea of an afterlife, and slowly I realised that I was prepared to believe, prepared to follow, that I
      needed to
            believe
                in

Carbon Copy of a letter from Rev. Archibald Nicol
to Peter A Scot,
October 21st 2001

c/o Mount Royal Hospital
Perth
Great Britain

Dear Peter

As I have not heard from you, I wonder if all is well? I am writing to
give you my new address, as I have had to leave the manse. It is another
distress I could well have done without, but in all honesty I was not able
to manage the house on my own. I had no idea how reliant I was on my
dear late wife.

Out of all the sadness and the misery of these last years, it is as if
something awful has been born – a new age of religious conflict I would
rather not be part of.

Now I am able to see it all as if in clear relief – at the midwinter of
my life, among those deep December days of occasional low glinting sun,
a brief daylight of extreme clarity, when everything is quite distinct, still
more so than in high summer, when vistas are distorted by hazy chimera,
by dreams and desires that have sprouted like leaves and obstruct the eye.
In winter all is bare, and when the clear light shines, everything is obvious
– the great peaks, the shadowed troughs; the ridge and the otherwise
hidden abyss.

You'll forgive my waxing lyrical, I trust, for now I understand the
great lesson all this has brought me, that, as for John Duns Scotus, reason
is not the way to faith. Life is indeed often absurd.

God can never be understood by Thomist exposition, nor by Aristotleian
principle. God cannot be known by the method of investigation – only
acknowledged, as He is revealed to us. Faith is an act of will – a practical
surrender to the divine.

I had, in the months after Margaret's death, begun to lose my faith. I
had forgotten that the fundamental act is that of accepting – of believing

in the bounty of God, even when that which we love is taken from us. I had been retiring not only from my ministry, but from my faith. But now that I have mourned her, I ask forgiveness. I have been reconciled to the Divine Will. Yet how marvellous are the ways of the Lord!

I am confirmed in my faith. I am ready.

Yrs in faith
Archibald Nicol

Letter from Philippa Gabrielsen
to Rev. Archibald Nicol
November 11th 2001

Bon Hoga
Serrafir
Tokumua

Dear Archibald

I haven't heard anything from you since I sent the last interview I did with Miss Jeromsen, and I am worried, especially as it seemed that she may be able to confirm the identity of the man you are looking for. I hope you're okay and not ill?

Sadly, I have to report that Miss Jeromsen died last week, at the age of one hundred and one. I had come to know her very well over the last few months of her life, which was an amazing one when you come to think of it, spanning the whole of the twentieth century. To have begun where she did at the time she did, and to have travelled as far as this is in itself a remarkable thing, but the more I have learned about her life both in Zetland before she came out here, and the life she lived when she arrived, the more in admiration I am.

Sadly,
Philippa

Postcard from Jerusalem
Image: 'The Via Dolorosa'

21.11.2001
Dear Reverend Nicol

I told you I was going to Jerusalem, and here I am at last. I just want you to know that I made it, as you were the signpost that brought me here. It is the heart of my mystery. I found my mother here, at Gethsemane – where else! Martin too, at the precipice above, where Jesus gave his Sermon on the Mount. It's the world of the stories she loved to tell us.

The Pilgrim

PS Have you realised who I am yet?

PPS These things that are happening in the world – it is the End Time
I think

Luath Press Limited

committed to publishing well written books worth reading

LUATH PRESS takes its name from Robert Burns, whose little collie Luath (*Gael.*, swift or nimble) tripped up Jean Armour at a wedding and gave him the chance to speak to the woman who was to be his wife and the abiding love of his life. Burns called one of the 'Twa Dogs' Luath after Cuchullin's hunting dog in Ossian's *Fingal*. Luath Press was established in 1981 in the heart of Burns country, and is now based a few steps up the road from Burns' first lodgings on Edinburgh's Royal Mile. Luath offers you distinctive writing with a hint of unexpected pleasures. Most bookshops in the UK, the US, Canada, Australia, New Zealand and parts of Europe, either carry our books in stock or can order them for you. To order direct from us, please send a £sterling cheque, postal order, international money order or your credit card details (number, address of cardholder and expiry date) to us at the address below. Please add post and packing as follows: UK – £1.00 per delivery address; overseas surface mail – £2.50 per delivery address; overseas airmail – £3.50 for the first book to each delivery address, plus £1.00 for each additional book by airmail to the same address. If your order is a gift, we will happily enclose your card or message at no extra charge.

Luath Press Limited
543/2 Castlehill
The Royal Mile
Edinburgh EH1 2ND
Scotland
Telephone: 0131 225 4326 (24 hours)
Fax: 0131 225 4324
email: sales@luath. co.uk
Website: www. luath.co.uk